CRAZY BEACH©

L. R. Welborn

As to not embarrass those still around, I've changed most of their names, to honor those that have checked out, this is the way the deal went down…..

Most of what follows…is most of what follows….

"…only those that risk going too far can possibly find out how far one can go…"-T.S. Eliot

Track 1-Summertime's Calling Me-The Catalinas (3:09)

You've probably never been to the beach where I grew up, but you know its real name. Showcased front and center most every year, usually between June and October on the Weather Channel. It's catnip central for hurricanes. More than two dozen have made landfall or passed close by in the last several decades.

The little beach community has been around 100 years or so, nearly burned down a couple of times, been TKO'd by a few of the aforementioned hurricanes, and scandalized by politicians run amuck. Somehow, it still manages to welcome tens of thousands of visitors every summer with a goofy, somewhat quizzical smile that screams, "wow, you guys came back?" Think Barney Fife or a deranged hyena on crack and you'll be heading in the right direction.

If ever a community could lay claim to the old Jimmy Breslin title "The Gang that Couldn't Shoot Straight", it's the one where our family received our mail, along with 300 or so other mostly middle-class families.

The beach in summer…summer man, summer is, has been, and always will be the best. Unless of course, climate change makes us all move in with Santa. Take a moment before you dive into phase one of my adolescent misadventures to remember some of the best times you've had at the beach or times you experienced the beach through song, film, literature, or television. Pretty good memories I hope. Mine sure are.

Growing up I got to enjoy almost all the great summertime experiences first hand. Our little island was nearly a magical place, if not for the near Twilight Zone-like absurdity of the things I witnessed. Sometimes, it was almost like we were characters in a Kurt Vonnegut novel. More likely, an about to be discarded short story he used as a tissue before tossing in the wastebasket.

That's the kind of place I'm going to tell you about, my hometown. A weird, cozy little island community. A funny, at times bizarre joint, filled with eccentrics, escapists, dreamers, enough small-town shenanigans for a whole state of small towns, and lots of good, fun folks. Oh yeah, and my trip to Woodstock in a VW van as an 11-year old stowaway.

Nearby communities had nicknames like "Fayette-Nam" or "Razor City", but there was nowhere like our little island where we'd all go reeling from one escapade to the next, enjoying or enduring whatever spectacle we were witness to, helped create, participate in, or heard about through the grapevine. It was a literal Crazy Beach. Life in Crazy Beach was a daily, wacky roller-coaster ride, getting clown-punched over and over, but once, just once, when we thought, well, perhaps things may settle down to some version of normal, this happened…

It was the Fourth of July, back in the early 1970s, our family; Mom, Dad, my little eight-year-old sis and I were walking to get some breakfast, quickly covering the short distance to the boardwalk from our beachfront home. We had in tow all the beach accessories required of the era, folding chairs, portable AM-FM radio, cooler, umbrella, and Mom's ever-present bag, full of what would likely qualify today as a small Wal-Mart.

We'd reached the stoplight (the last of three) at the town's main intersection which was packed with tourists and locals for the annual bacchanal. A bald man, 40ish, wearing only some ragged overalls, casually cruised through the heavy traffic and dropped his drawers in the middle of the frantic intersection. As horns began blasting and people started yelling, he calmly deposited some serious business in the middle of said intersection, turned to admire his unhandy work and bent over. Pants still around his knees, he retrieved a small American Flag on a stick that fell from his overalls. He gently and reverently placed the little red, white, and blue holiday icon into the middle of the heaping pile and simply walked away.

That fourth started not quite as dramatically, more like most I could remember. Our small oceanfront cottage home filled with music from the radio. Country if Dad was home, R&B or pop if not, the smell of coffee, the summer ocean breeze (yes, it smells different in winter), lots of cousins, and several maternal great-aunts. It was a continual small riot, summer at our house.

We'd moved to the beach a few years earlier before I started third grade. Family lore says it was to be close to my maternal grandmother. She'd relocated more than a decade earlier in 1954 because of her asthma. Yep, that's right, hurricane buffs, the year of the REAL BIG ONE, Hurricane Hazel. Hazel wiped away much of the coastal Carolinas just blossoming beach communities. Our little island was right at Ground Zero. Granny and most locals tried to take the hit in stride, but it took a long time for our little island to recover.

Granny's concrete apartment building, little more than a block from the ocean, was one of only a handful of structures within a half-mile of the beach to survive Hazel's category four winds. It still stands to this day. Hazel also unleashed a wicked storm surge made more mountainous by a full moon high tide. Buildings that survived the Great Fire of 1940 were swept away like Pharaoh and his chariots. One poor family had just put the finishing touches on rebuilding their hotel from the last disaster when Hazel leveled them again. They moved three hours inland to Raleigh. Beach life before the Weather Channel could be very hazardous, what with hurricanes, rip tides, sharks, drunken sailors, you or yours could fall victim to an odd assortment of Ripley's "Believe It or Not" calamities at any moment.

Granny always said of Hurricane Hazel, "I've never seen so many grown men cry... all the bars were destroyed". Man, Granny knew how to set one up. All were fair game for my maternal grandmother, the high and mighty, the drunkard, and the sacred. Prime example numero uno from family history; my mother, almost nine at the time, ran into the kitchen as my grandmother was washing dishes to deliver the news that President Franklin Roosevelt passed away one April morning in 1945.

"The President died Momma," little Ginny said.

Without turning around, my grandmother laconically responded;

"That's alright honey, they'll get another one."

My granny wasn't at the house that Fourth of July morn, she was working at The Landmark Restaurant in the dead center of Crazy

Beach's bustling boardwalk. The Landmark, the "Heart of the Boardwalk" was our initial destination when we happened upon our first-ever viewing of "performance art". My mom was speechless and looked to my dad for something, anything. I'm not quite sure what she was hoping or searching for from a man of so few words, but this is what she got.

"He did that in the war all the time," Dad muttered. "Shells whizzing by, cool as a cucumber that "Eggs". Most guys just crapped their pants. Not Eggs, he would stand right up and do his business."

Dad carried on as if it had been a horse at the end of the homecoming parade.

We continued our leisurely stroll to the boardwalk, as cars clanked into one another, people shouted, and the cops arrived to nab the poop artist. I turned to get one last glimpse of the spectacle and saw the coppers tackle Eggs just in front of the boardwalk's latest controversy, a fountain whose water feature was a three-foot statue of a small boy, pants around his ankles, taking a wiz into the circular pool below. A dude who shared a deuce with the world arrested under the smiling face of a little fellow sharing a number one. I guess the old axiom has some truth to it, art and beauty truly lie in the eye of the beholder.

By the time we got to the long, narrow, open-air breakfast and burger joint that was The Landmark, it was buzzing with Egg's escapades. Granny was laughing her usual hearty laugh behind the lunch counter as she heard the tale of Eggs' tail from two white-suited young sailors seated on a couple of the restaurant's 15 or so bar stools. Her sister, my great-aunt Nina, was doubled over laughing behind the circular nick-knack counter.

The counter was situated between the wide, western-facing front entrance and the identical north side one we entered through. She looked between the rows and rows of giant rainbow-colored lollypops at my mom and asked if it was really true. Mom nodded yes, and Aunt Nina continued her guffaws. We grabbed the first picnic-style table by the side entrance and my great-aunt Pat strolled over, an icy bottle of Miller High Life in hand for my dad.

"Wish I'd seen that," Aunt Pat said. "Eggs was here just a few minutes ago, talking to himself like always and forgetting to pay, again."

"It was a pile this big," lil'sis expressed with her left palm raised, facing down at her right, about a foot apart.

She was prone to massive exaggeration but really wasn't far off this time. Aunt Pat chuckled-smiled.

"Ok, ok," Aunt Pat said. "What you mean-nesses want?"

That fourth lives on in family lore and occupies a place on the family's greatest hits album (Vol. I) of all-time bizarre moments. That year's events almost require a greatest hits volume of their own. So many head-shaking, bizarre things happened, I started to just make a list, but it got so long…

Track 2-Saturday Night at the Movies-The Drifters (2:24)

That year the island's only theatre was sold to an out-of-towner. Our little resort community's businesses up to then were owned almost exclusively by locals, passed down from generation to generation with little outside ownership. No franchise joints, no hotel chains, no anything without the names of one of the founding fathers of the island attached to the place or some stupid, corny, beachy cliché.

The Wave Theatre had been around almost as long as the town. It burned to the ground in the fire of 1940, then rebuilt on its original spot near the north end of the inner boardwalk. The movie house was situated right across from the big arcade, squeezed into a little two-story spot between the single-story donut shop to the south and the two-story Benway's Gift Shop on the north side. Ms. Benway lived above her shop she opened after Hazel.

My friends and I were at the theatre a lot, I mean, like three or four times a week a lot. Matinees were only 35 cents. This was the dawn of the old school rating system. Midnight Cowboy had been the first X-Rated movie we'd heard of, and to this day still remains the only one to win a Best Picture Oscar. It was the first X-Rated film to be shown on the island, except of course those shown at the legendary Last Chance Saloon's upstairs lounge during stag parties.

We didn't dare try and see Midnight Cowboy. My best friend and I, along with a gaggle of friends, whose roster changed as fast as an ancient band trying to still sell tickets on the road, would make every effort to get into the R-rated fare. You had to be accompanied by an adult to get in. We were successful most of the time, thanks in large part to the ease of alcohol acquisition in those days for certain junior-highers on the island and a somewhat dependable wino who liked movies.

We got to see original showings of Bonnie & Clyde, The Good, the Bad, and the Ugly, all the Bruce Lee films, Billy Jack, and something called The Party. The Wave was a great place to watch a show, with an upstairs balcony for lovers and the unruly. We got kicked out more than once. The first time came during a showing of some Godzilla movie. The film broke and we "entertained" the crowd from our balcony perch with lewd hand puppet shadow images projected on the screen. It happened at least once a summer for many years. As we got older the shadow puppets grew more obscene. The film broke one summer night and we quickly drew the ire of the owner who knew our actions well.

"You two are banned," Mr. Brockington yelled as we raced down the single staircase, past his startled high school-age daughter Melissa, who ran the cramped concession stand. Melissa, light blond hair and rail thin, was, to my eye, one of the prettiest girls on the island. We bolted out the glass double doors into the midst of a packed boardwalk. The smell of fresh-baked donuts, aided by a giant fan placed strategically above the donut shop's frying vat, filled the night air. We ran over to the arcade, narrowly sidestepping an elderly, quite rotund couple wolfing down donuts. Their faces plastered with the sticky sugary, white creamy flakiness that was one of the biggest draws on the boardwalk.

After a brief re-enactment for our friends working at the arcade, we played a few games of skee ball, (only a dime a game back then), more re-enactment for some tourist girls we were trying to win a stuffed animal for (success) and then, we hoped, off to see the submarine races.

You see many of the blue-collar tourist girls (a new batch each week) had no idea our excited pleas to come to the submarine races was just a ploy to get them out on the sand and let nature take its course. We struck out most of the time, but like my dad's oldest brother Uncle C would say, "… with girls, it's like baseball, you can strike out seven out of 10 times and still make a million bucks getting those three hits...". Our batting average was a bit below the Mendoza line (.200) but we didn't care. We had a blast! Kissing girls on the beach was the best, no big-time sexual adventures YET, but lots of making out and assorted other goodies. Numbers were always exchanged with promises of keeping in touch or "next summer". Ah, youthful promises…

Mr. Brockington let us back in the next day, due to his daughter Melissa's insistence. Melissa always watched out for us because we were her surfing buddies. Plus, she knew I had a great weed connection.

"Boys, I'm selling the theatre," Mr. Brockington began.

"Why?" I blurted out before thinking of the inappropriateness of my inquiry.

"Melissa's mom always wanted her to go to a nice school up north and Ms. Brockington, God rest her soul, has family there," He continued. "Besides I'm ready to retire. So after this summer, we'll be heading to New York."

We were stunned. It took a moment before we gathered ourselves. We'd never suffered a loss like this before. No more Wave, no more Melissa, no more porno puppets. We shuffled into the theatre, slid into the middle of the back row and sulked.

We watched Clint Eastwood shoot up a bunch of cowpokes without our usual zest and filed out to the boardwalk. Night had fallen and so had the rain. It was really coming down and vacationers were crowded under the awnings of businesses on both sides of the boardwalk.

It's really a special feeling you get stepping from the darkness of the theatre experience into the beach night with rain falling. People are hurrying about and the night seems alive with the sights, smells, and sounds of the boardwalk in summer. The games are ringing, whistling, and buzzing. People are laughing, raffing, and snaffing at the weather. The glorious smells of cotton candy, fresh hot donuts, and grilled burgers were sometimes offset by the occasional puke artist. A poor soul who was often blistered, bewildered, and barfing from a day of excess on the beach. A real microcosm of vacationland gone slightly askew. Ah, vacation!

"Grr," I heard from behind as we exited the arcade.

I thought "what the hell?" I turned to see ol' Eggs standing there mumbling under his breath. He was a bit worse for wear after hours in the slammer due to his performance art.

"Grr," my buddy said back at Eggs.

"Eggs you want something, you alright?" I asked.

"Grr," he repeated. "Mumble, mumble, (long pause) raff, snaff, mumble, mumble."

The later part was Eggs usual vocabulary. Sometimes enhanced by and often accompanied by a threatening, somewhat odd, deep bayou drawl. Part animal noises, part something else, no one quite ever figured it out. Champollion had an easier time deciphering the Egyptian hieroglyphs.

My buddy shrugged his shoulders, grabbed my arm and urged me forward as two little blonds exited the other end of the arcade. I looked back over my shoulder and Eggs was still leaning on the arcade's west side brick entrance. He was mumbling, always mumbling.

"Hold up," I said to my buddy.

I turned and started back in Eggs' direction. He was talking to the brick wall. I made it about halfway.

"Come on," my pal B yelled. "Heath and Nathan are going to scoop them up."

I froze. I looked each way twice. The girls, decked out in little shorts and halter tops were heading right for our greasy-haired, arch girl-hunting nemeses, the carney duo of Nathan and Heath, who were leaning on the brick wall securing the entrance to the bumper cars.

I knew as Mom taught me, I should help someone in distress, but Eggs appeared in distress about 90% of the time. The other 10%, he just looked lost. Scratch that, he looked lost 100% of the time.

I turned my back on Eggs. I sprinted the 10 or so yards to catch up with B. It gave me just enough time to get the girls' attention before the Despicable Duo had a chance to speak. Just as Nathan, the self-proclaimed "horn dog with a corndog" (the only original thought to ever come out of his head), opened his mouth and took a step forward toward the girls, I touched the right shoulder of the blond on the left. The girls turned around quickly. They both smiled.

"Hey," I said excitedly. "Weren't you on the beach today near the pier?"

I could see over their recently sun-kissed shoulders Nathan and Heath fuming at my timing. The Despicable Duo began having words as they walked away toward the amusement park section on the south end of the inner boardwalk. They were play fighting, slapping wildly at one another.

"Ah, yea," said blond number one, the shorter by two inches of the pair.

"Was that you guys out there surfing?" quizzed blond number two.

"Could've been," I lied. "Where you girls heading?"

"We have to check-in with my mom," number one said.

"Oh," I shrugged.

"But it'll only take a minute," number two gushed. "Her mom's real strict, but she's right here at the bingo parlor."

Ah, that moment, that joyous moment filling each boy's heart when he knows, when he really knows, not hopes, a cute girl wants to spend time with him. Actually, it's one of the big seven, THE

SEVEN WONDERS OF BOYHOOD. It clocks in at number four. We'll get to the others later.

"Cool, cool," I beamed. "We'll be over by the putt-putt."

I walked away. You know the ol' Tao of Steve (McQueen): 1. Be Cool 2. Be Excellent in Her Presence, and 3. Be Gone. Check, check, and double-check. It took B an extra second too long to begin moving away from the girls, almost destroying my brilliant maneuver. He quickly adjusted and we begin strolling toward the putt-putt just around the corner.

"We didn't see them today, did we?" B asked, raising his left eyebrow, Belushi-like.

"No, of course not," I said punching him on the left shoulder.

Track 3-We Gotta Get You a Woman-Todd Rundgren (3:05)

You know how, sometimes, when you're growing up, you lose focus? Heck, we all lose focus as adults. When you're a kid and your hormones are raging, focus is hard to maintain. Well, right about then B and I ran into two of the biggest focus-losers on the planet.

"Hey Lenny, hey B, we got some live ones down at the Rec Hall," Hal, focus-loser number one said.

"Hurry, let's go they're really itching," focus loser number two, David said.

"Can't, we're meeting some girls here in a bit," B said.

"Don't worry B," Hal said sarcastically. "Lenny will get more, he always does."

"Hey, knock it off," I said. "So what's the deal?"

"Two jarheads down at the Rec Hall shooting pool want to play for some money and meet some local girls," David said. "Been there about an hour drinking. We tried to find you earlier."

"Ok, ok," I sighed. "Let's go."

"Man," B moaned at the potential loss of the two little blonds.

"C'mon, no worries," I laughed. "They make more every day."

That was one of the greatest things about growing up at a tourist destination, new girls every week in summer. The four of us walked toward the Rec Hall, past the Urinating Little Boy Fountain and Arcade #2 (there were three on the boardwalk in those days). The arcade was packed with tourists and locals, machines beeping, buzzing, lights flashing, folks celebrating, and having fun.

The Rec, technically not on the boardwalk, was just west of the arcade, a two-story building built after Hurricane Hazel. The concrete and wood building housed a Family Dollar Store for most of the 1960s, but was now and had been for a few years the centerpiece of the bad-boy beach lifestyle. The one main entrance was two big glass doors. The building's two large plate glass windows faced the u-shaped parking area signaling the beginning of the central boardwalk area. The other side of the u was anchored by the second incarnation of the venerable four-story Bame Hotel. The first, a three-floor wooden structure, burned in the 1940 fire. They wisely built with brick the second time.

We busted through the double doors, man the place was rocking! Filled with mostly young people age 14-25. I spotted the marks right away, a couple of buzz cut Marines playing pool at the far end of the hall.

"Get the table beside them," I told Hal and David. "You haven't told them about Marguerite yet, right?"

"No, no, no," said Hal.

"Good," I nodded and strolled toward the bar.

"Let me get a coke Dutch," I spoke to the owner tending bar.

Dutch turned and started to pour me a fountain coke. Dutch was about 5'8" and a belly-heavy 200 pounds. He was just past 50 with slicked back dark hair and had the vibe of a man who'd seen it all.

"Cubs won today," I said. "Looking good this year."

"Yea, I heard part of it," Dutch said as he handed me the clear plastic eight-ounce cup housing my coke with crushed ice.

Dutch was a die-hard Cubs fan. We talked baseball almost daily in the summertime. He was the first-person I thought of when the Cubs won their first World Series since 1908 in the fall of 2016.

"Bonham pitching tomorrow when the Mets come to town," I said.

"Should be," Dutch agreed.

I slid off the bar stool and walked past the third, and last, of the giant wooden columns separating the pool table area from the rest of the joint downstairs. When you entered the building, the seven regulation pool tables were on the left, with a ledge bar against the far wall behind the tables. A mirror ran the length of the wall above the ledge bar where drinks, chalk, and cigarettes made their home.

Cheap plastic orange-backed booths took up the middle section of the downstairs with a couple of foosball tables and a dart board on the right as you entered. The bar was in the back right section with the rest rooms just off the bar. A rear entrance was near the last pool table. It led to a narrow east-west alley, with the first north-south street just a few steps away to the left (west) and the alley connected to the inner boardwalk just 15 yards east between the Sugar Shack and Jim's Bingo.

The ball boy gave us a tight rack. Hal broke. Hal was a powerfully built, but somewhat heavyset guy with a round face, dark hair, and always cheerful demeanor. His shirts were always just a bit too tight for his belly making him appear shorter than he was. He split the balls up pretty good but failed to make one.

"Nice one, Hal," I said.

I nodded at B and he shot first. We were playing team eight-ball. B made a couple and David did the same on his turn, my shot next. I knocked home a couple of easy ones, three-ball side pocket and the orange five in the mirror-end left rear pocket. The next shot was a bit tougher, a rugged slice shot, but I was able to cut the heck out of the one-ball with a deft touch easing it in the side pocket nearest the Marines.

"Nice shot," Marine number one said.

Number two nodded.

"Thanks," I said smiling.

"Can we get the winners?" number one said.

I looked at my friends feigning I needed their agreement. David and B nodded their consent. I knocked in the last two solids and made a fairly easy eight-ball shot. The baited hook was dropped into place perfectly.

"Sure," I said. "You guys stay put, we'll come over there."

The Marines were playing on my favorite table. The last one, nearest the rear entrance. You know, the old Mafia-Baptist perspective; back row, in the corner, you can see everything unfold in front of you and not have to worry what's behind. Besides, it was the best table in the house, newish felt, but not too new. B and I were entitled to the break since they'd challenged us.

"Want to play for two bucks?" number one asked nibbling at the bait.

"Well, ok, I guess," I smiled again.

You can probably guess what happened next. Instead of a shot-by-shot replay, a bit of reader's digest consolidation is in order. We played them a little slow and split the first four games two-all just to make sure they were fully engulfing the hook. We made some decent shots, but nothing too great, no great runs, maybe three or four, but just biding our time. The talk turned quickly to girls.

"You guys know any local girls out tonight?" number two asked.

He was about six-foot, thin, with kind of big ears. He was dressed in dark jeans with a darker tank-top and worn-out black converse sneakers. He said he was from Akron, Ohio.

"Oh yea, there're some out tonight," I said.

"You got to work the ones from here," B said. "Tough to pick up local girls on the boardwalk."

"How's that?" number one inquired.

He was taller, stockier, and seemed a bit older than his buddy, and had a little bit of a ruddy complexion. Number one was wearing jeans, boots, and a Lynyrd Skynyrd t-shirt. He was from Macon, Georgia. They both appeared to be around 22 or so.

"Just takes a bit of time and money," B continued.

"Like those two over there," I nodded toward a couple of our friends who were sitting in a booth not far away.

Right on cue, B upped the ante as he was about to break.

"Wanna play for five bucks this time?" he asked.

"Sure," number two said. "Invite those girls over."

"Alright," I said. "After this game."

B made one on the break, then sank three more before a miss. He didn't leave them much. Number two looked at his options and attempted a two-rail shot that didn't have much of a chance. I cleared the rack without having to make any fancy or trick shots, just a solid win.

"Good one," said number one. "Double or nothing?"

"Sure," I said.

"The girls, the girls," number two impatiently nodded in their direction.

"On the way," I said. "Take my break B."

A clear breach of pool etiquette, especially with $14 on the line. The Marines didn't seem to care as I slid in next to Darlene, a tall, golden-haired blonde. Her friend Lexi, a cute, petite brunette with shoulder length silky hair sat across the way.

"Hey Lenny," Darlene said, running her right hand through my curls.

"Hey Darlene," I said. "You look rocking tonight."

Darlene always looked good with her thick mane of Farrah Fawcett-like hair. She had an extra just kissed by the sun glow beach girls get. Tourists don't, it's different, trust me. She gripped the back of my neck and kissed my cheek.

"So what you want?" Lexi asked dismissively.

"The first Marguerite of summer," I smiled broadly.

"I told you, don't even ask anymore," Lexi glared, first at Darlene, and then me.

"No, no, and triple no," Lexi said. "Darlene, you remember what happened to that poor soldier last Labor Day weekend. We said never again."

"Aw, that was just a freak occurrence," I grinned.

"No Lenny, no," Lexi stood her ground.

She could be a bit stubborn. She was a smart, practical girl most of the time and cute as hell. I'd known her for six years, since third grade.

"Yo, your shot Lenny," B yelled.

"Ten bucks each," I said to the girls. "It's always a blast, you know y'all love it much as we do! Back in a sec."

B dropped a couple on the break but missed his next shot. Marine number one made a good run, dropping five of his team's seven stripped balls. I'd some work to do, game-wise and girl-wise. I could see the girls' animated conversation as I looked over my table options. I needed to focus on the game for a few.

I made a couple of relatively easy shots, then came the moment of truth. I needed to make our remaining three balls. I stood with my back to the mirror, chalking my stick, surveying the landscape. The cue ball rested close to the lower left pocket. I could take a shot at either the red three at the far right end of the table up against the back rail or the yellow one near the rail on the right side of the table. It was just before the middle pocket requiring a bank shot. I also had the option of attempting a tricky slice shot on the purple four, resting a few inches above the one ball.

Now most players would take the bank shot. I'm lousy at banking. My forte is the soft touch, none of the banging and clanging you see with a lot of players. The soft touch and the slice were how I made many extra summer duckies. So I went with the shot on the four. I sank it! The Marines groaned. Their dismay was short-lived though.

"Lenny," Darlene said as she approached. "We're going to party at the house later."

Darlene was the quintessential beach girl. She was tall, athletic, tanned, great smile, and had a rocking beach bod. She was wearing a denim mini-skirt showing off the best teenage legs on the beach. Her toenails were painted white, further accenting her brown skin.

"Ok if I invite these fellas over?" I asked pointing to the Marines.

We were just close enough so the Marines could hear us. Sharp little Lexi, wearing cut-offs and a red bikini top joined us. She was the better actor of the two and critical for the success of our night of fun.

"Yea they can come, they're cute," she said loud enough for them to hear. "But," she glared at Hal at the next table. "Leave turd-face here."

Hal shrugged his shoulders and grimaced. Darlene gave me another kiss on the cheek for emphasis and turned to walk away. All eyes at that end of the Rec were on the girls. When they reached the second column, Darlene turned around and raised her right hand pointing to the sky.

"Marguerite's going to be there," She yelled-smiled, gave a signature wave (you'll hear more about later) and walked on out into the summer night. All the boys were enthralled by their exit, the spell broken only by….

"Hot damn," Hal said.

"You can't go," David said. "Lexi hates your guts and everything else about you."

"Bullshit, I'm going man," Hal said. "If Marguerite is there, it's on!"

And right on cue, as if he'd rehearsed his line and timing for months. The mark fell for the bait. He couldn't get it out fast enough.

"Hey, hey, who's Marguerite?" number one asked.

In this variation of a legendary, always slightly changing, Oscar-worthy script we performed a couple times each summer over the years, Marguerite (pronounced Mar-go-reet) was Darlene's sister. She was supposedly the island "easy girl". But I'm getting a bit ahead of myself.

"Double or nothing?" B asked as he broke.

"Sure, sure," number two said, not even contemplating the damage thus far. "Hey, so a beach girl party?"

"Yea," I said, nodding nonchalantly.

B once again knocked in two on the break. Then left one hanging on the cusp of the right side pocket. Marine number two missed an easy one, distracted I'm sure about the prospects of some hot beach girl lov'n.

"Marguerite, tell me about Marguerite," number one pleaded.

Number two came close to hear. I motioned them closer. I leaned in.

"Ok, ok," I whispered. "You boys are going to get to go somewhere we don't take many outsiders."

I motioned for them to come over toward the back corner. I looked around to make sure no one else could hear. I started to whisper again.

"One sec," I said, turning away from them. "Let me take my turn."

They both sighed. I ran the rack. You see, full disclosure for you, I grew up with a pool table in my house. Actually, under my house, on the carport. Our house, being on the beachfront, was built on stilt pylon beams. We made a lot of money shooting pool with tourists, at least enough to finance a bunch of our fun.

"Ok, ok," I continued. "Here's the deal."

B interrupted at the perfect time. We'd been best friends since we met the summer I moved to the beach after second grade. We had a system. Our system worked, most of the time, well, lots of the time.

"Let's square up guys," he started. "Twenty bucks each."

You're probably good at math. So you know our take should have only been $28 total. Horny servicemen, when they think they're going to a beach girl party, their math skills decline precipitously. They forked over the money without question. Not only was the hook set, the catch was working hard to jump in the boat!

"The party's on the back of the island," I said. "Did you guys drive?"

"No, no," B said, displaying his best enforcer persona. "Cops come by way back there, just one local car man. Otherwise, cops will think some big drug deal or something is going down."

"Yea, good idea," I continued. "Plus gives us an excuse to bring Hal."

Hal was the only dude in our crowd with a vehicle AND a license. He had a big, old, rusty, puke green International Scout four-wheel drive, which his older brother Terry had owned. Terry went off to Vietnam a few years earlier. Terry was one of the coolest kids the island ever produced and was a great athlete. He would haul his little brother and his buddies to ballgames and concerts for years. He included us in tons of fun things, beach shenanigans, and our first taste of real booze. A real top drawer guy that Terry. But see, Terry never came home. Hal was never the same and was always looking to fill that void.

"Lenny, we going to get some of your dad's beer or go to Graham's?" David asked.

"Pops is home, so Graham's it is," I said.

"So tell us about these girls," number one said as we began walking to the front.

"Hey Lenny," Dutch shouted from behind the bar. "Double down tomorrow."

"Yea, Dutch, thanks," I said.

I almost forgot I'd won $10 that day on my baseball bets, five on the Cubs and five on my Orioles. You see Dutch was more than just one of the dozen or so local bar owners. He was the island's number one bookmaker, procurer of female companionship, and supplier of "goodies" all rolled into one.

"Go easy kid," Dutch said. "And hey, make sure old man Norbett isn't home. Check for the boat!"

Dutch seldom joined in on the Marguerite fun, but I guess he was happy about the Cubs winning, plus I saw his cash stash was even bigger than usual when he added some bills to the money drawer. All the locals pretty much knew what we were up to and the Rec Hall's packed crowd was about half-local. Some said it was Dutch started the Marguerite fun back in the day. No one knows for sure. He would never say. Thankfully, Dutch just relieved me of explaining part of the set-up.

"Who's Norbett?" number one asked.

"Oh, no worries, he's just Darlene and Marguerite's dad," I said. "He's a boat captain, gone most all the time."

"We just need to make sure he's not around," B said. "He's been known to go after fellas chasing Marguerite."

"Aw, that's just talk," I said. "David, you talk to Danny and Donnie?"

"Yea," David said. "They're bringing the hard stuff."

David always played his role well, the outside set-up man. He looked like an accountant or an indie music guy, tall, skinny, black glasses, button-up shirts. David almost always took care of the off center stage set-up. A second unit director if you will. He was excellent at his job.

The six of us climbed into the door-less old Scout, Hal driving, with David up front, me and B in the small bench seat. The two jarheads sitting in the gate-less rear section on the bed.

"Oh man," I said, turning to face the Marines as Hal drove toward old man Graham's store.

The grizzled WWI vet with failing eyesight's store was near the fresh-water lake. Close to the boardwalk and only a hundred yards or so south of my house, it was the only place I could buy booze that young. I always had to check and make sure my dad's car wasn't there before entering.

"We're going to have a blast!" I continued. "Wait till you guys see Marguerite, if you thought Darlene and Lexi were fine, wait till you see D's big sis."

"Cool, cool," number two said. "That little Lexi is hot, but a little young, don't want to go to jail."

"Yea she's only 16 and D will be soon, and they don't put out," B said truthfully. "But that Marguerite, boy howdy, she does, oh man does she, and she's 20."

"Great," number one said. "I was a little worried about all the girls being too young. What does Marguerite look like?"

"A lot like Darlene, the taller one," I said. "But much bigger boobs."

I hated to throw Darlene under the bus like that, she had nice boobs. She'd let me play with them twice earlier in the summer and one time right at the end of the summer before, after eighth grade, but that was as far as I'd gotten. There was hope, but my timing always seemed to be a bit off with Darlene.

"Whoa, nice," number one said. "So it's just a party or what?"

"Ok, here's the deal, it's a small party, at Darlene's house on the river, back of the island," I said, as the Scout chugged into the store's parking lot. "It'll be us six, our two buddies with the hard stuff, Darlene, Lexi, couple other girls our age, and Marguerite. Umm, not to offend you guys or anything, but she might be too much for you to handle."

Their faces dropped. They looked at one another a bit dumbfounded. They quickly tried to recover.

"Oh no we got this man, we can handle any girl," number two said.

"Cool," I said. "Go grab a case of beer or two."

Without hesitation, and without asking for a contribution, the two Marines went into Mr. Graham's store. They stayed inside for a few minutes. It looked like they were shopping for snacks. They returned with two cases of Budweiser.

"Ah, the good stuff," David said.

David and most kids our age were used to the cheapest crap we could afford, stuff that was so gut-wrenching awful no one else would touch it, 99 cents a six-pack garbage, like Silver. Yep, that's right, a Silver can with a picture of the Lone Ranger's horse on it. What poor Silver ever did to get associated with such swill beats me. Even worse, wait for it, Tonto's 99 cents quart of wine. Even in those somewhat unenlightened times, we KNEW that wasn't right.

Eggs could usually be seen with a bottle of Tonto's firewater or should I say, a near-empty bottle of the brew.

Anyway, you might be saying to yourself, how did junior high kids (ages 12-15 in that era) get beer and wine in the first place. Well, the younger ones didn't (except under clause number two below).

Quick sidebar- a few ways and item number four reveals the Sixth Wonder of Boyhood:

1. Older dudes, like the wino mentioned earlier, the Marines or their ilk, or somebody needing some connection from us- party info, weed connection, or other goodies.

2. Steal it from a relative- pretty easy in the beginning, but my dad caught on pretty quick his old school fridge under the back deck was losing inventory. He switched from Miller to Pabst Blue Ribbon-yuck! That quickly cut one source short. We could tap other, not as observant friends' folks who were easier marks, especially around any holiday or grown-up party.

3. You may know the drinking age for beer and unfortified wine was only 18 back then (still had to be 21 for the hard stuff). Plus no one carded that diligently back in those days, so if you were kind of stout or had ANY facial hair, were somewhat composed, and not too many zits, you had a shot.

4. The fake I.D. card. Ah, THE SIXTH WONDER OF BOYHOOD, that first fake I.D. card. Mine would come a year later, from the back of Rolling Stone magazine for five dollars. The best five bucks I ever spent got me a fake birth certificate, Wyoming

Driver's License, and social security card. Said I was 22 when I wasn't quite 17. I made a killing off that I.D card, but that's a tale for another time.

Back to Mr. Graham's store-present day-for this story anyway. While the Marines were inside, we did a quick once-over of the game plan. We usually had few problems with the script.

"Everybody, ready to rock?" I asked.

All nods and yeas around.

Hal shifted the old Scout through its poor wretched gears, each shift a near death gurgle, as we rumbled down the main east-west boulevard of the island. That main drag still runs from the boardwalk to Killing Floor Road on the far western end of the island. Really just a couple of miles, but a journey from civilization to the wilds of nature. Beers were consumed, talk and laughter about girls filled the summer air, and we quickly reached the Killing Floor Road stop sign.

"Not much back here," said number one as we wheeled left, going south on rugged asphalt covering what had been an old plank road in Civil War times.

"Yea," I said, over the regular mechanical misfiring of the old Scout. "Feds won't let you build anything back here, it's what they call a buffer zone. The Storm Point Military Shipping terminal is across the river. They had a big old explosion over there during World War II, so they are afraid anything on this part of the island would get lit up by another big boom-boom."

Another round of beers and we were turning right onto little more than a donkey path. The Scout hit every pothole. One pothole, more like a sinkhole, almost bounced number two out the back before his buddy snagged him.

"They live back here?" number two quizzed. "Thought you said feds didn't allow any buildings back here."

"Grandfathered in, a couple of old fishing shacks that pre-date WWII are all that's left," I said. "Darlene and Marguerite's folks have lived here since before the island was an island when it was part of Federal Point Peninsula. Army Corps of Engineers dredged the Intracoastal Waterway in the late 1920s and early 1930s, splitting us from the mainland. Their folks, all fishermen, every single one since then has lived in that old cottage. Probably ends with old man Norbett though, nobody else left except Darlene and she's gone come college time and Marguerite, well you'll see, she'll be ready to leave with you guys if you'll take her."

The Scout came to a stop in front of the island's oldest and most overgrown graveyard. We were in the most heavily wooded section of the buffer zone. Near silence except for a lonely owl and some crickets.

The Marines were trying to keep their cool as we exited the vehicle. A bit of uneasiness began to show in their eyes. It happened to all who came before and those that came after. It was and still is at night, a very creepy spot. We popped a top on another round.

"We got to walk from here, can't risk taking the ride any closer, just in case ol' man Norbett's around," B said. "Turn the Scout around Hal, quick getaway and all."

The Marines' uneasiness escalated a bit. We let it simmer. They were looking all around and checking out some of the headstones.

"You sure about this man?" number one asked, trying to sound tough.

He was wavering. I could tell, seen it before. A few bailed on us at this point over the years and it still turned out hilarious. When they stuck in there, the real riot started. Number two, obviously the bigger horn dog of the two, made sure they were sticking in there.

"Man, I'm ready, let's move on," he said excitedly.

"Slow your roll, Johnny Wad," David said. "Got to wait your turn."

We could hear laughter up the darkened trail. Several voices headed our way. We could make out two distinct female and male voices. The guys were closer.

"What do you mean," number one started. "Our turn?"

"Well Miss M's a freak," I said. "But she's not THAT freaky! Hey, the guys with the hard stuff, Donnie and Danny sounds like them heading our way."

And right on cue, Donnie and Danny, both tall, brown shaggy 70s hair, athletic and 17, emerged from the pitch black path. They came within 10 yards or so, just where we could make out their silhouettes. Donnie was pulling at his zipper.

"Oh, man, she's on fire tonight," Donnie half-laughed, half gasped.

Danny was carrying two half-empty bottles of whiskey. He stopped just in front of us and took a swig. He put a serious dent in the contents.

"Man she let us do EVERYTHING!" Danny laughed. "She's ready tonight! Never seen her quite like this, I think she's been smoking a bunch of weed."

"Me next," Hal said.

"Me too," chimed in David.

"Don't think you little boys will be able to handle her tonight," Donnie said chugging whiskey out of bottle number two.

"Let these guys go first, they're soldiers or something, they MIGHT be able to handle her, the both of them," Danny said rubbing his head, referencing the Marines buzz cuts.

"Nope," I said. "Hal got us out here, he has next up. David can go next too."

Next up worked pretty much on everything back then, basketball pick-up games, shooting pool, even party, and girl-related stuff. It was the law of the land. No exceptions allowed. Donnie offered the Marines some whiskey.

"You boys gonna need this, I promise you," he said boisterously.

The Marines took a couple of good-natured swigs of the whiskey and kept drinking their beer. Hal and David grabbed another beer and headed down the sandy path. Just as they were about to disappear into the darkness, Darlene and Lexi emerged right at the dark to light transition point, smoking a joint. Hal and David continued their exit.

"You guys are animals," Lexi glared at Donnie and Danny.

They just laughed. Donnie and Danny clanged their bottles of whiskey together. Both bottles were draining rapidly.

"And I told you guys not to bring Hal," Lexi continued.

"Your sis is a real tiger Darlene," Danny said. "Hope you're like that by next summer."

"Hey," I gave Danny and Donnie a hard look.

"Whoa," Donnie said. "Don't get mad Lenny boy, we all know you got dibs on Darlene's cherry."

"Up yours Donnie," Darlene said, then turned to me. "I got the keys from Hal, Lexi and me are going to get some cokes at old man Graham's. Need anything, papers?"

"Nah, we're good," I said. "Set some of the beer on the ground though."

Donnie and Danny were engaged with the Marines, laughing, talking beer, and girls. B and I stepped over to join the conversation as the Scout chugged away. It was just us six in the pitch black.

"Man, when you going to nail that Lenny?" Donnie said punching me on the shoulder.

Donnie, two grades ahead of us, was always ribbing somebody, mostly in a good-natured way. He was a cocky sort, but one who could back it up. A solid ballplayer, he'd scored the winning TD versus our arch-rival that past fall on an interception return.

"Let it go Donnie," I laughed, shaking my head from side to side. "You'll never know, and besides you're just jealous."

"Whoa, I hear ya kid," Danny howled, bent over laughing.

"BOOM! CHA-CHA, BOOM! CHA-CHA, the unmistakable sound of two pump shotgun blasts split the night wide open. Everyone froze.

"I'll teach you to mess around with my damn daughters," A very loud voice bellowed in the distance.

"Run, run," we heard Hal yell as he emerged from the darkness. "It's old man Norbett!"

BOOM! CHA-CHA, BOOM! Hal flew forward out of the darkness. He landed face down in the sand twenty yards away.

"No Paw, don't," a female voice screamed just behind the male one.

"I'll kill all you sons of bitches," old man Norbett screeched from the darkness, but closer this time.

Everyone was already running (good Olympic times I'm sure) when we heard the fourth cocking of the pump shotgun. CHA-CHA, BOOM! Donnie was leading the Marines by a step, Danny and I close behind. We heard an uggh as B thudded to the ground behind us.

"Go, go, go!" I screamed.

Danny split right, Donnie had already left us in the dust and disappeared far ahead to the left. Marine number one fell, getting a face full of sand and sand spurs. His bud and I picked him up.

"This way," I said, as we turned right at the graveyard and sprinted 60 yards or so toward Killing Floor Road.

We three reached the road just as we heard another CHA-CHA, BOOM! The sound was much closer. Old man Norbett was at the graveyard. Crazy laughter filled the night air as he bellowed:

"Got another one of you fools!"

We were all bent over at the waist, panting.

"Town's that way," I pointed northeast, back toward the boulevard. "I'll hide over across the road till the girls come back. Got to keep them away from here."

The Marines were as frightened as anyone I've ever seen in my life, even to this day. They didn't hesitate and began running the three miles or so back to town. They disappeared in the far distance in a few minutes, never looking back, not once.

A few minutes later, with Darlene driving, the old Scout chugged up from the other direction just as all the dead and disappeared fellas emerged from the graveyard dirt road laughing. David brought up the rear toting "Norbett's" 12-gauge.

"Oh, man, that was one of the best," Donnie said slapping me on the shoulder. "Darlene, you play your older sister well, good job David, you're prob the best old man Norbett ever."

We were all laughing. B, Lexi, Darlene, and I got into the bench seat with Darlene sliding onto my lap behind the driver's seat. It was a tight, fun squeeze. B put his arm up on the seat behind Lexi. Hal took the controls with David at his side. Danny and Donnie took the Marines former spot in the back storage area.

"'My car's over on Powell," Lexi said leaning forward. "We got to get home."

The wind blew Darlene's long hair across my face. It smelled like flowers. She always said she wanted flowers painted on her first car. She'd be 16 come September and her dad had promised her a Chevy Malibu for her birthday.

"Mine's on Blair," Danny said.

We turned toward the south end of the island in the opposite direction the Marines took off in. We dropped the girls off first. B hopped out the right side and Lexi eased on out without saying much. Darlene grabbed my left knee with her right hand as she slid out onto the dirt road. I handed her the $20 I promised.

"See you tomorrow," she smiled, giving me a full-on kiss on the lips. "That was a blast."

"Geez, get a room, why don't ya," Donnie crowed from the back as he finished another beer.

We barreled on over to Blair. It was just a few streets away. We let the fellas out at Danny's car.

"Good work, Lenny," Donnie said. "I think the tall one shit himself."

He put Danny in a headlock with his right hand. He then stole half a case of our free beer. He howled at the moon.

"Thanks for the beer, boys," He laughed, releasing Danny and waving a festival queen wave as he got into Danny's green 1968 Camaro.

"Where to?" Hal asked.

"Let's go camp out at Boy Scout Lake," B said.

"Sounds good," said David.

And just like that, we were off to the next Crazy Beach adventure.

Track 4-Spinning Wheel-Blood, Sweat and Tears (3:41)

We drove toward my house to pick up some camping gear. There was only one way to get to our beach-front house by vehicle, as it was on a short one-way street running north-south. Our street was just three blocks total with the Steel Pier on the north end and the stop sign by Mr. Graham's store and the lake on the south end. About 15 houses in all, with an equal number facing them. Those houses backed up to the main highway if you could call it that, well let's say the main road instead.

The main road ran from the bridge over the Intracoastal Waterway all the way to the southern tip of the island. The main road and Killing Floor Road were the only two roads running the full length of the island in those directions. We turned right off of the main road onto the Steel Pier entrance way that was only a couple blocks long.

"Hold up, pull over," I said tapping Hal on the shoulder.

Hal dutifully obliged.

"Why are we stopping here?" David said.

"There's my uncle," I said pointing to a wobbling figure coming our way down the sidewalk.

I hopped out and approached my uncle. I knew he had a buzz. I wanted to make sure he was ok.

"Glad I caught you blondie," Uncle D said.

I could smell the booze from several feet away.

"What's the deal Uncle D?" I asked.

"Cops at the house," Uncle D slurred. "The fat cop too, bloat-o cop, said you boys pulled a fast one on some soldier boys."

Damn, that was kinda fast.

"Is Dad home?" I asked.

"Yup," Uncle D said, nearly bumping into me. Uncle D was a bigger version of me or I was a smaller version of him. My dad said when I walked on or off the ball field, I looked just like him.

"Will you tell Dad I told you I was camping with my friends at Sugarloaf?" I pleaded. "But say I told you earlier, be sure you put that in there."

"Alright, alright, move it on out," Uncle D said. "But your pops is pretty steamed. He's rolling his tongue up a lot."

"Crap," I said.

The tongue rolling bit was Dad's signature, "I am really pissed at you" move. He would take the tip and bend it back under his top two front teeth and glare. You knew you were about to have a bad day anytime it happened. It was serious business when it appeared. Thankfully that wasn't too often. I also figured if Uncle D was this loaded, Dad was well on his way.

"Thanks Uncle D," I said bopping him on the shoulder. Oops, almost knocked him down.

"Let's get out of here, coppers at my house," I said to Hal.

I know, I know, you want to hear about the poor Marines we left running down the road and Boy Scout Lake camping adventures. We'll get to that, but first let me tell you a bit about my Uncle D, my favorite. It shows some of the funkiness and insanity I come from.

Uncle D was a year older than my pops, they were both good ball-players, with my Uncle D being the best of the six full brothers (seven girls as well!). My dad was next to the youngest of the boys, so that made Uncle D, my grandfather's son number four by my grandmother (he had three older children, one son and two daughters whose mom died in the great flu pandemic of 1920). My dad had hurt Uncle's D's knee real bad in football practice Uncle D's senior year. Most folks said Uncle D would have at least played in college or maybe even the pros (in baseball) if not for the injury. My dad felt bad about the incident the remainder of his life.

After graduating, Uncle D followed the family custom and entered the military, choosing to enlist in the Air Force during the height of the Korean War. My Uncle C (the oldest) was already over there, fighting on the ground with the Marines, as he had in WWII. Dad would join them following his graduation the next year, turning down a baseball scholarship to become a jarhead. A son from our family served in all the major conflicts the U.S entered between 1776 and Vietnam.

My paternal grandfather never knew what patriotic boys he sired because he died at the hands of a neighbor. It happened on his own front porch in 1938 during a drunken card game dispute. My grandma raised 13 kids on a farm during the Depression and World War II with no husband and no government safety net. She never remarried. She lost two kids at early ages, one to pneumonia (J, age eight) and one to an accident so horrific it boggles the mind. Her daughter, Little E, age six, was walking to school with her siblings when she dropped her pencil. Once she noticed she'd lost it, she ran back to get it. Before her siblings could stop her, she was hit by a train backing up as she reached down to retrieve the pencil. I could write a book about my grandma and her heroic struggles. Stay tuned.

Well anyway, Uncle D served Uncle Sam, came back to the red clay of Piedmont North Carolina and began a checkered history of hard labor jobs, punctuated by long stretches of drunkenness and visits to the county farm. He never had a place of his own. He lived in the house he grew up in till the day he died.

He helped Dad build the house where I grew up, right on the beach. The house is gone now. It fell victim to Hurricane Fran in 96. If you google the Hurricane Fran Weather Chanel video you can see my house, it's the tan one floating out in the ocean about halfway through the video. On a positive note, you can visit the sand where it was, some of it's the same I'm sure. A big chain hotel sits on our old property and that of our former neighbors to the north, including the old Steel Pier.

The house was super cool, if not the best constructed. They always had a few when working on the house, well more than a few most of the time. This led to some parts being not quite level. All the windows didn't work just right. There was a door to nowhere in my folks' room. But we didn't care, we lived on the beach!

Uncle D was a frequent visitor, the only one I think Dad relished seeing. You know when you have a house ON the beach, ALL your cousins, and old friends from other areas of the state, people you forgot you knew, they love to visit. They love to visit often. Some too often.

Mom was always a great hostess. She loved having anyone and everyone, from far-flung third-cousins to people she didn't always quite remember. Sometimes Dad would disappear for a few days when certain family members from my mom's side of the ledger would show up, often unannounced or with just a prior day's phone call for notice. He would hang out at the VFW, golf course, or work extra shifts at the plant.

But Uncle D, he was the man! He and Pops would share beverages, stories, and wow, what stories; war stuff, ballgame stuff, girl stuff. Both of them had won best-looking their respective senior years so they always had that little bit of one-up-manship going on. They would often be joined by my "Uncle Nard", really my mom's first cousin Bernard. The trio would get feeling right and begin singing whatever God-awful country song was on the radio. "Abilene" and "Hello Walls" were among those on the frequently butchered playlist.

Here's one quick Uncle D story. Then we will get back to the poor Marines running down the road. We'll get back to the cops, the theatre, and all the trouble I would get into. Boy, there's a lot to tell…

Uncle D would always come down in October when fishing was at its peak. He loved to fish. He was fishing the day he died, age 37, just a few years after the main part of this story takes place. He was fishing on a small damn that crossed the river a few hundred yards from the family farm. The house was built by my grandfather in 1920 after he came home from World War I. We don't know what happened first and the coroner couldn't tell either, labeling Uncle D's death, "death by misadventure". He either passed out, fell into the river and drowned, or knocked his self-out by falling, striking his head on the concrete before rolling into the water or some other combination of those events. Anyway, I think that was the saddest I ever saw my father. The day his brother, Uncle D, died. Even more so than when his mom passed two years later.

But this is a fun Uncle D story.

It was a few years before the main events of this book when Uncle D was down at the coast for some fishing. He'd been down for a few days and was well into his beverage fun time. It was a Saturday and he asked if I wanted to go fishing with him after my little league football game that morning. I really care zero about fishing, but I took every opportunity to be with my Uncle D. Pops had to go to work after the game, so we took two cars to the game and Uncle D drove, more like zig-zagged, the rest of the gang back to the beach after the game. He'd already had several by this point.

We hit the shore a little after lunchtime and fished all day, all afternoon, and into the early evening. Uncle D was pulling in a few, and drinking quite a few. I caught zip but didn't care as I got to hear lots of great stories and jokes. When we left the strand the beverage cooler was half-full of empty beer cans, half-full of fish, and an empty Jack Daniels pint bottle on top. I had scored a couple TDs that morning, we won, and I got to spend the day with one of my favorite people of all-time. I was in great spirits and Uncle D was full of them. Life was good.

"We could walk," I said, noting it was only a little more than a mile or so north to the house from our spot down near Center Pier.

There were four piers on the island at the time. Today there are only two, one at each of the far ends of the island. The Steel Pier and Center Pier later fell victim to hurricanes.

"Nah, I can drive ok," Uncle D said stumbling as we reached his old beat up faded black 1949 Ford. 1949 was the first year cars had ignition keys. Uncle D struggled with his.

In those days, man people drove drunk A LOT. My pops, my uncle, neighbors, my friends' dads, they all did, regularly. But the thing was on the island, everyone knew everyone, and especially once the tourists left after Labor Day weekend, the cops didn't hassle the locals much, just us rowdy kids. Drunk grown-ups would usually get a pass, as long as they were polite, and the cops knew them. Often a police escort made sure the unsteady driver made it safely home. That evening we only made it about halfway to the house.

Pop! Sissss, sissss, thunkthunkthunkthunk, flat tire. Uncle D turned the Ford to the side of the main road. Almost zero traffic after Labor Day, so I wasn't real worried. It was dusk though.

"Want me to help?" I asked.

"Nah, nah," Uncle D started. "I got it."

I heard some rumbling in the trunk and a crash. Uncle D had fallen into the deep old trunk! His legs and feet wiggling back and forth like some of the fish he'd caught that day. A bit of cursing ensued and about the time Uncle D righted himself, a town cop car pulled up behind us. No flashing lights and I turned to see Chief Hall talking with Uncle D. I turned back around just as Chief Hall approached my side of the car.

"You ok Lenny?" Chief Hall asked, shining his flashlight into the passenger area, but not right in my eyes.

"Yes sir, Chief Hall," I nodded.

"Ok," he said. "You sit tight and I'll follow you home after your uncle finishes up."

Chief Hall walked to the back of the vehicle. The trunk was still up so I couldn't really see what was going on. Less than a minute later, Chief Hall briskly walked back to my window.

"Lenny, you go get your dad," he said aggravated. "Right now!"

'Why, what's wrong Chief?" I asked.

"Your uncle is changing the wrong damn tire," he fumed and turned around.

I got out in time to see Chief Hall handcuff Uncle D and put him in the back of the squad car. Do you know how drunk you have to be to try and change the wrong tire? I stood there on the side of the road for a second trying not to laugh. I failed.

The left rear was flat. Uncle D had the jack under the right rear and was trying to loosen the nuts on the right rear tire when Chief Hall put a halt to Uncle D's misguided mechanic effort. I started to change the tire, but it was getting pretty dark.

I jogged the remaining few blocks to the house. Dad's car was in its usual spot on the left of our two-car carport under the house.

Dad's 1967 burgundy Ford Fairlane was his pride and joy. Visitors parked on the street because the pool table occupied the right carport slot, mom didn't drive.

I sprinted up the 12 steps to our front deck and in through the screen door. It was a perfect October night with the moon hiding behind a few clouds every now and then. I walked into our kitchen and I could see Dad sitting it his customary spot at the far end of the table just past the counter bar. Mom had her back to me, messing with something on the stove. She never turned around during the ensuing exchange.

"Dad, Dad, you gotta go get Uncle D," I started, a little out of breath from all the running.

Dad had an almost empty Miller bottle in front of him. I could see a few empties on the top of the trash can beside the stove. He looked to be feeling no pain.

"What?" Dad said as he turned my way. "Why?"

I told a very Reader's Digest version of what I just told you.

"C'mon let's go get him," I said as if it were automatic, turning back slightly toward the front door.

"Nah," Dad said reaching into his pocket.

In what seemed like an eternity wrapped in a moment, I saw my dad toss me his car keys. They floated in an arc over the bar. I cupped my hands and caught them waist high against my belly.

"You go get him," Dad said matter-of-factly and turned back to face the other end of the table as he took a big swig of beer.

"But Dad, I'm 11," I protested.

"Go on, go get your uncle," Dad said dismissively waving his right arm and hand in my direction.

Hmmm, so no help from Mom here. I turned and walked out the door, half-hoping to hear her say "come back here" or something. There was no reprieve. I headed downstairs to my dad's prized possession, the only new car he would ever buy in his life, his Fairlane. It was only a few years old at this point. Dad was a Ford man through and through. I couldn't believe he was actually going to let me drive his car, on a real road no less, at 11 years of age. Heck, I NEVER thought I'd get to drive it on the road, ever!

The Ford was a "three-on-the-tree" manual transmission with the gear shift on the steering column. I was already 5'7", having gone through a big growth spurt that summer, so reaching the clutch wasn't a problem. Dad had in fact taken me to the old county fairgrounds on the mainland that summer and taught me how to drive. So I felt ok about the technical aspects. I knew Chief Hall was the only cop on duty, so no worries there. Our little island's police force was only four cops in fall/winter. One on for each shift, one off each day. We all knew the coppers schedule like the back of our hand, one of the main reasons we were able to have so much fun without getting nabbed.

I looked down the road both ways before I got in the car. All clear, I got in, put her in reverse and backed out a little unsteady. I hadn't done much driving in reverse at the fairgrounds. I made it the mile or so to the old police station/town hall by the marina without incident. I didn't grind the gears at all. I parked on the marina side entrance to be out of the view of Chief Hall.

"Where's your dad Lenny?" Chief Hall said from behind the glass communication window that resembled a ticket taker's booth.

"He's waiting," I said nodding toward the marina bar. "I think he's talking to Skippy about going fishing tomorrow."

Skippy ran one of the many charters that left daily for Gulf Stream fishing trips. Dad had been on plenty with Chief Hall and Uncle D. One or more of the three usually had to be helped off the boat.

Chief Hall turned and unlocked cell number one, Uncle D was its lone occupant. The other three cells were empty. Chief Hall opened the heavy jail entrance door that separated the jail from the town hall. Uncle D struggled out. He looked like he'd already been asleep or passed out for a while. Chief Hall clanged the door behind him. Uncle D and I headed out toward the marina. We got about five yards from the car before it struck Uncle D.

"Where's your dad?" he asked.

"Home," I said.

Uncle D got in on the passenger side, never saying a word about me driving, why wasn't Dad here, or asking if I could even drive. He just sat there. Uncle D slept on the back deck hammock that night. I went in the front, placed my dad's keys in front of him and his fresh Miller, turned and went to my room.

This story never came up again in our house and was never discussed by the participants with one another to the best of my knowledge. I'm glad you got to meet my Uncle D. Now back to the poor running Marines, the cops, and all that.

Track 5-Anticipation-Carly Simon (3:17)

As far as we know, those were the last two Marguerite "victims" to go to the cops. The Marines had run, walked some, I guess. It was quite a ways, three miles or so to the police station at the marina. Turns out they knew the way because they'd been fishing that day on a charter. So, unlike most Miss M "victims", who ran straight for their car and were never heard from again, these fellas went to the cops. Oh, boy...

My dad was waiting on the front deck when I got home from camping the next morning. He was sitting in his favorite old folding chair. That relic, along with three others, and an old card table served as the small front deck atmosphere.

Now Pops was a pretty serious guy. I saw the ex-Marine sitting there with his coffee, a lit Kool in the ashtray and a stern look on his face. I knew the next 15 minutes weren't going on my most joyous moments' list. Dad kept his gaze fixed straight ahead.

"Sit down Son," he said matter-of-factly.

Now when Dad used the word son, my heart sank, it was going to be bad, real bad. He only called me son when I'd disappointed him. Knowing that pierced my heart a little more each time. That day was far from the first and even farther from the last.

I did as commanded and took a seat across from him at the card table. The day was overcast and the salt air mist was more intense than usual. I wasn't feeling my best as we'd partied pretty hard at Boy Scout Lake the night before and I'd gotten very little sleep. Just as Dad turned his gaze toward me with a sternness I only ever witnessed a few times, Mr. Weaver from two houses down stopped his old brown Chevy wagon in front of the house.

"Hey want go play some golf?" Mr. Weaver yelled out the window.

Dad turned slowly away from me, his blue-green eyes moments before lit with the fire of a blowtorch, quickly eased back to their normal level of a still super-intense pilot light. It gave me a second to think. Uh, I came up with nothing.

"Sounds good Walt," Dad said waving. "I'll be right down."

You see, besides a Redskins, Cardinals, or UNC win, few things brought Dad joy like a day on the golf course. I regularly still say a prayer of thanks for Mr. Weaver. I believe I've had a couple of guardian angels in my time, probably too big a chore for just one. Mr. Weaver was definitely one. He was a retired military guy (WWI and II), walked slightly bent over, was well past 70 with white hair and a wardrobe to match.

"Get the clubs," Dad nodded at me.

"Yes sir," I responded.

I couldn't get out of that chair fast enough. I sprinted down the stairs to the storage closet behind the pool table where we kept sports and beach stuff. There were several golf balls on the green tarp-covered pool table. I grabbed those as I heard the screen door clang. Dad went inside to tell Mom our plans. I was exhausted and didn't really want to go play golf or anything else. I had to work at the doughnut shop later. Four or five hours of sleep was what I desired more than anything, well almost anything, but Mr. Weaver was my good governor granting me a pardon or at least a temporary reprieve from the electric chair.

We hit the local municipal course on the mainland, which was a Donald Ross designed gem. The links were aging poorly, were underfunded, and actually kinda sad. A day on the course with my dad was always a good time, even if I knew I was in for some real heat. We walked the course with our clubs pulled along behind, rolling on two-wheel carts.

"So Lenny how's your summer been so far?" Mr. Weaver asked.

"Pretty good Mr. Weaver," I nodded and smiled. "We're in first place in the Babe Ruth League (baseball ages 13-15). Lots of good waves this summer so far, and working a bunch on the boardwalk."

"You're always a hustling," My guardian angel said. "Boy's going to make something outta himself one day Raymond."

"Could be," my dad said, looking straight ahead.

By the time we made the turn after number nine, the sky had cleared a bit. The day was warming to a more late July-like temperature. I was hungry and thirsty.

"Let's grab a sandwich," Mr. Weaver said. "I could go for a cold one too Raymond."

"Sure thing," Dad nodded.

I was so happy to take a break. We entered the 40-year old clubhouse that smelled of old golfers, stale coffee, and moldy carpet. Mr. Weaver hit the restroom. Dad and I walked to the bar.

"Hey Barney, two Millers and a coke for my adopted son here," Dad said nodding at me.

"What's he done now G.R.?" Barney, the barkeep said, looking at me as if I'd robbed a bank.

My infamous deeds were already somewhat well known in the larger town of which our little island was a bedroom community. At 15.75, I was already solidly on the trail to the big house or at least the county farm. I stared at Dad kinda wide-eyed, not knowing what was coming next.

"Well, for starters Barney," Dad began. "Ever see me get a coke?"

"Nope, can't say that I have, either Miller, PBR, or Pepsi," Barney replied.

"You know what I drive Barney?" Dad continued.

"Always seen you in a Ford, Raymond," Barney answered.

Dad pointed at his UNC polo shirt and then at my Duke t-shirt.

"Boy likes Dodge, Coke, and Duke," Dad deadpanned. "He has to be adopted or the milkman's."

He turned and walked away. I was stunned. It was funny, but I was still stunned.

"Three bucks kid," Barney said holding out his hand.

That was the first beer I ever bought for my old man. Sadly, the only one I ever bought for Mr. Weaver. At the time, I didn't know if the tongue-in-cheek slight was my punishment for the coppers coming to the house, but Dad never brought THAT particular visit by Chief Hall and patrolman Big Bob up again. Maybe the punishment was the dreaded anticipation of "the talk". Perhaps the real punishment would come later. That dread would linger for about a week and then subside. That was a tough week.

I found out later that summer the tale the running Marines had told patrolman Big Bob. They ran into him about halfway to town hall. Kinda explains how the coppers were already at my house when we ran into my Uncle D. Still, the Marines must have been booking along at some serious mph.

One sweltering August night, B and I ran into an off-duty Big Bob in the arcade with his very pregnant, but still very hot wife, Nicole. Now Big Bob wasn't that much older than us, he may have been 25 or so. He was a gentle giant of 6'7" and well over 300 pounds. A better-looking Andre the Giant if you will. He often found our escapades a bit amusing and a few years later would save my life (look for it on Disc two-Crazier Beach-the High School Years). He relayed that the two Marines sprinted up to him as he was about to get into his squad car at the gas station.

Big Bob said the guys pleaded for him to "come quickly" an old man was "shooting kids" at the graveyard. Big Bob said patrolman Nick was in his squad car next to Big Bob's car number 28. There were only four police cars in town, so how it got to be number 28 no one knows.

"I knew right away it was you two little idiots," Big Bob laughed. "But I played them a bit myself."

Big Bob was looking at Nicole for approval for his performance. He most assuredly had already shared the details with his former head majorette wife and high school sweetheart. She looked bemused by Big Bob's fascination with our hijinks.

"I sent Nick to your dad's and told him to ask your dad to play along," Big Bob smiled.

The oh crap look on our faces must have given away that this was the first time we were hearing about it. Hence, my dad's lack of interest in my "punishment". Things made a lot more sense now.

"I told the service boys Marguerite's dad never forgot a face," Big Bob started. "I asked them a couple of times if they'd been "made". I made a fake distress call for back-up, told them to come to the station and I'd put'em in a cell for their own protection."

At this point Big Bob was smiling so big, you'd think his kid had just been born. Nicole was just shaking her head. A few of our friends were listening in as well.

"I took them into the station and locked them in cell one and turned to leave," he continued. "I went just outside the door but talked plenty loud so they could hear me. I acted like I was having a conversation on the phone with the Chief about calling in SWAT and how best to protect the Marines from ending up the same way as the last crowd that went out to the graveyard."

Big Bob went on to tell us he let the jarheads sit awhile in the cell while he smoked a cigarette. He said they were scared shitless. Well not entirely. One of them got sick.

"When I came back in, I let'em out and said old man Norbett had been nabbed and they should head on back to Camp Lejeune and stay away for a few years because old man Norbett had relatives on the mainland might like to get a hold of them," a beaming Big Bob concluded.

"O.K., O.K., Richard Pryor," a bemused Nicole said taking Big Bob's arm. "That's enough honey. You boys ain't right."

Nicole was pointing her finger at me. Her head tilted to the right with an expression that was part reprimanding and somewhat warm and fuzzy at the same time. She was smiling pretty big.

"You wouldn't want us any other way, would ya?" I laughed as we began to bail. "See you Big Bob, Nicole."

"Man is it just me," B started as we exited. "I would so still do Nicole."

"Of course, of course, you perv," I said thumping B on the upper arm.

Track 6-With a Little Help from My Friends-The Beatles (2:44)

We left the arcade and headed over to the Wave to see a six o'clock twin-bill show featuring "The Concert for Bangladesh". The film documented the first big-time rock benefit show. Organized by George Harrison, featuring Eric Clapton, Bob Dylan, and tons more people who became even more famous in the ensuring decades. A movie about Joe Cocker's latest tour, "Mad Dogs and Englishmen" was the opener.

"This is going to rock," I said as we paid old Marie at the window.

We slipped into the very cold AC the theatre always offered. Sometimes it was the best thing about going to the movies at the beach. We didn't have AC at the house, lots of folks at the beach didn't back then because the ocean breeze kept it tolerable most of the time. Some families would have a window unit AC in their living room or bedroom. Mom finally talked Dad into one for the living room a few years later. For years, Dad, the old farm boy, never set foot in there when the AC was on. He would always hang out on one of the decks.

"Lenny, can I talk to you a sec," Melissa said as we scored some popcorn and sodas.

She was wearing white pants and a black tank top. The contrast was striking, especially with her ultra-light blond hair and almost translucent blue eyes. She had the sweetest personality.

"Of course, of course," I said.

She stepped from behind the counter and touching my arm led me over to the far corner away from her dad's office. Mr. Brockington was hard at work in his tiny cramped office under the balcony stairs. It was about the size of a broom closet.

"There's a party on the south end tonight," Melissa started.

"Cool," I smiled.

"Can you get some goodies?" she asked.

"Oh yeah," I said.

"Variety?" she asked.

I nodded affirmatively. She looked over to see where her dad was, and then reached into her bra and pulled out some cash. She placed the money in my hand. I quickly shoved it into my pocket without counting.

"That's 40 bucks," she said. "Get me some herb, make sure it's nice, and as much cid (acid/LSD) as you can. You can get that right, from you know who?"

She'd almost whispered the last part. Melissa wasn't allowed in the Rec Hall. Many "nice" island girls faced the same restriction. Hell, I wasn't allowed in there until the year before.

"Don't bring anybody but B," she said. "It's a high school party."

"I got to get there, don't I?" I said.

She hesitated for a few. I reached into my pocket to give her money back. Now I had every intent of going to that party come hell or high water, but I was trying to seem like it wasn't a big deal. She pushed my hand back into my pocket firmly, her nails were blue.

Her hands were warm. She smelled like Love's Baby Soft, a light, sweet smelling fragrance popular with teen girls in the 70's.

"All right," she said, somewhat resigned to the fact that I was the only hook-up she trusted. "But Dalton's not going to like a bunch of junior high kids at his birthday bash."

Holy crap, Dalton was throwing the party! I was invited! By Melissa Brockington no less. Dalton was the big dog on the island among the 16-24 crowd. A former lifeguard and later beach icon, his parties were legendary and this was the first one I was invited to attend. It was his 21st birthday. Melissa grabbed my hand again as we reached the entrance to the concession stand.

"I'm counting on you," Melissa said.

She smiled, a rarity for her, as she squeezed my hand a bit harder.

"No worries," I assured her.

She let go and turned to enter the concession stand. I could see the outline of her tiny panties through her white pants. A massive boner building since she first touched me reached unprecedented (for me) heights. She'd never stared into my eyes for so long. It would be the first of several "salutes" induced by Miss Brockington over the next few hours. That night would become one of the cornerstones of the Lenny legend. My conversation with Melissa was the start.

The movie was rocking. Mad Dogs indeed! Joe Cocker slayed it. Cocker, wild, unpredictable as always, flailing around like a possessed man fighting several hornets' nests at once. He was backed by a plethora of great musicians, including Leon Russell on piano and keyboards and heartbreaker Rita Coolidge (the Delta Lady) singing back-up. They totally ripped through Cocker's best material from that era. The movie had plenty of split-screen shots and a raw, trippy, you're there feel. There was a great crowd in the place rocking along when "pop" tiktiktiktik…the film broke…

"Shit!" B yelled at the screen and instantly the crowd turned nasty.

The air immediately filled with flying food and assorted crap you only find on the theatre floor; funky paper, weird cups snuck in from people's houses, empty mini-bottles, popcorn, candy (the cheaper stuff), no one was such a dumbass they threw away the pricey goodies.

A chorus of boos and hisses grew louder by the second directed at the blank screen bathed in the bright white light of the projector's 1,000-watt bulb. We could hear Mr. Brockington scramble into action inside the tiny film room that housed an ancient giant projector behind us. He was cussing quite loudly.

"Watch this," I said, standing up from our balcony perch.

I proceeded to make shadow puppets appear on the screen turning boos and hisses into even louder boos and hisses with some laughter and catcalls mixed in. B joined me in the vaudeville fun, casting funky shadows of animals, mythic creatures, and ultimately, of course, dirty puppet sex. A piece of licorice was used as a whip for a little s/m blue farm animal action. The crowd roared with laughter just as Mr. Brockington, all buck 20 of him jetted from out of the film room in our direction. Imagine a leprechaun-sized version of Martin Scorsese and you got Mr. Brockington.

"Out, out!" He yelled. "You two have done this for the last time! Get out of my theatre now!"

Mr. Brockington called us every name in the book and I don't mean The Good Book. I'd only heard that hardcore language from my Uncle Ed, the Navy vet who used it like he was winning money by doing so. I didn't know regular folks spoke that way too.

We made a couple of really obscene last-second necrophilia animal puppet scenes then bolted down the stairs. Mr. Brockington was still cussing up a storm. We ran past the concession stand and I blew Melissa a kiss as we exited the dimly-lit theatre lobby into the bright neon lights of a summer evening on the boardwalk.

"Let's roll to the house," I motioned to B as we headed south on the boardwalk past the donut shop, bumper cars, and the Sugar Shack.

I'd told B about the party as the movie was getting going. He was pretty stoked. I was as excited as I'd been in a long time.

"When we get to the house you call Hal," I continued. "I'll get the camping crap."

"This is going to be crazy," B smiled. "You know how many girls are going to be at Dalton's shindig?"

"Several boatloads, I'm sure," I noted. "We gotta hit the Rec Hall on the way to the house."

"Right, right," B said. "Plus we got to get some brew."

We got to the house and bounded up the steps. The place was packed with relatives and friends. Beer cans littered the bar area.

"Hey boys," an obviously already tipsy Aunt Pat said, motioning us toward the dining table. "Come on over, we're about to get started."

Aunt Pat was standing with about six or seven others around the dining table between the bar and the back of the couch. The double sliding glass door leading to the beachside deck was open. The ocean breeze might as well have been seated as another player for game night.

"Would love to Aunt Pat," I said. "Going to a birthday party though."

Mom turned from her ever-present spot near the stove. She was wiping her hands on her favorite red apron. She smiled.

"Whose party?" she asked matter-of-factly.

I'd told my poor mother so many lies about my misadventures, I couldn't keep up. I should've kept a journal. Now, this is the part where I lie to Mom, again.

"Nancy's," I boldly declared.

I could see B freeze. His somewhat half-goofy smile that showed up every year for school pictures for a decade made an appearance. He stood there like a statue.

"That's nice," Mom replied. "Simpson or Beattie."

I continued to dig myself deeper. I felt I was standing in a hole. I continued to shovel.

"Beattie," I lied again. "Down at the air station."

"I thought she moved after school let out?" Mom inquired.

"This week, after the party," I said, hoping the mini-interrogation was over.

"Well, (this pause was realllly long) have a good time, but don't stay out too late, you have all-star practice after Driver's Ed tomorrow," Mom said as I headed to my room and B went to call Hal on the phone by the bar.

"Have you eaten?" Mom asked raising her voice above the din of the game players battling in what was surely a heated Monopoly contest.

"Party food Mom!" I exclaimed.

"Tell Ms. Beattie I said hi," Mom said just a wee bit louder.

Mom never yelled, not once I can recall, I'm sure she probably did, just don't remember it. Never heard her say a curse word either. A true southern belle (which was her middle name, Belle that is), her only vice was smoking Winston's. She never drank alcohol, tons of coffee though, and was always respectful of others, regardless of their race, origin, or religion. One of her most endearing traits was her thoughtfulness when it came to others. In our home or in public, we couldn't call fat people fat, or homosexuals "gay" (and we had several relatives and friends that were/are one of the two or both). I told her on more than one occasion it was acceptable to gay folks to refer to them as gay, especially as opposed to some of the other terminology used at the time.

"No, no," Mom would say. "Let's just call them "happy".

Fat folk were "fluffy".

"Isn't Ms. Beattie dead?" B asked.

"Yea, yea," I said. "She checked out years ago, old man Beattie ain't married to that lady that lives with them. See what you can swipe from Dad's fridge on the back deck and meet me downstairs."

I jetted down the front deck to the carport closet to grab a cooler. I grabbed the old blue one and put it on the pool table tarp. Wouldn't you know it, guess who picks right then to "stop by?" Yep, you got it. Darlene and Lexi in Lexi's mom's white Oldsmobile Cutlass (the biggest selling car of the 1970s).

"Hey Lenny, what ya up to?" Darlene asked.

"No good, I'm sure," Lexi, uninvited, answered in her best Lexi pursed lips fashion.

Damn, time to lie again. To my two best ladies in a row. Well technically, Darlene was probably third, as my granny was a solid second, and sometimes first. Sorry Mom, I can see them arguing in heaven now. If that's allowed.

"Going fishing," I said confidently.

This would be the only time in my life I ever uttered those words not associated with Uncle D.

"Really?" Darlene asked cocking her head to the side.

"Yup," I replied, a little less confident.

Many say that in life, timing is everything, and for the most part, timing was not on my side this night.

"Hey, hay party time," Hal yelled pulling up in the open-air Scout that seemed to have a new ding in the left rear quarter-panel.

No way! B just called him and Hal got there in what? Three minutes, five at most, ok maybe seven, I did have to scrounge around in the closet for the cooler. I also paused to look at some old trophies in a box. Narcissism, the bane of man, and on this night, the slight delay had me in the muck of the summer.

"So, fishing?" Lexi asked sarcastically. "When you ever go fishing?"

Darlene got a disappointed and slightly angry look on her face. Lexi would've made a great prosecutor. Lexi would've made a great anything.

I weighed my options for a millisecond (seemed like about a week). I knew I had to act fast to save my shot at rounding the bases with Darlene before summer ended and still getting to the party and Melissa. About a gazillion options raced through my mind.

"Yea, we're going to fish down by the rocks, heard there might be a shindig down that way tonight too," I said, gesturing with my hands like I wasn't sure.

"He KNOWS there's a party down there!" Lexi declared triumphantly. "And not just any party, Dalton's birthday party!"

Darlene crossed her arms and tilted her head as if to say "well?"

"Oh yeah, that's right?" I said in a mock, slightly surprised voice. "Wow that's cool, we'll stop by."

I continued matter-of-factly, glancing at both girls to see how my reaction was playing. Lexi wasn't buying it. Darlene appeared undetermined at this point. I knew I needed more. I piled it on.

"B said he heard about it at work today," I offered, dragging B into my fabrication.

I knew Darlene would need more info to be assured I hadn't just told her a bold face lie. Which of course, I had. Not the first time either.

B worked with some of the high school kids at a local fish restaurant and often smelled like fried fish himself after work. Not really good for picking up the chippies on the boardwalk, but that's another tale. I was hoping this fake corroboration would suffice, as Lexi's brother was Dalton's pal. Lexi's potential future sister-in-law worked at the same restaurant as B. Whew, I'm tired just remembering how I came up with the logic for that part of the fairy tale of "How Lenny found out about the party of the summer".

Once again, timing, oh timing, you giver of fortune and slayer of dreams showed she wasn't through with me this night, not by a longshot.

"Oh hey girls," B said turning the corner after descending the beachside stairs.

"Hey B," they responded in unison.

The next millisecond was one of the most critical of the night. If Lexi got to question B first, we were doomed, likely forever. If on the other hand, I got to B first, I could attempt to put another notch in my relationship ladder with Darlene by weaving an even more intricate lie and dragging B farther down my rabbit hole.

Thankfully Hal was preoccupied with letting Bluto, his dog, drop a deuce in our tiny side yard. He brought his damn dog? But in this

68

case, the dog was good karma as it kept Hal out of a conversation he would have surely sabotaged as easily as the Harlem Globetrotters beat the Washington Generals.

"B will you grab Dad's two Garner rods and his tackle box?" I asked my best friend, turning enough to give him a wink without the girls seeing.

I'd also turned enough to see Bluto, Hal's massive eight-month-old, technically still a pup, but more like a miniature horse, mastiff-pit bull depositing a major load by mom's hydrangeas near the road. Bluto barked loudly. Hal was laughing.

The question hung there, like Ralphie's flying lug nuts in "A Christmas Story". In retrospect, I was hoping it wouldn't be an "O Fudge" moment. So there, I've managed to work my favorite holiday movie from 1983 into my primarily early-to-mid-70s fable.

B hated lying, still does to this day. Yep, we're still great friends. We're having a party soon to celebrate 50 years of friendship. A YO! A Golden Anniversary of Dudeship PARTY!

"Sure," B said, raising one eyebrow, Belushi-like again.

The eyebrow raise was his way of saying what the hell is going on?

You see, we NEVER FISHED. Not once in our 50 years of friendship, ever. I know you're saying, huh? You grew up on the ocean, on an island and never fished with your best friend? B probably did, I'm not sure, never asked him, but me and him fishing together, no, not once, and this was the only time it ever came up.

69

Hell, I only went fishing with my dad once, when I was like six, and I hated it to the extreme. I caught one fish, begged my dad to throw it back and that was that. Never wet a line with him again, just Uncle D. Just the couple times when, as you remember, I was 11. I concentrated on girls and sports. So I could never take that sage Dude advice to "quit, dump her, go fishing". Probably kept me employed a few times and helped prolong a few relationships. I wonder if it's too late to start.

The girls were a little leery of my tall tale, but once B appeared with the fishing gear, I thought I was in the clear. They seemed to start buying my bit. I wish I were so lucky.

"We're going fishing?" Hal asked as he helped B load the cooler and other gear into the back of the Scout.

Bluto sat there drooling massive quantities, unencumbered with my teenage dilemma. Lexi came a step closer. She started to say something. I quickly cut her off.

"Yea, stop and grab some bait at Mr. Graham's," I said, giving Hal a "shut the hell-up face". "I'll ride with the girls, damn it, that dog stinks."

We all pulled into Mr. Graham's store as the sun was going down. Sunset in August is a wonder to behold on our little island, you watch it rise over the ocean in the morn and set over the river to the west as night draws nigh. This night's was especially brilliant, as it was to be the night of the full moon and along the coast that usually brings the best sunsets of summer. It was sinking, slowly sinking, and I couldn't help but think my summer goal of getting Darlene to say yes was dropping with it.

We got the needed goodies from Graham's store and I poured a bag of ice over a case of beer. Bluto lustily licked up the spillage and began licking the cooler. He shared his slobber, making the cooler a mess.

"He's going to be a good one," Hal beamed, patting the mutt on the head.

"Yea, he'll be alright," I agreed.

"The bait was $2.25," Hal said.

"Well that'll get ya several beers," I said.

"That'll work," Hal grinned in reply. "I sure do love beer."

The girls chatted excitedly as we made our way to the southern tip of the island. I was trying to figure what to do once we got there. Edward Bear's "Last Song" was playing on the radio.

"All the lifeguards will be there," Lexi said, wide-eyed to Darlene. "Benny has been eyeing you all summer."

Lexi's obvious attempt to make me jealous went nowhere with me or Darlene. I knew boys lusted after Darlene. Who wants a damned girl people don't lust after? And Darlene was one of the most lust-worthy girls I'd ever see.

"He's an idiot," Darlene laughed. "A cute one, but an idiot."

"And he pooped his pants in fourth grade," I laughed, popping a top on the first cold beverage of the evening.

"Damn Lenny!" Lexi exclaimed. "What if we get stopped?"

I pointed my right index finger to my watch-less left wrist as I took a big gulp.

"Shift change, no worries," I smiled.

"Still," Lexi whined.

"Let me have a sip," Darlene demanded, turning toward me in the back seat.

I passed her the can and she took a swig.

"What the hell," Lexi said, shrugging her shoulders.

She took the can from Darlene and finished it off in one big chug. She tossed the empty back at me and demanded another one. When she wanted to (rarely) Lexi could be loads of fun.

"Whooooo," I yelled out the open window. "That's what I'm talking about. Let's rock!"

"What the…?" Lexi said quizzically as she looked in the rear-view mirror. "Hal pulled over and somebody's getting in the back."

"I think that was Eggs," Darlene said.

"That dumbass," I said, meaning Hal, not Eggs.

"He better not bring him to the party," Lexi said.

"Hal's not that dim?" Darlene half-asked looking at me.

I shrugged my shoulders. The weirdness had just begun. This night was going to get Hall of Fame-level weird.

Track 7-Theme from the Good, the Bad, & the Ugly-Ennio Morricone (2:45)

We call them "The Island Trinity", those of us that grew up on the island in the 60s and 70s, "Cappy", "Eggs", and the "Hermit". Almost mythical in character and nature, they were huge influences on a generation of young people and an inescapable part of the lives of the adults who lived on the island in those years. These three men embodied the varying attributes the counterculture was trying to ascribe to, but never came close to emulating; rejection of tradition, true personal freedom, living with as few material things as possible, and even more, becoming part of nature… well two of them anyway.

The most mythological first, the Hermit. You see, there's plenty written about the Hermit; articles, books, and a play. You can research more stuff about "Mr. Robert". Some are ok, but there's a lot more story out there, especially from locals, those of us who spent time with him at length or regularly interacted with him. Mr. Robert came to the island in 1955, the spring after Hurricane Hazel's October knock-out punch of the Carolinas. After Hazel, Mr. Robert is probably what the island was most famous for, with the donuts being a close third. In the 21st century, the donuts are likely number one.

He was the Hermit to those over 25 or so and to tourists and sadly, now to the world. "Mr. Robert" as the young called him, was anything but a hermit, and in private, adamantly detested the term, but publically embraced it in his later years. Sure he lived alone in a secluded area, but he was never stand-offish and regularly interacted with almost all who came his way. He lived in an abandoned World War II bunker by the ocean on the far southern end of the island. He had some very eccentric ways and philosophies, but a hermit, nah, no way. He was funny, respectful, often witty, and charming in an earthy way. He always told us he was going to write a book about his philosophies (I wish!). A treasure trove of his letters resides in the East Carolina University archives.

He regularly walked the island scavenging and would wander into town on occasion. He could be counted, like clockwork, to appear at our house late each fall, when our side yard's persimmon tree was ready to start dropping its sweet joy, helping Mom gather up the bounty. Most folks like their persimmons in a pudding or other desert concoction, but Mr. Robert liked his fresh off the ground, unwashed, the way nature delivered them. Mom considered him an "old soul", an acclaimed title in my mom's simple vernacular.

To most of us kids, Mr. Robert was just an interesting old guy, who was wiser than most, lived the way he wanted, and had few material possessions. We would check on him more in winter than in summer. In summer the tourists would help with his needs and take up lots of his time. When the late fall and winter came, the island settled into its annual six month-sabbatical from the outside world. Those were the times we enjoyed most with Mr. Robert. He was usually good to go, the most self-sufficient and efficient person I've ever met, but every now and then he would say, "If you boys run across so and so…". We always made sure we did.

I could write a whole book about Mr. Robert, but there are several out there already. He was one of the most interesting people I've ever met. He is a character definitely worth exploring more about at your local bookstore.

The second spire of the Trinity was Henry Dominic "Cappy" Capillary. Picture one of Z.Z. Top's grandfathers as a George Hamilton-level tanned leprechaun and you have an idea of how Cappy appeared to the world. For over four decades, starting in the early 1940s after he graduated from college, he would arrive on the island when the water became warm enough to go swimming and would depart when it wasn't in early fall. He had a wide and varied career; a teaching degree from Elon, a civilian employee at Ft. Bragg, a stevedore at the local shipyards, and a couple stints at a local factory. He lived out of his 1969 Cadillac in the years I spent around him, a man at peace with his choices. Greatest swimmer the island ever knew. His daily sunrise ritual was to walk to the beach just behind The Landmark restaurant and the putt-putt. He would stroll straight into the water, no stretching, no warming up, just straight into the ocean, swim out past the breakers, swim the mile or so down to the North End Pier, (sometimes the other direction to Center Pier) turn and swim back. He went so far out sometimes, unsuspecting tourists would call the police or coast guard to report a man "lost at sea". He definitely wasn't lost, more like at one with the ocean.

His best friends were the dolphins who often accompanied him on his journey. I swear it seemed like they were waiting for him each morning. You could see them jumping, cackling dolphin talk, Cappy swore he could understand them a little bit. He would emerge from the ocean, like Neptune covered in ocean debris, his beard soaked, making him appear somewhat sinister, but nothing was farther from reality. Cappy was perhaps the most joyous person I've ever encountered. Always smiling, offering a kind or uplifting word, sharing a cold ocean-side beverage with the rapt audience who gathered around him on the evenings he would magically appear on the boardwalk. He talked of nature, the ocean, its creatures, life, and happiness. He seemed to be a living, breathing part of each.

The third spire, "Eggs", you've met already. Shaken to the core by the horrors of war, Eggs wandered through the rest of his life seemingly eternally looking as if he was searching for something he'd lost. He just couldn't remember what it was, or where it might be.

Eggs was about 5'8" and maybe a buck fifty. He had a severely receding hairline and a pock-marked face with a ruddy complexion. He often wore clothes that looked a bit ill-fitting on the loose side, appearing as if he'd lifted them from a larger man's clothesline. He was a curiosity, an enigma, and a riddle no one quite ever solved. He bounced and bounded around the boardwalk and island like the dimension splitting singer from A'Ha's "Take on Me" video.

On this one night, at one of the biggest and best island parties of the decade, they came together for, by all accounts, the first and last time. An epic meeting of island quasi-deities that shook the souls of most who attended. Well, that may be just a bit dramatic, judge for yourselves.

Track 8-We're Having a Party-Sam Cooke (2:29)

I'd love to claim I was responsible for the almost mythical evening about to unfurl, and most islanders of that time lay the blame or credit, as I view it, on me. The truth is, I only deserve partial credit. Karma, Elvis, or whatever deity you believe in likely should get half the royalties on this one.

We pulled up to the beach parking area near the Civil War museum. There were already a couple dozen vehicles parked by the edge of the dunes. Most we recognized, on a small island you get to know the vast majority of the vehicles either by family or place. Plus, I was always good with i.d'n cars, make, model, and owner. When I was a little kid, before we moved to the beach, my dad would take me to his local hang-out, an old-school Shell gas station run by one of his school buddies. Dad would challenge non-locals who stopped by for a repair or pit-stop to ask me a baseball question or challenge me to identify any passing car for a bet of a beer. Dad got to drink A LOT of free beer!

So I almost knew who we'd see when we walked the couple hundred yards to the party site by the parked cars present. The old 55 black Buick was "Salem's", Dalton's uncle, a hard-core partier, about 30 and sometime drinking companion of my Uncle D (who'd already passed at this point). Just an older version of Dalton, a kinda island Iggy Pop, wiry, and full of piss and vinegar, an avid fisherman, who made his money on the sea and spent it in the local bars.

The shiny, new gold Datsun 260Z belonged to Melissa, a gift from Mr. Brockington, for Melissa's birthday back on Valentine's Day. B and I always joked whoever ended up with Melissa would at least only have to buy just one gift on Valentine's Day. If, pretty sure this was a gargantuan if, they could talk her into getting married on V-Day, presto, Wham-O, only one gift for three major occasions! I could go on and on about the cars/trucks/dune buggies/jalopies, but you get the idea. I wasn't expecting any surprise guests.

"Whooooo-hoooooo," Hal screamed at the top of his lungs sliding the Scout in next to us on the sand. "Party time!"

Bluto was sitting on the lap of the hitchhiker in the back and obscured the view. B made it around the Scout. He patted me on the shoulder.

"Not my fault," he said and continued toward the dunes.

Bluto leaped out the Scout and there sat Eggs. Sad sack Eggs, his shirt wet from Bluto's slobber (I think, hope?) Hal grabbed the cooler, hoisted it up on his broad shoulders and began walking in the direction of the party.

"Yo, Hal," I said, nodding my head toward a still seated Eggs.

"What could he hurt?" Hal shrugged and walked on.

"Eggs, how ya doing man?" I asked.

"Mumble, mumble, raff, snaff, mumble, mumble," Eggs said, looking at me.

"Oh, ok," I said.

I could've been agreeing to the most reprehensible thing of all time, I'd no idea. I also had no idea how to proceed. Crap, I just didn't know what to do.

"Did you want to come here or go home?" (no one knew where THAT was) I continued.

"Mumble, snaff, raff, raff, mumble," Eggs said, a bit louder.

Usually, these were Eggs most used words. Depending upon the inflection, the best one could hope for was to discern, anger from less anger. That was what we thought at the time.

There've been few times in my life, I felt as unprepared and/or at a loss as I did at that moment. I wanted to hurry on over to the party and begin shindigging, see Melissa, laugh with Darlene and Lexi, drink with Hal and B, and enjoy an evening on the beach. I was now thinking that if things went really well this might be "the night". I could see the bonfire was already going and I could hear the music, some sweet soul music. If I remember correctly it was Al Green's "Let's Stay Together."

"Eggs, do I need to get you home?" I asked.

Most of my being wanted to simply walk on toward the party. My friends had already crested the dunes. I watched them disappear into Partyworld.

"Lenny," I heard a familiar voice say from behind.

It was Mr. Robert. Maybe he was a ghost, he sure popped up sometimes with little or no approach or warning. I turned his way, west toward the river.

"Hi Mr. Robert," I said.

I felt like I was in an episode of the Twilight Zone. I was waiting for Rod Serling to appear. Talk about the universe coming to call at unexpected and inopportune times.

"I could use a ride to town," Mr. Robert said.

"Sure, sure, Mr. Robert," I blurted, before calculating the possible consequences and/or repercussions.

I guess I was on autopilot. I certainly wasn't thinking clearly. I'd only consumed about half a beer and no drugs but was clearly out of my mind. Mr. Robert walked around to the other side of the Scout and had his hand on the windshield frame. I watched it all unfold as if I was having an out-of-body experience. At that precise moment, a familiar vehicle pulled up blocking the path of the Scout.

"Lenny, is this the party spot?" Cappy asked, leaning out the Caddy's window, its engine chug-chug-chugging in rhythm with the surf.

Words can't begin to tell you what that moment felt like. I'm sorry for not being able to better explain. If someone has had a more existential moment, cheers to them! I think I was so dumbfounded, so utterly confused, I just kept saying "yes". I don't know how many questions, or how long before I recovered my senses. The next thing I knew, Cappy was standing right in my face. He was in Seinfeld parlance, a "close-talker".

"Dalton told me to come, said it was his birthday," Cappy offered with his usual ultra-positive countenance and smile.

"Yes," my eloquence continued.

"Over there?" Cappy pointed beyond the dunes.

Steppenwolf's "Born to be Wild" was now playing. The crowd noise was rising. The waves were louder, crashing, and the full moon high-tide would be coming in soon.

"Yes," I retained my consistency.

Cappy put both hands on my shoulders. He looked at me intently. He changed angles and did it again.

"You alright boy?" he asked with a concerned grandfatherly look on his face.

"Yes." One last time, I muttered and hoped.

I glanced at the Scout. Mr. Robert was sitting in the front passenger seat. He was adorned in his usual attire; big straw hat, dark tank-top, and ragged denim shorts. He was looking straight ahead. Eggs, directly behind him, was having a sweet conversation with himself as usual. I think the voices in his head might have been fighting. Somehow in this bizarreness, Bluto had returned and was sitting as erect as any human in the driver's seat, slobbering profusely on the steering wheel.

Cappy began to walk toward the sound of "…like a true nature's child…we were born, born to be wild…" He stopped and turned around. He pointed at me.

"Got any weed?" he queried with a smile.

You already guessed the answer. We had popped by the Rec Hall and "scored" a bit earlier. I was armed for bear. If bears wanted to get really, really high.

"Yes," I robotically said.

I'd smoked with Cappy a couple of times that summer. He was fun to get stoned with, lots of laughter. We'd caught a buzz around the pier one morning after his swim. He'd passed me as I was sitting on my board, waiting for some waves and asked the same question.

"Fire one up," Cappy said as he walked the eight or so steps back to the Scout.

The robot complied. I reached into my mostly blue Hawaiian shirt's (hey, it was the 70's!) only pocket and produced a joint Dutch had given me as a sample of what I was buying. I hadn't yet dipped into today's fresh stash I'd gotten for Melissa, me, and my friends. Just as I was about to light it...

"It's not what goes in a man that defiles him," Mr. Robert said, quoting the Bible. "But what comes out."

Well, I couldn't get much out. I've replayed these moments in my mind a gazillion times, searching, reaching, looking for something I could've said or done to alter the evening's outcome or enjoy this moment more. You ask a lot of folks what they would change about their lives and sometimes they come up with something profound, sometimes something cool or silly, or the self-indulged say...nothing, I wouldn't change anything. That's probably a lie in most cases, they just wanna sound super cool.

I passed the J to Cappy, who took a nice, long, slow drag. He looked at me and nodded toward the Scout. Using proper stoner protocol to see if I wanted to share with the others since it was my herb. If it'd been Cappy's, the protocol would've allowed him to pass it wherever he wanted.

"Yes," the stuck record answered.

Cappy offered the joint to Mr. Robert, walking around the Scout to the passenger side avoiding any possible interaction with Bluto's slobber, keeping his brown Cuban-style shirt clean. Mr. Robert nodded as he accepted the joint.

I've no idea how much time had passed at this point, 10 minutes, 20, 45? Don't know, guess I was hoping some of the others would return and help me with my dilemma. Man, I wanted to go party, but this was too unreal to disturb.

Mr. Robert leaned over the driver's seat and handed the joint back to me, never acknowledging Eggs in the backseat, who was still deep in his own mind, out loud. Bluto seemed to be staring straight ahead at some unseen (by us) person or thing. He was a slobbering statue. Perhaps he was getting a "contact" buzz.

I inhaled. I was getting a little high. Cappy was smiling. Mr. Robert was smiling. Bluto was smiling, and for the only time I ever saw, had stopped slobbering. I became concerned we were leaving Eggs out, but for some reason, I decided to forego passing the joint to Eggs and decided to blow Bluto a "shotgun".

If you are unfamiliar with drug culture, let me explain. A "shotgun" happens when one herb smoker takes the joint, flips it around and places the lit end in his/her mouth. The next step is to blow smoke to the person receiving the "shotgun". You can really get stoned VERY quickly using this method.

Bluto loved it, lots of creatures don't. I have a story about getting some goats high you'll hear about in Crazy Beach-Disc II-the High

School Years. He took in the smoke and immediately leaped like a deer out of the Scout and ran toward the party. Smart mutt, maybe he smelled the hot dogs roasting in the fire pit.

Cappy laughed, Mr. Robert laughed. I wish Eggs had laughed, but he was somewhere else, in his mind I'm sure, but now to my great alarm, physically as well. It was as if he were a wizard and had vanished, much as Mr. Robert had appeared in such a flash earlier. Also time, time, as Steve Miller sang, "keeps slipping into the future". I'd lost all concept of how long it had been…

In ensuing days and weeks, my friends said they thought I was dealing with Eggs, which at some level had a bit of truth to it. But now Eggs was gone. I stared at his empty seat. I briefly entertained the thought he'd been "raptured" the Christian belief that the good ones get "swept up" to glory on Judgement Day or something like that. Why would I think that? Well, Eggs' clothes were still in the seat.

Cappy slapped me on the shoulder. He complimented me on the power and flavor of the dope. He shook his Medusa-like long brown/gray hair violently. He had some ashes in his beard.

"Time to roll that way," he said pointing to the dunes and the source of the music, which was now Little Feat's "Dixie Chicken".

Before I could say anything, probably yes, again. Cappy was what seemed like far away, disappearing over the dunes to PartyWorld. I meanwhile was still stuck in the surreal world. Mr. Robert still sat quietly in the passenger seat. The "roach" portion of the joint, the very last, little bit, burned my fingers. I let it fall to the sand. I kept thinking where the hell did Eggs go? The music grew louder.

And no lie, at that very moment, Mr. Robert said. "I really need to get some eggs, Lenny."

"Mr. Robert," I said breaking my "yes" spell. "I don't think I should drive."

Number one; because I'd been drinking, number two; because I had no license, I was just finishing up driver's ed, and number three; I had to find Eggs.

I turned to look at the ocean to see if Eggs had decided to go swimming. I didn't see him and I would've, the late summer's rising best moon was giving it, like in Clement Moore's poem, "the luster of mid-day below".

I swear in what couldn't have been five seconds, I turned back toward Mr. Robert and poof! He was gone just as he'd arrived, instantly and without warning. I was beginning to think all of this was a dream.

I was alone, dumbfounded, slightly, or mightily stoned, and certainly confused. Dutch told me the sample joint was herb called "Maui Wowie', my first encounter with non-mainland weed. I told myself to relax, I was just a little high. My next few moments made me wish I was much higher.

Track 9-Dance to the Music-Sly & the Family Stone (3:00)

I could hear the incoming tide making its appearance known. Again, no track of time as I stood by the Scout. I looked south toward the dunes, I could see flames from the bonfire, I could hear Zep's "Black Dog" wailing. I looked west toward the river in the distance, nothing. I turned north toward town, nothing. I completed my 360 gazing east back at the ocean. I stared at the glistening sea, moonlit, and inviting, I thought of going in, but thought better of it.

"Raff, mumble, snaff," I heard, but didn't see.

Was Eggs calling to me from the other side? Was this what he'd been trying to share with me all summer? Did it have anything to do with his performance art? Was I in one dimension or alternate reality and everyone else in another? I concluded boy, was I stoned!

"Raff, mumble, snaff," I heard again.

"Eggs, Eggs, where are you?" I yelled.

"Raff-n-snaff'n, mumble, mumble," Eggs beckoned from somewhere.

It sounded as if he was coming from another world, down below perhaps?

Poor Eggs, had I anything to do with him going to the underworld? Should I've helped him that night on the boardwalk when I left him to talk to the two little blonds? I felt despair, but in another instantaneous appearance, Bluto was back and sliding under the Scout. I bent over and yep, you guessed it, there lay Eggs, completely naked, face up, getting his forehead slobbered on by Bluto.

"Eggs, Eggs," I said, unsure what to do next.

"Lenny, I got some eggs," a magically re-appearing Mr. Robert said from in front of the Scout's hood. "Let's go cook'em on the fire."

Yep, Mr. Robert had beamed down (in?) on the passenger side of the Scout. He was holding a half-dozen or so eggs. I pointed down at the belly of the Scout.

"Eggs," Mr. Robert said without looking down. "Come on up outta there, we're going to go eat."

For the first time in my life, I saw Eggs respond directly to a request. Like Lazarus coming forth from the grave at his Master's command, Eggs climbed out from under the Scout on the passenger side and stood there naked looking at Mr. Robert's hands.

"I like eggs," Eggs said.

That was the only complete sentence I ever heard him say.

We all started to walk toward Partyland. We'd only covered a short distance and must have looked like the three unwise men. What a trio; a hermit holding some eggs, a stoned out kid, and a naked quasi-lunatic strolling leisurely in the sand.

"Your pants Eggs, go get your pants," Mr. Robert said, gesturing with his shoulder back toward the Scout.

Mr. Robert and I were treated (mistreated?) to our second full moon of the night as Eggs made his way back to the Scout. Bluto had long disappeared across the dunes to party central. Eggs got his pants alright. He just didn't put them on right away. He was waving them vigorously over his head, like the hot girl starting a drag-race in old-school flicks or the Fast and Furious series. Just as he reached us, Mr. Robert instructed him to do so.

"How's your mother Lenny," Mr. Robert asked, as Eggs managed to button his drawers.

"Fine Mr. Robert," I said. "I'll tell her you asked about her."

"I'd like that," Mr. Robert said.

"Raff, snaff, snaff, snaff," Eggs said emphatically.

"Now Eggs, you be nice, there'll be young ladies here," Mr. Robert said.

"Mumble, mumble," Eggs nodded an affirmative (I think?).

We crested the northern dunes to an amazing sight, a huge bonfire bouncing into the night sky as if propelled by a trampoline. A few yards away from the main fire, closer to the western dunes, was a food fire-pit surrounded by young people with sticks, roasting and toasting various meats and other goodies. They all seemed to be having a great time.

Bluto was running in and out of the ocean, several people were swimming, basking in a bright lunar glow, a portable stereo was blasting Harvest's "Dancing in the Moonlight". A dozen or so people were doing just that, dancing, some in couples, others just groups of girls, twisting, gyrating, and having fun. Like CCR sang, "…barefoot girls dancing in the moonlight". It was beautiful.

There weren't many stars out, just a big, bright summer moon. As I recall, it was perhaps the closest the moon has ever appeared to me. Perception? The weed? Science! Who knows? All I know is I felt as if the best of the night and the best of the day had merged into one magnificent new reality.

"Glad y'all finally made it," Cappy said as we approached the bonfire. "Was beginning to wonder what had happened to ya."

"Eggs had a problem with his tailor," Mr. Robert said.

"Sounds bout right," Cappy nodded. "Where you get those eggs Robert?"

"Was going to town, then I remembered those ducks over by the museum," Mr. Robert noted.

"Lenny!" It was Melissa. "Bout damn time!"

She'd changed into some cut-off shorts and a hippie-girl woven tan blouse. She was barefoot, like most of the girls. She looked relieved to see me.

"Where ya been?" she asked, putting her left hand on my right shoulder and tilting her head to look me in the eyes. "Shit, you're stoned already!"

She laughed her cute, little-girl like-laugh that I wish I had heard more. I could see Darlene, Lexi, and B over by the fire-pit roasting something. I was immobile. I smiled and said nothing. Eggs, Mr. Robert, and Cappy headed toward Dalton and his buddies by the bonfire. Hal and the dog were running up and down the beach. There was laughter from the swimmers. The fire was crackling, dancing in rhythm to the sounds of BTO, "You ain't seen nothing yet". How true, how true…

Melissa gently took me by the arm and led me away from the others toward the western dunes which separated the main road from the beach. She looked a little concerned. The ocean breeze was blowing her hair toward the river.

"Is everything alright?" she asked, big sister-like.

I nodded yes.

"Do you have the stuff I wanted?" She continued.

She still had a hold of my arm and was standing very close to me. The summer breeze brushed her platinum blondness across my face. I was getting a little excited. I nodded yes again.

"I want a kiss," I broke my silent spell by saying something that had been on my mind for a long time.

I had to be wrecked to make such a request, right? After all, Darlene was only 30 yards away, Dalton just a bit closer. Melissa's head twisted a bit as if trying to comprehend what I'd said. She smiled. She looked at me as if I'd asked for a million dollars.

"Boy, you're really are stoned," She smiled bigger and let go of my arm. "Have you had some of Dutch's new batch?"

I nodded and smiled. The wind now blew just the tips of her hair near my lips and nose. I'd never been so happy.

"You know I'm three years older than you right?" she again tilted her head, like she knew something I didn't. "And with Dalton, right?"

I nodded yes.

"I want a kiss," I repeated, cocking my head for emphasis.

"You know I'm seeing Dalton, right?" she sounded more stressed than light-hearted now.

I nodded yes again. I reached into my board shorts pocket and retrieved her weed and a three-quarter sheet of acid in a cellophane pouch. I handed them to her. I didn't want the kiss to be one of "you don't get your goodies" unless you do kinda thing. She quickly shoved them in her shorts.

"Lenny, you're just too much," she smiled again, placing her right index finger on my lips, she quizzed with tilted head again. "Besides, aren't you talking to Darlene? Like, since kindergarten or something?"

With that, she turned and walked away.

I hope you've heard the Jimmy Carpenter (from Greensboro, NC) blues classic, "Sometimes I Wish You'd Leave Me" (just so I could watch you walk away). Well, this was THAT moment. The combo of setting, my raging 15.75-year old hormones, the herb, and my interaction with one of my dream girls produced a raging boner the moment I saw her ass in those barley there cut-offs. I mean, earth-shaking, gotta grab it sized boner, where your back involuntarily arches and it feels soooooo good! Praise Elvis! And praise Elvis again I was a good 30-yards or so from other human beings.

I watched her walk back and had all the perverted thoughts a 15-year old boy has about a fantasy dream girl. Yes, I was really into Darlene, but my fantasy dream girl (and really she was only 2.75 years older than me) had made close physical contact with me on multiple occasions already this day. The smell of her sun-kissed skin, the hint of Love's Baby Soft body spray, the touch of her hair, her finger on my lips, and finally the sight of her nearly perfectly heart-shaped tiny little beach butt had finally driven me the last few paces to being totally out of my mind. I just stared at the ocean and sky doing math problems until my pieces parts calmed down.

Track 10-Celebrate-Three Dog Night (3:07)

"You just going to stand over here?" Hal inquired. "You're ripped!"

I petted Bluto. He and Hal had been in the water. They smelled like the ocean.

"Dude, you better get over to the party, a bunch of those older boys hit'n on your girl," he continued. "She looks super-fine tonight. Lexi does too!"

I glanced over at the two fires. There was a crowd around Darlene, Lexi, and Jade, 18, a long-haired sandy blond. She looked every bit a woman of 25. People were dancing everywhere. I nodded. Hal slapped my arm. I looked at the mark his hand left, boy I was feeling more stoned every second.

"C'mon, man, let's go play!" he almost shouted and began to jog with Bluto toward the fires.

The fires were spinning and appeared to dance together high above the revelers below. It finally struck me, I was tripping! I'd only done acid once before and wasn't really experienced handling the stuff. I knew you weren't supposed to let it touch your skin till you were ready to ingest it. I must've touched the sheet too much when I split it into two cellophane envelopes. Most of the sheet was for Melissa and the smaller portion for me and my close friends. Trails of multi-colored lights were flowing behind Hal and Bluto. Yes, I was definitely tripping.

I began inching, so it seemed, toward the fires. The bonfire was blasting skyward and the food-pit fire was doing the same in a mini-version. Their yellow-orange talons were spiking higher by the moment and seemed to be engaged in a sword fight over the dancing party-goers.

I felt like it took me forever to reach the outer bands of dancers, a group of high schoolers about 10 yards away from the bonfire. There were about a dozen people celebrating by gyrating, jumping, and moving rhythmically to the sounds of Brownsville Station's "Smoking in the Boys Room". They all seemed to be smiling, laughing, and having a really good time.

One girl in particular, a tall redhead was bounding higher and higher. She almost seemed to defy gravity. I slowed my gait to observe. She had on cut-off jeans and a too small for her boobs purple bikini top. Her girls had me transfixed. They seemed to move to their own beat. One was dancing wildly and the other more steadily. I kept to my, hopefully, straight walking path, bringing me within a foot or so of the redhead.

"Hey Lenny," she said in a second of momentary contact with the sand.

"Thanks for the goodies!" Red said laughing. "I'm so light!"

How long had I been standing out there? I remember seeing Melissa visiting her friends. I guess she was passing out her party favors. It usually takes 20-45 minutes for acid to "kick-in", had I really been out there long enough for them all to be tripping already?

I passed by another group. Next up was a few guys talking and drinking beer about five yards from the bonfire. One of them seemed to have on Mr. Spock ears, or were those his real ears? The acid was really kicking. Sea, sand, and sky were so noisy and beautiful, like nature's train rumbling by and then through me. I was close to the bonfire now.

"Hey," it was Dalton, the man of the day. "You did damn good Lenny boy!" he slapped me on the right shoulder and handed me a joint. "You scored some great weed too!"

"Thanks Dalton," I said. "Happy Birthday".

"Kid, don't know where you scored this shit," Salem said. "But it's kicking my ass!"

I never looked at them. I just wandered off to the right, away from the bonfire and toward the fire pit. A group of guys were drinking and talking to Lexi and Jade.

"Where's Darlene?" I asked Lexi.

She moved her shoulders and head to the right. I looked over. Darlene was about 10 yards away with another group of partiers.

"Hey Lenny," Jade said. "Want to go for a swim?"

"I'll go," about three guys said in unison.

I just nodded no. I chose, for some reason, to turn back toward the bonfire and the ocean beyond. I could see Eggs, a soaking wet Cappy, and Mr. Robert on the other side of the bonfire eating boiled eggs and wieners without buns. Cappy was laughing. Mr. Robert pointed his hot dog at me. Eggs never looked up, munching away on his namesake meal. CCR's "Proud Mary" was just finishing up.

As I approached the fire my friend Tyler was switching off the music. He pulled his acoustic guitar from its case and began playing Buffett's "Come Monday". Cappy began to dance around Tyler. Mr.

Robert began to sing along. Eggs just glared at them all. I wish I'd a picture of that moment to include in this book. It was way beyond cool.

The acid was playing all kinds of wonderful tricks with my senses. At various moments, I felt I could hear conversations from far away. Then I heard the dunes shifting. I also heard and felt a few other things, if mentioned at the time, would've gotten me committed to Dorthea Dix, the state mental hospital.

I don't know how much time passed. Tyler had played many songs, I think. I hadn't moved or talked to anyone in a while.

That portion of the night, I felt more like an observer or chronicler. I guess I really was, as you are reading my account of those events. I felt the sand as never before or since. The ocean permeated my every cell. The sky rushed by and I played connect-the-dots with the few stars making the scene. The man in the man-in-the-moon seemed to be partying with us and winking at me. I could touch the breeze. Suddenly, as if in a time travel moment, I was standing by the bonfire.

"Lenny," It was Darlene. "What the hell are you doing just standing here? You alright? You've been here a long time by yourself."

She passed me a joint. I nodded yes and took a hit. Her eyes were rolling like a casino slot machine. Her hair was dancing. This was the peak of my trip, I thought.

"You want something to eat?" she asked.

As I nodded no, I noticed a couple of guys standing just behind her. Water was springing from their heads like a collective fountain. Damn, these were good drugs!

"We're going to hit the waves and do some bodysurfing," dude number one said.

"You wanna go?" Darlene asked.

I nodded no. She shook her head as if she couldn't figure out what I was doing. I should have told her I was tripping, but I didn't. I didn't have a clue as to what I was doing. I was just watching. I like to watch. I really like to watch a lot.

Darlene dropped her shorts to reveal a rainbow-colored bikini bottom. Damn, she was fine. Her legs were spectacular. Her toenails had what appeared to be a fresh coat of blue paint matching the blue of her suit. The rainbow was pulsating, especially in one spot. She and the two high school dudes raced past me. I stared down at her jean shorts, they were dancing too!

A conga-line type dance group was circling the fire, about 20 people strong, including the redhead, her dancing friends, Cappy, and Mr. Robert. "Jumping Jack Flash," by the Stones was blasting from the stereo. Eggs was doing a funky witch doctor dance in an outside orbit around the conga line.

"Yo Lenny," it was Tyler, carrying his guitar case. "We need to get together and play some parties before school starts."

I nodded ok, Tyler and I (on drums), along with David on bass, sometimes tried to be a band. We were never very good, but we had fun. I'd no idea where David was. He may have been at work or vacation. His family took a lot of vacations.

Mr. Robert slapped me on the back as he congaed by. Where was B? I looked around, didn't see him, Hal, or Bluto. The fire pit was now deserted; someone tossed a hot dog into the bonfire from behind me. The next one whizzed by and began sizzling as it struck the bonfire. A couple of Dalton's close buddies broke thru the conga line to deliver more wood for the fire.

Whack! A hot dog smacked me upside the head. Now normally a person would turn to see who'd hit them with something, but in my drug-soaked mind, I simply bent over to pick it up. Bluto appeared and I tossed it to him. He got rid of it quickly. At that moment, I felt an arm around my shoulder. It was B.

"Hey man!" he started. "You sure are an easy target. You've been standing here forever. Can I get my hit?"

I nodded and reached into my pocket. I handed the small cellophane envelope to him. He took a square and put it in his mouth and returned the envelope to me. I placed it back in my pocket.

"You going to drop?" he asked.

"Already have," I said, not knowing how much I'd absorbed in cutting up and transferring the acid.

Lots of acid can make you crazy. It happened to Pink Floyd founder Syd Barrett, the subject of the band's "Wish You Were Here". My little 11-year old cousin claimed he'd been dosed by someone at the Rec Hall earlier that summer. We were never sure if it was an accident or he took the stuff on purpose and blamed others.

He swore some perv was trying to get him. His mind was toast after that incident.

"Ok, ok," he said. "Let's hit the water."

"Pass," I said.

I didn't want to go in while tripping. Hal appeared and we repeated the give and take acid bit. He and Bluto followed B to the water. Over half the party was now in or at the water's edge, I watched the dance of bodies, some swaying in the water alone, others splashing each other, some swimming, and a few bodysurfing. One couple was making out and appeared as snowmen from the waist down.

Then out of nowhere, a light rain began to fall, more like a mist from one of those sprayers at modern-day musical festivals. It was a really weird rain. I couldn't recall ever having experienced one quite like it before, nor have I since. Maybe it was the acid, but without much of a breeze; it came down in soft cross currents. It was nice and didn't seem to slow or deter the partygoers from their appointed rounds.

Several people passed by, commenting on the goodies, most were laughing, and/or dancing. The conga line made its way to the water. The tide was beginning to come in stronger now or so it seemed. The full moon high tide is truly something to behold, one of nature's grandest displays; power, beauty, majesty, and grace all wrapped in a violent behemoth thrashing at the shore. The waves were bigger now and a few folks had to be helped from the "breakers" area where waves begin their tumble down to the shore. The ocean emptied of most of its occupants rather quickly. Dalton and a couple of the other guys were or had been lifeguards. They were urging everyone to come back to shore and return to the fire.

I heard Bluto bark in the distance. I turned and began walking in the direction of his noise, which was north, back toward the vehicles. The mist continued to fall as I crested the northern dunes and looked out at the makeshift parking lot. I could see a couple of people milling around, no sign of Bluto. A small gazebo was about halfway between the cars and where I stood. A lone female figure sat inside. As I got closer, I could see Melissa's long, platinum blond hair being tossed by the mist-filled now stronger night wind. I approached the gazebo. Melissa's back was to me.

"Hey Melissa, whatcha doing out here?" I asked, regaining my voice as I came into her line of sight and entered the gazebo.

"Lenny, you did us right, man," she started. "This stuff is unreal, everyone is having a blast. The moon is….."

Her voice trailed off. I sat down next to her, on her left. She looked at me smiling.

"Yea, I'm feeling pretty tight myself," I agreed. "The herb and the Cid are both rocking."

"I never knew I could feel this good," she said. "The moon, the mist, the smell of the ocean."

I have to interject if you've never smelled the beach after it rains, put it at the top of your sensory experiences to enjoy in the future. It was always my favorite pick-up line with the tourist girls in summer, a real show-stopper. "Ever smell the beach after it rains?" I would say to some random cutie in the arcade or elsewhere as the rain began to slow or stop. It worked every time, the only line that did! Anyway back to Melissa.

"Everything seems so perfect right now Lenny," she said gazing at the moon.

"Yea, it does," I said.

She turned her translucent blues eyes to me. The ocean danced behind her. She had a halo. It's probably as close to an angel as I'll ever be.

"Just this once, she said. "Our secret."

She leaned over and kissed me, softly, at first. It was almost too good to be true. Then her lips grasped mine more firmly. Every cell in my being wanted to explode. Everything was more alive all at once. Her mouth tasted like the first snowflakes of winter on my tongue. It was as if all of creation was enveloping us, my senses overload warning lights and sirens were creating a mini-symphony. Fuses were blowing left and right. Her left hand touched my right, both resting on the bench. I could feel the electrical current between us, like the moment when Dr. Frankenstein sees the lightning jolt his creation to life. You know what happened to my down below.

Bluto howled right beside us. Melissa slipped away, returning to her previous position. The spell was broken.

I instinctively stood up. Bluto howled again. I stepped out of the gazebo to see why he was barking. He howled again looking right at me, this time shaking his hindquarters violently. Then I saw the problem. A crab had latched onto his right rear section. Melissa saw it the same moment I did. We both began laughing. I'd a bit of a time removing the clamping crustacean because Bluto was a hoss and wouldn't hold still. I finally managed to free Bluto from the free rider and both scurried away.

"I need to go find Dalton," Melissa said as she began to head back to the party.

"You seen my dog?" Hal asked, approaching from behind some vehicles. "I heard him, but haven't seen him."

I pointed toward the dunes.

"Will you help me get him?" Hal asked.

"Sure," I said. "A crab had latched onto him."

"Holy shit," Hal laughed as we strolled to the party walking about 20 yards behind Melissa.

"Damn, that's so unreal," Hal said, looking at Melissa.

"Um-hum," I nodded.

Track 11-The Battle of Evermore-Led Zeppelin (5:38)

Hal and I made our way back over the dunes. About a dozen or so tents had popped up in our absence. The rain, lighter now, not having slowed the party much, continued to be an uninvited, but not an unwelcome guest. Bluto appeared from behind a red tent, wagging his tail. Hal stooped down and loved on his pal. I walked on toward the new shanty town. Most of my crowd was gathered around the bonfire. Small groups of high schoolers were in little packs of four-to-six spread around the tents and the two fires. A few couples had retreated to their tents to enjoy one another's company.

"Where ya been?" Lexi asked staring right at me.

She was obviously very high. Darlene was just behind her and appeared a bit stoned as well. I saw double of them a couple of times.

"Helping Hal find his dog," I said.

"Do you have another joint?" Lexi asked.

"Uh, yea," I said dismissively, remembering one I still had left over from a prior batch.

Darlene looked at me, head tilted, lips pursed, in response to my treatment of her best girlfriend. I reached into my shirt pocket and pulled out my last rolled J. I handed it over to Lexi. Darlene grabbed my wrist and pulled me closer to her. She whispered in my ear.

"You brought us a tent, right?"

Crap, I hadn't, didn't even think about it. My mind, as you saw earlier, was elsewhere in my evening preparations. I knew Hal usually had one in the Scout. Trouble was it was probably the only one we had for five people and a dog.

"Yea, we got one," I said hopefully.

She pulled back placing her hands on her hips. She was always so extra fine when she was upset. And boy was she upset.

"We have one?" she asked in an accusatory tone. "Just that one big stinky one of Hal's the dog sleeps on in the Scout?"

"I grabbed another one," B, the lifesaver said. "We got a few sleeping bags too."

For the gazillionth time, B rang the bell just when I was about to be counted out. As if to put an exclamation point on B's saving statement, the mist halted. Now some partygoers could sleep outside in the bags if they wanted. A lot of beach people usually prefer to sleep outside, weather permitting, so it probably wasn't going to be a big deal for Darlene and me to get the smaller tent to ourselves. The girls had arranged the ol' I'm sleeping at the other one's house ruse to get away for the night.

More logs appeared for the fire, I looked around for the Unholy Trinity, but they were nowhere to be seen. I hoped they were all ok. I was a little concerned.

"Hey B, you seen Mr. Robert and those guys?" I asked.

"Nah, beats me," he said, turning from a high school girl named Debbie he was talking with.

B appeared older than he was, at 15.5 he was already well over six feet tall and could grow a solid small dark mustache. He was also very smart, the middle of three children his mother was raising alone. Dylan, his older sister was at the party. A notorious wild and crazy girl, Dylan was also one of the prettiest girls on the island. She was also one of the most argumentative and bull-headed.

"What are you shitheads doing," she said, addressing us for the first time that night.

"Inventing a time machine," I said sarcastically.

"Let me get a hit," she demanded.

I looked at B, he nodded his assent. I reached into my board shorts' pocket and produced the cellophane envelope. Most of the Cid was gone by now. Dylan plucked the envelope from my hand.

"Hey," I protested.

She walked away.

"Don't worry, I'll cover what was left," B said.

"Nah, no biggie," I said. "Prob two hits, three left at most."

I would only be out about three bucks my cost. I could've sold them for $12-15 total or saved them for me and Darlene or B. Getting rid of Dylan quickly was worth taking a small loss.

The unmistakable sound of the Scout, along with a couple of other four-wheel drive vehicles roared up close behind us. The other two were filled with high schoolers, new to the party with more beer. Hal had followed them over the dunes. Bluto leaped from the passenger seat and crashed into a nearby tent, partially knocking it down.

"Hey, watch your damn dog!" one of Dalton's friends, Joe, said from the other side of the bonfire.

"I'll fix it," Hal said, attempting to make things right.

He made it worse, the tent collapsed. Joe and another beefy high school guy sprinted over. It looked like trouble was about to become a party guest.

"Get away from our stuff," Joe said.

The two of them glared at Hal. B stepped over to intervene. He had years of martial arts training and never backed down. Dalton arrived just as things were about to escalate.

"Lenny, what the hell's going on?" he asked, quickly getting in between the two potentially combative groups.

"Hal's dog landed on Joe's tent," I said.

"Damn, that's all?" Dalton laughed. "Shut the hell up Joe and go get me a beer."

Joe and his buddy sulked away, returning in a moment with a cold one for Dalton. They had several in their hands. Dalton took them all and gave me and B one.

"It's my damn birthday and ain't no fussing and fighting going to be going down, understand," he proclaimed loudly.

He slowly scanned the crowd to make sure everyone heard and understood. Dalton was the alpha male of his age group and all quickly nodded their agreement. Then he flashed a huge smile, and spreading his arms wide let out a whoop of joy.

"Hey Jade," he yelled. "Play some Zeppelin. Hal, keep an eye on your mutt."

Bluto licked Dalton's hand that was pointing at the culprit. Dalton laughed. Bluto barked.

"It prob should be the other way around," Lexi intoned, drawing laughter from everyone.

"Everybody, we got a whole bunch of new cases just arrived!" Dalton yelled, arms raised. "Drink up!"

Everyone yelled and howled at the moon. A dozen or so partygoers grabbed brews from the fresh cases delivered by the newcomers. One case disappeared quickly. Dalton put his hand on my left shoulder.

"Got any of that Cid left Lenny?" he asked.

"Dylan took it," I said. "Not ingested, she grabbed it." I laughed the last part out.

"That hootchie," Dalton laughed.

Dalton and Dylan had been on again off again boyfriend and girlfriend until Melissa had come in the picture the year before.

"I'm going to get her," Dalton laughed and headed off in her direction.

She was standing with her best girlfriend Candace about 15 yards away. Dalton quickly covered the distance and a very animated conversation got underway. Dylan put her finger right in Dalton's face.

"Lenny, can you give me a hand with this?" Hal asked.

I turned to see Hal tugging at his ancient army tent that slept eight. It smelled really awful. It looked even worse.

"Coming," I said.

B, Darlene, and Lexi were talking with the new arrivals I didn't recognize. Must be from town, I thought. One had on an academy t-shirt. Hal and I struggled to pull the decades-old Army surplus canvas tent from the back of the Scout. It smelled like wet dog and other stuff I won't mention.

"Hal, it might be time to get rid of this ol' thing," I offered.

"Nah," Hal said. "Bluto loves it!"

He proceeded to get all the equipment required to hoist an ancient statue from his toolbox. Putting a tent of that size up in those days required an engineering degree, a ton of patience, and a lot of alcohol. I would've chosen even more alcohol.

"Got the last one," Dalton said, from just behind me.

I turned in time to see him show me the square on his tongue. He smiled as he closed his mouth. Showing your "dose" before you "dropped" was a time-honored tradition in the drug culture. No pretending to "trip" allowed.

"Tonight's big for you Lenny," he said. "When I roll outta here you got a shot at being cock-of-the-walk you keep this up. And man, you're really lucky too, you've got the "Queen of Light" as your woman!"

He slapped me on the back. I smiled thinking about his use of Darlene's nickname, lifted from a Zeppelin song. I thought since I had him right there…..

"Hey Dalton," I began.

I immediately took advantage of my newfound status as a confident and ally of the beach's number one dude. I probably should've asked for something grander. I maybe even could've asked for something spectacular. I didn't.

"Could you get a few fellas to help Hal out?" I asked, nodding over toward hapless Hal's construction project.

We glanced over at Hal, who was tangled up in some ropes with Bluto pulling on one end. We both laughed. They both fell to the sand.

"Uh-huh," Dalton smiled. "Ricky, Joe, David, get over here."

As if summoned by the highest court in the land, Dalton's three friends left the ladies they were talking to on the other side of the bonfire and heeded the call of their master's voice. He instructed them to assist. They weren't happy.

"You got to be kidding me," Joe said, looking at Hal's mess.

Yep, you guessed it, the same Joe that moments earlier was going to bop Hal on the nose for messing up HIS tent. Now he was being told to help his near former boxing opponent erect a mini-building. It would be a monumental chore.

"Just help the kid out, will ya?" Dalton said palms raised.

The three grumbled but set about the pyramid-esque project.

"You got any more of that killer Maui-Wowee or Acapulco Gold?" Dalton asked.

Melissa made her way over. She smiled demurely at me and put her arm around Dalton's waist. Her hair was still dancing.

"Yea, sure," I said. "But none rolled up"

"You can use mine and Melissa's tent, over there," he said, pointing to a blue tent about 40 yards away near the far south end of the party's reach. "Go with him will ya and bring back my pint of Jack."

Melissa looked at me and I looked at her. She motioned for me with her right hand to follow her. We got to the tent and she unzipped it. I started to enter.

"Wait a sec," she said, putting her left hand on my chest. "Let me grab his booze."

Well, you can imagine all the thoughts crossing my mind during that 40-yard stroll. We'd spoken not a word and the silence was deafening. She bent over to enter. She had to get on her hands and knees. This dream sight was too much for me and made my soldier salute her for the fourth time that day. She reappeared seconds' later, head and hands first, eye level with my crotch.

"Geez, Lenny," she said as she rose. "I left some papers in there if you need them. I'm going back."

Embarrassed, but proud, I adjusted myself and waited a moment for some blood to flow to other places. I took one last look at Melissa walking away and entered the tent. Melissa's overnight bag was right there and wouldn't you know it, two bathing suit bottoms peaked out from inside.

I know what you're thinking.

"You Perv!"

Well damn, wouldn't you at least be tempted to touch them? But that was all I did, I swear. I didn't mess with them or sniff them or any crap like that, just moved them out of my way. I'd seen her wear the red one a few times that year. The other, a white one with tan stripes, I hadn't seen before. I knew I had to focus, couldn't afford to lose track of time again.

I sat about my work, quickly rolling three excellent, tight (but not too tight, a mistake many make) joints. Just as I was finishing up, Lexi poked her head inside. I could see Darlene's legs behind her.

"Can we come in?" she asked, one foot already inside. Her toenails were painted bright pink.

"Nah, I am coming out," I said, quickly rising and making my way out. "Zip that will you?"

Darlene was just standing there. In my mind, she was asking questions without asking questions. My guilty conscience likely showed more on my face than it should. Or was it just the drugs messing with me?

"Dalton sent us over," I said, assuming she'd seen me and Melissa together. "For me to roll some joints and her to get his Jack."

Darlene smiled.

"I ain't worried about you pretty boy," she laughed and gave me a quick peck on the cheek. "You don't have a death wish. Let's get high."

Lexi gave me a slightly more negative questioning look. Maybe I was paranoid. Had somebody told one or both of them I'd been with Melissa earlier also? My stomach turned a bit as we headed back to the bonfire. Darlene's left hand and my right were pretty close together. They touched, she held on, I held on back.

"Can I get a joint?" Lexi asked. "There's one of those new guys that just got here, Ted, I want to talk to a bit."

Now Lexi was never this nice to me and I could've flatly and justly said no. I knew my summers-long romance with Darlene was impacted by her. So the likelihood of us losing our virginity anytime soon was also probably partially dependent on her.

"Sure," I said. "Here ya go."

I reached into my shirt pocket and gave Lexi a J. This time it was the "killer" new stuff. She was already pretty stoned. I was hoping the J might send her to bed early and improve my chances of more alone time with Darlene.

"Thanks Lenny," she said.

She blew me a kiss and jogged off ahead. She trotted past the bonfire, the construction of the Coliseum (which didn't appear to be going well), onto the Scout and by now, the not-so-new arrivals. We could see her smile light up the area around her. It was the biggest I'd ever see from her no smiling ass. Our astronauts on the moon likely saw it too.

Track 12-What Becomes of the Broken Hearted?-Jimmy Ruffin (2:57)

"Going to be heading out Lenny boy," Mr. Robert said as Darlene and I approached the bonfire. "Cappy's going to give me a ride. Heckuva good party though. And don't worry bout Ol' Eggs, we'll take him along too."

Mr. Robert held out his hand. I shook it. I thought about riding in the Caddy with the three of them sometime. That would've been fun, bizarre, and probably short story worthy, at least. But of course, that never happened. I also considered a comic book about them as weirdo crime fighters but didn't want to disrespect them.

"See ya soon, Mr. Robert," I said, as he turned away.

He stopped and turned around, the bonfire dancing behind him.

"Tell that mom of yours I said hello," he said nodding his head.

"Will do," I replied.

I could see Cappy and Eggs out past the Scout heading toward the dunes. Mr. Robert strolled by the erect-a-set bunch. He paused to speak to B, who had joined in the construction frenzy. That was the last I would ever see of Mr. Robert.

"Damn, Lenny this shit is madness," Dalton said, his pupils dilated.

The acid had definitely kicked in good with him. I nodded. Mine was leveling off a bit, but I was still tripping.

"Here ya go Dalton," I said handing him the joint Darlene had just fired up.

He took the J and inhaled deeply. He began nodding his head up and down, an enthusiastic positive response to the weed's taste and power. It was delicious! He passed the J back to Darlene.

"Damn, that's the best-tasting bud ever!" He exclaimed. "Melissa come on over here."

Melissa was talking to Jade and Julie on the other side of the fire. All three girls headed our way. They appeared to float on an invisible beam of something.

"Shotgun?" Darlene asked me.

I nodded yes. Darlene placed the lit end of the joint in her mouth and cupped her hands around her mouth and mine, gently blowing a powerful blast of the sweet leaf past my lips. Her hands felt warm. I loved having her this close.

"Get a room you two," Jade laughed as the trio approached.

I nodded to the herb's power as well. I bowed to Darlene's skillful shotgun as I took a half-step back. It was the best-tasting bud I smoked until I traveled to Jamaica later in the decade.

Darlene offered a shotgun to Melissa. Without looking at me, Melissa stepped between us and Darlene repeated the act. Yea, you guessed it, I'd all the thoughts a 15-year old boy would have watching the hot dream girl he'd kissed not long before having her lips, face, and body that close to his quasi-girlfriend.

"They should get a room," Dalton said with a hearty laugh.

"I'd pay to watch that," Jade chipped in.

Julie, a long-legged, rising senior, and the most skilled surfer on the island, just shook her head in agreement. Melissa slowly lifted her head back. She smiled at me, like, "you wish". I scratched my forehead. Darlene passed the joint to Jade. She took a toke and passed it to Julie.

"Lenny, can I buy a dime bag of that from ya?" Jade asked.

I shook my head no.

"Just got one joint left with me," I started. "I'll hook you up tomorrow though, get with me before the game."

"Alright," she responded.

"Me too," Julie smiled, looking me up and down. "Too bad you're only what, 16?"

I nodded.

"Almost, Halloween," I said. "Two days before."

For some reason, I always captivated the older girls' attention. Darlene smiled. She placed her arm around my waist and pulled me close.

Dalton took a swig from his pint of Jack Daniels and offered me the glass bottle. I took a small chug and passed it back. He handed it to Melissa, who declined and passed it on to Julie who took a small sip, as did Jade. The bottle made its way back to Dalton, who took another hearty belt. The Doors' "When the Music's Over" was now playing.

"I love the Doors!" Jade exclaimed, excitedly bobbing her head to John Densmore's pounding drumbeat.

"Morrison was so hot," Julie said. "Lenny, you guys have the same hair."

The other girls nodded in agreement. Darlene placed her head on my right shoulder. She rubbed my chest.

"Guess I might want to watch out for those late night tub times then," I smiled.

Morrison had famously overdosed (or so the official story goes) in a bathtub in Paris a few years before. Some of Dalton's buddies joined our little conclave and began chatting up Julie and Jade. They all talked excitedly about the party being one of the best ones ever.

"Let's go set up our tent," Darlene said, lifting her head and looking into my eyes.

"Cool," I nodded.

Dalton pointed his bottle at me. He finished off his pint with one mighty gulp. He pointed again.

"I hear ya dragon slayer," Dalton said.

I looked over my shoulder and smiled at Dalton and Melissa. Melissa smiled. There was now three of her. I told myself the effects of the acid were still in full force as fire, sand, and night mixed in a swirl of colors and patterns as we glided by the now completed eighth wonder of the world project. B nodded at us, sipping a beer. Bluto was running around inside the massive tent. Joe and Hal apparently found some common ground. They were in a beer chugging race, won quickly by Joe, who smashed the can on his forehead as his pals erupted in cheers and laughter.

"Another," Hal bellowed.

They both reached into an almost empty cooler for another round. Lexi and her new friends were drinking, leaning on a black four-wheel Chevy missing its driver's side mirror. Darlene stopped us to catch up with Lexi. Her new buddies offered me a brew. I gladly accepted. My mouth was a bit dry from smoking weed. I made some small talk with the guys while Lexi and Darlene chatted, huddled in close together.

"Beer?" one of the guys asked Darlene.

"Thanks," she said. "I'm going to hang here with Lexi for a bit."

I could tell they needed to talk some more. She squeezed my hand and smiled. I brushed the hair from her face.

"Ok," I said. "I'll go get the tent."

"Good idea," Lexi's object of affection Ted chimed in. "Reese help me get ours set up."

I strolled on over to the Scout as the two guys went to the back of their truck and began unloading gear. More Doors, "LA Woman" rang out. I grabbed a couple, three bags B had tossed in the Scout. The unused fishing gear lay there in a tangled mess. I toted the stuff back on the western dunes side of the trucks. I could see Lexi and Darlene talking. They started to walk toward the northern dunes that split the parking area from the beach.

"Where y'all heading?" I asked as they passed by on the other side of Reese's green Ford truck.

"We'll be back in a bit," Lexi said. "Gotta get something outta the car."

Darlene was walking with purpose, head down, Lexi right behind. Girls are funny like that; you never know what they're up to. Plus, Darlene and I had a history of losing one another in large crowds.

I made my way to a little clear spot just in front of the western dunes and about 20 or so yards past the food fire pit, which was now nothing more than a few burning embers. I dropped all the camping crap and decided to stoke the fire. A small white cooler, its blue lid tossed aside, was down to its last beer. I grabbed it, opened it, and took a big swig. Delicious! I tossed a couple of small logs into the pit and drank some more beer.

Most of the crowd had started to head toward tents, sleeping bags, or the parking area. A few small groups still milled about. There was one group of three around the bonfire, a couple talking by the water's edge and another group of four standing outside the small tent city between the trucks and the water. I finished the beer and turned to work on our tent.

It was just a small two-person tent and only took a few minutes to set-up. I thought about all the effort that went into erecting Hal's ancient canvas monstrosity and laughed out loud. In the far distance, I could see Darlene and Lexi heading back just over the dunes. Hal, B, Ted, and Reese had all retired to their respective sleeping quarters. I took one of the sleeping bags over and tossed it inside Hal's tent. Hal, Bluto, and B were all sitting in a semi-circle discussing Hal Lindsey's book "The Late Great Planet Earth". Bluto appeared to be sitting still and listening to the conversation as intently as any moderator.

"Thought you might want this B," I said.

"What do you think Lenny?" Hal asked.

"Not getting into all that right now Hal," I said. "Maybe tomorrow, later guys."

"Oh that's right, you got work to do," Hal laughed.

"Later," B said. "Good luck!"

I headed back to our tent. Darlene was standing alone just outside. She appeared pensive.

"Lexi?" I asked.

Darlene waved over at the tent city. She gave me a little half-smile. She placed both hands on my shoulders.

"Ted's tent," she smiled fully.

"You ready to head in?" I asked.

"Yes, yes I am," Darlene said, ducked and went in.

I followed thinking how lucky I was. I'd made us a pallet on the floor of the tent using the tent case and my sleeping bag. It was warm enough that we could sleep or do whatever on top. She moved our bags into the corner.

Darlene laid on her right side and I plopped down on my left after zipping up the tent. She looked so beautiful. I placed my right hand on her hip and leaned in to kiss her. Just as I did, the wind kicked up a bit and a steady rain began to pelt the tent. Darlene laid back and we kissed more deeply. My right hand felt her left breast. She moaned a bit and then pushed me back gently.

"Lenny, I need to tell you something," she began. "I want this like you do, but…" Her voice trailed off. "Promise you won't be mad?"

"What is it Darlene, just tell me," I responded, trying not to sound too eager or hurried, though parts of me were raging to go.

My heart sank quickly, other parts not so fast. That was when I first felt the night might not go as planned. Damn, and I'd bought condoms at Graham's.

"Depends on what it is," I said, ignoring the golden rule of just saying "It doesn't matter".

"I hooked up with Reese last week," she lowered her head. "We didn't go all the way. I didn't let him get in my pants, but we did hook up. Don't be mad, please."

The other parts finished sinking. I pursed my lips and as my mother taught me, counted to 10 before responding. Of course, during that count to 10, I had tons of images of the guy just 30 yards away doing things to and with "my girl". Of course, I was a horrible hypocrite. I'd kissed Melissa only a few hours before and several other girls that summer and every summer since I met Darlene. While I was debating myself internally, Darlene continued.

"It was just once, I'm so, so sorry," she said. "You know you were my first kiss, the summer I moved here after sixth grade, you remember, don't you? You're the only boy I'd ever kissed, I'm so sorry."

Track 13-The First Time Ever I Saw Your Face-Roberta Flack (5:22)

Oh hell yes I remembered, or as Bob Seger sang, "I remember, I remember, I remember". It was three years earlier, the first time I laid eyes on Darlene. I'd just finished sixth grade. I was 12.75 years old and working one of my many "hustle" (the good, young Pete Rose kind, not the crooked, older Pete Rose hustles) jobs that day.

I was sweeping off the old putt-putt (no longer there during the main events of this book) on the outer boardwalk's north end. I was sweeping off number 18 right next to the boardwalk when Darlene Alexandra Winter breezed into my life on a July morning. She walked by, her legs catching my attention first when they came into my line of sight. Her legs were long, beautiful, and she was barefoot. She was wearing a bright orange one-piece bathing suit leading up to a very pretty face, smiling eyes, sparkling white teeth, and the most glorious, shiniest hair I'd ever seen.

She was laughing with her mom and Dad. She was about 10 yards away when our eyes first met. You know how in the movies this scene would be in slow motion? Well, it wasn't. It was at full fast forward speed. She took my breath away, smiling as she passed and mouthed the word "hi". Dumbfounded, and totally mesmerized, I did the same and gave a little stupid four-finger half-wave at my waist with my right hand. She passed by but turned as she did and gave me the same stupid half-wave. Her wavy golden locks fell just below her shoulder blades. I watched transfixed as she made her way across the dunes and onto the beach.

I immediately hatched a plan to meet her. I'd run over to the bath house just a block north (site of a brand new Hampton Inn today). I would ask Bobby T if I could work a bit. The bathhouse, for a small fee, let folks change clothes, shower, or rent a locker. We also rented beach crap like umbrellas, chairs, bodysurfing rafts, and floats. Pleased with my plan, I finished sweeping 18, collected the trash, and quickly ran to the bathhouse.

Trying to act cool, I approached Bobby T, a serial entrepreneur before there was such a term. He always had his hand in several island businesses at the same time. He was a young curmudgeon, not yet 40, but crotchety old acting, a great athlete in his youth, his sports' dreams cut short by a knee injury that could be easily repaired today.

"Hey Bobby T, need a hand this morning?" I asked.

"Damn Lenny, glad you showed up," he started. "I was just about to call your house, dumbass David (yep, that David) didn't show up today, didn't call, he's fired! Stan will be here in an hour though."

Seizing on my friend's misfortune, I readily jumped on the opportunity. I was elated. David had forgotten to tell Bobby T. his family was going to Six Flags in Atlanta on vacation that week.

"I got it no problem," I said, trying to act nonchalant.

"Ok," he said. "The change bucket is in its usual spot. I gotta go to the damn restaurant, Clara didn't show up either. Can you wash dishes tonight?"

"No sir," I said. "I have a game."

"How's the team doing this year?" he asked.

In those days there was only one little league baseball team on the island, now it's in the double digits. We played the mainland teams. The island has its own league now.

"Middle of the pack," I said, telling a slight story, we kinda sucked.

The regular season was over. It was All-Star time now. I was the only kid from our team to make the squad. We'd won a couple and were set to play a team from Raleigh next.

Bobby T started walking away. He was bouncing a yellow tennis ball. He waved over his head with his back turned to me, he yelled.

"First-pitch strikes Lenny, always throw first-pitch strikes."

A great philosophy, I always tried, but really had no idea where the damn ball was going. I was a way better hitter than pitcher. I could blaze it, but walked so many, my pitching career ended in high school. I once pitched a no-hitter and lost the game 1-0 because I walked the bases loaded and David (yep, that David) made an error.

Anyway, so the next hour would be one of the longest of my life, waiting for Stan to get there, so I could go "run the beach". One person always opened the shop, putting stuff out front for display, rented stuff, and got the day underway. A second kid would arrive an hour later, and the first would begin the rounds to collect rafts that were rented for just an hour or collect money for more time.

The single-story bathhouse was on the last east-west row at the far northern end of the boardwalk with two-story bars on each side. There was also a small walk-up hot dog stand wedged in between the "Bank'n Ours" bar that anchored the far northwestern end and the bathhouse. I worked at the hot-dog stand sometimes as well. The "OP" bar with its big, second floor Oceanside deck was the northeastern anchor of the entire boardwalk. The opposite row had a bar, a restaurant (Blue Marlin, where I would work some washing dishes the next summer), a couple of games of chance, and the "ring the bell" amusement welcoming visitors to the boardwalk's north end.

The minutes dripped by. Just a handful of customers helped inch time forward. Finally, Stan approached. He was whistling the theme from the Andy Griffith show.

"Hey Lenny!" Stan said. "Where's David?"

"Tell you when I get back, got to go collect," I said, telling another fib.

I bolted to the dunes before Stan even got to the big open-air entrance of the bathhouse. I sprinted the 30 yards to the dunes and surveyed the landscape. I looked left toward the North End Pier at the far end of the island. It being mid-July, the beach was already teeming with sun bathers, swimmers, and families. No sight of an orange bathing suit. I turned right to look south.

"Hi," a girl's voice said.

It was her! She was by herself. She was right up on me before I could think. She had money in her hand.

"Can you tell me where I can buy some cigarettes for my mom?" she asked, flashing a sparkly smile so bright I felt like I was caught in an alien tractor beam of light. "She forgot hers."

I just looked at her, wow she was even prettier up close. Her skin was the color of peaches, her face delicate with long, light-colored eyelashes. Overall, she had a definite Nordic aura. The ocean breeze blew her hair toward me.

"A, yea, sure," I said, trying to sound cool again.

I was sure I wasn't. Thinking quickly, I offered to help. A gazillion thoughts raced through my poor almost adolescent brain.

"I can show you, just down here," I said pointing back past the bathhouse.

"Risley's store, I can show you," I offered, a bit too eager.

"That'd be great," she said. "We just moved here a few weeks ago, I don't know where anything is yet."

She closed that statement with a laugh. A light, almost wispy laugh, that was at once both alluring and sweet. She stood there as if waiting for me to say something.

"I'm Lenny," I said, remembering my manners.

"I'm Darlene," she responded.

Risley's was a block and a half west, just across from Bank N' Ours. I was determined to make a good impression. Stan must have been inside as we passed the bath house.

"We moved here three years ago from the Piedmont," I started. "Where did you move from?"

"Ft. Bragg," she said. "My dad just retired from the Army, we've moved a lot!"

The laugh again, I was already hooked. How badly? About as badly and totally as you can be at that age.

"My dad was Marines, in Korea," I continued.

"Mine too," she said. "And before that Japan."

"Yea my Uncle C was there as well, he just retired after 30 years in." I said.

We walked past the "Ring the Bell" game at the entrance to the main north-south inner boardwalk walkway.

"What part of the island are you on?" I asked. "If you're on the island I mean."

"We're back by a school," she answered.

We passed a beachwear shop on the left and some of the first traffic heading to the north end on our right. The cars crawled by and made the quick left turn onto the one-way road just in front of Bank N' Ours. They were likely headed to one of a dozen mom and pop motels crammed together on Carolina Avenue North or the North End Pier. We reached the stop light. It turned red fast, and I grabbed Darlene's arm to keep her from walking into traffic. I quickly let go.

"That one comes up on you fast," I said.

She smiled. We crossed over the narrow street to just outside the Royal Palms Hotel, the largest on the island. Morning revelers were already gathered outside its Dancing Bear Bar. It was really the Wagon Wheel, but someone put a Grateful Dead sticker on it. We then faced north and crossed the street to the corner where the family grocery store was. We got to Risley's much quicker than I wanted.

"Hey Lenny," Mrs. Risley said.

"Hi Mrs. Risley," I said.

"This young lady needs a pack of cigarettes for her mom," I continued.

Risley's was a wooden two-story building, where the Risleys, an island fixture for decades, lived over their business. Darlene completed the transaction and we made our way out into the bright mid-morning sun. This time we crossed on the north side of the intersection and were quickly back at Bank N' Ours.

"What grade will you be this fall?' I asked.

"Seventh" she answered.

"Me too," I said, more excitedly than was cool.

I thought she might be a grade ahead. I was big for my age, but she was tall for her age too, already 5'6" or so. She was just a touch shorter than me.

"We'll be going to the same school on the mainland," I said. "The school back by your house is just k-sixth."

"That's great," she said.

"Hey Lenny," Stan said as we approached the bathhouse. "Watch things a sec, I'm going to get a burger, you want one?"

"Nah, I'm good," I said. "Darlene, this is my friend Stan."

They exchanged a hi and Stan headed over to the Blue Marlin.

"So you work here?" Darlene asked. "Weren't you just working down at the putt-putt?"

"Yea, I help out here sometimes," I said, and anticipating her next question. "And the putt-putt, and a couple other places on the boardwalk."

"Wow, that's really awesome," she said smiling. "Well, I better get these to my mom."

"Ok," I said.

"Can I rent one of those rafts?" she asked.

"Sure," I said. "It's 50 cents an hour."

She handed me a couple quarters and I wrote down the raft number, seven, and her name. A few years later she told me she got the raft to make sure she would see me again that day. I was glad she did…

"About where are you and your family on the beach?" I asked.

We had to write down the approximate location in case somebody else had to go get the item. She laughed, my favorite new sound. She touched me for the first time with a light tap on my shoulder and pointed toward the dunes.

"Right in front of where you were standing a while ago silly," she laughed taking the raft and turning to go.

Boy, I've never been so elated and felt so stupid at the same moment. I remembered, I definitely remembered. I'd never forget!

Darlene had her hands on her face now and was sitting up.

"Lenny, I didn't mean for it to happen," she said. "We were just hanging out at the arcade and Reese and Ted invited us to go four-wheeling with them. I got a little buzzed, I'm so sorry."

I could tell she was really upset. I put my left arm around her shoulder and squeezed her. I was so mad, at myself, at her, at Reese, but also very touched by her obviously heartfelt apology. I felt a gazillion different emotions.

I really had zero right to be so mad. After all, we'd never officially said we couldn't hook up with others, and Elvis knows I'd been doing it a lot over the last couple of years. Still, I was hurt. Even though we'd never, ever, said boyfriend/girlfriend to one another or allowed others to call us that more than once, it hurt. We were both so fiercely independent we never even said we were "going together", the common teen slang of the time for bf/gf. But still, it hurt. It was my first big heartbreak and that, my friends, is the FIFTH WONDER OF BOYHOOD-knowing your heart can be broken and feeling it for the first time.

I could tell she was about to cry. I'd never seen her cry, not even when her dog, Connor, got run over the year before. What to do? I've replayed that moment in my mind a thousand times. Not many weeks ever pass without it playing on the non-stop video in my head. She put her head on my shoulder for a moment, sobbing. I held her as close as possible. The rain was coming down harder now.

"Can we get in the sleeping bag?" she asked, raising her head, tears on her cheeks.

I nodded. It was already unzipped and she slid in. I don't know if it was any one thing or most likely a combination of factors, drink, drugs, emotional turmoil, the lateness of the hour, but I think she was asleep before her head hit the ground. I thought of our first day again.

I watched her walk away from my 12-year old self. Once again, I waited for an hour to pass. Damn, it would be a long hour.

"So who was that?" Stan asked, munching on his burger.

Stan was the first person I met when we moved to the beach. We rented a house about halfway into the island while Dad and Uncle D were building ours. The one we rented was about a mile south past old man Graham's store, in a u-shaped neighborhood of only two streets. We were at the bottom end of the U. Stan's family lived behind us.

Across the street from the base of the U were acres and acres of woods where we spent many great hours playing, talking, and dreaming. He was two years older and one grade ahead (he'd flunked fifth grade). He was one of the first guys I talked girls openly with. Stan had dark hair and bad skin. He already smoked cigs and was the first person I knew who was high most of the time. Case in point, this morn he already had the 10 in the morn munchies. He was also the first person I got high with, in those same woods, the next summer.

"Her name is Darlene," I answered. "Just moved here."

"Nice, that is reallll nice," Stan smiled a pervy smile.

"I'm sure Tina would love to hear that," I countered.

"What Tina doesn't know, won't hurt her," he laughed.

Stan was also the first person I knew to have a relationship with a person of another race. Tina was black. She came over from Seabreeze most every other day that summer to see Stan. Seabreeze was a black neighborhood, with its own beach, bars, and nightclub just across the waterway. Tina was a super nice, funny girl, none of us could figure out why she liked Stan. Maybe it was the bad boy thing. Stan was already in junior high on the mainland and met her at school. On the island, there was only one black family at the time, an Air Force family stationed at the air base near the museum. Their only child, a girl named Reba, was the only kid of color among the island's school population of 180 or so kids. She kept to herself mostly and was two years younger. To most of us, she was just another kid.

"But boy if she did," I responded. "Plus I'm the one going to get that raft."

Stan chuckled.

"Whoa, Lenny boy," Stan laughed. "Knock yourself out."

As soon as the hour was up, I started to race to Darlene. I hadn't gone 10 feet when her family crested the dunes, raft in tow. I tried not to stare as she approached. I did math problems in my head to distract myself.

"Thanks," she said.

"Sure," I smiled, taking the rope of the badly frayed blue and yellow old number seven.

"Mom, Dad, this is Lenny," she said. "Lenny, these are my parents, Mr. and Mrs. Winter."

I extended my hand to shake her dad's. He was tall and rugged, fitting the military type you imagine of a G.I. Joe. He had an obvious old bullet wound on his left shoulder.

"Pleased to meet you sir, mam," I said.

"Hey aren't you G.R.'s son?" Mr. Winter asked looking me directly in the eye. "I saw you at the VFW the other day."

"Yes sir, he's my dad," I smiled proudly.

"I think I'm coming to your game tonight," he said. "Your dad invited me, we're hitting the VFW after."

"Oh, wow, that'll be great," I said. "Hopefully, we'll play a good game."

"Darlene, why don't you go to the game and watch your new friend play?" Mrs. Winter, my new favorite person asked.

Darlene looked at her dad. I could tell by the way she turned her head and the look in her eyes she wanted to go. What would she say?

"Would that be alright Dad?" Darlene asked.

The next moment seemed longer than those two earlier hours.

"That'll be fine," Mr. Winter, my second favorite new person said. "We'll see you at the game. Now let's move it Winters, we got to get your mother to the doctor at one."

I smiled as they walked away.

"Go Lenny boy," Stan said in a most hubba-hubba way.

"Shut-up Stan," I said.

Damn, was I happy! I watched her walk away. She looked back over her shoulder, smiled and gave me that stupid half-wave. I did the same. It became our go-to sign of affection. Three years had passed really fast.

I watched her sleep, how long I don't know. It produced that feeling you get when something you long for is so close you can almost touch it, yet you know in reality it's far away. On a night I'd high hopes of us losing our virginity, I felt like I was sinking. I was sitting inches away from a girl I truly cared for, who earlier said she wanted the same thing. Yet, here I was, my heart and mind all screwed up.

"Woof, woof," What I assumed was Bluto broke the melancholy spell. It sounded like he was just behind our tent, in the dunes maybe? I knew their tent was zipped, I did it myself when I dropped off the gear. How did he get out?

It was raining pretty steadily, but I knew, if it was Bluto I better corral him. I got up and wandered outside. Sure enough, it was Bluto, up on the top of the western dunes taking a dump. When number two needs to be processed most dogs are super shy. Not Bluto, he had the odd habit of barking when he did his business. Proud? Relived? Who knows?

He finished up and I called him to come on down. He ran eagerly through the rain and I walked him back over to his tent. It was still zipped. He'd wiggled out of a hole in the corner of the tent. I'm sure Hal and B appreciated the effort. I managed to get him back inside after working the old-ass wet zipper for a while, getting soaked being my reward.

I kicked some sand on the canvas to seal up the hole and made my way back to our tent. I was now wet and a bit cold. Darlene was still solidly asleep. I took off my wet shirt and board shorts and grabbed another pair from under the sleeping bag. I slid in next to

Darlene. I kissed her forehead. I drifted off to sleep to the sound of the rain and thoughts of what might have been.

"Heard you ran rafts for Bobby T today," Dad said from the back deck as I approached beachside.

"Yes sir, he asked me to fill in for David, they went to Six Flags," I said.

"Well you know Mr. Snow doesn't like you boys swimming on game days," he said sternly. "Go get ready."

I just nodded as I got to the top of the stairs. Old school coaches believed swimming took away your freshness for the game when actually it helps loosen up your muscles and really just makes you stronger. Living on the beach certainly helped me become a much better athlete. Go run in the sand. It takes a lot of work and years of doing it made my leg muscles rock hard. Swimming and surfing had done the same for my torso and arms. Never seen many fluffy surfers or hardcore swimmers have you? All that resistance from the waves and the sand can make for a pretty mean athlete and a super fit physique.

I showered and put my uniform on, my regular island uniform, sponsored by the only bank on the island. I was number 14, Pete Rose's number. The uniform is in the permanent collection of the museum down there if you ever make it that way. The uniform's there not because I was anything great, seems I was the only one who still had a jersey from way back. My mom kept that kinda stuff, you know, one-legged G.I. Joe, newspaper clippings, wrecked Hot Wheels.

Kids who made all-stars back then just wore their team jersey with new matching hats displaying their league's logo. During the season we mostly all rode in the back of Mr. Snow's pick-up truck to the game. We played on the mainland fields by the bridge and next to the train tracks. Stop cringing, it was the 70s! But since it was All-Stars and I was our team's lone representative, Dad would be driving me.

I walked out on the front deck. Dad was now at his more customary spot drinking a PBR, but also sitting there was Mr. Winter. Darlene was standing behind him. Holy cow! She looked amazing. To this day when I think of youthful beauty, what she looked like in that moment is what enters my mind. She had on a yellow sundress and black flip-flops, her hair in a ponytail with a tiny white ribbon. She was a sun-drenched goddess. I was almost speechless. She smiled and did the half-wave. I did the same.

"Go introduce Darlene to your mother," Dad said.

'Yes, sir," I said, nodding my head for her to come my way.

I held the screen door open for her. She smiled. Mom was talking to Aunt Pat by the bar. I made the introductions.

"I'm going to ride with your Aunt Pat and Uncle Ed," Mom said. "So your new friends can ride with you and your dad."

"You're going to have a big fan club there tonight Lenny boy," Aunt Pat said. "We lost count at 12 or so."

Oh swell, nothing like a new girl and your whole family coming, some sure to be under the influence, to an All-Star game against the defending state champs to make your stomach turn a bit.

"Great," I managed to say without choking.

I managed to drift off to sleep after a bit. Later that night, Darlene began to move around some as if having a bad dream. I held her, she awoke.

"It's ok, just a dream," I said.

She held me tight, her head nuzzled under my chin. The rain was lighter now, but still thumping that wonderful sound against the tent making it easy to fall asleep under normal circumstances. I treasure that moment, just that moment, holding her, our first night spent together, the rain falling, and her sleeping in my arms. I tried to make it last as long as I could. I fought sleep for as long as possible.

Dad and Mr. Winter sat up front on the way to the game with Darlene and me in the back, behind our respective parent. The ride was about 20 minutes to town. Dad and Mr. Winter talked baseball. They were both St. Louis Cardinal fans and were discussing that year's team. Dad would pepper me with questions, something I usually loved but didn't right then. I wanted to talk to Darlene more. After about the fifth or six baseball quiz question, I looked at Darlene and rolled my eyes. She reached over and took my hand smiling. That my friends is the FIRST WONDER OF BOYHOOD- the first time a girl takes your hand, on purpose, no less! The feel of her fingers and skin, the gentle clasp of our intertwined hands. I couldn't stop smiling.

"It's Ernie Lombardi, dad," I said answering my dad's query as to who won the National League batting title in 1942.

"One of the first catchers to do it," my dad, an old backstop himself, proudly kicked in.

"Boy knows his baseball G.R.," Mr. Winter said.

"Yes, yes he does," Dad responded. "Let's hope he plays like it tonight."

"Ok Lenny, you're at third tonight," Coach Thompson yelled, calling out the lineup.

Coach Thompson's team had won the regular season title, earning him the right to coach the All-Star team. He had five players from his team in the starting line-up. We were a seven-team league, so there wasn't a lot of room left for players from other teams after six of his players made the 15-member squad. The coaches voted on the roster of the All-Star team. We were a solid group, 11 would go on to play college sports.

I took the field and made some routine warm-up throws to first. We had the first base side dugout, so family and friends were in clear view from my spot at the "hot corner". The stands were packed on both sides as the team from the Capital City had brought a large group of supporters. I could see Darlene sitting next to her dad near the end of a row, about middle way up, smiling. She gave me another little half-wave. I was so proud to have so many of my family and especially my new friend there, but I was still a little nervous. I had to remind myself to concentrate on the game.

Surprisingly, the game was somewhat uneventful as both pitchers, the best in their respective leagues were in command and neither team could get much offense going. I had a good rip the first time up, but it was a hard-liner straight at the shortstop. On defense, I only handled one easy pop-up in foul territory the first half of the game, which was set to go the standard six innings for our age group.

My second time up came in the bottom of the fourth. The Raleigh pitcher had issued his first walk of the game. My teammate advanced to second base on a ball in the dirt after it bounced away from their catcher. The guy ahead of me struck out. I stepped to the plate with a runner in scoring position and two outs.

I'd been studying their pitcher's first pitch habits the whole game. He always threw a fastball first to try and get ahead of the hitters (like Bobby T said). He'd been very successful so far. Coach Thompson preferred us to take (not swing at) the first pitch, but I was determined to look first-pitch fastball and take my cut if it was in the strike zone. I glanced at the stands just before I stepped into the batter's box. I could see my dad nodding as he knew my strength was first-pitch fastball hitting. I nodded back. I noticed the rest of my large contingent of family and friends clapping, cheering, and whistling. Only Darlene sat there still, just smiling, helping bring me some much-needed calmness.

I glanced out at second. My teammate was a fast kid, any type of hit to the outfield would break the scoreless tie. The pitcher went into his stretch, he turned and delivered. I was right! A blazing fastball, probably a little higher than he intended was right in my wheelhouse. I turned on it and made solid contact. I blistered a rocket toward left field. I started down the first baseline, a sure double in the corner I thought. My heart sank as I saw it curving foul at the last second, foul by just a few feet, about 20 feet from the outfield wall. Groans escaped from our side, a huge collective sigh of relief from theirs.

I trotted back to the batter's box, picked up my bat and stepped back in. So close, but now I was in the hole 0-1. I was lucky; the next two pitches were breaking balls well outside the strike zone. I guess he was being extra careful because the two swings I'd taken against him I'd hit the ball real hard. Ahead 2-1, I figured he'd come back with another fastball. I wasn't as sure as the first time.

He looked over at his coach. I took a practice swing in the box. He delivered, it was a breaking ball, twisting and spinning its way quickly to the plate. It looked like it was going to be a strike on the outside part of the plate. I just went with the pitch making solid contact and lacing a clean single to right field, our runner scoring easily. Our side roared with joy, theirs went silent.

Our first base coach was all smiles as he gave me a high-five. Their manager called time and walked out to talk to his pitcher. My coach gave me the situation. They looked like they were going to make a pitching change and did. I stepped off the bag to talk to my coach. I could see my dad in the stands smiling and talking with Mr. Winter. I could see my mom and great aunts talking, laughing, and having fun. I saw Uncle Ed take a swig from his flask. I caught Darlene's eye. I half-waved, she did the same. My run-batted-in (RBI) had given us a lead we wouldn't relinquish. We added another run against a different pitcher in the bottom of the fifth inning and ended up winning 2-0.

There was quite a celebration! No team from our area had advanced as far in the state tournament in a long time. To see so many of my family and friends smiling, laughing, and together was something else. They had a big cook-out for us behind the field after the game. I enjoyed the time with my teammates but was ready to talk to Darlene more. On the way home, we held hands almost the entire time. I remember little of what was said by the grown-ups in the car or really what she and I talked about much. I just liked looking at her and touching her fingers and hand.

The sound of truck engines firing up jostled me awake. I didn't want to move and wake Darlene up. Damn, she smelled good and her skin was warm. More people stirring and Bluto barking brought her out of her intense slumber a few minutes later. Her left leg was wrapped around me. I kissed her forehead. She started to speak. I beat her to it.

"Just this day forward," I smiled.

She smiled.

Track 14-Games People Play-Joe South (3:34)

Summer days were filled with family at the house, the sounds and smells of the beach, boardwalk, and work. I seemed to always be working, daydreaming about what it would be like to just run the beach all the time, having fun. But alas, that wasn't my deal. My deal was to rise super early, if I wanted to catch any waves before work, hit the beach, come back in, and shower up. I'd hustle to the boardwalk, open up the donut shop, work till three or four and hit the Rec Hall for a bit trying to win some money shooting pool. I would head home, shower, and either do something baseball-related or hit the boardwalk for some fun. That would last a few hours, then I would try to score some more dough by helping close either the big arcade or one of the boardwalk restaurants.

The best thing about working and hustling? I always had some cash. This enabled me to have the freedom to do tons of things. Most importantly, I could go to the movies whenever I got a chance. The Wave Theatre was my home away from home. I couldn't begin to count the hundreds of hours I spent there in my youth. It was a special place from a time long gone, the single screen, local one owner theatre. It was a sad day when we all learned Mr. Brockington was selling out. The day after the big beach birthday party shindig would be the day I met the new owner for the first time.

I was making my way to the donut shop after catching some tasty waves. I was pretty psyched about how I'd handled Darlene's confession and was certain I'd scored enough points with her the deal was going to go down and soon. I strolled by The Landmark and said hi to my granny who was just opening up for the day.

"Ms. Hazel wants you to help her with some yardwork Lenny," Granny said from behind the counter as she flicked switches and brought the building to life.

"Will do Granny," I said leaning over the counter to give her a peck on the cheek. "I'll stop by the bumper cars."

Ms. Hazel operated the ticket booth at the bumper cars for as long as anyone could remember. She was a boardwalk fixture, a small round woman prone to excessive rouge with a great husky laugh that sounded as if it belonged to a lumberjack. She was always smiling and was a great friend of my granny. In contemporary lingo, more like a frenemy, as they shared meals, but were fierce competitors in the bingo parlor chess matches taking place nightly on the boardwalk. Several rivalries were quite longstanding, with Granny's and Ms. Hazel's being the Yankees/Red Sox version.

At one time there were three bingo parlors on the boardwalk: Jim's, Corner Bingo, and Red & Eve's. The boardwalk bingos each had a vibe all their own. From the back-room card game feel of small, smoky, and dark at Red & Eve's, to big, open, and airy at the touristy Corner Bingo, to the more modern, and air-conditioned Jim's. Most of the older lady crowd of locals back then were players, and several, like my granny and Ms. Hazel, made some extra bucks "calling" bingo a few nights a week. If not "calling", they were playing. One of the main competitions was between local women who prided themselves on the number of cards they could play.

Novices played either three or six cards, experienced pros played 12. Granny and her frenemies played 18-24, tough stuff.

"Can you and B help me move some stuff tomorrow?" Granny asked as I was leaving.

"Sure, no problem," I said as I unlocked the open-air north side entrance for her.

I strolled north past the Corner Restaurant, arcade number two across the way, Mr. Bob's shooting range, a clothes shop, and then the bumper cars.

I made arrangements with Ms. Hazel to take care of some painting she wanted done. I stopped for a second and looked up the east/west walkway between the clothes shop and the bumper cars. I spotted a group of my friends carrying boards to hit the waves. They passed quickly on the outer beachside boardwalk. I headed on to the donut shop.

That was when I saw Mr. Brockington and a tall, dark-haired man shaking hands in front of the theatre. Mr. Brockington handed the man a set of keys as I was approaching. I started to turn down the alleyway.

"Oh, hi Lenny," Mr. Brockington said. "This is Mr. Warpole, Gerald Warpole. He's the new owner of the Wave."

I walked past the shop and over to the theatre. Well, he'd warned me it was coming. I figured it would be after Labor Day, the traditional last hurrah of the tourist season summer.

"Mr. Warpole, this is Lenny boy," Mr. Brockington began. "He works next door at the donut shop, and most other places on the boardwalk."

The way Mr. Brockington said it, with a smile and a little laugh, I knew it was a sign of respect. As much as he and I had our problems caused by my misbehavior we "got" one another. Mr. Brockington had been a hustler his whole life and he knew I was one too.

"Hiya kid," Mr. Warpole said with a very obvious northern accent. "Call me Gerald."

"Nice to meet you sir," I said turning my attention to Mr. Brockington.

"When will you be moving Mr. Brockington?" I asked, my mind quickly shifting gears to Melissa.

"Well the old girl (the theatre, not Melissa) is Gerald's starting today," He sighed. "Eve's already bought our house, so as quick as I can get a moving company we'll be heading up to NYC, where Melissa will be going to college. My guess is the end of next week."

"Wow, that's quick," I said.

"Yea, I know," Mr. Brockington said. "But all this has been in the works for quite a while."

I shook Mr. Brockington's hand.

"Good luck son," Mr. Brockington said.

"Thank you sir, take care," I managed.

Gerald was already unlocking the Wave's glass double doors. Mr. Brockington turned and walked away north down the otherwise deserted inner boardwalk. I didn't know it right then, but that was the last time I was to see Mr. Brockington. Funny how that is in life, people are a part of your life for a while, sometimes years and years, and then that's it, they no longer are…

I walked down the narrow alley leading to the shop's employees' back entrance, opened the screen door and unlocked the old wooden door. I would do this for four years, five or six days a week in the summer. This morning was nearing the end of the second.

Besides the obvious demarcation points like middle school, high school, or college, another one of the funny things about life is when you're in the middle of some period of your life, you have no idea that it's part of a time parcel you will one day look back on as part of a certain segment or chapter. As I walked in to make the first batch of hot glazed goodness from a secret recipe, I'd no idea that a major segment of my life just ended. The Wave as I and countless others knew it, would soon be nothing more than a memory.

Track 15-Woodstock-Crosby, Stills, Nash & Young (3:59)

I started my usual morning routine of mixing the secret ingredients with the usual suspects to make a doughnut that has become quite famous. There's even a book about it, you can look it up (Britt's!). Well, this is long before one of the nation's most visited doughnut shops became famous, in fact, it was in transition. The original owner, who opened the shop in 1939 across from its current location, had retired just the year before and sold the shop to a former employee, Bobby Nivens, who happened to be my dad's close friend and carpool buddy. Bobby and his wife Maxine were now the owners. They wisely elected to keep the original owner's moniker as the name of the shop and it remains so today. They still work there, late March/early April to just past Labor Day every summer. Pop in and say hi if you get down that way. There is a great poster as you enter on the left showing our crew circa mid-70's. I'm the one in the middle with the white t-shirt.

"Hey Lenny," I heard a familiar voice banging on the back screen door.

"Just a second Davey," I yelled back, my hands were busy mixing up the dough. "Come on in its unlocked."

Davey made his way past the 50-pound bags of sugar and flour that took up one whole side of the rear of the kitchen.

"Thanks man for helping me get this job," he said.

"No worries," I said. "You just gotta be on point, no screwing up."

Well telling Davey that was like telling a dolphin not to make fun of humans. You know they're going to, come on, that cackling laugh, you've seen it and heard it, they're laughing at us man, just laughing at us.

"I won't, I won't," Davey stressed. "Just show me what I need to know."

I walked him through the process. First the prep stage; mixing the dough, putting it away to let it rise, rolling it out, cutting out the doughnuts, putting them on a wooden tray, and putting them in a warmer to help the yeast rise. The second stage was cooking, which started by moving the doughnuts to a dunkable iron tray, submerging the tray in a big round deep fat fryer and turning with drumsticks until they were a perfect light golden brown. The final stage was placing them on a long wooden stick to roll in the glaze and hanging them on a drip rack. After a moment to let the glaze soak in, they were ready for the counter crew. The crew filled orders, putting the treats in bags or on wax paper to serve up.

Most people ask questions when learning a new job. Davey asked zero. Of course, he'd always been that way. Davey was a year younger than me, the youngest of four siblings.

"Have you got any of our stuff from Woodstock?" Davey asked somewhat desperately.

"Yea, sure," I said. "I have MY stuff from Woodstock, why?"

Davey was always a bit of a schemer. I was sure he was heading that way. I was right.

"I hear there's a big demand for stuff from the festival since a bunch of those suckers have died," he said. "Let's sell it and we can take another trip."

I could see the $$$$ signs in his eyes. Davey was always longing for that next trip. Trouble was, he never had any money.

Our first trip together had occurred in the magical summer of 1969 alluded to in song and film. I was about to turn 11, big and developed for my age. Davey was a little past 10, a tiny, skinny, good-looking, dark-haired ball of disaster. He and I'd already gotten into trouble once that summer, putting glass bottles across the main cruising drag late one night and then hiding in the alleyway watching the cars smash'em up. It was a glorious mess and we laughed our asses off. We were so lucky no one got hurt (except some pride) and luckier still we didn't go to juvey. We did have to wash police cars for a month. But that's a tale for another time.

"Hey Lenny," 10-year old Davey in 1969 said. "Let me borrow a dollar. I'll pay you back, I promise."

"My money's at the house," I lied, and continued sweeping off the putt-putt carpet.

"C'mon," Davey pleaded. "I want to get a corn dog."

"Get one from your mom," I said.

"She's not working today," he said, looking down.

Davey's mom, Robin, was a notorious booze and man hound, prone to skipping work and all other sorts of poor mom behavior. At the time she was supposed to be working with my granny at The Landmark. Granny always tried to cover for her.

"Oh, alright," I said. "Here."

"Hey I got a cool idea," Davey said taking the money.

Important life events sometimes happen by accident. Who knows what would've happened if I hadn't handed Davey that dollar for a corn dog. But I did, and it was the best dollar I ever spent, and no, I never got it back.

"You know that big music festival they're going to have next week up in New York?" Davey asked.

"Yea, yea, Woodstock," I said. "The Who is supposed to be there and tons more cool bands."

"Well Leslie and Hitch are going," Davey said.

"Wow, now that's rocking!" I said, a lot jealous.

"Well, how bout we go too?" Davey smiled.

"What?" I said. "They would never let us tag along and my folks would never let me go anyway. Are you crazy? Check that, I know you're crazy, but this is way crazy."

"No, no, no," Davey said.

He then proceeded to tell me a plan he'd concocted only hours earlier after hearing his 18-year old sister Leslie and her 20-year old hippie boyfriend, Hitch, finalizing their travel plans for the festival. Davey said we could stowaway in the back of Hitch's VW bus, a bright orange rolling party! Leslie and Hitch were going to load everything Tuesday night. They wanted to be ready to take off first thing Wednesday morning for the 15-hour-plus drive to Wallkill, NY where the festival was supposed to be held. Davey said we could sneak in the back early Wednesday morning (they were leaving at 6:30). They'd be none the wiser until it was too late to turn around.

"Ok, ok," I said. "I don't think that would work, besides what would I tell my folks?"

"Just tell them we're going on a Cub Scout camping trip," Davey smiled an in-your-face smile.

Pretty insane, huh?

Well, common sense and fear of my father should have ended the conversation right then, but my love for The Who and all things rock counterbalanced my good sense. I let him continue, pulling me into his grand delusion, but perhaps the greatest accomplishment of Davey's life: "Our Journey to Woodstock!"

I worked my end of the deal to a pretty high degree of perfection. I busted into my piggy bank, actually an old Quaker Oats carton. I could just see the old Quaker (William Penn?) on the box questioning my judgment. I think I may have even carried on a bit of a conversation with him.

"Len, son," William Penn said. "Is this a prudent use of your hard earned $72 dollars? You've mowed a lot of lawns this summer, worked really hard cleaning the putt-putt, and helping your grandmother."

"Really?" I said. "A talking Quaker Oats box?"

"Well, someone has to question you at this point and try to make you see reason," Mr. Madmen creation intoned in a very Preacher-like cadence.

"It's my money," I countered. "What would you have me do?"

"Keep saving for that surfboard you want, give some to your church, tell the truth, etc.," A beginning to look bored box-man said.

"But it's The Who, Janis Joplin, and a ton more bands!" I exclaimed.

"Very well, I tried," he said, giving in rather easily as my "good angel" always has. "Bring me a souvenir, I'll be keen to hear about your adventures young master."

Too late, I was already out the door.

Mom had bought the scout camping trip bit. We were going to a nearby National Forest on the fake trip. My pops was at work, so things couldn't have been proceeding more smoothly. I'd packed a small bag with the things an 11-year old needs for his first big Tom Sawyer-like adventure. As I recall, I had several t-shirts, a matching number of shorts, socks, and underclothes. I'd remembered to grab my toothbrush, some toothpaste, and of course, some snacks. Mom made sure I had snacks. She even tried to give me some of her money. I refused, saying it was only $10 and I wanted to pay. Her trying to give me money for my big lie would come to be the only part I felt guilty about.

Davey and I camped out in his yard the night before departure. We were so amped up we hardly slept. We sure didn't want to oversleep and miss our VW bus to paradise. We managed to be awake when needed and slid easily into the rear of the VW van. Davey had a "check run" the night before to make sure we could get in and have enough room. We could see the lights coming on in the house just as we slid in behind Hitch's ample camping gear.

"You sure you got everything?" Hitch asked Leslie just outside our hideaway.

"Yep, told you 12 times already," Leslie, always in control, said.

The VW sprang to life, jarring the darkness as the engine fired, the lights and music creating a new world.

"You remember the camera?" Hitch said over the sounds of Steppenwolf's "Magic Carpet Ride".

"Duh, yea," Leslie said.

Davey and I sat really still for quite a long time leaning up against the driver's side frame in the far back of the VW. We could make out certain landmarks early on, the spires of familiar churches in the nearby downtown, and markers as we rolled onto Interstate 95 near Dunn, NC an hour or so later. You may remember Jack Kerouac also rolled through Dunn once (they dropped off a hitchhiker) in "On the Road". Well, Davey and I were definitely on the road and that little symbiotic tie to my second favorite book (To Kill a Mockingbird is first) made it all the more sweet. We both fell asleep at some point shortly thereafter. The next thing either of us remembers is the sound of Leslie's voice.

"What the hell are you two doing back here?" an animated Leslie asked from just a couple feet above our heads.

Hitch had stopped in Richmond, Virginia to get some gas. Leslie went to the back because she thought something was wrong with the engine. The engine was fine, our snoring asses gave us away!

"Davey, I'm going to kill you," Leslie said. "Get your ass up."

We all scrambled out the bus in a helter-skelter about-to-be a street fight kinda way. Leslie, not a small young woman, grabbed Davey and shook him pretty hard. Hitch was returning from the bathroom when he saw us. He started laughing.

"Right on, right on little men," Hitch wailed, bent over at the waist.

Leslie bopped him upside his head with her right, while still holding Davey's shoulder with her left.

"You two are going to get it," Leslie continued her rant. "I'm still going to kill you Davey. And oh shit, Lenny, I wouldn't want to be you when your dad finds out about this!"

"Oh man, you can't rat the little dudes out," Hitch protested.

Leslie punched him in the shoulder.

"Owwww, cool down, cool down!" Hitch strongly suggested.

"Rat them out?" Leslie asked, contorting her face and head into a Shining-like "Here's Johnny" moment.

"I'm going to kill them," she said. "No better yet, I'll make them ride the bus back home. Hitch go ask where the bus station is."

Hitch shook his head no but dutifully responded. Now Hitch was about 6'4", but only about a buck sixty so he was no match for Leslie's badger-like response.

"Lenny, you go call your house," she started on me. "No wait a sec, let me get some insurance on you first."

I trudged over to the pay phone. An old wino wearing raggedy overalls sat on a couple of used tires drinking a bottle of Night Train wine. As I reached for the phone, the old wino looked at me and started to speak, then stopped, mouth partly agape, and just slowly lowered his head. I glanced back at Leslie, she was pointing at the wino, a good 20 yards away, but intimidating enough to keep him from speaking his piece, her hand still firmly attached to Davey's collarbone.

Well, as I called the house a few scenarios crossed my mind. Busy, no worries, I'll try to lie to Leslie, but what if she wants to speak to whoever answers? Oh my God, what if my dad answers? I wondered what my obit would say:

Lenny the Kid, nearly 11, died from fear of what his dad would do to him once he got back in the same zip code. They say everyone poops their pants when they check out. If that scenario had unfolded I would have got a head start.

"Hello,"

Praise Elvis! It was mom. Dear, sweet, lovable mom. At least death wouldn't be quite as instant and much less painful. As luck (whatever gender or non-gender specific it is) would have it, Dad was at work. On the big ones, non-gender specific luck has pretty much always skewed my way with only a couple of exceptions. This time it was with me once again.

"Hello?" Mom asked with her beautiful, light southern drawl.

"Hi Mom, it's me," I said.

I watched the wino kinda slump on over onto the pavement blocking the walkway to the two exterior service station bathrooms. He blasted a massive one as he toppled on over, perhaps he was pooping his pants for me. Or maybe he was playing wino-possum, to avoid Leslie, who was closing in on us.

"Hi Son, is everything ok?" she said with a slightly worried tone.

"Great, everything is great Mom," I lied.

Davey continued to take a serious tongue lashing from Leslie. At least she'd let go of his shoulder. Hitch appeared from inside the station and the ruckus also brought a couple of names-stitched on their greasy overalls employees out as well. No lie, one was wiping his hands with the dirtiest rag I've ever seen. They all converged just as I admitted to the biggest lie I'd ever tell my mother.

"I'm not on a camping trip Mom," I quickly started. "I'm with Leslie, Hitch, and Davey, we're going to Woodstock."

Just as a clamoring of voices gathered around me, all of them talking at once, except the wino (just acting?). Guess we will never know unless...

SIDEBAR:

"Dear Wino from Richmond, August 69,

If you're still out there (wouldn't that be super cool?) please contact my agents and disclose whether or not you were "playing possum" during the above exchange. They'll buy you a case of wine. I promise, it's in my contract."

Ok, back to the service station in Richmond.

I heard the phone hit the wall, we had a wall mount model with a long cord. I clearly heard the sound of it hitting the wall. Had my mother fainted? Had I killed my dear, sweet Mother? I waited as the chaos around me reached a crescendo.

"I think my mom fainted," I said quite loud at no one in particular, but at the whole congregation. They went silent.

"Oh sorry Son, I dropped the phone," she said quite matter-of-factly. "What was it you said, you're camping in Woodstock? Where's that?"

So I quickly and briefly as possible told the truth, the whole truth, and nothing but the truth so help me Elvis. Leslie nodded angrily, Hitch smiled a great stoner smile. The stitched name tag guys smiled and returned to work, but not before Leslie asked to borrow that aforementioned greasiest rag on earth from mechanic number one and shoved it in Davey's face, aiming for his mouth. He turned just in time. The wino laid there like a slug (just like Randy in "A Christmas Story"). As we know from Ralphie, his brother, his only defense!

"Ok Son, you shouldn't have lied to me and we'll deal with that when you get home," she started. "We won't tell your father for now."

I unleashed the biggest sigh of relief I've ever had in my life. I expelled so much air I could have inflated a truck tire. The rest of the conversation, in interview form, went like this:

Mom: How much money do you have?

Me: $72 (another lie, but a white one, I forgot to subtract the 75 cents Ma Bell charged me.)

Mom: Well, you mind Leslie.

Me: I will.

Mom: Be careful.

Me: I will.

Mom: I love you.

Me: I love you.

Mom: Let me speak to Leslie.

Me: (thinking: "Oh shit!") ok, bye Mom.

Mom: Bye son. You be good.

Leslie took the phone and as I handed it to her. I'd such a feeling of euphoria I've seldom experienced since. I guess my young brain was flooded with endorphins. I was in a temporary state of ecstasy, like the death row inmate who gets a reprieve from the governor at the last moment or the guy who gets called into work just before his wife makes him watch "The Notebook" or any other Nicholas Sparks' work for the gazillionth time.

I had to fork over some more quarters to Leslie as she and Mom talked. They were bingo and boardwalk friends. Leslie was an old soul, who probably was a ruler or a wizard or something like that in a previous life. Leslie was nodding a lot and not talking much. A good sign? I hoped so. Then it happened. Leslie laughed and laughed some more. This stirred the wino a bit.

"Ok, Ginny, I'll watch after him," she said giving me the evil eye. "See you Tuesday, maybe Wednesday at the latest."

With that, the iceberg was avoided, not all clear sailing ahead mind you, but choppy seas at worse. I didn't have the balls to tell my dad about all this until I was almost 30. His response?

"I thought it was funny, a cub scout camping trip? You were never in scouts. I figured your mom had screwed up the details."

My mom never mentioned it again. Detect a pattern here? A couple decades later, I ran into Leslie for the first time since the 1970s. We were both trying out for Jeopardy at an open test event held in of all places, a shuttered mall cafeteria restaurant on the mainland.

Of course, we talked life events. When we talked Woodstock, I asked her what Mom had said to her on that call. She smiled and giggled a bit throughout recapping the conversation. Besides general Mom to basically babysitter talk, Mom told her a story from the spring of 69, just before school was out. I'd got called to the principal's office for the some number in double digits time that year. The Principal was an ancient World War I vet who I helped send off into retirement at the close of the school year. He'd told my mother, in front of me, mind you, that I'd finally "worn him out" and he would rather go back and fight the Krauts than have to deal with me and my crew for another year!

"You know Ginny, at heart I think Lenny is a good kid," Mr. Wilkes, the Principal said. "He makes A's, he plays sports, hell, he was in here twice for stomping that bully's behind, the transfer kid, what was his name, Rory. Sent him packing, which was a good thing. But you and I both know, he's got a little dark side. Like he has an angel on one shoulder and a devil on the other."

"Oh, Mr. Wilkes," My sweet, Godly Mother said, looking directly at the grizzled trench warfare veteran. "You don't know my son at all. He doesn't have an angel on one shoulder and a devil on the other. He has a devil on both shoulders."

My own Mom, dear sweet Mom, chunked me firmly under the bus. With that, she gave me "the look" and away we went. So, now you know what saved my trip to Woodstock, the devils on both my shoulders! Anyway, after Leslie got off the phone with Mom, she herded us all back to the VW. Davey and I slid into the middle section.

"Oh hell no," Leslie said. "You two are in the back, and I don't wanna hear no mouth from ya."

We were all just bit players in Leslie's Woodstock trip. She wasn't going to have a couple little hams steal her spotlight or spoil her trip. Davey and I sat in the back as we rolled through the mid-Atlantic region and crossed the Chesapeake Bay Bridge. On the other side, we saw the worst accident I've ever witnessed.

An 18-wheeler southbound on I-95 had just completely run over a little VW Bug dragging it, attached to its midsection, a good piece before crashing into a guardrail and collecting a bunch of other vehicles ala "The Big One at Daytona or Talladega". Awful, simply, awful, the accident had stopped southbound traffic. As a result, we witnessed our first true traffic jam (stoppage actually). Our side slowed to a semi-stall/crawl and it took us an hour or so to clear the disaster zone.

Davey and I'd sat there silent throughout all this. Leslie took notice and offered to move us up to business class. We excitedly shuffled into the middle section and started talking up a storm. We blabbered on and on excitedly about the wreck, the wino, the trip, and of course the festival. We were going to Woodstock!

"Man, I have to see The Who," I said excitedly.

"Me too," Hitch said, turning around slightly and nodding.

"Eyes on the road fool!" Leslie popped Hitch in the shoulder. "Did you not see that shit back there?"

Donovan's "Sunshine Superman" came on the radio. We were listening to a station out of D.C. They were jamming and talking about the festival a lot.

"Who do you want to see the most Sis?" Davey asked earnestly.

"Janis, CCR, the Dead," Leslie said without turning around.

"I want to catch those dudes from Buffalo Springfield," Hitch said. "I love "For What It's Worth!"

We powered through PA without much fanfare or discussion, a couple of uneventful pit stops, but lots of good music on the radio; Cream, Iron Butterfly, Strawberry Alarm Clock, The Beatles, Stones, and Led Zeppelin kept us rocking the whole way. Radio was different back then, not the oh-so-formatted crap of today, but a real eclectic mix on most stations (but country). You might get the rockers listed above, followed by some Ray Charles, Motown, Philly Soul, or Ike and Tina followed by some folkies like Joan Baez or her buddies. Several disc jockeys went on about whether Bob Dylan was going to appear at the festival since the word was he lived within walking distance of the festival site. He did neither.

We made into the Empire State close to midnight. Leslie fed us peanut butter sandwiches a couple times, but everyone was hungry and Hitch said he was tired of driving. We decided to camp for the night. Hitch spotted a cool little area just below and beyond a bridge that was near perfect. A small stream rolled along as we came to park near an open grove of apple trees about 60 yards from the bridge. We made our way out and stretched our legs a bit before Leslie the taskmaster put us all to work.

"I don't want to put that damn awning and tent up," Hitch said. "It's a pain in the ass."

"We're putting it up, in case it rains," Leslie said. "Besides, I ain't sleeping in that van with those two."

Putting up the awning and tent was a hassle, just like Hitch had predicted. His VW minibus was a 1960 Westphalia Camper model (it didn't have the traditional bench seating) complete with all the camping crap you could ever need. His dad had bought it brand new while serving in Germany in the early 1960s. VW would ship servicemen's purchases back to their homeland in those days. Hitch's dad had toured around parts of Europe with this one for about four months before heading back to the U.S. It was Hitch's dad's pride and joy. Hitch said he always kept it in immaculate condition. Sadly, he was killed in Vietnam during the Tet offensive in 1968. Hitch's mom went into a deep funk from which she never recovered. Hitch spoke of them often.

"Ok, that'll do it," Hitch said making the last adjustments to the awning/tent that attached to the side of the VW. "Let's pull out the food."

"We're going to have to hit a grocery store before we get up there, we're feeding four instead of two for the weekend," Leslie noted. "So let's not all make pigs of ourselves."

After some Vienna sausages, crackers, and a couple of potato chips we all settled in for the evening. Leslie and Hitch slept in the tent while Davey and I slept under the awning. The August night air was nice and cool. Hitch had hooked the tent flaps to the awning so they could enjoy the breeze as well.

"This is gonna be a blast," I said.

"I know," Davey said.

"I'm going to blast you two if you don't shut up and let me sleep," Leslie said. "We got a big day coming tomorrow."

Track 16-Melissa-The Allman Brothers Band (3:34)

Davey didn't make it a week at the shop. He did usual Davey things, being late, being slack, and not bothering to show up on our busiest day, a Saturday, was the final straw. Davey and I never really hung out much after he was fired. He'd made me look bad with the shop's owner since I'd gotten him the gig. So that was kinda my final straw with Davey as well.

"What are you getting into tonight, Lenny?" my co-worker Tammy asked.

"Going to see a movie, I think," I replied. "That shark movie is supposed to open next door tonight."

"Oh, I think me and Randy are going too," she said.

We were washing up after our day shift ended a few minutes earlier at four. I was ready to get out of there. I bolted out the back door and strolled over to the Rec the back way, along the street. I entered through the alleyway door. The place was pretty deserted. I headed to the bar and asked Josie, who usually ran the place when Dutch wasn't around if he left my envelope. I'd been doing pretty well with my baseball bets the last month. I'd let him know earlier I wanted to take out some of my winnings.

"Here ya go, Lenny," Josie said. "That's a pretty good little wad."

"Yea, been lucky," I said, tucking the little brown "pay" envelope in my right front pocket.

It was simply marked "L1". Dutch had a little code system and my code was L1. I'd been betting with Dutch since the summer after I turned 13. He'd heard me talking baseball with some older fellas and started picking my brain on games. Baseball was my passion, along with ROCK! I knew the game backward and forward at a young age, its history, its players, strategies, and most importantly for betting, the best match-ups.

In baseball betting, it isn't always the best team. The smart bet is to wager on the best pitcher in the day's most lopsided match-up. Say, if a team, we'll use the Red Sox, has its best pitcher going against another team's fourth or fifth best pitcher, that's a good bet. How much to bet is another book altogether. They're out there, go make yourself some money. The key is discipline and staying within your budget.

Josie turned to talk to the boy racking the balls and I rolled out the way I came. This time when I exited I headed up the alley to the inner boardwalk. I stopped at the Sugar Shack to get a chocolate milkshake. Made with the old green three-spindle blenders, the best, simply the best. It was creamy, thick, and oh so cold. After a super-hot August day in the back of the donut shop making thousands of donuts, it was just what I needed to recharge myself. I decided to walk back past the shop to the theatre and see what time the shows were for "Jaws".

Gerald, the new owner was out front talking to a tall red-headed dude whose hair was the longest I'd seen on a guy in the south, over halfway down his back. He had on a tank-top and basketball shorts. He had on Chuck Taylor Converse tennis shoes and red-striped tube socks up to his knees.

"Hey, how's it going?" I said, disrupting their conversation.

They both turned and gave me a quizzical look.

"I'm Lenny, Mr. Walpole," I said. "Mr. Brockington introduced us last week."

"Oh, yea, right kid." He said, scratching his head. "Remember to call me Gerald. This here's Sid. He works with me."

We exchanged pleasantries. I was looking at the poster for the movie. Sometimes we'd get the new releases later than the mainland cinemas, but hey, it was better than driving to town.

"Hey, you want a job kid?" Gerald asked. "Mr. Brockington's girl quit when he sold out, so I need some people."

"Thanks Mr. Warpole," I said. "I really appreciate it, but my plate is kinda full right now. Baseball just ended (we'd recently lost in the 13-15-year-old All-Star tourney) and besides the donut shop, I help at the arcade and football practice starts soon."

"Busy boy," Mr. Warpole chuckled. "And again, please call me Gerald."

"He couldn't work here anyway after Labor Day," The redhead said. "He's way too young."

Then came the moment I sensed something wicked had our way come.

"Shut-up Sid," Gerald said, shooting lightning bolts out of his eyes at the redhead.

"Never mind kid," Gerald said pushing the redhead by the shoulder toward the theatre entrance.

I stood there and watched the door close behind them. Gerald proceeded to administer a severe tongue-lashing at the redhead.

After a moment, they saw I was watching and disappeared into the office. I was intrigued but knew to move along. I headed over to the arcade to see if Mr. G was going to need my help late-night.

I saw a couple with their four or five-year-old daughter playing skee ball trying to win a stuffed animal. They were struggling to get past 250. I always played the first machine at the northwestern corner of the arcade, right up against the wall. I rolled a few games between 280 and 320. You had to get 350 to win. On my fourth or fifth try, I rolled nine consecutive 40s for 360 and a win. I let the little girl pick the animal she wanted. She selected a pink zebra with white stripes.

Mr. G came over and I got my marching orders for the evening. He wanted me to come in late-night and help him close up. I headed down the boardwalk toward home guessing the Yankee and redhead's conversation subject. I decided to go to the pier and maybe hustle a game or two of pool if there were any good marks around. I finished my shake as I entered the pier house. It was pretty deserted as well. The day fishers were gone and the supper/nighttime crowd wouldn't be around for a while. I passed by the counter and strolled onto the pier.

A pretty decent breeze was blowing in from the east and a sweet summer pier breeze on a sweltering August day felt pretty righteous. I leaned on the railing and contemplated the breeze, the sea, the bikini-clad honeys laying out and walking below. In just a week or so school would be back in and football practice would be taking up a lot of my time with two practices a day for a week starting week two.

I got a bit of a knot in my stomach about summer ending, the theatre being sold, and Melissa moving. Most importantly, I was thinking about Darlene. Damn, it seemed summer was slipping by so fast and with it my chances to get Darlene in the right situation where "it" might happen. Since the big party, we'd only talked on the phone a couple of times.

Now anyone that knows me will swear I detest talking on the phone, even today in the technology crazy age. Screw mobile phones, yea I have one, wish I didn't need it, but it's sadly a part of daily existence in the 21st century. Let me emphasize once more, I really, really hate phones.

If time travel could be achieved, many people say they would go back and hang with Jesus or Elvis or some such, not this dude. I'd head back to the 1870s and put a cap in one Alexander Graham Bell. Well check that, I wouldn't want to kill anybody. Maybe I could get him into something other than inventing the telephone, opium perhaps? Or maybe lurid pictures of Queen Victoria or some other sweet 19th-century porn? Imagine how out there he must have been to come up with the phone idea: "Oh wow, I want to talk to people who aren't even here!" A true potential stoner if there ever was one. But anyway, you get the picture, I hate talking on the phone more than Count Dracula hates the sunrise.

So my conversations with Darlene were pretty bland, on my end anyway. Any phone conversation I'm on, I just want it to end, even with Darlene. For someone who can talk your ears off face-to-face, I suck at phone conversation. I just want it to be over. Plus, she'd gone away with her family to visit her aunt and uncle in Raleigh and wouldn't be back till Tuesday. That would leave us only a few days before school started to make something happen. The same thing had happened our second summer knowing one another, her family left for an extended visit with relatives so we didn't get to spend as much time together as we both wanted.

I found out years later from Lexi they were really away for such long periods due to her mom's health. You may remember the day I met Darlene several years before, they were taking her mom to the doctor. Well, it turned out, her mom was quite ill and had been for some time. Multiple Sclerosis (MS) ran in her family and Darlene's mom had received the same diagnosis many years before. Darlene's maternal grandmother had died young at 49 of complications related to MS and Darlene's mom seemed to get a bit worse each year.

Darlene's mom was born in Minnesota to Swedish immigrants, who were farmers. Darlene's mom, Anika Signe Enberg, was a striking woman of obvious Nordic heritage. Youthful photos of her in the family home depicted a tall, lean, muscled athlete with a million watt smile. That had all but faded by the summer after our ninth grade year. The eyes though, the Liz Taylor-like luminescent deep blue-violet eyes, retained more than a hint of their original wattage. Darlene had the same smile and eyes but was always pretty private about her family, and especially about her mom's health.

I spent a few more minutes on the pier and then headed home. I could see dad's car in the carport from the pier and I wanted to talk to him about my sports physical for the coming year. First, I made a quick pit stop in the pier toilet to transfer my envelope money into my shoes, my big hiding place. I had 14 $20 bills, a 10 and a couple ones-$292 dollars. It took me two weeks with all my regular jobs to make that much!

I'd been saving my job money for a new surfboard and toward buying a car. This pile would make a nice addition. I had my own bank savings account (with Mom as co-signee) since the bank came to the island after my fourth-grade year. I was a diligent saver. Mom never really paid any attention to my finances and Dad never said a word about money to me. In fact, I never really ever remember money or finances being brought up much in our house. Mom had helped me start the savings account and for the most part that was it. I knew I was expected to work in the summer for my "fun" money, but Dad always paid for my sporting gear, school clothes, and other essentials. Extra stuff, I knew I was on my own.

After sorting out with dad what was needed before school started, I decided to head over to B's and see what he was up to. I hopped on my bike and made my way toward B's. About halfway there, I saw him coming my way on his bike. We met right at the midway point between his house and mine, right near the island lake.

"Still want to hit the movie tonight?" I asked.

"Sounds good to me," B replied. "A big moving truck is at Melissa's house. Thought you might want to know."

"Thanks, let's roll back that way and check it out," I suggested.

B nodded his agreement and we biked the ½ mile or so to the school and Melissa's just beyond. Two older men in grey uniforms were loading the Brockington's green couch into a big yellow van the size of a transfer truck. We climbed the three steps to the front porch and knocked on the door, which was open for the movers. No one answered.

"Only one here is a young gal," Mover number one, the older and beefier of the two said as he made his way past us and into the house. "I think she's upstairs."

"Hey Lenny, hey B," It was Melissa, leaning out a second story window.

"Hey Melissa," I said. "Just stopped by to say hi before you got gone."

"Come on up," she said. "I'm just finishing up."

B and I entered the old frame house with the giant first-floor picture window. I'd broken the window two summers before with a batted ball from the schoolyard across the way during a pick-up game. My dad and I replaced the window. So this was my second time in Melissa's home. The first visit was when my crush on her started. She was on the downstairs kitchen phone that day, in cut-off denim shorts and a red billowy top, barefooted, and chatting with one of her friends about a party. I'd been seeing her for a couple of summers at the theatre and always thought her attractive. The day of the window repair, some switch went off in my 13.75 year-old head, sending me spinning into young lust run amuck. She didn't even say a word to me that day, but I was hooked, and as you know, on this, the day of her departure well over 700 days later, I still was.

B and I got to the bottom of the wide stairwell. Melissa was on the top landing waving us up. She had on pink cotton shorts and a sleeveless white top. She was barefooted. Come to think of it, the only time I ever saw Melissa wear shoes was at the theatre.

"I'm glad you guys stopped by," she started. "I hadn't seen you this week to say goodbye."

She was somewhat matter-of-fact in her delivery. I was a bit unsure how to take it. She looked so pretty, but sad.

"I know you're going to have a blast at college," I said. "But it's not going to be the same at the Wave without you or your old man."

"Yea, it really is bittersweet," she said looking out the landing window into her backyard. "Like I said, I'm glad you two are here, cause I need a couple favors."

"Fire away," I said, a little too eagerly.

"Ok, one," she started. "I have to stay here till the movers finish. They're done up here, but I want some beer. B, would you run to Graham's and get us a 12-pack?"

B nodded yea and Melissa motioned for us to follow her down the hall. The upstairs had a bedroom on each end of the hall and a bathroom on the way to Melissa's room with a large closet across the hall. Melissa led us to her room. She picked her purse off the now empty floor-to-ceiling built-in bookshelf and plucked a $10 bill from inside.

"Whatever you guys drink is cool," she said, handing B the paper.

B looked at me, raised his eyebrow and left. Melissa turned and looked out her bay window that allowed for a panoramic view of her backyard. She flung open the double window and a cooling drift of summer breeze floated into the room.

"Guess, I'm going to have to get used to a lot smaller space at college," Melissa said wistfully.

"You going to be in a dorm?" I asked.

"Yea, pretty small," she noted turning back to face me.

"What was the other favor you needed?" I asked.

"My stash is in one of the dressers already loaded in the back of that truck," she began. "You wouldn't happen to have anything on you would you?"

I shook my head no. I seldom carried drugs, just when I knew I was about to consume them or get rid of them to someone else. A policy that always served me well.

"Damn, oh well," Melissa said with the first big smile of our visit. "That's ok. It's just six blocks up to Graham's, hope B remembers to hide his bike so the old man doesn't see it. That one story is so funny."

"Yea, I think he's learned his lesson on that kinda thing," I chuckled, recalling that episode at Graham's the year before.

I'd always grabbed the brew for us that first year we started attempting to get it ourselves and not rely on winos buying for us or swiping it from the fridge. It was nearing the end of summer after eighth grade and B wanted to give it a shot. We both went in the musty old concrete-bunker like building that had a dive bar feel. Mr.

Graham was a tall, thin man in his mid-70s. He wore spectacle-type glasses and dressed like it was still 1942. A 48-star U.S. flag had hung behind the counter for decades.

"That all you need Lenny?" he asked as I sat a six-pack on the counter.

"Yes sir," I said.

"That'll be $3.19," he said.

I paid up and began walking out as B placed his six-pack on the counter. It seemed to go ok and I waited for him by the door. B smiled as he passed and walked on out as I opened the door.

"Lenny, could I speak to you?" Mr. Graham called.

Oh crap… I thought this can't be good. I walked back over to the counter.

"Here, your friend forgot his change," he said.

Whew! I breathed a sigh of relief. I started to exit again when Mr. Graham spoke quite loudly.

"Next time your friend might not want to wear his Sunset Junior High shirt."

"Miss, Miss," we heard mover guy number two yell from the bottom of the stairs. "We're about to head out, anything else you know of?"

Melissa and I bounded downstairs. Mover number one was closing up the back of the truck. He waved.

"I think you guys are good," Melissa said. "Thank you."

"All right then," number two said as he walked to the passenger side, removing his hat to wipe his brow.

We watched as the big rig pulled out of Melissa's yard with her family's belongings for the long trip to New York. We just stood there silently as it pulled past the school heading for the main road. In a moment, it was gone.

"Let me give you the grand tour," Melissa said smiling, way more upbeat than I'd expected. She looped her right arm in my left and we re-entered the house. We paused in the living room by the fireplace. Melissa told a few family stories, mostly holiday stuff, and about one birthday party her mom had thrown here when she was nine.

"Mom loved piñatas," Melissa said. "So every year I can remember, I had a birthday piñata my mom made herself. It was one of the last things she did before she passed last year."

"I remember one of those," I said. "It was a unicorn, I think."

"You remember that?" Melissa looked at me quizzically. "That was two years ago."

"Yea, I was here with my dad fixing that picture window. I was the one broke it," I said. "It was an accident, baseball crap. I remember the unicorn being on the kitchen table."

"That's right, that was you!" she exclaimed and bopped me on the shoulder. "I remember now, I was on the phone when you were here, sorry if I seemed rude."

I shook my head no. I was elated she remembered me being in her house. I didn't think she knew I existed then.

"You were always bigger than the other kids your age back then," she said. "I thought you were older."

She actually thought of me like that? Wow, I was stunned! Happy, but stunned, definitely stunned, and now a little out of sorts.

"I thought you were cute," she said smirking.

I blushed. What should I do with that? I did nothing.

"Thanks, I guess?" I sheepishly responded.

"Oh don't be acting all shy, Mr. Big Stuff," she said. "All the little girls love you."

I was always good with animals and girls. Not much else, but those are two pretty good things to excel at, I guess. If Melissa only knew it was one big girl I'd wanted to win the affection of instead of a bunch of little ones.

"The tour continues," Melissa said re-enveloping my arm and pointing out Brockington gems about their kitchen, laundry room, and master suite downstairs. "And now, my boudoir."

We walked arm and arm up the stairs. I couldn't help think back to the day two years earlier when I could only dream, and a very big dream at that, about EVER seeing Melissa Brockington's bedroom. Now here I was being escorted there by the fair maiden herself. I guess sometimes dreams do become reality, or parts of them anyway.

We took a peek inside the spare upstairs bedroom. Melissa informed me it also served as her mom's sewing and projects room. Melissa noted the room was where most of the piñatas and other assorted crafts Mrs. Brockington was known for reached fruition. Then we headed back down the hall to Melissa's room.

"Well, I killed the suspense, since you've been in here already," Melissa said. "But this is my room, the only bedroom I've ever known."

I couldn't tell how much of the emotion in the last part was put on comedy and how much was melancholy. The phone rang. Melissa's phone was on the floor, but by the carpet indents, I imagined it had once set on a nightstand next to her bed.

"In a bit, I'm pulling out," Melissa said, a stressed look came across her face. "I'm staying at my aunt's in Virginia Beach tonight."

The other person talked for several minutes. I stood there kinda awkwardly looking out the window. I wasn't trying to eavesdrop, but it was hard not to hear.

"I can't," Melissa said firmly. "I don't think that's wise. For either of us."

The other voice got louder. I understood it was probably Dalton. Word on the boardwalk was they'd broken up a few days before.

"Please don't leave it like that," Melissa said earnestly. "I know you don't mean what you're saying. I'm hanging up now."

Dalton beat her to the punch I guess, because Melissa just raised her hand holding the phone and scratched her head. She gently placed the headset back on the cradle and the entire thing back on the floor. She appeared a bit shaken.

"Sorry you had to hear that," she said. "He's not taking all this very well."

I just nodded, I felt for the both of them. For Dalton, to lose a girl like Melissa must be a crushing blow. For Melissa, well because, just because she was Melissa.

"I don't know what he expects," she said. "He knew when we started I would be going to THE CITY to college! It was my dad's call for us to move lock, stock, and barrel. But it's what Mom wanted, and I really wanted to experience college life in New York, the city, all the stuff."

Melissa touched a small dragonfly that was painted above where it appeared her headboard used to be.

"Your mom?" I asked motioning toward the dragonfly.

"Yea," the smile came back to her face as she continued. "She painted it on there when I was really little. One of her favorite things to say was "… dragonflies are smart, they know they've only a few months to live and they make the most of it…"

She told me her mom talked often about dragonflies, teaching her almost every culture uses the dragonfly as a symbol of change. She gazed at the colorful painting. She took a couple of steps, leaned over, and gently kissed her mom's artwork.

Just then B came clamoring up the stairs and into the room, a big paper bag under one arm.

"Ice cold beverages," he started in a loud, barker-like, funny voice. "Ice cold beverages, get your ice cold beverages right here!"

"Well alright," Melissa said.

We each drank a couple. The first kinda quick and mostly standing up. Then Melissa sat in her bay window for her second, and last.

"I gotta drive, so just two for me," she said.

B and I sat on the floor for our second Budweiser. I sat cross-legged mostly. B stretched out, having grown so much in the last 18 months, he was now well over six feet tall, way taller than me. We talked about movies, summer, school, Melissa's college choices, and other random crap that popped into our heads. It was one of the best, but most melancholy half hours of my life.

"You guys take the rest," she said pointing to the remaining beers. "I got to get on the road."

"Oh, here's your change," B said, pulling a few dollars and some coins out of his pocket.

"Thanks," Melissa said.

"Guess we'll roll on then," I said.

I was kinda at a loss for what to say. I damn sure didn't know how to say good-bye. B started out the bedroom door, holding the bagged beer under his arm.

"I'll send Lenny down in a minute B," she said, grabbing my left wrist.

B looked down at her gesture. He smiled. He just nodded.

"Bye Melissa," B said, nodding again.

"Bye B," Melissa said.

I turned to face her. We were a couple of feet apart. She smiled. I smiled.

"I wish we'd spent more time together Lenny," she said, her eyes a bit misty. "You're a lot of fun to be around."

I just nodded, once again, speechless.

"You're a good guy, Darlene is so lucky to have you." she continued. "Take care of your crazy self and your friends, especially B."

She was tearing up. I was trying not to. I failed.

She let go of my wrist as a slight breeze came in through the bay window. She moved closer, the breeze blew her hair on my shoulder. She placed both her hands on my cheeks and tilted my head down, kissing me on the forehead.

"Bye Lenny," she said releasing me and stepping back.

"Bye Melissa," I said.

I left without looking back. I made it halfway down the hall. I stopped. I turned and walked resolutely back toward her door. She was standing in the doorway, leaning against the frame. She was wiping a few tears from her eyes. They probably weren't all for me, but I hoped a few of them were. All of mine were for her. Well, maybe one or two were for me. I paused a couple feet away. She stopped leaning.

"I love you," I said, doing my best to hold back more tears.

"I know you do," she said half-smiling, half-crying. "I'm going to miss you the most, wild and crazy Lenny…."

She paused and caught her breath.

"Now please get outta here."

She said the last line pointing down the hall. I obeyed without looking back.

Track 17-Time of the Season-The Zombies (3:32)

Leslie cut up some fruit for breakfast Thursday morning as we prepared to hit the road to Woodstock. Davey and I ate ours down by the riverbank, where some rapids bounced by several old silver jutting rock formations. The morning was kinda cool, but nice, a definite break from what we were used to an August morning being in the south. Over the years I've tried to find the place on a map, but haven't been able to hone in on it. With Google Earth I should be able to, but really haven't made the effort. I know, I should. I've thought of mapping the whole trip via Google Earth, along with my trips to Woodstock in 1994 and 1999 and pile them all together in one dossier. That would be kinda cool. Maybe those tales will be in Crazy Beach Disc Two and/or Disc Three.

Anyway, while Davey and I were eating, Leslie and Hitch took a stroll through the apple orchard. They were gone for a quite a bit. It was probably only 15 minutes or so, but that's A LOT to a kid eager to get on with his first big life adventure.

"Let's roll boys," Hitch shouted as he and Leslie reappeared, giving a big windmill arm motion, ala Pete Townshend.

Leslie had a big smile on her face, as did Hitch. Davey thumped me on the shoulder and smiled too. I thought, hmm… apple orchard lov'n? We were just behind them as we approached our magic carpet ride. Hitch's gait was like those of the fake Bigfoot pictures you see, real long and loping with arms swinging way out. Hitch stretched real big. Being a tall, gangly fellow, he seemed to almost fill up the sky. As his arms descended he pinched Leslie on the right ass cheek and she reached to slap him, but he'd already begun an evasive maneuver to his driver's side perch.

Davey and I sat right behind Hitch and Leslie as we rambled back up to the main road to continue our northern trek. That's when it hit me, and I think it hit Davey at about the same time, a very strong, pungent, but pleasant odor. I didn't know but suspected what it was. Davey mouthed the word "dope". I mouthed the word "marijuana" back at him. He shook his head in the affirmative. My first encounter with "Mary Jane".

Now I'd seen ads and been told in school about the evils of marijuana, but we all knew, even at a young age, that scare tactic crap was all pretty much bullshit. I'd heard the older kids talk about it, some even claimed they'd tried it. I'd yet to see any in person, but that was about to change.

"Damn," Leslie said reaching down for something falling out of her pocket. She grabbed at a small plastic bag landing near my left foot. I instinctively reached for it as well. Her eyes locked on mine as we reached it simultaneously.

"I got it," she said, averting her brown eyes as she quickly snatched up what appeared to be some greenish/brown stuff in a sandwich bag.

"Y'all been getting high!" Davey exclaimed. "I knew it!"

"Shut-up," Leslie demanded.

"What's the big deal?" Hitch asked. "He knows we get high. I'm sure Lenny knows the deal by now."

"He might not have dumbass," Leslie said. "But I guess he does now."

Leslie turned up the radio. The Strawberry Alarm Clock's "Incense and Peppermints" was drawing to a close. And no lie, for real, the next song that came on was The Byrd's "Eight Miles High". Leslie turned the radio back down.

"Look, you two," she started.

We knew we were about to get "the drug talk".

"Hitch and I are old enough to decide what we want to do about booze and drugs," she continued. "You two aren't. So don't, not yet, anyway. I'm sure you're going to see plenty of pot smoked at the festival. Somebody will probably offer you some. Just say, thanks, but no thanks. I swear, if I see either one of you smoking, I'm going to beat both your asses, you hear me?"

We, of course, in unison, nodded yes, but I was thinking… "oh boy, somebody's going to give me free drugs?"

Then Davey pulled another classic Davey.

"Hey Sis, why not let us try some now, that way you'll know where we got it!"

Leslie turned three shades of red as she whirled and threw a half-full can of soda at her brother. It popped him squarely just above the left eye. Blood immediately gushed out. Cola spilled all over Davey, some on me, and a bunch on the floor, seat, and inside panel of the VW.

"Hey!" Hitch said loudly, the first time I EVER heard him raise his voice that wasn't a positive sound. "Geez, Leslie, you're going to clean that up."

Davey bent over and grabbed at his eye, cussing.

"No, I'm not!" Leslie retorted at the same volume. "That little shithead is. Now let me see your eye Davey."

Davey raised his head, blood covered most of his right hand and the left side of his face. He bent over in obvious pain. A puddle of blood quickly formed beneath him.

"Lenny move to the back," Leslie said.

She slid in next to her brother. He tried to push her away. She manhandled him.

"Let me see, shitwad," she said. "Let me see."

Davey moved his hand. I couldn't see really well from my angle, but by the look on Leslie's face, she was concerned. She was pressing her right hand on the wound to try and stop the bleeding.

"Lenny look in Hitch's toolbox and get me some duct tape or rubber cement, something like that," she demanded, her voice as shaky as I'd ever hear it.

I hurriedly began dismantling Hitch's old, dinged up red toolbox. Nothing on the top shelf. I lifted it off and sat it on the rumbling floor. It bounced around like Mexican jumping beans for a bit till I moved it.

"Find anything yet?" Leslie asked excitedly. "Grab some pepper out of the food bag!"

"Not yet," I yelled over the din of the motor.

I rummaged through the bottom section. It was greasy and smelly and had lots of crap in it. I moved stuff around and moved it around some more.

"Hurry up Lenny!" Leslie demanded.

"Here, here I found something," I said.

It was a small container of drywall paste. I also spotted some horribly dirty and barely still there duct tape as well. I grabbed both of them as well as the plastic pepper shaker.

"Hand'em here," Leslie said reaching with her left while applying pressure with an old mechanic's rag to Davey's eye.

I passed along my first triage kit. Leslie gave Davey a field dressing to remember. She covered the wound with pepper to stop the bleeding. She then reached into the plastic cup and gooped about two fingers worth of white oozy paste above Davey's eye. She held her hand parallel against his forehead, just below his wound and just above his eye. It looked like she was saluting for him.

"Lenny," Hitch called from the front. "Lenny get up here, look at this map."

I stepped kinda over/around Leslie. Her straight as a straw shoulder length jet black hair was bouncing in time with the rhythm of the engine. Her purple underwear was showing. Hey, 11-year olds find any titillation interesting! Don't judge you pervs.

"See if you can find the road I'm supposed to take once we get to White Lake," Hitch said.

Well, those of you that know your music history, realize the "Music and Art Fair" was originally supposed to be held in Wallkill,

New York. I won't belabor the reasons here (you can google'em up), but at the last minute, it got moved to Max Yasgur's Dairy farm in the little town of Bethel.

Of course, I'd no idea what Hitch was talking about, but I earnestly pretended to look as hard as I could. Using my right index finger to trace several roads that ran from Pennsylvania to that part of New York. I did luck up finally and find White Lake and Woodstock and reverse engineered myself back to my best guess of where we might be.

Hitch had been a storehouse of info as we traveled along about the various places we were going past, passing through, or were about to approach. Thank goodness he was prepared a bit because you likely know the traffic jam history of the New York Throughway during the festival and all the problems it caused. Well, we would miss it, because of our early start and the decisions Hitch and I made right that minute, but mostly because of some invaluable help from a couple folks you are about to meet.

"Huu, maybe this way?" I offered, pointing to a route that looked reasonable to me.

"Ok, ok," Hitch said. "Looks as good as any. We should be getting to that turn in another hour or so, I think, maybe."

He looked at me smiling and shrugging his shoulders. Hitch had always been ok in my book. At that moment, I felt like we became friends.

Leslie's concoction of pepper, paste, and duct tape managed to stop Davey's bleeding. That area of the VW was a disaster though.

Blood, Coca-Cola, duct tape, and gobs of strewn-about paste made it resemble Dr. Frankenstein's lab. Poor Davey, he really looked the part too. Covered in make-shift bandages, blood everywhere, he was the embodiment of the creature come to life. Leslie was pretty messed up as well.

"We gotta stop and get this crap cleaned up," Leslie demanded of Hitch.

"Ok, ok," he said. "Next place I see. Lenny keep a look out for a service station or a mom and pop store."

We pulled into a two-pump gas station. There were a number of cars near the pumps and we noticed a lot of young people milling about. This was early Thursday afternoon, August 14, 1969. The festival was supposed to start the next day. We were about to encounter our first co-festival goers.

"Oh my gosh, are you all ok," a raven-haired, needle-thin girl in a peasant skirt asked Leslie and the group as we exited the VW.

"We're all ok," Leslie, her shirt covered in blood, said dismissively. "Davey go to the bathroom and clean yourself up. Lenny help him out. Hitch you go get some water and extra rags and start on the bus. I gotta get this crap off me."

Davey and I hurried over to the bathroom on the side of the building. Two teenage girls were exiting the ladies' room. They were startled to see a bite-sized Frankenstein.

"Is he alright?" a tall auburn-haired girl asked.

Her ample boobs, barely held in check by a white tank top were right in Davey's face.

"Can you help us?" Davey plaintively asked.

That was when I knew Davey was going to milk this (the situation, not the boobs, but he would have if he could have) for all it was worth. The girl basically took over Davey's care. I was left outside the bathroom with the girl's friend. She was a cool-looking, cocoa-skinned girl with a medium sized dark afro. She was wearing jeans and a Levi vest covering a yellow bathing suit top. She was wearing boots. I feel in love immediately.

"Hi, I'm Dani," she said.

"Hi, I'm Lenny," I responded.

"That accent, where are you from?" she asked.

"North Carolina," I replied.

"Wow, that's a trip," she continued. "We're coming in from Cleveland."

We talked about the festival. Dani really wanted to see Janis Joplin and Joan Baez. I told her of my love for The Who and some of the other acts I wanted to see. She said she liked The Who as well.

"We're kinda stuck right now," she said. "Our car broke down about a mile from here and my friend's brother is trying to get it fixed."

"That stinks," I said.

Davey and the other girl emerged from the men's room. Davey didn't look much better, only somewhat cleaner, but he was smiling a really big smile. The girl had her arm around him and he was nuzzled in her bosom. I guessed the girls were both late high school age. The girls, not their boobs, but I guess they were too.

Introductions were made and we headed back to the van. Hitch had finished cleaning up his prized possession as best he could. Leslie was still inside the store or bathroom, we weren't sure which.

While we were talking, the girls' male companion lumbered into the parking lot and said their car was shot. He was carrying three bags and a tent with him. He was very muscular, just under six-feet, looked to be about 20 with dark hair and some facial hair. He had on jeans and a Cleveland Browns t-shirt.

"I sold it to some guy down the road for $100, looks like we'll be taking the bus or hitching back to Ohio," he said.

"I'm still going to the festival," Dani said.

"Me too Melvin," the other girl said. "I don't care if you're my brother, I can decide for myself."

"Mandy you know Mom told me to watch after you," Mandy's brother declared. "And I say we need to head home."

"We're only an hour or so away," Mandy replied. "I'm going to this concert to see Joe Cocker and you can't stop me. I'm 16 and I'll do what I want!"

The two argued for several minutes. Her brother finally relented. He picked up one bag and turned to walk away. He stopped, dropped the bag, and walked back to his sister.

"You call Mom and tell her," he said. "I'm going to start home. Dani, you going to get up with your dad, right?"

"Yea," she replied.

Melvin shook his head, reached into his pocket and pulled out a wad of bills. He handed Mandy several 20s and walked away. Then

Hitch stepped in and offered the girls a ride to the festival. Davey and I were ecstatic! Two super-hot teenage girls going to Woodstock with us? Hell yea! The girls readily agreed and thanked Hitch for the offer.

Leslie reappeared and quickly assessed the situation. Surprisingly, she was fine with recent developments. We made sure everyone was properly introduced. The girls grabbed their bags. Hitch and I strapped their tent to the top of the VW. Davey and I headed to the back and the girls occupied the former hospital zone. They talked excitedly about their journey from Cleveland and about their hopes for the next few days. Davey and I just stared and listened. Mandy went on and on about Joe Cocker, while Dani focused on her love of Janis and her desire to see lots of other "cool people".

"I wonder who else is going to play?" Mandy asked.

"According to the radio, the Grateful Dead, Credence, and Hendrix are supposed to play," Hitch said.

He was right, with the keyword "supposed". As we all found out later, the concert line-up was influx during the whole festival. Some artists were delayed because of the roads or weather, others declined at the last minute. Still, others pitched in and filled a gap or two on the bill. Almost no one would come on at the time they were "supposed" to, but nobody seemed to care. There were many great surprises, but they were yet to be, as we were still a few minutes from the site and a day away from any live festival music.

"You know the festival is not really in Woodstock, right?" Dani asked. "It's nearer to Bethel, in Sullivan County."

"Uh, no, I didn't know that," Hitch replied.

"Yea Woodstock is about 40 miles away from where we're heading," she said. "My dad lives nearby, that's the only reason my mom let me come, to see him. He told me on the phone Tuesday night about all the stuff that's been going on up here. Then last night when we stopped in PA, I called and he said it was beginning to get crazy!"

Dani went on to tell us her dad was a postman in the area, that he was white, and lived in nearby Monticello. She had visited him each summer since her folks split up when she was eight. This was her father's home area. She and her mom had moved to Cleveland after the divorce to be near her mom's folks. Dani's knowledge of the local area would save us much time and heartache the next few days.

"We're rolling in the best way possible," she said as she directed us in from the west side of the festival site. "My dad said a boatload of people are already here."

I'm not sure what would have happened to us if Leslie hadn't beaned Davey and we hadn't stopped to clean things up. Meeting the girls would turn out to be one of the best things that happened to us on our Woodstock journey. Hell, we were going to Woodstock proper before we met them. Now we had a better sense of where we were going and the best way to get there. As you likely know from history, many others didn't.

"My dad's family are cousins to the people who own the land where the festival is going to be," Dani said. "They're dairy farmers."

"Are there any stores between here and where we're going?" Leslie asked, speaking for the first time since we re-entered the VW.

"Yea, I'm pretty sure there's a little store another couple miles up the road," Dani responded.

"Pull in there Hitch," Leslie directed.

The VW chugged along past farms and wood. We'd been on a two-lane road for a long time and while the scenery was great, we were all anxious to get "there". We finally got to the little store Dani told us about and we pulled in by the gas pumps. Gas was 29 cents a gallon.

"I'll top off the tank," Hitch said.

Another wise move, as we wouldn't find gas or supplies for three hours after we left the festival. We all disembarked. Leslie headed to the store with Dani and Mandy, while Davey and I hit the restrooms on the side of the building.

"Man you see those boobs," Davey said punching me on the shoulder. "I snuggled real close to them!"

"I know, I saw you! You lucky turd!" I noted. "How old do you think Dani is?"

"Well Mandy said she was 16," Davey replied. "So I think she may be bout the same, maybe a little younger?"

"Yea, I think so too," I said. "Think I can pass for 14?"

"Nah, nah," Davey said shaking his head. "You look older than you are, but don't go higher than 13 or 13.5."

We took care of business, washed our hands, and bolted out the door, almost knocking each other down to get back to the VW and the girls. They were all still in the store. Hitch was talking to several other fellow travelers who had pulled into the store in a caravan-like line of station wagons, pick-ups, and cars. At least eight, maybe 10, don't quite remember.

I heard some of them say they were from Pittsburgh and a couple others from places in western PA. They'd met along the road and decided to caravan to the festival. They all appeared to be late teens or early 20s and were a little more "clean cut" than most festival goers we would encounter. One was a Vietnam veteran who had a big scar on his left leg from mortar shrapnel. Davey and I listened for a bit but headed into the store. I hadn't spent any of my money yet (except Ma Bell's toll) and neither had Davey. He brought a grand total of $12.

"I'm going to get a Mars bar," Davey declared as we entered the old, grey cinder-block store with chain-pulled ceiling fans.

A young guy wearing a "Make Love, Not War" t-shirt behind the counter was ringing up Leslie's purchases. She had two whole grocery bags full of stuff. I saw him stuff a new roll of duct tape into one bag along with some rolling papers. Mandy and Dani had a drink each and some snack stuff in their hands. Davey quickly made good on his promise and got in line right behind Mandy with a Mars bar and an Orange soda. I decided to treat myself to a coke and some ice cream. I handed Leslie $20 for my part of the food and stuff.

Everyone else was already outside when I made it back to the bus with my small paper bag. Hitch was still engaged with the PA folks and Leslie was sorting out her purchases with the front passenger door open and her grocery trove on the seat. Mandy was looking at Davey's makeshift field dressing and suggested more duct tape. She stepped up into the VW to get some and Davey gleefully followed her in. Dani was drinking a 7-Up when I approached and pulled two ice cream sandwiches out.

"Here," I said. "I got you one too."

"Aww," she said. "Thank you, that's so sweet. I love ice cream sandwiches!"

Mandy and Davey re-appeared. Davey was sporting some more tape and bandages. He could have easily gone trick-or-treating.

"Well Dani," Mandy started. "Looks like you have your first Woodstock admirer."

Dani smiled. I did too. We both tore into our ice cream sandwiches.

Leslie laughed, "Yea too bad he's going in sixth grade."

"Do what?" Dani laughed. "You little devil, I thought you were at least 13 or 14."

Trying the hardest I ever had in my life to be cool while dying inside, I managed this response.

"Yea, that's what I was going for."

Everyone was laughing so hard, even some of the PA folks. But my stomach was in knots. My first shot at Woodstock romance exploding all around me on the launch pad.

"I still think you're sweet and cute!" Dani said, running her left hand through my blond curls. "And you have great hair. But Lenny, I'm 14, I'm sure some sixth-grader will fall for your charms."

Lots more laughter all around. I felt a little better, but not much. We got back on the road after promises of meeting up with the western PA crowd near the stage. The road was getting more and more congested.

"Those were nice people back there," Hitch said. "Give me some food, I'm starved."

"We got to ration this stuff out," said Leslie sternly. "We're going to be here till Sunday night, we only packed for two. Now we got six mouths to feed."

"We got plenty in our bags for us," Mandy said. "And we'll share too."

So we had our first rolling commune, four beach people, and two girls from Cleveland with one having ties to the festival area. We were set, or so we thought. We were all getting hungry, so Leslie had me pass up her food luggage bag. Mandy asked for hers too. I pulled the bags from the back and Mandy passed our food bag up to Leslie. Leslie doled out some fruit, crackers, and a few cans of Vienna wieners for us to share. Mandy passed around a big bag of chips and a huge bag of oatmeal raisin cookies. We all ate our fill. Just as we were finishing we began to notice cars on the side of the road and dozens of people walking eastward.

"We're getting pretty close," Dani said. "We can turn off about another mile up the road to the left and try and find a spot."

"Sounds good," said Hitch.

It was probably about three or four that afternoon when we arrived at the festival site. People were everywhere. We all wanted to get down close to where they were still building the stage. Hitch, using his dad's imparted military logic, denied our pleas.

"No, and hell no!" He declared. "We'll get down there, but on foot. We're going to camp up here on the top of this ridge. Dad always said take the high ground in all things military and camping, so that's what we are going to do."

No one bucked him after that. It was perhaps the smartest move we made the whole trip, the high ground. As you know, the rains would come. In fact, the ground was still somewhat soft and mushy from wet weather earlier in the week. We set the VW Westphalia's camping apparatus up, with awning and all. Davey and I were a little more help this second night on the road since we'd one whole night of experience with all the camping crap.

People were everywhere, tents were everywhere. We'd a great spot though, no one else had set up very near us yet, but there were hundreds of tents on the slope below. From our spot on the high south side ridge, we could see down several hundred yards to the stage construction site and a quite large pond beyond. Hitch brought his dad's binoculars and Davey was checking things out below.

"Look at all the people," he exclaimed and handed me the field glasses.

It was quite surreal looking through the lenses at all the people and activity. I saw tents being erected, tents falling down, people kissing, people smoking what I guessed was dope. Then it happened. THE SECOND WONDER OF BOYHOOD-Seeing your first set of boobs live! I saw my first set of live, uncovered female breasts through those lenses. She looked to be 20 or so, long brown hair, denim shorts, beads around her neck and head, and topless, most importantly topless! They were so nice, small and pert, but so nice. She was about forty yards or so away, just casually talking to two other mostly clothed girls and a guy.

"Tits, 12'oclock," I whispered to Davey and handed him the glasses.

I was a good friend.

"Where?" He asked desperately.

Trying to scope out boobies with his damaged eye was proving problematic. He also had no idea how to locate using the face of a clock. So, I reluctantly pointed. Davey was never going to get that Rhodes scholarship.

"Whoa!" he exclaimed, way too loud.

Plus, he wouldn't give the glasses back.

"What you guys checking out?" Dani asked with a smirk on her face.

"People, tents," I tried to respond nonchalantly, shrugging my shoulders.

"Titties," lots of titties," Davey smiled, lowering the glasses.

"You little perverts," Mandy laughed. "Come on Dani, let's go walk around."

"Ok," Dani said. "Bye boys."

"Later pervs!" Mandy exclaimed waving over her shoulder.

"Idiot!" I yelled at Davey, punching him in the shoulder pretty damn hard.

"Ouch," he said hitting me back.

"You two cut it out and get over here," Leslie said. "Your job is to find out if there are any portable toilets and to check out those woods over there for a possible latrine site."

Damn, from the highs of seeing your first boobies in person, to looking for a place to poop. Such was this, what would always be remembered as an epic, beyond epic adventure. Boobies! Music! Girls talking to us!

So Davey and I set out to find poop palaces and girl watch. We did great at the latter, the former, not so much. There were so many pretty hippie girls around in various states of dress. Most were adorned with the garb of the day. I'm sure you've have seen pictures from that time, so you know what I mean. Lots of peasant skirts, cut-off shorts, jeans, billowy blouses, tank tops, and some without tops. It seems at each succeeding Woodstock festival more and more people got naked. By the time of the third one in 1999, I'd seen more boobies in person than Hugh Hefner. While not as many as 1994 or 1999, there were a ton of topless girls that first day we arrived.

Davey and I made our way down to the stage area, thousands of folks were already staking their spot for Friday's music. We moved to our left at my suggestion. It's much easier to navigate crowds if you go left. See 90% of the world is right-handed, so they instinctively move right, we lefties know to go the other way. You can get right to the front of most any general seating/standing venue. Trust me, I have been to over 400 concerts and it's worked 95% of the time. It would work this weekend as well. We easily made our way to the front of the stage on the left side. It still looked like they had a lot of work to do.

The history of Woodstock suggests the promoters had to make a decision the day before, build the ticket booths and fences, or the stage. They wisely chose the stage. They would lose their shirts to start, as it become a free event and Woodstock Ventures would be sued a gazillion times, but the film and soundtrack profits allowed them to eventually get everything settled and paid. It's been profit city ever since. On this day, things were definitely in a state of upheaval and chaos.

We were never asked for a ticket or saw anyone else asked for one. Leslie did have two three-day passes for the festival she had bought from an address in NYC. The passes were $20 each or eight dollars a day. Leslie's three-day set had little symbols (a star, a crescent moon, etc.,) on them and was green. The single day tickets I saw didn't have the symbol. They were numbered. I found an eight-dollar Saturday ticket as Davey and I were strolling near the stage. I still have it to this day.

> WOODSTOCK MUSIC and ART FAIR
> SATURDAY
> AUGUST 16, 1969
> 10:00 A. M.
> $8.00   Good For One Admission Only
> 02887 B   NO REFUNDS
>
> SAT.
> AUG. 16
> 1969
> 02887 B

It started a tradition. I've kept almost all my concert tickets since. As I noted earlier, there are well over 400 of them. If Providence and my editors allow, you might get to hear about some more of them and see some of the copies if there's ever a Crazy Beach II and/or III. Oh, the stories I can tell you...

After I found the tix, Davey and I made a hard left and attempted to flank the stage area. They hadn't secured that portion of the performing section yet. We were easily able to wander around in the back of the stage area. We didn't see anyone famous or any security, just a couple of guys doing rigging yelling for us to get the hell out of there. They basically paid us little or no attention right after.

We followed a few people down to what we thought was a lake. I later found out it was called Fillippini Pond. It was at much lower elevation and would serve as the far northern boundary of the festival site. There were naked people there! Lots of them. Holy Crap Batman! Lots and lots of naked folks. I tried to act cool, but it was impossible, remember, even though I was big for my age, I was still a few weeks shy of 11-years old. My eyes were thoroughly dotted. For the only time I ever witnessed, Davey was speechless. We just stood there by the edge of the water watching naked people laugh, splash each other, toss one another around, love on one another, and bathe.

We walked east along the waterline. We started to make our way back when I noticed some clothes I thought I recognized on the ground. Holy shit, they were Dani's! No sooner had I made this startling observation, it happened-The SEVENTH WONDER OF BOYHOOD-A GIRL YOU WANT TO SEE NAKED is in the BUFF RIGHT in FRONT OF YOU! Emerging from Fillippini Pond were a very naked Mandy and Dani. Needless to say, they had my full attention, especially one area of my person. I imagined Davey was likewise at attention. I thought the moon landing a few weeks earlier would be the greatest thing I would ever see. Boy, was I wrong!

"Hey boys," Mandy said.

Now, we were both speechless.

"What's wrong, never seen a naked girl before?" Dani smiled.

"Of course not, they're like 12," Mandy said, missing us high by a year for me and two for Davey.

They both giggled and slowly reached for their clothes. Their girl business was not more than four feet from us. It would be as close as I would come to that wonderful destination for quite a few years yet.

"You just always remember," Mandy said proudly. "The first pie you ever saw, was Cleveland pie."

And to this day, as all my friends and former girlfriends will attest, that's what I call a lady's end zone: Cleveland!

Track 18-Will It Go Round in Circles-Billy Preston (3:12)

I was excited to see seventh grade start. We island kids would be going to school on the mainland for the first time. Since meeting Darlene a few weeks before, she was on my mind a lot. I was hoping we would be in the same homeroom. Homeroom would be another big change about going to junior high for the first time. In elementary school, we had the same teacher for the whole day, in the same classroom. Junior high meant switching classes and having several different teachers. You had a homeroom teacher the first couple of hours giving instruction on a subject or two, then you would switch to another class and another teacher for the next two class periods before lunch. Then after lunch, two or three more classes, two or three more teachers.

Another big change would be the opportunity to play school sports. The school I was to attend, Sunset Junior High had been around since the early 1940s in a building built by the Works Progress Administration (WPA), one of President FDR's "New Deal" programs that provided otherwise hard-to-find jobs during the Great Depression. The WPA and other programs like it helped build tons of schools, roads, and other infrastructure. My new school was one of those. It was also our first introduction to widespread integration.

The south had been in the throes of Jim Crow for so long and was just beginning to reluctantly accept the Supreme Court's landmark 1954 ruling in Brown vs. the Board of Education. That ruling called for school desegregation and the integration of school children of all races. The ruling struck down the history of "separate but equal" (unequal) schools, not just in the south, but in all areas of the country.

Sadly, one of the things to come about in the south as a result of all the school adjustments was the rapid rise in the establishment of private schools. Our county had zero private schools before the Civil Rights Act in 1965. The first was established right after. I hated the place because even as a kid I knew what its founders were doing, charging money for a "private" education, but mostly to keep their kids away from others not like them. Now I know you folks reading from other places than our part of the south have had private schools for a long time and so this may or may not apply. Where I'm from it did, and everyone knew it, though the founders of these academies denied it. Liars!

Tryouts for the football team and cheerleading were being held the week before school started. The only girls' sports junior high offered back then were cheerleading, track, and basketball. Darlene and I managed to meet on the boardwalk a couple of times as the days counted down till the first bell.

"I know you're going to play football Lenny," she said as we played a game of putt-putt behind The Landmark.

"Yea, tryouts start tomorrow," I said. "Are you going to go out for cheerleading?"

We were about to start the third hole and she was positioned to tap in an easy next-to-the hole-shot. She paused and looked up at me.

I could tell by her expression what was to follow wasn't going to be to my liking."

"No, Dad has enrolled me in that private school near the junction," she said scanning my face for a reaction.

"Really?" I managed as my heart sank about a mile.

"Yea, he did it Friday," she started. "I was going to call you, but my dad doesn't think girls should call boys. I guess I'm going to try for cheerleading and track this year."

She tapped her putt in and we walked over to number four. It was a pretty easy hole, you just had to clear two triangle-shaped obstacles facing one another about five yards from the start. I've cleared that obstacle a million times in my life. I clanked my ball off the left one.

"Wow, I don't know what to say," I tried. "Did he tell you why?"

"He told me and my mom it was for the best," she said. "He didn't allow many questions. My mom tried, but he just went and did something else."

We left it at that till we finished our round. We held hands as we walked south on the outer boardwalk past a couple of bars and a clothing store to the Steel Pier. Darlene had to be home by six and it was closing in on that time.

"Let's ride the Skyliner chairlift!" she said excitedly.

"You sure you have time?" I asked. "I don't want your dad pissed at me."

Both our families were aware that Darlene and I were "sweet" on one another since the ballgame a few weeks before, but her dad was really strict about where she could go and what time she had to be home. I didn't want to risk getting on his bad side.

"He's playing golf with your dad silly," she laughed. "They probably won't be home for hours. Mom won't care if I'm a few minutes late."

I didn't know they were playing golf. I'd been working washing dishes and doing other stuff all day at the Corner Restaurant for Carlos Holland, a boardwalk fixture for decades. Darlene had come by when I'd got off at four. We played in the arcade, walked the north end, and played the game of putt-putt. We now were about to embark on the first of many chairlifts we would take out over the old Fisherman's Steel Pier.

The chairlift started before you even got on the venerable old pier structure (site of a chain hotel today), rose up over the pier house and out nearly to the end of the pier, 50 yards or so away from the pier house. The ride was about 100 yards out and back the same amount. It took little more than 10 minutes to make the circuit. That's it on the book's cover.

"This is going to be fun!" she said as we paid our 50 cents for the ride.

Darlene, in the early years of our relationship always insisted on paying her own way. She grabbed my hand as we made our way into the two-person chair. The attendant placed the iron bar down in front of us to secure us in place and off we went. Darlene looked at me excitedly and gave me a peck on the right cheek, a first! The chair jerked quite a bit as we ascended up and over the pier house. It was a kinda cloudy day with a nice breeze and the beach below was sparsely populated. The time of day, the advent of school and the clouds did their work to empty the sands. We could only see one other occupied chair. It was at the far end of the pier, making the turn to head back. Darlene let go of my hand and looked over the right side of the chairlift.

"It's so cool to look between the boards," she said. "This is so exciting!"

I used the opportunity to slide my right arm onto the top of the chair. She noticed and smiled as she turned around. She slid a little closer to me. Our bare legs were touching. The breeze was drifting her hair away from me and her smile was radiant. I was very happy.

"I'm glad we found each other," she said as she laid her head on my shoulder and placed her left hand on my right thigh.

I just squeezed her shoulder in response. We stayed like that for a bit. It was such a great feeling, it's hard for me to capture. It was as if all my dreams had come true at the same time. We stayed in that embrace until we'd almost reached the turn. She rose her head slowly, smiled a little smile and leaned toward me. I leaned toward her and just as our lips were about to meet, the chair jerked violently as it made its turn back toward the shore. She giggled, I laughed. Then it happened in spite of the creaky old chair, our first kiss.

She placed both hands on my face and just planted one right on my lips, just for a couple of seconds. It was warm and salty. Her skin smelled so clean. I didn't know what I was supposed to do with my hands. The one that had been on her shoulder, I let slip to her waist.

She let her hands drop and looked at me for a second. She smiled. I smiled. She leaned back in and I leaned toward her. Kiss number two was much longer and involved more entanglement. We kept kissing, her hand once again resting on my thigh.

"Whooo-hooo!! Go Lenny!!!"

I heard familiar voices yell. We broke our lip lock. Damn if it wasn't the dumb-ass duo, Nathan and Heath, they were approaching on the other side, walking down below. They repeated their calls and chant. I gave them a dismissive wave.

"They're just jealous," Darlene said proudly.

"Yea, I know," I said. "But what crappy timing."

I laughed, she laughed. We would always laugh a lot. It was one of the best things about our relationship, then in its infancy. We got off the ride and headed toward the lake.

"I'll walk you home," I said.

She smiled. I smiled. We held hands for the six-block walk back to her house. We didn't talk much. It was one of the best walks of my life.

"Have fun at football tomorrow," she said climbing the steps to her house. "Let me know how it goes!"

"I will, I'll call after," I said.

She smiled. I smiled. She gave our quirky, awkward little half-wave. I did the same.

Track 19-Sundown-Gordon Lightfoot (3:34)

The days after Melissa left were mostly a fog. I worked, I surfed, went to ball practice, Groundhog Day that a bunch. I was actually kind of lost. I was waiting for something to happen. I wasn't making anything happen. I kept an eye on the movie theatre and noticed there were some seedy type fellows going in and out the emergency exit in the back. I even overheard a couple of heated arguments in the back parking lot of the donut shop between Gerald, the redhead, and another older, skinny, dark-haired guy. The theatre was still showing its regular fair in the prime time hours and matinees, but a new thing was happening to the late night shows…"dirty movies".

I first noticed it the Friday after Melissa left, just before the start of school. I was closing up the arcade late night and I saw a small line of mostly men, but quite a few couples, standing outside the box office window. I looked over and inside the lone glass movie poster holder hung just to the left of the box office window was a poster saying "Special midnight showing". The poster was for "Behind the Green Door", an X-rated adult film starring former Ivory Soap model Marilynn Chambers. Another hand-written sign hung over the box office saying "18 and over ONLY!"

I strolled home thinking about the movie and wondering how it had come to be shown at our little island theatre. I didn't tell anyone about it that weekend. When I went to open the donut shop the next morning, the poster was gone.

I was about halfway through my day shift when bikini-clad Darlene, Lexi, and one of the Ransom girls (the eldest of the three little hoes) came into the shop. I was sitting at the far end of the counter facing the entrance, as it was an unusually quiet Saturday. I was caught up on all my back room responsibilities. My co-worker Tammy and the trio talked for a bit by the front drink fountain. Tammy and the Ransom girl kept up their chatter as Darlene and Lexi made their way back to me.

"Ladies," I said.

"Hey Lenny," Lexi said.

"Hi Lexi," I replied.

Darlene gave our little wave. I smiled. The girls sat down on the two stools nearest me.

"What's rocking?" I asked.

"Not much," Lexi said. "We're going to clean up and head to town to get some school clothes."

"Nice," I said. "Sears?"

"I think we're going downtown first," Lexi replied. "My mom loves Belk."

"I got to get some new jeans," Darlene said. "But I've to get academy approved skirts and blouses first. Blah!"

"You always look cute in your little school-girl uniforms," I teased.

Darlene gave me a sarcastic smile.

"What are you and the fellas up to this last big weekend before school starts?" Lexi asked.

"Don't know," I started. "Been busy with work and practice, haven't really talked to 'em much."

"Oh," Lexi said. "Figured you guys would be lighting it up."

She stood and excused herself to the little girls' room. Darlene scooted down one bar stool to Lexi's unoccupied seat next to me. We talked about their day on the beach, prospects for our 10th-grade year, and random other things until Darlene moved the conversation in a direction to make something happen.

"Let's go see a movie since you don't have any plans with the guys," Darlene said.

"Sure," I said. "Tonight?"

It was kinda hard to keep my eyes off of Darlene's breasts which looked to be trying to escape from their perch. Her figure had gone from athletic young lady to healthy in all the right places a teenage girl would want over the last few months. She was breathtaking.

"That should work," Darlene replied. "Let's meet at the arcade bout quarter till nine."

"Ok, sounds good," I said.

"What's playing?" she asked.

"Not sure," I replied.

Lexi returned and plopped down on Darlene's former stool.

"Doesn't matter," Darlene said placing her left hand on my right wrist as I leaned on the bar. "If we don't like it, we can do something else."

"We better get going," Lexi said tapping Darlene on the shoulder.

They got up and started toward the front. They both looked so good in their bikinis, Lexi's was light red and Darlene's white. They were both so tanned from a summer outdoors.

"See ya Lenny," Lexi said without turning around.

"Later," I said.

Yep, you guessed it, Darlene did a full turn and gave me our little wave. I blew her a kiss.

As soon as my shift was over I went out front and walked over to the theatre to see what was playing. It was "Dirty Mary and Crazy Larry", a robbery caper starring Peter Fonda and Susan George. Gerald came out the front as I was staring at the poster.

"How ya doing kid?" He asked.

"Good," I said. "Might come check this out," I said pointing to the poster.

That was when I noticed that the "Behind the Green Door" poster wasn't taken down, it was just covered by the "Dirty Mary" one.

"You showing the other one again tonight?" I brazenly asked.

He chuckled.

"Yea kid, you saw that huh?" he quizzed.

"Yea," I replied.

"Stuff's just for grown-ups though," he said. "But you probably know that don't cha?"

I nodded. Now I knew what the redhead meant when he said I was too young to work there. From what I'd seen lately, I wouldn't want to work there anyway. My stomach knotted up a little.

Gerald turned and went back inside. I just had a funny feeling all these changes were leading to something funky. What? I'd no idea. Had I known, maybe I would've alerted someone, an adult, or the cops. But at that point, I was somewhat clueless about what was happening behind the green door, the theatre door, and the me and Darlene door.

"I have some pintos on for supper," my mom said as I entered from the front porch.

"Great," I said.

I walked over to the stove and gave her a kiss on the cheek. The house always smelled so good, especially when Mom was whipping up a meal. If a Hall of Fame for great moms were established, my mom would be a charter member.

"Board games tonight," Mom noted as I made my way to my room.

My tiny bedroom was an afterthought. Dad and Uncle D forget to build me one. So they just half-assed walled-in the right side of the ocean-side deck. Don't get me wrong, I loved it, best room a boy could ever have, three-window ocean view, private beachside entrance, but still, geez guys!

"Can't Mom," I yelled. "Going to the movies with Darlene."

"Oh," Mom said back. "Bring her by, I haven't seen her much this summer."

"I'll try Mom," my yelling continued. "But we're probably going straight to the show."

She let it die at that and I went to grab a shower. I was showering pretty quickly until I started thinking about the girls in their bikinis. Darlene had just the most killer hot beach bod now and Lexi's little body was way too sexy in that tiny red number. I stayed in the shower much longer than I'd anticipated.

"I gotta use the bathroom," lil'sis yelled, banging on the door.

"Ok, ok," I yelled. "I'll be right out."

"Hurry, I gotta go!" she yelled again.

"Coming!" I yelled as I stepped out of the shower, wrapped a towel around my waist, grabbed my shorts, and bolted to my room.

"Uh, hey," B said as he sat at my work desk.

"Yo," I said. "Give me a sec."

B nodded and went out on the deck. I put Grand Funk's "We're an American Band" in the eight-track player. I threw on a Baltimore Colts' t-shirt (with the Colt kicking a football with its hind legs) and some black baggies and headed out.

"Darlene called," my mom said as I exited my room. "She said to meet her by the picnic tables at eight instead of the arcade."

"Thanks Mom," I said stepping out on the deck.

"What's going on?" I asked.

"Not much," he said. "Just wanted to touch base on school and practice stuff."

We sat on the deck and watched a couple kid surfers try their hand at some decent sized waves and talked about the coming school year.

"Guess we're going to have to ride the bus till I get my license in October," I said. "The Scout has been in the shop more and more lately. Dad and I are going to look at those two cars again Sunday."

"Cool," B said. "Which one are you leaning toward?"

"Tough call really," I said. "I like them both bout equal, but I can get the Duster for $1100 and the Chevelle is $1500."

"Four bills, that's a big difference," B said.

"I know," I said. "But Dad has given me an option. I can pick the car either way and also choose to either pay for the car or the insurance. I got the feeling he's trying to teach me some kinda financial crap here, so I don't know what to do."

"Well?" B asked.

"Man, I got a lot on my mind right now," I said. "Melissa leaving, school starting, trying to play both soccer and football this fall, the car stuff, and Darlene, just too much going on in my head right now."

"You'll figure it out," B said. "Bunch of the guys want to camp out tonight. You wanna go?"

"Nah, heading to the movies with Darlene," I said.

"Cool," B said. "After?"

He raised his eyebrow Belushi-like at the end of the question with the clear inference being about possible sex stuff and me hitting the campout after Darlene's curfew.

"Geez, I don't know," I said. "We got nowhere to go except the beach. I don't want that to be the deal."

B just sat there. Then he sprung up and motioned for me to meet him at the front of the deck like he had just uncovered Deep Throat, the Watergate informant, not Linda Lovelace of the porn movie of the same name.

"How about the donut shop?" B said as if he'd just discovered a great cure. "You have a key. It'll be closed after you guys get out of the movie."

"Are you for real?" I asked, though somewhat intrigued by the possibility. "That's crazy."

"It would work," said B.

He was probably right. It would work. Logistically anyway. No one ever went in the shop after closing time. We could be alone with little or no fear of being found. There were huge 50-pound bags of sugar and flour stacked like mini mattresses in the back. I began to wonder why I hadn't thought of it before. At least for a make-out session.

"Too far out man," I said. "I want this to be great for Darlene."

The little surfer dudes wiped out on a wave a bit large for their skill level. Kudos to them for giving it a shot. You could tell they were a little woozy as they exited the surf just as sundown began closing the books on another beach day.

"I think that's your best chance man," B said. "She's going to 10th, like us, so that means the high school side of the academy Monday. Going to be a ton of junior and senior dudes there just dying to get into her pants."

"I know, I know," I said. "I'll think of something."

Track 20-I Think We're Alone Now-Tommy James & the Shondells (2:07)

For a couple years now, Darlene and I'd been meeting at the lake whenever we were going to the boardwalk together, just the two of us. Most of the time though, we were always with our friends and would just meet at the Rec Hall, putt-putt, arcade, or wherever we ran into one another on the boardwalk. There were a couple of picnic benches around the lake and whoever got there first would just grab a table and wait. We didn't spend many total hours there over those years, but it was a special place for us because we seldom got a chance to be alone what with family, friends, and activities.

"That's three in a row," she said laughing as I approached. "I mean make a girl wait why don't cha."

"Sorry, sorry," I said. "B was at the house when I got home and wanted to talk school and sports crap."

I joined her sitting on the table portion. We shifted around to face the lake. A couple of cars honked as they passed. Friends or pervs, or both, don't know. Darlene really looked hot. Tiny white skirt and a light blue, belly-button baring billowy top. She had on a touch more clear lip gloss than usual, but it looked sexy.

"Mom really wants to see you," I said.

"Ok, tell her I will pop by tomorrow," she replied. "My mom wants me to bring that casserole dish back to her anyway."

"Cool, cool," I said.

"So what's this movie we're going to see, dirty, crazy something," she began. "My mom wasn't too happy about the title."

"Dirty Mary, Crazy Larry," I said. "Peter Fonda, Susan George, it's a car chase, cops, and robbers thing."

"Oh," Darlene shrugged. "I get to stay out till 11:30. How long is it?"

"Ninety minutes, two hours, I guess," I said.

Her normal curfew was 11, but since it was the last Saturday before school, she got to stay out a bit later with the usual caveat that she couldn't leave the boardwalk until she was heading home. Also, per usual, when it was just the two of us, I was obliged to walk her home, per both our dads. Of course, I didn't mind. We'd about an hour before the movie started.

"You want to grab a bite before the movie or wait for popcorn?" I asked.

"We just finished up supper before I came," she said.

"Oh, ok," I said. "I had a bowl of pintos and slaw, but I'll be ready for some popcorn."

"Let's go out on the beach and walk up that way to the show," she suggested grabbing my hand and not waiting for an answer.

We crossed the main road and made our way past an old Mom and Pop motel and out onto the beach. The exact same sign for the motel we passed by is still there today. We both took off our flip-flops. She grabbed my hand again and led us toward the water. We walked north along the ocean's tidal edge with the water cascading over our feet. It was a near perfect late summer evening.

"This summer has flown by," she said wistfully, looking out at the ocean.

A few lonely gulls circled overhead crying for bread or companionship, or some other seagull thing.

"I know, just seems like a minute ago we went swimming the day school got out," I said. "That was a blast!"

It was kind of our gang's tradition, to meet at the pier and go swimming on the last day of school. We'd started it after fourth grade. The girls joined in a few years later.

"That was a good day," she said looking at me, her violet eyes twinkling with laughter. "I thought Hal and David were going to have a stroke when Lexi lost her top!"

"Oh hell yea," I said. "Hal didn't stop talking about that for weeks!"

We walked slowly toward the Steel Pier, holding hands along the shoreline, letting our feet and ankles sink in the wet sand. The water felt great and a few rogue waves splashed a little higher up our legs.

"We should all go swimming tomorrow!" she said releasing my hand and thumping my chest.

"Sounds good," I said. "We can make a day of it. Let's have everyone meet at my house after I get off."

"That'll be so much fun!" she giggled. "I know Hal will be hoping for a repeat performance!"

We walked past my house and a couple more before we reached the Steel Pier. I could see the lights were already on and made out a few game-night relatives standing around the table. The noise of the boardwalk came into play as did the sounds of Skyliner cable car riders as we headed under the main pier house.

We held hands facing one another. I sighed, she smiled. We kissed. As good a kiss as I'd ever received or participated in up to that point. Not sure why, it just was. You know the kind, the one or ones that stay with you, and when you think of romance, love, sex, or just kissing, it's the first one that pops in your mind most of the time? Yep, that one.

We continued our under the pier make-out session till we were both significantly hot and bothered enough to know it was time to break. Like two boxers, hanging on for dear life nearing the end of a grueling match and the ref steps in and says "break". We both knew we needed to break and we did. Part of me wanted to pull her further up under the pier and get the real proceedings underway. But I knew that wouldn't be right for her, so I did math problems in my head.

"Math problems, again?" she asked smiling as big a smile as I would ever see from her.

I nodded.

"Let's go to the show," she said, starting to walk away without me.

"No more math problems Lenny," she said motioning with her head and shoulder for me to follow her.

I caught up with her just as we exited the pier pylons. We climbed the couple wooden steps leading back to the outer boardwalk and began making our way toward the putt-putt.

"This movie better be good, it's our last one before school," she began.

Darlene was always big on firsts, lasts, and anniversaries. She could reel off every seemingly important first and last thus far in her young life. She especially was air-tight memory-wise concerning things that happened when we were together.

"Remember last summer, that last movie we saw?" she asked.

I didn't.

"What a turd," she kept it up. "The Abominable Dr. Phibes or some crap. Who picked that pile?"

"B, I think," I said, placing the blame squarely on my best friend.

"This better be much, much better," she continued on a roll. "The first one this summer was good though, Cooley High. I wish my school was more like that."

"Don't we all," I said.

"Well yours will be more than mine, I'm sure," she said. "You're heading to one of the best 4A schools in the state and I'm stuck at that stupid academy. Big deal, I get to cross campus to start high school. You get a whole new school."

She looked a little ticked and continued her tirade against her father's choices for her academic life.

"I mean, he's even trying to pick my college choices, all private schools," she kept railing as we turned left just past the putt-putt, leaving the outer for the inner boardwalk.

We passed my dad's favorite bars, Loretta's and the Silver Dollar. The Silver Dollar is still there. Stop in and have a few cold ones sometime.

"Yea but that's still almost three years away," I said. "Things can change a lot in that amount of time. Just look at us."

She stopped on a dime, right outside The Landmark's side entrance and turned to face me with fire in her eyes. What just moments before were the softest kindest portals of affection turned into a turbulent sea of wrath. I'm sure several customers and staff heard what came next. Thankfully, my relatives who worked there were all at my house for game-night.

"What did you say Leonard Raymond Melton?" she demanded in as loud a voice as I would ever hear her use and the only time she ever used my whole name. "You got the three years right! But that's the first time you've ever said us! Not once in three years, not once in the three years I've followed you around like a stupid puppy!"

To say I was dumbfounded gives me too much credit.

"Why?" she begged. "Why now, why not ever before?"

Wow had I opened a can, no check that, a supermarket full of cans of worms. I had no idea what to say or how to say it. I could feel tourists gawking at us. Then I did it. Without rhyme or reason and certainly no planning or hope of a certain result. I just did it.

"Because I love you," I fired my best, most sincere shot. "And I want this to be us."

I felt the wrath abate ever so slightly. Her instantly icy demeanor began to melt. I thought she was going to cry. Boy was I wrong…

"Us?" she asked. "Do you even know what you mean or intend to mean by that? You love me? You tell me now, out here in the street, after all these years. What is wrong with you?"

Well, I've never felt more lost my entire life. Several people were just staring. Mr. Smith, the owner, came out of The Landmark.

"Lenny, Darlene, you two ok?" Mr. Smith asked. "Why don't you come in and have a coke on me?"

She looked at Mr. Smith and then me. She seemed to simmer down a notch or two. She closed her eyes for a moment.

"Do you want to go in here?" she asked pointing past Mr. Smith.

"Sure, that's fine," is all I could manage.

She shook her head and walked in all the way to the back, past the jukebox and up the one step to the very back where no locals ever set. Thankfully that section (four booths, two on the left wall, two on the back wall, bathroom and storage on the right)) were empty. She plopped down in the second booth on the left facing the way we'd entered. She was in the back corner as far as she could be. I sat down across from her.

"I'm sorry, I upset you," I tried. "You know I'm not good at that kinda stuff."

"Lenny," she started. "You're the most silver-tongued devil walking this earth! I've seen you charm the crap out of anyone that suited you, so don't hand me that bullshit."

"It's different with you," I tried again. "Other people are just, people. You mean more to me than them."

"Oh, so now you tell me all this?" she quizzed. "Why now, huh, why not ever before? We've been talking to one another for over three years and it's obvious as shit to everybody else and always has been since day one that we like each other. It's obvious as shit to us too, so why now huh, why now? Is it because of the sex stuff?"

"No, no, no," I kept trying. "That's not it at all."

Well you know that was at least partly a lie. Every teenage boy with a girl that likes him, he's thinking about the sex stuff and it's always, at least partly, about the sex stuff.

"I just felt tonight was a good time to make something concrete," I said.

"Dumbass, we have something concrete," she tossed at me. "To be so smart, you can be such an idiot sometimes. Mostly about me."

I detected another trace of glacial thaw.

"I know we've had this great unspoken thing forever," she said. "And it was cool for a while, but a girl likes to hear stuff. I'm not stupid either. I know your reputation. I always thought that was one of the reasons you never said anything like that, because you liked a lot of girls and I was just one of them, maybe the top one though, maybe. You've shown it more the last year or so anyway. I could tell you were trying a little harder. Hell, even Lexi noticed. But just when I thought you were going to come through, make us official or some shit, you would slide back to your old ways."

I sat there in silence, my hands folded on the table. Mr. Smith brought us two cokes. He started to speak, just pursed his lips and quickly left without saying a word.

"I'm 16 in two weeks and come Halloween you will be too," she continued. "You'll have your license and a car. So, what do you want this to be?"

She pointed at me and then placed her hand on her chest.

"I want it to be us," I said, reaching for the hand that covered her chest. "All the time."

I felt the wrath turn to softness as she thawed some more. I thought maybe she was going to cry again like the night of the party. Boy was I wrong, again. I was stupid to even think that. I knew

Darlene and she wasn't about to cry right then. I only ever saw her cry a few times, one you know about. Another you'll hear about. This wasn't the second, not even close. Like she said, I can be a real dumbass sometimes.

"Ok, look, here's the deal," she said matter-of-factly. "And don't you say a damn thing! I want this to be US too."

She said this while repeatedly touching all her fingers on her left hand with the same ones on her right, kinda like what quarterbacks do when they are motioning for their teammates to huddle up.

"You think about all this until your birthday," she continued. "If you still feel the same, I want a promise ring on your birthday. But I know you, you say this stuff now, but by next week some girl at school or pretty little tourist beach bunny will bat her eyes at you, hell they do it right in front of me all the time, and there's no telling what you will feel then, except horny! Like I said, don't say anything, but that's the deal. Now let's go see that stupid car chase movie."

Track 21-Freedom/Motherless Child-Richie Havens (3:40)

Hey folks, from this point forward, I'm not (and haven't been) trying to tell a perfectly historic account of Woodstock 1969. They're plenty of great books, documentaries, and videos that nail it. I'm just relaying my experiences to the best of my recollection from notes I made in the weeks after, as a birthday present to myself. I used them for a school paper on "What I did this summer". I thought my teacher, poor Ms. Ward, was going to faint. Thank goodness she didn't call my folks. So if you have a historical account that reflects a different viewpoint or remembrance of a particular thing, that's cool, but also remember, as Henry Ford once said, "History is pretty much bunk!"

It took Davey and me a minute to compose ourselves after seeing Mandy and Dani in their birthday suits. We wandered around the pond area for a bit, just kinda zoned out really, Invasion of the Body Snatchers, Stepford Wives-like. Kinda the same as when you get the Christmas present you really, really wanted but didn't think you were going to get, like Ralphie's Red Ryder B-B gun.

It was that amazing, and as I noted, makes it the Seventh Wonder of Boyhood, your first, in the real, live flesh, sighting of a naked girl, a girl you want to see naked. All boys (except happy fellas) dream of that moment and when it happens, pure joy! The female form is, well I take it you've seen one, so you know. It's truly a work of art, beyond description, unable to be captured by artists, or director. The real, in the flesh woman or girl is breathtakingly, achingly, the most beautiful thing on earth, and likely in the universe. Women are the best evidence that there is a God because that stuff didn't just evolve. So, whatever deity you believe in (if you do), if that deity made something better, they kept it for themselves.

We eventually made it back to the campsite as darkness was beginning to fall. Hitch was roasting some hot dogs over a little fire pit he created. He had a spit and everything, with chili in a pot cooking over the open flame.

"You boys go grab some more wood before it gets pitch black," Hitch instructed.

Davey and I meandered over to the closest woods, just east, a couple hundred yards away. We passed other folks just setting up their tents, some smoking pot, a smell that would become more prevalent as the festival got underway. Music was playing everywhere from portable radios and acoustic guitar players. The coming night was going to be full of music, chatter, and people wandering into the fields and woods around us. The crowd had grown appreciably in the last few hours. We looked down toward the stage as the last few rays of Thursday disappeared to quite a sight. It was getting packed! We were just getting to know Woodstock, the world was about to as well.

We didn't go to sleep right away of course. Hitch and Leslie slept in the big tent, while we camped on a pallet we made under the Westphalia's awning. The girls came in later and crashed in their quite small pup-tent Hitch had set up for them a few feet from where Davey and I bunked in.

"I can't sleep," Davey said.

"We gotta though, tomorrow is going to be so much fun, I want to get some rest," I answered.

"What's that?" Davey wondered about some clanging nearby. "Is it Dani and Mandy?"

"Roll over and go find out if you wanna know," I said.

That was the last I remember of Thursday.

"Breakfast time kiddos," Hitch's voice boomed. "Come and get it! Eggs, bacon, and sausage. A sandwich any way you want it."

The smell was incredible. The delicious aroma of an outdoor breakfast cooking on a fire spit. The sizzling bacon smell alone was worth a sprint to the fire pit. I opened my eyes to a gorgeous morning with a lot going on already. I had to punch Davey a couple times to get him up. The girls stumbled from their tent, sleepy-eyed, but so lovely, as young women often are when they first awake. They still had on their clothes from the day before. I hustled over to the fire pit, shirtless.

"Well look at little Lenny," Mandy said. "Quite the strapping lad for a boy of 12."

Glad she made me a year older, but I was a bit embarrassed and turned red in the face, a life-long malady I'm afraid.

"He's big for his age," Dani said smiling.

"Big idiot," Davey said, punching me in the shoulder.

"Ok everybody, dig in," Hitch said. "Make a sandwich, if you want. Paper plates over there."

Leslie, as usual, had thought of almost everything. She was standing near a small card table just in front of the front passenger door. The table's inventory contained all the things we would need to help with meals; paper plates, utensils, napkins, condiments, and other assorted crap, I'm sure not many others thought to bring. Leslie pretty much slayed everything about the trip, save one thing, but that comes up Sunday.

"Go easy on the paper towels," Leslie said. "Davey don't use more than one."

Davey had already made a mess, spilling mustard on the table while failing at making an egg and sausage sandwich. We sat around on logs, the ground, and a couple blankets eating and talking away about the trip thus far. Other festival goers were heading to the woods to heed the call of nature or engage in other activities.

"Oh man that old drunk back in Richmond, he was a riot," Hitch said. "I bet he thought Leslie was the devil."

"Screw you Hitch," Leslie laughed.

We recounted that part of the story for the benefit of the Clevelanders.

"That's too funny," Dani said. "Wouldn't it be bizarre if you saw him again on the way home?"

"Oh, I sure hope so," I laughed. "And those gas station dudes. They looked like they were expecting a riot!"

"Ok, enough reminiscing," Hitch said. "Time to get ready to rock!"

"Davey, Lenny, you got KP (kitchen patrol) duty," Hitch said directing us east toward a nearby creek.

"Man, do we have to?" Davey asked.

"You wanna keep eating, don't ya?" Leslie said.

"Girls if you will get all the garbage together, we will use it for fireplace fodder," Hitch requested. "I got a bucket in the van for cans."

"On it," Dani said.

Davey and I collected the frying pan and pot Hitch used in preparing us our powerful start to what would be an epic day. We'd need every ounce of energy our bodies could glean from Hitch's fuel to endure and boy would we have to endure.

"This sucks," Davey said, as we made our way east again a few hundred yards to a small, shallow quick-moving stream.

"I'll wash the pan, you fill those two empty water jugs and that pot with water," I commanded.

"Alright," Davey said. "But you gotta help me carry them back."

The stream was just out of sight of the VW in a small set of woods, with pasture land on each side. There was right much cow poop in the area leading down to the stream.

"Uh, let's go up a few yards, up that hill," I said.

"Why?" Davey asked. "We can get water right here."

"Dumbass, cows pooped all over right behind us," I started. "The rain and stuff brought some of that crap right here. The water up there will be cleaner."

Davey grudgingly trudged uphill another 20 yards to a cleaner spot. I made quick work of the pan using a creek-bed stone. Davey filled the jugs and pot and we began our trek back.

"Mind if we get a drink out of one of those jugs?" said a tall, dark-haired guy with a beard. He was clad only in some brown boxers.

"Sure," I said, handing over one of our jugs.

He drank heartily and passed it to a little girl who looked to be about six, who was clad only in her little light green panties.

"Thank you, thank you," he said. "We didn't bring any containers."

The little girl smiled.

"You're welcome," I responded. "I saw a couple of cans down by the stream, you might use. I'll show you. Davey go on, I'll re-fill this one."

I showed the guy where the cans were and quickly refilled the jug. I hurried back to the campsite. Everyone was standing around looking at me when I returned.

"Lenny, that was cool to share your water with those people," Leslie said. "But everyone, we have to be careful of our food, we're going to be stretched pretty thin by Sunday night, we might run out before then. We have a long way to go. There're going to be a ton of people here, so just be careful."

We all nodded. I noticed the girls had changed. Mandy was wearing a substantially wrinkled white sundress and Dani had on red shorts and a matching tank top. Neither had on a bra. Howhowhow!

"You boys brush your teeth and wash your face over there," Leslie said pointing to a lone oak tree about ten yards directly in front of the VW's grill which faced west. "Hit your pits and put on some clean clothes."

When we returned, the four of them were smoking a joint.

"Hey," they aren't that much older than us!" Davey protested.

No one responded. I just stood there and watched my first real, up-close encounter with marijuana. Davey and I'd seen folks smoking in the distance the day before and that morning, but this was the deal, the real deal just a few feet away.

"I think that stuff stinks," Davey said. "And it stinks you won't give us any!"

He stormed off.

"So we're all going to the front together?" Mandy asked.

Boy that sure sounded great.

"I doubt it," Leslie said. "Look down there already."

Tens of thousands of people filled the pit near the still under construction stage area.

"Oh wow," said Dani. "That's really changed just since breakfast."

The only thing I had to compare it to at that point in my young life was The Exodus, depicted on film in Cecil B. DeMille's landmark three-hours and 40-mintues 1956 biblical epic, "The Ten Commandments". They showed it every Easter weekend on TV. I made the comparison out loud.

"Hope Moses' arms don't get tired," Hitch deadpanned.

In those days there was no instant way to know who was playing and when, just stuff we'd heard on the radio. We also had very little idea of when the first act would come on or who it might be. We heard lots of rumors from tons of different people. By mid-morning, the VW had become a gathering place for a dozen or so fellow festival-goers from all over. Hitch had hoisted a peace flag, along with our state flag atop the rear of the van on a fishing pole strapped to the back by duct tape. Curious hippies and others of all stripes popped by to talk music, where they were from, our state, and lots more. It was quite the interesting bunch.

"So tell us about your ride man," a stoned-out guy, who claimed to be from New Mexico, said to Hitch. "It's super cool."

Hitch gave the guy a bit of the VW's history. Some girls talked to Leslie about buying some food from her. Leslie was reluctant to sell.

"Nah, not going to sell any," Leslie said.

"Money-changers in the temple and all that," Hitch laughed.

"Shut-up," Leslie said. "Kiss my ass."

Hitch promptly took two steps left, leaned over and kissed Leslie's very generous, denim-clad hindquarters.

"Idiot," she smiled, gently pushing his head away.

"Here, take these crackers and a couple cans of Vienna," Leslie said.

"Oh, how cool," a girl from Vermont said. "You need to come visit us in the Green Mountains after the festival. We live in a commune up there, it has a great vibe. We're trying hard to make it work."

Davey and I were all ears to the sound of a commune. I imagined more pond-bathers, lots of free love, and who knows what else. Just a total rejection of the "establishment".

"It's a lot of work and we could sure use all of you," she continued.

Whoa, a lot of work, not what I had in mind. I was more about the nudity and free love. Leslie just nodded.

"We could go check it out," Hitch said hopefully to Leslie.

"What would we do with these two," she motioned at us.

"They can come," Hitch said. "How far away is it?"

"Not that far, not as far as you guys drove," hippie girl from Vermont number two said.

"They have school next week," Leslie said.

"It's in two weeks," I corrected her.

She shot me the evil eye.

"We have our own school," Vermonter number one said.

"Heck yea," Davey said.

"No way," Leslie said. "I promised Lenny's mom I'd have him back before school started."

Another boyhood dream destroyed and at such a young age. Oh, the inhumanity. My devastation didn't last long though, as Dani and Mandy returned with tales of lots of herb-sharing and boys. They were obviously really stoned, giggling, and talking really fast.

"These guys, about half-way to the stage said they would save us a spot!" Mandy gushed. "They're from Rhode Island, really cool, and gave us this."

She'd been holding her right arm behind her back and quickly brought it out front for all to see.

"Holy crap!" Hitch exclaimed. "That's the biggest joint I've ever seen."

It was a monster. I wouldn't see anything close to its size until the 1993 Pot Festival in Atlanta.

"Fire it up," said another male visitor, wearing only some kind of homemade robe, alongside his very-pregnant, string-haired blond girlfriend clad in a short white dress with lots of tiny red polka-dots.

Mandy didn't have to be told twice. She put a spark to the six-inch submarine-sized doobie. The strong smell and cloud of smoke instantaneously generated smoke signal features that had the same message of communication.

"Here gather a tribe of potheads, bring Dorito's and doughnuts!" our smoke-fest seemed to say with its wafting odor and billowy clouds.

People on their way around our campsite suddenly decided to stop by to see what the gathering commotion was and see if they'd interpreted the signals correctly. Of course they had! Our small band soon became one of the largest congregations outside of the masses in front of the stage. So many people gathered around the VW, it could've served as a poster for the counterculture or a United Nations meeting. It also worked to mine and Davey's advantage as tons of girls were in the throng. In just a few minutes, we met people from eight or nine states, two Canadians and a small band of gypsies from Eastern Europe.

This little revelry lasted a good hour or so, long after the Zeppelin-like gagger had been consumed. Many joints were blazed. Everyone was stoned, except Davey and I. Davey had tried to snag the big joint when it passed near us, but Leslie made a last-second interception and smiled as she took a long drag staring at Davey as she did so.

"Don't worry Lenny," Dani said turning her back to Leslie and whispering. "I'll get you high later."

Well, you can imagine all the things that went through my head right then.

"Man, I am ready to hear some bands!" Hitch proclaimed loudly.

"Here dumbass," Leslie said to Hitch and pulled him close to her.

Leslie placed the lit end of another, nowhere-near-as-large, but still jumbo sized joint into her mouth and pulled Hitch's face near hers, blowing him a fast-paced blast of smoke out the other end, my first time seeing a "shotgun". The new jumbo joint had receded to about the size of a normal doobie by that time and a chorus line of "shotguns" ensued. Dani gave Mandy one and their lips were so close, it appeared they were kissing!

Yep, you guessed it, that my friends is the THIRD WONDER OF BOYHOOD-The first time you see girls kiss, or in this case a very close approximation. Whoops! No, it's not, that belongs on another list for another time. The real THIRD WONDER comes later.

That gathering was one of the coolest impromptu parties I've ever been fortunate enough to attend. If I could take you back in time in more than story form, those few hours just before Richie Havens took the stage on Friday, August 15, 1969 would be one of our first stops. As all cool parties do, this one just drifted into something else, as many new friendships were created, some that would last only a few hours, others that would endure for quite some time.

"Ok boys," Leslie said. "We're heading down the hill, fix yourself a sandwich before we go. Hitch will have the canteen, so don't stray far away."

Davey and I quickly wolfed down a peanut butter sandwich and a couple of cokes.

"Bring a pack of those orange crackers each," she said. "No more!"

In another moment of crowd shock, when I turned from the van and started downhill, it appeared the crowd had doubled in size since the early morning, filling about half the bowl.

"Stay close boys!" Hitch said as we made our way down the hill on the left side facing the stage, Hitch knew the lefty secret too. "If we get separated meet back at the van for supper at seven."

Davey wore a watch so we'd that covered. I've never worn one, not one day. I saw Peter Fonda toss his in the opening sequences of Easy Rider and that was good enough for me. Freedom. Say it again. Freedom!

The first afternoon of music was fun and I really liked Richie Havens' passion. He opened the show and while most of the other acts would play relatively short sets of 90 minutes, an hour, or less that first day/night, Havens played for over two hours. I hope you've seen the Academy-award winning Woodstock documentary, it really does do a good job of capturing Havens and what the festival felt like those first few hours of music.

Havens' played a few Beatles' songs," Strawberry Fields", "I Get By With a Little Help From My Friends", and some others. It appeared he was ready to stop several times, but he kept coming back and playing more. We found out many years later it was because some of the acts were stuck in traffic and the promoters had him keep playing. He closed with an old gospel-like number, "Motherless Child" that he improvised into what became known as his now-classic "Freedom". At the time, we just thought it was one of his songs. It was powerful and moving in a way I hadn't experienced from music before. Richie Havens will always hold a special place in my heart because he was the first major act I ever saw play live. I had the good fortune of seeing him again many years later (1995) at a local venue. "Freedom" and Havens was just as powerful in 95 as all those years ago.

While I liked the rest of the music that first afternoon okay, it was the people that were the story for me on the first official day of the festival. I met people of other nationalities for the first time. I interacted with people of different faiths for the first time. It was a true melting pot, the only thing missing was an inflatable Lady Liberty. Those were the days before all the "extras" you see at festivals and concerts nowadays. It was pretty much music, people, a few flags, and a handful of homemade signs.

We snagged a spot on the very far left (facing the stage) about 150 yards back. Our motley crew of the basic "Woodstock Six" as we would come to call ourselves, coined by Mandy later that night, were joined by the Vermonters. I swear, I've tried to remember their names, if you girls read this, contact my publisher and we will update in future editions. There were also two dudes from NYC, same for you guys as well. They were basically following the Vermont girls. Also tagging along was the guy in the robe and his pregnant girlfriend. Those two stayed with us through most of Havens set and said their goodbyes just before "Motherless Child". And yes, same as you, I've often wondered if she was the girl who gave birth at Woodstock. Her due date was sometime in early September, so maybe it was her, or maybe not. I can't recall their names either if I ever heard them. I wish I had.

For you six, maybe seven, if the baby was born at the festival, no joke, call the publisher. There will be a short quiz to make sure it's really you. Hope you remember some details about our crowd.

Another cool thing day one was the official opening of the festival by a pink-robe wearing true-life Indian guru, Sri Swami Satchidananda. Please don't check my spelling on that one. He came on after Havens and said some cool things about music being the greatest force in the world. He was accompanied by several really pretty hippie chicks and a few guys in white robes.

The band Sweetwater played and then we headed back to the van for supper. We could hear Tim Hardin and Bert Somer play while we were at the back chowing down on hot dogs. We'd lost the NYC guys sometime earlier and now the female half of "The Woodstock Six" and the Vermont girls said they were going to hang at the van for a bit. Campfires were glowing when Hitch, Davey, and I headed back down into the bowl just as George Harrison's buddy Ravi Shankar introduced us to the sitar played live. The first of the legendary rains came along somewhere in this span of time.

Accounts vary, but I remember it happening just as we began to make our way down.

Like much of the confusion surrounding the stage, the next events are told many different ways, but we'd been told a folk band was supposed to play next, but instead, Melanie (Safka) came on and one of my first "adult crushes" blossomed. She had dark hair and seemed very nervous and shy. She also seemed genuinely moved by all the people, which now filled about 75% of the bowl. I remember "Birthday of the Sun" in particular from her very short set.

The mood of the crowd was very relaxed and festive despite the rain. I saw many joints being passed, a lot of laughter, singing, and hand-clapping. We stood the rest of the evening as the ground was getting a bit mushy around us. Hitch moved us to higher ground just as Arlo Guthrie began singing "Coming into Los Angles, carrying a couple of keys (kilos)". It was well after midnight when Arlo finished up and Hitch made the command decision to start back.

We ran into Leslie, the Clevelanders, and the Green Mountain Girls halfway back up. I remembered Leslie said she wanted to see Joan Baez the most. I was trailing the pack a bit and didn't hear the Hitch/Leslie conversation. We all passed by one another single file. Dani was last in the all-girl conga line and grabbed my hair as she smiled going past.

"Good morning," Baez said.

It was around one in the morning Saturday, August 16.

Track 22-13 Questions-Seatrain (2:45)

I paid our way into the theatre. It was four dollars. This was the first time Darlene ever let me pay everything for both of us. There'd been times when she would let me pay more than half, but never all. Was this my first test? Was she just preoccupied with our conversation and situation? I never asked. I paid ol' Marie the entry fee.

As soon as we entered, we noticed right away things were already different. The carpet looked like it hadn't been vacuumed in quite a while. The three-shelf, glass candy-case always filled to the brim with tasty treats, was now less than half full. The bottom shelf was completely empty. I noticed a large, clear plastic bag half-filled with popcorn on the floor by the popcorn popper. Melissa had always made popcorn fresh each day. This was my first experience with "pre-made", aka "saved" popcorn. The place even smelled different. The vibe was different. Not quite sure what, but it was definitely different.

"Popcorn and two cokes," I said to Gerald's red-headed buddy behind the counter.

"Buck-fifty," he replied.

First time I was ever required to pay first before I got my stuff.

"You want to go upstairs?" Darlene asked.

I nodded affirmative and she walked up ahead of me. It was always a joy to follow her up any flight of steps. We sat in the front row of the balcony. We were the only ones upstairs and the theatre was about a quarter full downstairs.

We nibbled on the not even warm popcorn and sat quietly through the previews. The movie began (caution: spoiler alert if you haven't seen the movie) with a sequence showing a freight train rumbling by and the movie would popularize the term "dingle berry" for a bit. The train would come back to deliver a crushing blow in the film's final fiery sequence. It was the first time I saw such a "coda" type beginning and ending. From then on, I always paid close attention to what happens in the opening scene of a film, even if it appears to be just a pan-in or otherwise innocent-looking scenery.

About halfway through the movie, Darlene reached over and took my hand and held it throughout the rest of the film. She said nothing, but her touch let me know that she wasn't so powerfully upset any longer. I was somewhat relieved we didn't have to talk.

Darlene liked the movie ok. She asked about the actors and I told her what I knew of Fonda and George. We exited the theatre onto a somewhat deserted boardwalk.

"Should we start walking toward your house?" I asked.

"Probably," she said. "Do you have the key to the shop?"

I was dumbfounded, but the crazy thoughts that shot through my brain, quickly evaporated when I heard her next words.

"I gotta go to the bathroom and I wasn't going in there," she said.

We made the quick right down the alley by the shop and entered through the back.

"First time I've been back here," she said. "Wow, that's a lot of flour and sugar."

I nodded.

"Back in a sec," she said, walking briskly to the front area and into the ladies' room.

I waited by the counter. Oh man, the thoughts I had those few minutes while she answered nature's call. How unreal she would ask to go to the shop late-night within hours of when B suggested we consummate our relationship in the very same spot. Fate? Coincidence? Crap? Should I make an attempt to kiss her and see where it goes? Should I offer her a drink and just talk? Just leave?

She re-appeared smiling.

"Can we get a drink?" she asked. "I'm a little thirsty."

I grabbed a plastic cup and poured her a coke, little ice, like always. She was smiling really big as she took it from me with both hands and took a big gulp. She got a little naughty look on her face.

"And kind sir, why has thoust not thought to bring me hence a forehand?" she curtseyed.

She was a bit of a Shakespeare nerd.

"I thought about it," I smiled.

She gave me a scornful, "speak the language fool" look.

"But thoust being a lady, I thought ill of my mind," I replied in weak mid-evil times vernacular.

I did think to do a sweeping arm across the waist bow though.

She sat her coke down on the counter and immediately kissed me really hard with both her hands behind my neck. She just as quickly pulled back. If I knew Shakespeare talk made her this hot, I would've been spouting soliloquies out my ass for years!

"You truly are a dumbass," she laughed and began walking toward the back door.

Once we made it to the back door, she looked to her left at the big 50-pound bags of flour and sugar. She slowly turned around. The turn was plenty slow enough for me to have lots of fun thoughts. She pointed at the stacked ingredients.

"Let me guess," she began. "You were thinking back here?"

She nodded her head at the bags. I grinned sheepishly. I was embarrassed again.

"We could've brought a blanket and went out front," she smirked and went out the door.

A day late and a dollar short. My lot in life, I guess. Dumbass Hall of Fame, here I come and at such a young age. What an achievement!

"Did you see the moon last night, hung like a Chinese ball," the jukebox wailed from The Landmark as we made our way by.

"What's the name of that song? And who's that singing?" She asked. "I really like that song."

"Uh, the name of the band is Blues Project, I think," I started. "Uh no, that's not it, that one dude was in Blues Project, don't know what they're called now. "13 Questions" is the name of the song."

"I really, really like that song," Darlene stressed.

It was (is) a great song. We walked hand-in-hand down past the south end amusements and rides. We turned right to head to her house. She stopped us.

"Who's at your house?" She asked.

"Not sure, it was pretty crowded earlier," I replied. "Do you want to stop by? Think we have time?"

"Dad's at some retired army-guy thing at the VFW with your dad," she said. "I can call Mom from your place and ask to stay a little later."

She seemed to know where my dad was more than me lately. We came up the street-side steps and entered what at first appeared to be an empty house, but only for a second. We could hear everyone out on the beachside deck. The living room was deserted and the Monopoly game was still out on the dining table. The radio was playing some smooth Percy Sledge.

"Let me wrap you in my warm and tender love....tender love."

"Hi everyone," Darlene said, walking out on the back deck.

"Well hey sweetie, so good to see you," my mom said, giving her a big hug.

My great-aunts were dancing with one another and my grandmother was smoking her ever-present Camel non-filtered. My aunt was dancing by herself. The simple, pure joy of being together and dancing. They always danced a lot.

"Girls asleep?" I asked.

"Yep," my aunt replied. "In your sister's room."

My aunt's seven-year-old daughter, Danielle, my only first cousin on my mom's side, often came with her to game night.

"Will you check in on them?" my mom asked. "Give us ladies a chance to talk to Darlene."

"Sure," I said. "No problem."

I smiled at Darlene. She smiled back. Signature move exchanged.

The girls were of course totally zonked out, splayed across my sis's big four-poster bed with a canopy that took up most of her room which was just off the dining table area to the left. I meanwhile, as you know, basically had a cot on a closed-in portion of the ocean side deck. I, of course, loved it.

I was hoping to sneak a beer, I knew my great-aunts never kept count. I grabbed a plastic cup from the counter and quickly popped a top inside the fridge and poured. I hit the bathroom and gulped it down pretty quick (delicious!) and made my way back outside. Mom had the tiki lamps blazing on the front corners of the deck and the ladies were all talking away.

"So 10th grade, huh?" My great-aunt Nina asked.

I nodded.

"Are you two going to be in the same school this year?" she asked.

"No, I'll be at tripH and Darlene will still be at the academy," I answered.

Darlene gave me the ol'headset to ear pantomime to let me know she needed to call her mom. I walked over and said as much to my mom. My great-aunt Pat spilled beer on herself as she was getting twirled by her sister.

"Oh honey, you go ahead," Mom said. "I'll speak to her if you want. It's the last weekend before school starts anyway."

Darlene got a big smile on her face, took my mom by the hand, and they went to the phone. The same exact phone my mom had

246

dropped years earlier when I thought she had fainted speaking to me on my first Woodstock adventure. My aunt was telling me some stuff about her new job with the newspaper when some fireworks exploded out over the ocean. It was a brilliant light display with multiple bursts featuring a lot of red, white and blue. I guessed they were leftovers from the Fourth of July celebration.

"She gets to stay," Mom said as the pair returned. "She has another hour!"

Good ol' Mom, she had come through for me again.

After a few minutes of small talk, I took Darlene's hand and led her away from my gaggle of relatives. We headed down the back deck steps, past the shower, and out on the beach. The maternal masses gave a very boisterous good-bye to her from the top of the deck, kinda like the Beverly Hillbillies, waving and saying "Y'all' come back now, ya hear?"

We left our flip-flops by the shower and walked barefoot in the sand. Walking barefoot in the cool sand at night in summertime is one of those "got-to-experience it" things of life. For you landlocked folks, if you haven't, put it on your list. For those close to the beach, what are you waiting for?

We walked just a hundred yards or so southward down the deserted beach. The ocean was at low tide, with very little wave action, if any. Very serene and peaceful under a starless night. We were at the water's edge and she turned to face the ocean. She looked at me.

"You want to go in?" she asked.

Taken aback, I just nodded yes. She was always the first to seek adventure. I was pretty quick myself, but nothing like Darlene. I always imagined one day she would climb Mt. Everest or dive for shipwreck gold.

Darlene quickly removed her top and skirt, revealing a matching set of light blue undergarments. I took off my shirt, we held hands, and splashed in. We played in the water, sat in the water, and generally goofed off for about 10 minutes. I picked her up and tossed her in from above my head a couple of times and she splashed the hell out of me in response. We were laughing really hard.

She came close, smiling. She got real close. We were holding both hands underwater at our sides, our bodies touching.

"I love you too," she said. "I always have, from day one."

Track 23-Soul Sacrifice-Santana (6:22)

"Griddlecakes, come and get your griddlecakes!" Hitch's voice boomed.

Not sure if it was the delicious smell or his voice that roused me from my second Woodstock slumber. I'd dreamed of an empty stage and standing alone in a field, but the stage wasn't the stage here and the field wasn't the field at Max's farm. As we all often do, I was a bit disoriented when I awoke after such a powerful dream. Thirty years later the dream became reality when I stood alone in a field in front of a large stage in Rome, NY on Thursday before Woodstock 1999 began. I have a cool photo of that moment. It will be in Crazy Beach III (Craziest Beach).

I punched Davey to wake him up, he just rolled over. By the time I got to the breakfast pit, the other four of the "Woodstock Six" were chowing down by the card table and engaged in conversation about Joan Baez's set.

"Well, there's the 10 o'clock scholar," Hitch said. "Is Davey dead?"

I just nodded yes and helped myself to two griddle cakes that were just a perfect crispy brown. I'm normally a glacially slow eater. Later in life, my friends would always tell me to go start eating 30 minutes before they'd arrive so we could all finish near the same time. But this morning, there was no need, I got rid of those two hot stacks really quick.

"Lenny, I need you to go gather some wood, we're running really low," Hitch said. "Make a couple of trips if you don't mind. I'll make Davey handle KP."

"Brush your teeth first," my Woodstock mom yelled.

"I'll give you a hand," Dani chimed in (with the wood, not the teeth brushing).

"Davey, Davey, get your sorry ass up!" Leslie bellowed.

I quickly brushed my teeth by the old oak as I watched Dani and Mandy have a laughter-filled exchange. I was just close enough to pick up some bits and pieces of talk about some guys they'd met the night before. Mandy pointed to a spot on her neck and the laughter grew louder. Leslie was cleaning up the card table area and Hitch was dragging Davey out of his slumber.

"Ready?" I asked Dani.

She smiled and joined me. We walked toward the wooded area where Davey and I'd handled our KP chores the morning before. She always had a slight bounce in her walk and seemed full of mischief.

"Who all you think's going to play today?" she asked.

"Not sure," I started. "But I heard from some fellas last night that The Who is supposed to play tonight."

"That's your favorite, right?" she said as we paused under a large poplar tree.

"Of the ones I know about that are supposed to play here, yea," I said. "I like them right up there with The Beatles, Zeppelin, and the Stones."

"I'm really happy for you," she continued. "I can't wait to see Janis. But I heard she and her band broke up, so I don't know what's going on there or who she might play with, the Dead maybe?"

We spotted a decent size limb that was once part of the poplar and grabbed it. We also snagged some smaller limbs and a small log that seemed out of place, perhaps a leftover from some long ago camping experience or land clearing. We gathered as much as we could handle and made our way back, talking some other acts we'd heard might play.

"Mandy wants to see Hendrix sooo bad!" Dani exclaimed. "She plays his albums all the time."

"I'm pretty psyched about that too," I offered.

Dani told me some about their trip in with Mandy's brother and Mandy's home life.

"She's just totally boy crazy," Dani explained. "Has been for a couple of years now. Her dad is really strict on her though, but he's usually away working. He's working in Alaska this summer, that's the only reason she got to come, and because my dad is close by too."

"When are you supposed to meet your dad?" I asked.

"Mr. Max's farm is one of the first stops on his route Monday," she said. "So I'm just supposed to meet him at Mr. Max's mailbox. I saw it coming in."

"That's so cool," I said as we lugged the much-needed fuel back into the campsite.

"You guys see Davey?" Leslie asked.

"Nope," I responded.

"Hell, he's probably lost," Hitch chuckled.

"That's not funny Hitch, well, if he's not back in about 10 more minutes, we gotta go hunt him," Leslie said dejectedly.

Mandy emerged from her tent wearing some denim cut-offs and a dark blue top.

"Hey, I was going to wear that today," Dani laughed. "That's my favorite."

"Sorry," Mandy said. "I can change it real quick."

"No, you done got your funk on it," Dani laughed some more as we all joined in.

"Clean up girl," Mandy said to Dani. "We got some fellas to go see."

Dani looked at me and smiled.

"Told ya," she said and walked to the water jug by the big oak we used for quick cleaning and teeth brushing. "Give me a minute."

Hitch was checking the VW's engine. He then adjusted the fishing rod flag pole. It had titled significantly during the night.

"Lenny grab me some more duct tape," he called. "And bring me a coke."

I found the needed items and was exiting the van as a cleaned-up Dani and Mandy walked by. Dani had on a little black skirt, black cowgirl boots, and a light orange sleeveless shirt that said "Texas". She pointed to her chest.

"Get'n ready for Janis," she smiled.

I just nodded and stared as they walked down into the bowl.

"Sometime this century, you little perv!" Hitch exclaimed. "You might need to empty your drool bucket."

I snapped back to reality. I handed Hitch his coke and the duct tape. He handed it right back.

"Put some fresh duct tape on that pole," Hitch directed. "I got to start her up."

Now the poor excuse for what we had left of a small, nasty-ass roll could still be barely called duct tape, but the last remnants did the job. I couldn't find the new roll Leslie had bought Thursday. I think Mandy was using it exclusively in her role as Davey's nurse. Hitch fired the VW's engine and let it run a bit.

"I don't like to let ol'Henreitta rest too long without putting her through her paces," Hitch said.

"Henrietta?" I queried.

"Some German broad at the VW dealership Dad took a liking too," Hitch said. "I don't say the name round Mom."

Hitch said the last part with a knowing smile and I left it alone. But the VW had a name and from that point forward I always referred to it as such, except in front of Hitch's mom. Davey came dragging back in.

"Where's my frying pan?" Hitch asked sternly.

Davey had one pot and two jugs of water.

"I dunno," Davey shrugged his shoulders.

"Damn Davey," Hitch said. "Lenny go back with him and see if you can find that pan. You might as well pick up some more firewood as you go too."

"I'm tired," Davey said.

"Get your ass back down to that creek and find that damn pan," Leslie demanded.

I had a pretty good idea where Davey cleaned the stuff and gathered water. Yep, you guessed it, the easy elevation spot with all the cow poop from the day before. I walked straight to the pan.

"Damn Davey, that's lazy as crap," I said. "Get some wood."

By the time we got back to the campsite Hitch and Leslie were preparing to head down into the bowl carrying a couple of towels.

"Good job Lenny," Hitch said, as I dropped the pan into its rightful place at the campsite. "We're hitting the pond, you guys stay close, we'll be back to get you before the music starts."

Davey went and plopped down on his pallet under the awning. I leaned in on Henrietta's open side door. I surveyed the landscape. The bowl looked to be about 80% full. People and campsites were now creeping closer and closer up the hill. Some were less than 20 yards away now. The sea of people below was truly one of the most amazing sights I've ever seen in my life. The most amazing to that point and for many years to come. Besides the naked girls, of course, that's in a different league altogether.

"Hey man, how's it going?" it was bathrobe guy, sans pregnant girlfriend. He had another goofy guy in tow.

"Cool man, you?" I responded.

"Groovy man, real groovy," He was nodding a lot as was his new companion, a rotund young guy sporting the first mullet I ever saw. He had on an orange "The Monkees" t-shirt way too small for his frame and a pair of ill-fitting muddy jeans. He was barefoot and smoking a doobie. Bathrobe guy's robe was starting to look even more shopworn and was a bit too open.

"Man, we're kinda hungry, got any grub you can spare?" he asked.

The rotund one offered me the doobie.

"No thanks," I said. "Trying to cut back."

Bathrobe guy laughed. Rotund nodded and kept smoking.

"Let me see what we can do," I said.

There was some stuff on the card table, but I knew that was probably Leslie's lunch prep. I motioned for them to follow me on over to Henrietta's open side door. The VW, when set up for camping, resembled a middle-eastern bazaar.

"Here ya go," I said, handing them a couple packs of saltine crackers and a can of spam.

No one had touched the half dozen or so cans of spam in our pantry inventory. I wouldn't eat that crap. Well, I guess if I was hungry enough. We ended up giving them all away.

"Oh wow man, that's cool," Robe guy said continuing to nod. "Oh and my ol'lady said to tell you, you were a really cute little guy. She's going to appreciate this."

The rotund guy was nodding. I smiled and handed him another can of spam.

"Tell your family we said hi," Robe dude continued.

"Will do," I said.

Family, that was too cool. I hadn't thought of it that way till right then, but they were my Woodstock family. Anytime I'd go to a festival for years, it felt that way, a sense of community, a sense of family, like-minded souls sharing some of life's great experiences together.

Davey was sleeping away and I was restless. I knew Hitch told me to stay close, but I thought about exploring the west side woods, a few hundred yards past the "clean-up" oak. I grabbed a coke and headed off on my first solo, non-cleaning or gathering Woodstock excursion.

I passed a couple of campsites where people were milling about, one topless girl waved, I waved back. I passed a couple making out under a young birch tree. They seemed to be having fun. The dude gave me the peace sign. I gave it back. My first one.

"What's rock'n little dude?" a stoned-out shirtless black guy with a big floppy hat and matching yellow bell bottoms asked. "Where your people, you lost?"

"Nah, I'm good, thanks," I answered. "They're just over there."

He gave me a little two-finger wave. I did the same as I passed by his mixed-race group of about eight or so friends. Four of them were holding hands in a circle and dancing around to some tune I didn't recognize blasting from a portable eight-track player. Yes, those were real, they had to have like a gazillion "D" batteries. It was some kind of music with chants if I recall correctly. I pressed on.

Every 30 yards or so, I would take a glance back to check my bearings and make sure I'd some good markers for my return trip.

Floppy hat guy's crowd had several orange tents so I set those as a mental marker. I also passed a lonely old mimosa tree that was in full pink flower. It was stately and beautiful. I stopped for a moment to admire its trunk and flowers. I've always had a thing for solitary trees and the stories I bet they could tell. I remember it was the first time on the trip I thought of Leslie's camera. I wish I'd brought it along on this trek. I would love to have a pic of the floppy hat guy's crowd and the mimosa, and heck, even bathrobe guy, but would have to make sure about the angle.

I entered the woods, a much thicker and older grove of several different types of trees dominated by maples and fir trees, with a couple dozen oaks around as well. It was the freshest smell of the weekend. The pure summer smell of healthy trees, fresher than clean linen, crisper than the falling leaves of autumn. I inhaled as much as my young lungs would hold. I closed my eyes. Mom always said when trying to take in Mother Nature, close your eyes and feel through your other senses, especially smell. A practice I follow, like it's my religion, to this day.

I heard some animal sounds and quickly opened my eyes. I didn't spot anything right away but followed the sound. It was kinda soft, so I was expecting some small creature or creatures. I looked around. I was alone and about hundred yards or so from where I'd entered the tree line. I might as well have been a mile. The commotion and emotion of the festival drifted away. I was alone with the sights, sounds, and smells of the forest. I kept following the animal noises. I crested a small hill that overlooked another stream. Much more robust than the east side one, it appeared a bit deeper as well. I began descending the hill toward the stream when I heard more of an animal ruckus. The same sounds, only louder, now desperate.

The noises grew even louder. I passed a seven-foot section of a fallen oak's trunk. It appeared to have been tagged by lightning long ago. I finally saw the source of the bellowing sound. A litter of baby foxes nestled in a much larger, hollowed out end of the same oak's trunk. This portion of the tree had fallen downhill about 20 yards away and just a few feet from water's edge. The little kits were raising holy hell as their mother was fending off a predator. I couldn't tell right away if it was a wild dog, a small wolf, or something else. The two combatants were both showing their teeth, waiting for the other to blink or make a mistake. I froze.

Once I regained my composure, I could see there were four baby foxes. Their mother was already bleeding from a cut on top of her head. The other animal looked ready to pounce. I knew I should quietly back away, but I couldn't. The other animal menacingly moved forward two steps, the momma fox held her ground for a moment, then backed up a notch, now only a few feet in front of her babies.

I started to back away, but stepped on a piece of the fallen oak, a limb about four-feet long and a half-a-foot in diameter. I started falling but caught myself with my right hand before I hit the ground. I saw the predator, which I now thought could be a lynx or something like that, advance again, one step this time. The momma fox backpedaled, she didn't have much more ground to give.

In a moment I've replayed countless times over the years, as to why or exactly how, this is my recollection of the next few seconds. I have no good answer. I grasped at the oak limb I'd stumbled over. Why? To steady myself? With intent to protect myself? With some other intent? I don't know. I just did.

The next thing I know, I'm running headlong down the hill toward the creek at full speed, yelling a blood-curdling Rebel yell like I'm advancing with Pickett's men on day three of Gettysburg and waving the oak club at the predator. Of course, the momma fox may have thought I was yelling and waving a small tree at her. What the hell was I doing? I don't know, but the next thing I know, I'm face down in the creek!

I was in about two feet of water. It took me a second to move, I'm hurt I know, but I also know there are wild animals behind me. I pulled myself up on my knees and looked over my right shoulder. I slid around and stayed low. I could feel myself bleeding from my forehead, knees, and I thought at least one elbow. The fox lair was just a few yards away. The predator was gone. The momma fox was on top the hollow oak trunk looking at me. The babies quieted their squawking a bit.

I decided to backpedal very slowly into the creek. Well, I told you it looked deeper, it was. Mr. Grace tripped again over something in the creek bed and splash! I was in deeper, cold water. I started to swim and then realized I could touch the bottom, barely. But I could, so I inched my way southward away from the animals and gradually made my way back to shore. The momma fox and I kept our eyes transfixed on one another for a good few minutes as I slowly reached the shore about 20 yards away. I purposefully continued southward along the shoreline a good 30 yards, glancing back every now and then to check momma fox's status and also to keep an eye out for the predator or other threats. Momma fox gradually began to shift her eyes elsewhere and attend her young.

I struggled back up the hill, about halfway up I stopped to check my injuries. My right knee was skinned pretty good and had several tiny pebbles embedded in the skin around my kneecap. I picked the pebbles out and several slow streams of blood began to run down my leg. I packed some mud on my kneecap to try and stop the flow. There was bruising. My left knee had a few scraps and the skin was broken in a couple of places, but already clotted, so there was no longer any loss of blood. I touched my forehead and found it caked with a good chunk of creek-bed mud. I'd face planted pretty hard and was kinda woozy. I could feel some blood had run down my forehead and my nose. I left the mud intact, thinking it might stop any additional bleeding.

My clothes were muddy and I'd lost one tennis shoe. The other was caked in mud. My elbows were muddy, but I didn't see any blood. I crested the hill and after about 50 yards ran into a couple in the forest who were close to engaging in sex by a maple tree. They quickly halted their proceedings once they saw me about 10-15 yards away.

"Hey kid, you alright?" the guy, mostly naked, asked.

The girl gathered her dress about her frontal area with one hand while holding the other to her mouth, shocked by my appearance.

"Hey, kid, you ok?" he asked again.

I nodded yes.

"Help him Dwayne, help him," the girl said, still clutching her dress.

Dwayne buttoned his pants and ran over to me.

"Come on kid, come with us," he said grabbing me by the left bicep.

"Connie, run on ahead and get some water," Dwayne said.

Connie put her dress on and took off.

"Where you hurt the worse kid?" Dwayne asked. "What's your name?"

"Uh, Lenny," I said. "My forehead hurts the worst."

"Ok, ok, I'm Dwayne and that was Connie," he said. "We got you, you're going to be fine. We'll get you cleaned up and back to your people."

Dwayne and I emerged from the woods back to the sights and sounds of the festival. It felt like I'd progressed from one century to another. I could hear music playing below. I knew Hitch and Leslie would be worried because I wasn't around like I was supposed to be. We walked north, down along the wood line about 40 yards or so to a group of tents. Connie came running up with a cup of water and a rag.

"Take a drink," she said.

As I did, she took the rag and after dropping to her knees, wiped off mine. The rag was wet and initially felt good, then the pain began to heighten as the wounds were cleaned. Dwayne took the cup from me and splashed the rest of the water on my face. Mud ran down my cheeks. He took the rag from Connie and began cleaning my forehead. That was when the smell hit me. Connie was standing right beside me and Dwayne was right in my face. It wasn't a bad smell, just different. Strong and earthy, more her than him. I'd never smelled it before. I couldn't make it out.

Dwayne and Connie were a bit older (I guessed early 30s) than most of the other concert goers I'd seen. Dwayne was about six-foot tall, stocky build, and had a big bushy dark beard. Connie was about my height with brown shoulder-length hair and some of the kindest eyes (green) I've ever seen. She had a little yellow daisy painted on her right cheek.

"That's a pretty bad gash," Dwayne said, eyeing my forehead. "But that mud helped, we got to get a bandage on it or something."

Connie reached down and after some struggling managed to rip the hem from the bottom of her light blue sundress. She tore off a long strip and wrapped it around my head. My first of only two headbands I would ever wear.

"There, that'll do!" she said.

I had my first nurse fantasy.

"Yea, I think it will," said Dwayne. "How ya feeling kid?"

"Ok, ok," I said. "Thank you."

"Oh wow," Connie said. "You're a mess. Might as well get rid of that one shoe and that shirt."

She pulled my t-shirt off as Dwayne tugged at my mud heavy shoe. I leaned on his shoulder for support.

"You have more clothes?" Connie asked. "Are your friends close by?"

I nodded yes.

"They're that way," I said, pointing southwest at the top of the bowl.

"Ok, ok," Dwayne said. "We'll get ya back to them."

"He really should get cleaned up some more," Connie said. "We could take him to the pond."

"No, no, thank you," I said. "I really need to get back to my friends, they're probably worried about me."

"Oh, that's cool," Dwayne said. "You may want to lose that one sock though."

I looked down, I still had on one soaking wet sock. Connie giggled a bit. Dwayne smiled and put his hand on my shoulder.

"Wardrobe by Woodstock style!"

We all laughed. I was hurting a bit but felt better since I was cleaned up some. I was tired. Dwayne put his arm around my shoulder.

"Let's go find your folks," he said.

Connie grabbed ahold of the back of my hair.

"Now that's a lion's mane," she said. "You're a tough kid. What happened to you?"

So I told the tale as we made our way past folks heading north down toward the stage. We walked around the upper ridge slowly getting closer and closer to the campsite. It was a much longer walk back.

"Oh gosh, you were lucky nothing worse happened," Connie said.

The rest of the "Woodstock Six" were standing by the fire pit when they caught sight of me from about 20 yards away. They all began running in my direction. Dani got there first.

"Lenny, Lenny, you all right?" She asked grabbing my shoulders.

"Damn Lenny, what the hell happened?" Hitch, arriving second, asked.

I looked at Dani, I could see the concern in her eyes.

"I'm ok," I said. "This is Dwayne and Connie, they took care of me."

"Thanks," Hitch said.

"Geez Lenny," Leslie said. "Let's get you back to the van. Mandy put some water on to boil, Davey, grab that brown towel over the door."

The two of them ran back to the van. Dani wrapped her arm around me. Dwayne told my story to the others.

"We were so worried," Dani said. "I didn't know what in the world was going on with you."

"Hitch tear that towel up," Leslie ordered. "Dani check him for any other wounds. Thank you guys so much for watching after him. Mandy get them some food and cokes. Davey grab two more pieces of wood for the fire."

Leslie hustled over to the van. She began tearing through things, searching for something. I lost sight of her as Dani demanded my attention.

"Where else are you hurt?" Dani asked looking me directly in the eye and holding my shoulders again. "Did you hit your head?"

"Nowhere," I said. "I don't think."

Dani was running her right hand over me checking for injuries. I liked it. I liked it a little too much.

She was bent over looking at my knees and legs. She was touching my right knee. She glanced up.

"Damn Lenny," she said smiling.

"Sorry," I said shifting my stance.

She stood up.

"You're too much," she said smiling even bigger.

"Doesn't hurt as bad now," I laughed.

She pinched my cheek.

"I feel for the girls your age," she laughed.

Leslie returned with the paste she'd used on Davey and some medical stuff she'd bought at our last pit stop. She dipped one of the rags Hitch made from the towel into the steaming water over the fire pit and began cleaning my wounds. I could tell she was worried.

"Damn Lenny, you're messed up," Hitch laughed. "Where are your shoes and socks?"

I just shrugged my shoulders as Leslie poured some hydrogen peroxide on my knees. It stung a bit. She placed a couple of gauze pads on my right knee and taped them down. Two Band-Aids took care of the scrapes on my left knee. She cleaned my elbows and didn't find any skin damage severe enough to warrant bandages. My forehead was a different story. I could tell by the look in her eyes once she removed my sundress headband.

"I did the best I could," Connie said munching on a sandwich.

"It'll be fine, fine, ok, fine," Leslie said.

I couldn't tell if she was reassuring Connie, herself, me, or lying to us all.

"Mandy get me another hot towel," Leslie demanded.

She gently took the towel and wiped slowly across my forehead. She turned and mouthed something to Hitch. The rest of the Woodstock Six were my trauma team.

"Ok Lenny," Leslie started. "Here's what I need you to do."

She instructed me to sit on my knees (on the used towel) and lean my head back. Hitch bent over to support my back. She poured some peroxide over the wound. It burned, but I held my ground. Dani and Connie stood over me, both grimaced.

"Another towel Mandy, another towel!" Leslie demanded. "Davey stoke that fire."

Leslie cleaned the wound some more and washed my whole face with warm water. She applied some paste to the gash, then ripped a gauze pad in half and placed the two halves side by side on my forehead. She secured them with another homemade headband fashioned from one of the towel pieces. She motioned for Hitch to help me up. I was still a little woozy from the fall, having my head upside down for a bit made me even woozier.

"Davey, get Lenny a shirt from his bag," Leslie ordered her brother.

Dani smiled and shook her head side-to-side as she washed off my chest and back with a nice, hot towel. Damn, if I could get that kind of treatment, I wanted to get hurt more often. Davey returned and I put on the clean t-shirt. Standing beside one another, with his bandaged eye and my bandaged forehead we looked like 2/3rds of the famous Revolutionary War print of the marching trio, one playing the flute, a flag-bearer, and a drummer boy.

"This keeps up," Hitch started. "We won't have any boys to take back home."

Everyone laughed.

"Let's go hear some damn music!" Leslie said. "Dani make Lenny a sandwich, he can eat it on the way down."

Track 24-30 Days in the Hole-Humble Pie (3:45)

I made sure the coast was clear as we approached the house. I needed to get Darlene a towel and get her on the way home before any of my crazy relatives could corner us. We approached as close to the dunes as we could get. Darlene waited by the side of the house as I went underneath the back deck and snagged a couple towels from the china cabinet. It housed all manner of beach stuff, old keepsakes, and who knows what else. We managed to dry off undetected and Darlene made me turn around as she slipped out of her wet undergarments and put her clothes back on.

"What are you going to do with those?" I asked.

"Your problem," she said, tossing them to me. "Think of them as a souvenir!"

"Funny," I said. "Very funny."

"Besides the bra is getting too small," she said.

"I noticed," I smirked and reached to grab her.

"I gotta get home Lenny," she pleaded as I wrapped my arms around her.

We kissed for a minute or two. Things were warming up rapidly. The sight of her in that tiny white miniskirt, knowing she didn't have any panties on was driving me insane. I reached up under her skirt and grabbed her cute little butt with both hands. She moaned a little and kissed me harder…. then the front screen door clanged closed!

"Everybody loves somebody sometimes…"

It was a very drunken Great-Aunt Pat trying to get down the street side stairs along with my great-aunt Nina. We reluctantly, but oh so quickly, broke our embrace. I stashed Darlene's sweet nothings in the cabinet. We waited for my great-aunts to leave and started on our way to Darlene's house.

"That's the first time we've ever gone swimming at night, just the two of us?" Darlene asked looking at me for agreement as we reached the lake.

"Yea we went in a couple years ago with a bunch of folks one night," I said.

"That was fun, we should do it again," she continued. "I really liked it."

"Sounds good to me," I smiled.

We made it back to her house a bit past her new curfew. I playfully grabbed at her skirt again, she smacked my hand away smiling. She went in through the side door. I waited for the signal that all was ok (two flicks of her light switch) and headed back home. I should've gone straight to the house, but I didn't. I made a left at the lake and headed over toward the tennis courts and library. I was going to stop by B's and see if he was still awake.

"He and Max are over at the water tower camping out," Dylan, his sister said.

She was standing out front with two of her girlfriends you may remember from the bonfire.

"Got any herb, Lenny?" Jade asked.

"Nah, not on me," I said. "Later ladies, I'm going to go check them out."

"Why don't you hang out with us?" Candace asked. "We're going to the Rec Hall, we'd have four for foosball or pool."

"Thanks, but I need to talk to B," I said.

"Oh come on, Lenny," Dylan said. "You'd rather hang out with my stupid brothers than us three?"

"Of course, I'd rather hang out with you girls," I said, bending over into a hunchback pose, leering at them with a lecherous smile while rubbing my hands together. "But I really must be going, monster's work is never done."

And I limped off hunched over. They all laughed, except Dylan. She was a dyed-in-the-wool turd.

"Come get us some damn weed and we'll give you some!" Dylan said.

I stopped about 12 feet away and turned around slowly.

"You'll give me some what?" I continued leering, staying in character.

The other two laughed.

"Oh, you're never getting that," Dylan said. "You been wanting this powerful shit since you were little. Never gonna happen! I just want some damn herb!"

"Speak for yourself," Candace said smiling. "You never know Lenny boy. Come on with us. Pleeeease?"

I straightened.

"Oh, alright," I said. "And screw you Dylan."

"Keep dreaming, little boy," she smirked.

Jade clapped. Dylan started walking toward the Rec Hall. Candace came over and looped her arm around mine.

"Ok, Lenny boy," she started. "Let's go have some fun."

The Rec Hall was pretty packed when we got there. All the pool tables were full and so were the two foosball tables. Dylan went over and put a quarter next to a couple more already on the closest table to the door. Jade went to the bar and started talking to some older construction guys.

"Hey Lenny, over here," Hal called from pool table number four behind the second post.

"Back in a bit," I told Candace and Dylan.

Dylan grabbed my arm.

"Will you go get my stuff before you get tangled up with those losers," she said nodding at Hal, David, Nathan, and Heath.

I looked over at the foursome. They were a sad sight. Some of them may still be virgins; Grouchy (Nathan), Doc (David) Mopey (Heath) and Dopey (Hal), the Despicable Duo and Simon and really Garfunkeled, the Mount Rushmore of Girl Repellant…….etc. etc. etc.

"Ok," I said, looking down at her hand holding my arm. "I didn't know you cared."

"Bullshit," she said. "But get my damn stuff first."

"Nice mouth," I said. "I think I suddenly forgot where to get any?"

"You little turd," she continued. "I know so much shit on you and B, you better not screw me over."

"I don't need to screw ya," I said. "But how bout a nice blow job? You do have a pretty mouth."

She smiled menacingly.

"Funny, always trying to make these dumbass little girls laugh," she said. "That crap doesn't work with me. Just go get my stuff, please?"

She let go of my arm and as she did, she pressed some money into my hand.

"That's $30," she continued, leaning in close. "I want some ludes (Quaaludes) and a quarter (ounce) of grass."

I nodded and seeing Dutch wasn't downstairs, I figured the upstairs crowd demanded his attention. The center-set stairs were just to the left of the bar. I hustled up to the second floor. It was only about ¼ full and Coven's "One Tin Soldier" was playing on the jukebox. Dutch was sitting at the end of the bar by the back wall watching some late night sports recap. He gave me the signal (moving his cup toward the barkeep) not to approach. I grabbed a stool at the other corner of the L-shaped bar. It was half the size of the one downstairs.

"Coke please Regina," I said.

"Sure Lenny," she didn't smile, another sign something was amiss.

She brought me my drink. I handed her a buck and told her to keep the change. Cokes were only 50 cents. I asked Dutch if the Cubs won.

"Yea," he said. "But had to use up a lot of the pen."

I nodded.

"See ya Dutch, Regina," I said, sliding off the barstool.

I got back downstairs and went over to the foursome playing pool.

"Hey Lenny," David started. "I think we can make some money tonight."

He nodded over toward the bar at a couple of military-looking guys.

"Nah," I said. "The girls are in for the night and I've no idea where Donnie and Danny are."

"No, no, no," Hal said. "Pier stuff."

"Man guys," I continued. "Don't know if I'm up for that either."

"C'mon Lenny," David said. "We haven't done that one once this summer! It could be a sweet bag of cash."

David fancied himself an old black bluesman and was constantly trying to sound like one and making up blues songs. That's why he injected the "sweet bag of cash" line. It was from a blues tune he and I wrote the year before and played at gigs sometimes.

"Maybe next time," I said.

The guys all looked disappointed. But I didn't feel like threatening to jump off the end of the pier after midnight. It was always a sucker bet that made us probably a couple grand over the years, a few hundred at a time. The deal would go down something kinda like this.

We would talk up pier jumping between two to four of us near the potential marks. This was usually service guys because they had money, liked to take risks, and either considered themselves brave or were full of themselves. We would argue amongst ourselves about jumping off the end of the pier. The bit was always done at night, always at night, during the day it's intimidating but doable, but at night pure plain ol 'scary to everyone. Bets would be made and this is where the mark(s) would set their own hook(s). They would ask if they could get in on the bet.

We made sure they weren't too drunk. Drunks will do almost anything for a buck and we didn't want anybody to get hurt. We'd ease them into the bet and set the parameters. Bet always started at $200 a person, sometimes we would back it down to $100 if they showed signs of trying to ease out. One of our group would back out of the bet and act as the banker holding the cash. We'd stroll out to the Steel Pier. We knew the tides, the currents, how to "read" the ocean and we always did it on moonless or cloudy nights. All of those things and a few intangibles made it more of a sure thing for us and way more daunting for them.

The bet was once you stepped on the pier, your money was in, you back out, you lose your cash. One of our crowd, usually one of the girls, but David was good at this role as well, would start talking about people drowning and how treacherous the currents were around the pier, recent shark attacks (lies!), generally poop yourself nighttime swimming talk. Plus, as a bonus, Jaws had just come out, so there was that.

We would always walk slowly, giving the marks plenty of time to see how high above the water they were and let the creakiness of the old pier, the wind, and the waves work their magic. Before we reached the end of the pier, most just forfeited their money. About 20% would make it to the very end, look over into the utter darkness below, and then cave. Over the years, I guess about 10 dudes or so were still in past that point. Almost all of those bailed as I started to climb up on the end railings. Only two ever dared climb the railing. The first made it into in a seated position straddling the rails before quitting. Only one ever attempted to stand up and immediately got back down once he was on his knees and looked down.

And me? I jumped off the pier about a half-dozen times, the first when I was 13, the last when I was 22. But those jumps were all in the daylight (usually very early morning) at low tide in very calm seas. No sweat, with nothing on the line but pride. Would I have jumped at night? Yea, but probably only once. There's scary shit in the ocean. A few good tales there for next time.

"So?" Dylan asked.

"I got to go somewhere else," I said. "I'll be back in a few."

"Wait, what?" Dylan asked.

"I gotta go somewhere else," I restated. "Not cool here."

"You better not be messing with me Lenny," Dylan said.

"Here, you want your damn money back?" I said. "I'm doing this for Candace, not you."

Candace smiled.

"We're up Dylan," Jade said putting their quarter into the foosball table.

"Can I go with you?" Candace asked.

"Better not," I said. "I'll be right back."

She smiled and twirled her really long sandy blond hair in her left hand. I smiled and watched her for a moment. Yep, you know that feeling. I turned and busted through the doors into the late night air. Just so you will know, the deal that went down upstairs was this:

Dutch suspected narcs (undercover narcotics officers) were in the Rec Hall. He had a system for when he thought there was "heat". The drink being moved was the signal to not approach. The Cubs' reference was kinda like a code or a baseball catcher's signals. My question was: Did the Cubs' win? This was the code/sign inquiring as to whether I could get anything in the building. I often asked Dutch if the Cubs' won, but the only time it meant anything drug related was if he had initiated the "don't approach signal". The rest of the time it was just two baseball nuts talking. A different protocol was used in winter.

Now once I'd put the query into motion, Dutch would respond with one of the following:

1. He would say some result. A win meant to see someone else in the bar for directions. A loss meant to come back in an hour. A rainout-no dice.

2. If he said a win, this meant to talk to his designated local flunky who would be somewhere in the building with a Cubs hat on. A set question was to be asked concerning the Cubs (changed regularly) to make sure you had the right Cubs' hat person, a little overkill I always thought. There just weren't many Cubs fans down

south in that era. The hat-wearing fella would then tell you where to pick up your stuff.

3. So, I needed to go to a backup location, at the time it was the bumper cars. When it was the bumper cars, Duff, a burly old carney who wore filthy tank tops in summer and just as nasty overalls in winter was the "pivot" man. Duff was missing two fingers on his left hand as a result of a tilt-a-whirl mishap and was a "third-level" in Dutch's hierarchy. There were usually about four at this spot on the chain-of-drug-command.

Duff had a thick eastern European accent and communication could be difficult. He always took tickets with his full fingered right hand, but as a "fourth-level" or "street-level", I knew the deal. You put your tix in his left hand and asked for a specific color of car depending on what you wanted. Green for grass and blue for "ludes". He'd tell you which numbered car to get into. They would always be parked in the very back of the room.

There were usually four to six level fours. Dutch would usually keep two adults, one college-aged person and one high school kid as his street-level people year-round and add a couple more in summer. I got to start a couple years early due to timing, luck, and Dutch's realization I could be trusted, was good with numbers, and people.

I scored Dylan's stuff and got myself about the same amount. You were always supposed to go to the designated broken car first, get your stuff, which was always in a box under the seat, act like the car was broken (it was intentionally disabled) go get another one and ride out a turn. You could only get grass and ludes. Acid was never dealt this way to my knowledge.

Dylan and Jade were still holding the foosball table when I returned. I slid in next to Candace, who was sitting across from another girlfriend, Sabrina, at the table nearest the door.

"All good?" she asked.

I nodded. Dark-haired, 16, an Audrey Hepburn look-a-like and just as delicate, Sabrina was talking about school and her boyfriend. Candace was telling her to dump him. Dylan squeezed me over into Candace and Jade piled in next to Sabrina.

"Well?' Dylan asked.

"All good," I responded.

"Just like Lenny, hogging all the women," Nathan said staring at the girls.

"Beat it Nathan," Jade said.

"Y'all come on over and shoot some pool," Nathan said, ignoring the girls' disdain for his presence. "We'll pay."

He was pointing at Heath, who was by his side, as usual, grinning from ear to ear. Hal and David wisely kept their distance.

"Get your sorry asses back over to the pool tables," Dylan said. "Don't ever try to talk to us again!"

"Whoa," Nathan said. "Must be you bitches time of the month!"

I quickly stood up and started to rearrange his face, but thought better of it because of all the drugs I had on me. Candace grabbed my arm as well. The despicable duo went back to the pool table.

"Let's go Lenny," Candace said.

"Yea," Dylan agreed rising to leave the table but not before yelling. "You two turds are lucky I don't kick both your punk asses!"

Sabrina headed to the bar and the rest of us left through the front doors. It was thundering. Lightning was attacking the ocean in spectacular bursts. Mother Nature was sending those still out and about a message; go home!

"Shit, I was going to say we'd go on the beach," Candace said.

"How bout the pier?" Jade offered.

"Not with that lightning," I said. "You do know it's a steel pier right?" I said.

"Let's just go to the house," Dylan said.

So we walked back down the main east-west boulevard on the island, past the intersection where Egg's had done his performance art, the old A&P store, that's now a local Mom & Pop grocery, and on to Dylan and B's street.

"Here," I said handing Dylan her stuff.

"Damn Lenny, right on the sidewalk," Jade said.

"The cops are all on the boardwalk," I said. "There's no one around. I'm going over to see B."

"Thought you were going to hang with us?" Candace asked.

"He's afraid his little girlfriend will find out," Dylan teased.

"Nah," I said. "Just going to share my drugs with your brothers."

I walked away.

"Later," Candace said. "Let's shoot some pool tomorrow."

"Thanks Lenny," Jade said.

I waved over my shoulder. It was only another 50 yards or so to the big, flat, circular water reservoir on town property behind the grocery store on the west side. There was a tennis court, a small library (where we saw our first boobs in a National Geographic magazine), a standard vertical water tower, a playground, and a field where we played pick-up games of baseball when we were younger. A long split-rail fence separated the field from an old Mom and Pop motel.

I went through the gate, which was rarely locked. The two water structures were enclosed by a relatively new wire fence. The storm had died down.

"Yo, coming up," I yelled.

"Yo," B yelled from the top of the ladder.

I climbed the dozen or so rungs up to the asphalt covered roof of the squat, flat tower. Max, B's baby brother, was pouring some liquid out of a gallon jug into cups. He handed me one.

"My first batch," he beamed proudly. "Homemade beer!"

B shook his head, a hard no, behind Max's back, but I had to take a sip. I took as small a one as possible. I immediately spit it out.

"Damn Max, that's gross," I said.

Max, two years younger than us, had a big rep as a practical joker.

"I know," he said. "You owe me a dollar B, told you he'd try it."

B forked over the dollar.

"Hope you got something else," I said.

"Oh yea," B said, handing me a Budweiser.

"Better, much better," I said taking a big ol' chug.

"Where's your sleeping bag?" Max asked. "We're camping out."

He pointed at four sleeping bags a few yards away.

"Hal and David will be here in a bit," Max said.

"I'm not staying," I said. "Just brought some goodies to share."

We smoked a joint. The storm cranked back up. The thunder grew more intense than before and a light mist began to fall. Thankfully Ma Nature eased up on the thunderbolts. I handed B an unlit joint.

"I think I'm going to bail," I said.

With that, we heard the sound of a car turning down Third Street aiming right for us. It was the cops. Oh crap!

"Time to jet," I said.

The squad car pulled right up in front of the ladder blocking the only apparent exit. Max dropped the gallon jug of crappy beer. It burst as we ran to the other side of the tower and hopped over the side. We knew the earthen works supporting the structure were much higher on the west side and it was just six-to-eight feet from the top to the first bit of dirt. We slid on down the hill, climbed the fence and ran in three different directions. Max headed straight west down Raleigh Avenue, toward the river. B bolted north into a residential area and I high-tailed it behind Deputy Temple's house, the old motel (now a nursing home), and then south toward the school, Darlene's, and Melissa's houses.

I ran through many familiar properties and hid out in Melissa's former backyard. I waited about a half hour, then slowly made my way back east toward the ocean and my house. I thought about ditching my drugs a couple times or at least hiding them, but I was pretty confident the two cops that were on duty would never catch me.

I was right and confidently slid into my bed. I was awakened early the next morning by a familiar voice speaking through one of my open windows, from the ocean side deck. At first, I thought I may have been dreaming. I wasn't.

"Hey man we gotta go down to the police station," B said embarrassed.

"Whatdaya mean," I said. "Did they catch you?"

I was still a bit asleep, but alert enough to know, I hadn't been caught, wasn't seen, and didn't leave any evidence anywhere. I knew B and Max if they'd been caught, would never tell. That was Crazy Beach rule number one, never rat, you could kill your mom, you'd be forgiven, but a rat never is, and has to look over their shoulder till the day they die. Even Michael Vick got a second chance, but not rats! Not Judas, not Benedict Arnold, never!

"Nah, of course not," B said. "But Max left his sleeping bag there."

I looked at B as if I didn't understand because I didn't.

"His name and address are on it," B explained. "So the coppers were at the house this morn. Mom was gone, but Big Bob says me, you, and Max got to go wash police cars today."

So that was how I spent the last Sunday before school started back and I entered the 10th grade, washing stupid police cars in 95-degree, humid-ass weather. It wasn't the first time, and it damn sure wasn't the last. But this one sucked the most, due to the timing, the stupidity of how we got nabbed, and the weather.

I called Darlene from Vito's (my co-worker Tammy's dad) Bar, Bait & Tackle across from the police station during a break. She laughed her ass off. I could hear Lexi laughing in the background too.

"What dumbasses!" Lexi howled.

Track 25-Sugar Magnolia-Grateful Dead (4:20)

The Woodstock Six rolled down the left side once again, but we could only go about half as far as the day before. The crowd now swelled to the epic proportions you have seen in the movies, newsreels, and photos. We got to a decent spot just as Country Joe showed up, without his band, the Fish, and played a rocking set best remembered for the "Fix'n to Die Rag" slamming the Vietnam War. Some of our fellow festival goers let us know we'd missed a band called Quill.

Mandy and Danni asked everyone within earshot if they knew when Janis and Jimi were supposed to play. There were lots of rumors, but no one knew for sure. The sun was beating down pretty good. I may have been a little woozy from my fall and/or the amount of second-hand marijuana smoke floating around, but I was definitely impaired to some degree.

I really don't remember a lot about John Sebastian or Keef Hartley. I talked a lot to people around me, including two guys from Baltimore, who were Oriole fans like me. Every now and then one of the girls would check on me to see how I was doing.

"You sure you're ok?" Dani asked for the gazillionth time.

I shook my head yes...

The defining moment, for me, of the second day of the festival came next. A new band from the San Francisco Bay area were introduced. They were the first mixed-race band I'd seen. Latino, black, and white musicians meshed to blast a sonic masterwork. They were led by the guy the band was named for, Santana, as in

Carlos Santana. Their set just plain rocked. Even before Michael Shrieve's legendary drum solo during "Soul Sacrifice" we knew we were hearing and seeing something powerfully unique. It was also the first time I witnessed tons of people dancing. There had been some swaying and a few dancers on the first day, but this was the first, who-gives-a-shit who's watching, everybody bust a move moment embraced by the majority of the crowd.

The crowd just exploded with noise, becoming part of the rock symphony emanating from the stage. Once again, it may have been due to the second-hand Mary Jane or my head injury, but the crowd appeared to become seamless in places, masses of humanity coalescing into a ball of rhythm. The Woodstock Six became part of the mix and it's the first time I can recall dancing in public. I danced with Dani and Mandy in a little circle and Davey even joined in. Hitch was spinning Leslie around and our twirling made me even more "high". It was my first time experiencing an elevated spiritual sense of belonging. Everyone was happy.

"I'm getting hungry," Davey broke the spell.

"Me too," Mandy chipped in.

Sunset greeted Canned Heat's appearance and we ventured back to Henrietta.

"Damn, they're rocking," Hitch said, pausing to turn and watch the band.

"C'mon Hitch," Leslie demanded. "Let's get everyone fed and get back down here before Janis comes on."

We had fire-roasted hot dogs, chips, and dip for supper. It was a blast shoving the wieners on sticks and poking them into the flames. Davey lost one to the fire below and Leslie gave him another tongue lashing.

"You're going to eat that tomorrow dumbass," she said.

"I'm going to feed it to you when you're asleep," Davey laughed.

The rest of us chuckled and smiled.

"I'll shove it up your ass if you do," his sister promised.

Even louder laughter from the peanut gallery. Hitch and the other girls were sharing a joint when Dwayne and Connie wandered into our campsite. I was happy to see my saviors again.

"Hey guys," Dwayne said, waving as he approached the fire pit. "We wanted to check on the ol'Lenny boy. How ya doing kid?"

"Good, really good," I said, finishing off my second hot dog.

"Glad to hear it," Dwayne continued. "Connie here was worried boutcha."

"You guys want something to eat?" Hitch asked. "We're out of dogs, but we got some chips. And how bout some spam?"

"Oh, thanks," Connie said, still wearing her torn blue sundress from earlier. "We ran out this afternoon."

"Looks like folks are running low everywhere," Leslie said. "We were down at some of the organizers' tents earlier and it was getting worse. Bunch of people needing water and food."

Dani brought two cans of spam over and handed them to Connie. Mandy shared the water jug. Dwayne whipped out a joint and handed it to Hitch.

"We're about to head back down," Hitch said. "You guys want to roll that way with us?"

"Cool, cool," Dwayne said.

"I got to use the bathroom," Davey said.

"Thanks for sharing," Leslie said. "Just go, no need to tell everyone."

"Where's the latrine at again?" Davey asked.

"Just behind that big pine right there," Hitch said pointing to the edge of the eastern wood line.

Davey retrieved the toilet paper from Henrietta. He ran, the only time I ever saw him do so that didn't involve the cops, toward the woods. Hitch had done the rugged duty of digging us a latrine the prior afternoon.

"Pretty cool, bringing the young ones to the festival," Dwayne said.

"They were stowaways," Leslie offered. "Little bastards hid in the back of the van, we didn't know they were there till we were almost halfway here."

"Oh shit," Connie laughed.

"Damn that's ballsy," Dani said.

"Yea, yea it is," Hitch said. "I'm glad they're here though, as long as they survive."

He patted me on the shoulder and laughed. Everyone else did too. I was a little embarrassed.

"Ok turd face," Leslie said to her re-appearing brother. "Let's go see Janis."

The eight of us didn't come close to reaching the spot we were before. We were at least 50 yards farther back, maybe more. We didn't hear any music on the way down. We waited and waited. We'd been there quite a while when Hitch asked a few people next to us what was going on. We got a bunch of different answers, but most involved problems on stage.

"Grateful Dead having some issues," said a small-framed girl with a Boston accent and dark braided hair. "They've tried to start a few times, but no luck. Parts of a couple of songs, not very good."

And so it was for the next hour or so, the Dead would come on, play some, have some kinda problem, electrical, equipment, or otherwise. They struggled to get through more than one song at a time. My first exposure to the seminal jam band wasn't good. Now I've had religious experiences at more than one Dead show over the years. I've also walked out a couple of times. "St. Stephen" sounded good, otherwise, not a good night for the Dead. You never hear a Deadhead say, "Let's cue up the Dead's performance at Woodstock." Nuff said.

Mountain was next followed by CCR (Credence Clearwater Revival), both rocked out really hard. CCR especially lit up "Proud Mary" and "Bad Moon Rising". It was after midnight when CCR came on and they ripped through about a dozen songs. They had what crowd was still awake jamming. John Fogerty has famously said that "...it looked like Dante's Inferno, bodies everywhere..."

Finally, about two in the morning, the Pearl appeared. If you were never able to see her during her oh too brief life, I'm so sorry. Her stage presence was almost unrivaled. The crowd was full of oohs and ahhs at her every move. She gave as commanding a performance as I've ever seen. Everyone, especially Dani and Leslie were completely enthralled. Who knows where all that power came from? God? DNA? Something else? A combo? Guess we'll never know. But I saw it, I heard it, and no one, anyone, has ever come close.

Janis left everyone around us a bit drained and many more began retreating to their campsites or crashing on the ground where they were. Tons floated back during the later parts of first Mountain and then CCR's sets. Only about 10 percent of the crowd still appeared engaged.

That changed quickly when Sly and the Family Stone took the stage and ripped the crowd a new one. It was as if the paddles had been applied to the collective chest of the group and wham! Back to life! "Dance to the Music" "I Want to Take You Higher" If you haven't listened to or watched videos of those lately, STOP READING, GO DO IT!

TOLD YA!!!!!

Well, WHO could possibly follow that?

Sorry, couldn't help myself....THE WHO, of course.

Davey had petered out after Sly and was fast asleep on the ground beside Leslie, who was also fading and sharing a joint with Hitch.

"I think I'm going to head back," Mandy said. "You coming Dani?"

"Nah, I'm going to stay and watch The Who with Lenny," she said.

"Man, we're beat kid," Hitch said tapping me on the shoulder. "I really want to catch your boys with ya, but I'm toast. I'll rock with ya from afar. We're head'n on back up too."

Well, it was about five Sunday morning, August 17. Hitch scooped Davey up like a bag of flour and threw him over his back. So four of the "Woodstock Six" slowly trudged back up the bowl, Dwayne and Connie had left after Janis. By this time almost everyone was asleep or seated.

At that moment I realized I hadn't sat down all evening. It was a pattern I would follow my entire life. I simply prefer to stand, at shows, at bars, at restaurants (if they have those cool, waist-high tables) and pretty much anywhere else or at least, lean on something. I'm a big leaner, posts, bars, high backed chairs, the chart you stand in front of when they take your mug shot, etc...Heck, I've a few long-term friends have never seen me sit on regular furniture. I sit on the floor or a barstool when I choose to sit.

"Thanks for sticking around," I said.

"No worries Lenny boy," Dani said wrapping her right arm around my shoulder. "Wouldn't miss it!"

The Who took the stage about an hour before sunrise, most chroniclers say it was five, but I think it was just before, maybe closer to 4:45 or else the watch the guy passed out next to us was wearing was wrong. I remember that distinctly, because it was a Mickey Mouse watch and my best friend back home B, yep that B, wanted one.

After an intro of "Heaven and Hell", The Who played one of their first hits, "I Can't Explain" and then launched into the full rock opera "Tommy". About halfway through, a spaced-out hippy dude (Abbie Hoffman) came out and tried to disrupt the set and say some political crap. Well, Mr. Pete Townsend would have none of that and promptly bashed him in the back with his guitar, chasing him off into the wings stage left. The crowd roared and the music fired up again with the pervy "Fiddle About".

The band was spot on as they blasted through the rest of "Tommy" and as the concert film shows, a beautiful sunrise came into view around six, Roger singing "See me, feel me..." A couple more powerful songs, including their great cover of Eddie Cochran's "Summertime Blues" brought one of the highlights of my life to a close and a first to my soul.

"That was unreal," Dani said turning to face me.

I was so spent I could just nod. She looked at me kinda funny, then shook her head slowly in a "no" motion, then smiled, and leaned in and kissed me! A really good one! Well, it was my first, so I don't know about that, but to me it was. And there it is, I know you've been waiting for it: the THIRD WONDER OF BOYHOOD- Your first Kiss!

"Our secret?" she asked.

I just nodded. You're the first other folks to know. Sorry Dani, figured enough time has passed you wouldn't be pissed.

"Wanna go now?" she asked.

I looked at the stage, the roadies were changing stuff up, so someone else was coming on. I didn't know who and everyone around me was in a coma. Dani and I were literally the only ones standing for hundreds of yards. I felt like poor Scarlett O'Hara looking over all the Confederate wounded at the Atlanta train station just as intermission comes to "Gone with the Wind".

"Why don't we see if anyone comes up quick?" I asked more with my spirit than my body or mind.

"Ok, ok," she said surprisingly upbeat. "But I gotta sit down."

The next thing I remember was the booming sound of Grace Slick's voice as the Jefferson Airplane took the stage. I was flat on my back and Dani was asleep on my chest. I guess I dozed off as well. Grace's unmistakable voice began to rouse Dani. She sheepishly looked at me as she lifted her head and ran her hands through her hair. We didn't say anything but slowly got back into a standing position. I was still way exhausted and I could tell she was too.

"You ready for some morning maniac music?" Grace asked.

A subdued and mostly spent Woodstock crowd did their best to respond. Grace looked really sexy in a mostly white outfit and the band seemed sharp. We made it through a few great songs before Dani took my hand.

"We gotta go get some sleep and I'm hungry," she said.

I just nodded and let her lead me away, it was about nine Sunday morning. We held hands until we got within about 50 yards of our campsite.

She stopped me. She leaned close and kissed me again, a little longer and more moist than the first. She held her right index finger up to her lips and smiled.

We went to our respective sleeping areas. Our crowd and most everyone else within sight was out cold. She smiled, waved, and went inside. I looked around at the sight of hundreds of thousands sleeping people. I took a deep breath. What a day…

Track 26-Ring of Fire (2:45)/I Walk the Line (3:20)-Johnny Cash

So school started. Darlene went to the academy's high school side and I went to my big ass high school on the mainland. The first few weeks before I got my license, B and I rode with a friend, Jimmy Davis, or took the bus. Darlene and I talked on the phone most nights the first week after I got home from football practice. On Thursday night she told me she'd given Lexi a note to give me at school Friday. She made me promise I wouldn't let anyone else see it, read it, or talk about its contents with anyone. I agreed and asked what was so secret. She said she couldn't talk about it on the phone.

Our first game was that Friday night and it being game day, all the guys wore their jerseys. I wore number 43 that season in honor of my NASCAR hero, Richard "The King" Petty. The cheerleaders wore their cheer uniforms as well. As I was heading to homeroom, Lexi spotted me from across the courtyard and called out to me. She was in uniform and her hair had grown out enough that it was in short pigtails. She looked really cute.

"Here dumbass," she smirked, handing me an envelope and then punching me on the shoulder. "Just kidding, you're alright, I guess."

She turned and ran to join a group of other cheerleaders by the fountain. She sure seemed happier than usual. I started to open it, but remembering my promise, I hustled to the closest boy's room and an open stall. The envelope was taped shut with Darlene's signature over the tape. Damn, must be some secret shit if she went to all that trouble and even hid it from Lexi.

Well, it was some secret shit alright! I locked the stall door and leaned my back against it. I peeled the tape back and opened the envelope carefully. It was much more than a note, it was a damn "War and Peace" letter, at least three pages long. I just got into the first paragraph of her beautiful cursive handwriting that looked like something from the 1700s with lots of loops and flare....

"Dear Lenny,

Please destroy this after you read it. First, please know that I love you and that's never going to change. This has been an unreal summer....."

THE DAMN BELL RANG!

Well, ballplayers couldn't be late for class or risk not getting to play. So I quickly folded the mini-novel back up and stuck it in my right front pocket. I ripped the envelope up and flushed it down the toilet. I hightailed it to class. I was in one of the damn mobile units. I made it just in time before the second bell (death knell!) rang.

I wanted so badly to open the note/letter in home room. I had a really great teacher, Mrs. Davis (no kin to Jimmy), who I already knew well enough that she wouldn't hassle me. There were prying eyes all around so I resisted. I didn't have enough time between periods to read it either. It was going to have to wait for lunch. There were so many students at our school there were two lunch periods. I had the second, B and the rest of the beach crowd you've met had the first.

"What ya going to do between end of class and six o'clock?" Jason, our quarterback that year asked.

"I dunno," I answered as we left our history class and headed to the lunchroom. "I'll meet ya in there, going to hit the head first."

I found an open stall near the back wall and pulled the letter from my pocket.

"…I can't believe it's over already and school is back in. It went by so fast. Good luck with the game tonight. I'll get there quick as I can, our soccer match (her private school didn't field a football team) should be finished before kick-off. I'm glad it's a home game for both schools (our schools were only a few miles apart). Well, here's some big news, Lexi gave it up to Ted, that guy from Dalton's birthday party Tuesday night. She swore they were careful and he used protection. I hope she's telling the truth…"

She wrote about Lexi and Ted in-depth. Ted had just started senior year and was my football teammate. I only knew him from the party and practice. I'd never really had many conversations with him.

"…Do you think maybe you can talk to him and see if he's serious about Lexi?" page three of her opus began. "I know you don't like that kinda stuff, but please, please, please, for me? She's driving me crazy and won't shut up talking about him and "doing it". I'm so glad we've settled some things and we have lots to look forward too!"

She drew a smiley face in a heart at that point, cheesy, but sweet, hey it was the 70s and we were stupid teenagers.

"… Anyway, I can't wait to see you tonight, I don't like going this long without touching you! Please be good and think of me when all those little hoochies from the dance team try talking you up. Lexi and Sabrina are keeping an eye out for me. Just kidding! Maybe we can double with Ted and Lexi tomorrow night? I love you, I love, I love you! Oh yeah, one more thing, I lust you too!"

She signed off with a big D encased in a heart with our initials linked by a plus sign underneath. But holy crap, I didn't know she knew Sabrina that well. Damn, I'd have some explaining to do (again!) if Sabrina mentioned seeing me at the Rec Hall last week with Candace, Dylan, and Jade. I damn sure didn't want to get involved in the Lexi/Ted thing, but she obviously wasn't going to take no for an answer.

I ripped the letter up into little pieces and flushed them down the toilet. I made it to the lunchroom in time to grab a bite and eat on the run before my only class of the afternoon. On game day players got released one period early for home games and several periods for away games depending on our distance from the opponent.

"Why don't we go to the Par Three when we leave?" Jason asked.

"That'll work," I said. "Who's going to drive?"

"Vince said he would," Jason replied.

The bell rang to close out my first week of official high school. I went to a school (Williston) that was ALL ninth graders the year before. Jason and I went to meet Vince and two other teammates under "The Zero Tree". The giant oak was the preferred parking lot hangout area for the ballplayers that weren't "jocks". The ones that did other things like getting high and liked to talk about something besides sports all the time.

The tree got its name because our Principal, a middle-aged ex-Marine, still sporting a buzz cut, walked by the first day of school and looked at all of us mostly with shaggy or somewhat unruly, or long hair hanging out by the tree and said, "…bunch of zeroes, all you'll ever be, a bunch of zeroes." So from then on, that was the place and that was our name, "The Zeroes".

By Thursday night someone spray-painted a giant white goose egg on the tree facing the entrance. Eighty percent of student parking was past the tree, so it was a great spot to watch the comings and goings of our classmates. Plus over the years it became a prime spot for my illegal business ventures expanding by the next year to include, selling booze out of my trunk, fake ids, and all other kinds of teenage insanity.

"Yo, Lenny, got any weed?" asked Justin, our fullback, who was sitting up front in the 1967 light blue Mustang.

"Not on me, nope," I said. "I don't keep it like that."

"Oh," he said. "Well can I get some for tomorrow night? Ike's having a party down at Knotty Beach. Bet you could make a bundle if you hit it up."

Knotty Beach was the rich kid beach, and while only 15 miles away from Crazy Beach as the crow flies north, it was a way different universe. Crazy Beach was, and still is to a large degree, a mostly blue-collar beach. I was thinking I'd love to go to the party, but I wasn't sure I wanted to jump in quick dealing drugs to that crowd. Plus, I needed to check with Dutch first concerning expansion, pricing, quantities, etc.

We'd a blast playing the nine-hole par three. We laughed our asses off at one another, none of us were any good at golf, but boy did we have fun. Vince hit one into a shallow pond to the right on number four and promptly discarded his shoes and attempted to hit his ball out of the water hazard. He thoroughly soaked himself with swing after swing that accomplished nothing but to lower the water level of the pond. Finally, he reached down and threw the ball up on the green.

"I quit," he laughed yelled.

Of course the ball he tossed rolled right into the cup from 15 yards away.

"That counts, that counts," he yelled some more.

Two holes later, I bounced my tee shot off a tree left of the green and scared the shit out of some poor birds that were snoozing in a nest.

"Crap," I yelled.

The ball ricocheted back to the green.

"Hell yea," I yelled as the ball approached the pin.

Yep, you guessed it, the ball just kept rolling. It rolled all the way ACROSS the green and into a deep sand trap on the other side. I didn't even bother trying to hit it out.

"Damn," I said.

Everyone busted out laughing.

We survived par three and stopped at the store to grab a snack before heading back to school. As we were leaving the store we caught a red-light. Vince yelled…

"Chinese fire drill!"

The car emptied quickly and all five of us had to change seats. I'd been stuck in the middle of the almost no back seat, so I was last to arrive at my new seat, the driver's spot. I hopped in just as the light changed to green. I gunned it, spinning the rear tires, making that great rugged sound, and producing an intense cloud of smoke. The Mustang roared forward and fishtailed hard as I shifted into second gear and made a quick left onto the main drag toward the school.

"That fool's crazy," said Big Will, one of our tight ends/defensive ends, the biggest guy in the car and now occupying the smallest spot where I'd been earlier.

"Lenny, you even got a license?" Vince asked from the front passenger seat holding on to the dashboard for dear life with both hands. "I just got this car last month, don't wreck it."

I floored the Mustang shifting gears as I barreled down the boulevard, hitting the brakes pretty hard, and sliding the 'Tang' sideways into the school parking lot. I blazed past the Zero Tree toward the fieldhouse.

"Damn right, now that's some driving!" Jason said loudly as we exited in a cloud of dust.

Most of the 60 or so guys on our team were already milling about outside the fieldhouse. Coach just shook his head as I tossed Vince the keys. The dust began to settle. It had just begun to stir on my notorious driving escapades.

"Not bad, for a Ford," I said. "But wait till I take you for a ride in my Mopar."

"Can't wait!" Jason said. "Let's go kick ass!"

The game was pretty uneventful. We did kickass. We won big, 34-0. We'd a great team and almost 20 guys went on to play college sports. I ran back kicks and played some at wide receiver on offense and safety on defense in the second half. We'd a ton of seniors and they got most of the playing time. I spotted Darlene and her dad sitting with my family at halftime. We did our usual little half wave and I went back to the business at hand.

My first high school game went pretty well and the coaches showed a lot of confidence in me playing me as the number one kick returner. Since we shut them out, the only kick-off I returned was to start the second half. I broke through an open space on the left side and had a really good return to almost midfield. I got to return four punts, no big returns, but a total of 82 yards for a 20.5 average. I picked off a late desperation throw by their quarterback as time expired. I was really happy with the way I played.

"Solid game," my dad said.

That was about as high as my dad's level of praise would go. He'd driven to the field house to pick me up.

"We're meeting the Winters and your aunts at the pizza place," he continued.

Great, I thought. I'd get to spend some time with Darlene tonight.

The pizza place near the school was packed with players, their families, and other students celebrating the season-opening win. Several teammates stopped by our booth to talk a bit and a couple reminded me of the Knotty Beach party set for Saturday night.

"Cool, cool," I responded to most. "I'll try and make it."

Lexi was there with Ted. The two carried on an out-of-place public display of affection for quite some time. They finally took a break and stopped by our table. Lexi asked Darlene the same thing.

"We'll see," Darlene said.

Darlene and I were sitting next to one another in a corner booth. She was drop dead gorgeous in her academy cheerleading uniform. Her school colors were green and white so her uniform stood out boldly against our school's sea of navy blue. Her hair was in a ponytail when we arrived, but she went to the bathroom shortly thereafter and took her hair down. As she returned to the table, all the boys were eyeballing her hard. She was so tanned and her hair was so golden blonde and full of bounce she could've easily been a model for some shampoo company. I felt so lucky.

"Darlene's next match is Tuesday after school," Mr. Winter said looking at me.

"I'd love to be there," I said. "But I have a soccer match away."

"Boy's biting off a lot don't ya think G.R.?" Mr. Winter asked.

"He says he can handle it," my dad replied. "It'll be a little easier once he gets his license."

Darlene looked at me and smiled. She placed her left hand on my right knee. I squeezed hers pretty good.

Playing both football and soccer during the same semester took some logistical planning, but physically and mentally it was no sweat. I loved playing and years on the beach and in the water, along with some great sports DNA from both sides of my family tree helped give me an athletic advantage over tons of folks. Sports and music were my passions, and girls, of course, girls!

"Yea, Dad's having to switch up a bunch of his shifts at the plant now," I said. "To make the games and stuff."

"When do you get your license?" Mr. Winter asked.

"Couple days before Halloween," I said. "I bought my car last weekend. Having a few things done to it. Should be ready soon."

Dad let me pick what I wanted within my $1500 budget. I narrowed it down to the 1970 Chevelle or the 70 Duster you heard me mention to B. I picked the Duster. It was in great shape, white with a black vinyl top, keystone mags, a built-in eight-track player, and a 340 turbojet engine. It had way fewer miles than the Chevelle and was in better shape. The Duster was a one owner local car and the Chevelle was on a car lot. The Duster will be a central character in Crazy Beach-Disc II-Crazier Beach.

Dad also taught me a very important financial lesson with the selection without saying much. Once I decided on the Plymouth, he gave me a choice; I could pay for the car ($1,100) and he would pay my insurance till I graduated from college or the reverse, I pay for the insurance and he would buy the car. Well, like a dumbass, I looked short-term, and let him pay for the car, thinking I could hang onto my $1,100. My insurance was only going to start at $35 a month. So figured I was making a smart call. Boy was I wrong! You've already seen how I drove back then and it only would get tons worse, but those are tales for other days.

Mr. Winter asked one of my great-aunts to drive his car back to the beach because he wanted to talk to my dad. Those two loved talking sports, military stuff, and who knows what else. Darlene and I were happy with the new arrangement. On the ride home, Darlene and I sat close together in the back seat and talked about the weekend.

"So you're going to that party tomorrow?" Darlene asked.

"I dunno," I said. "You wanna go?"

"If you want to?" she said her voice lilting in a higher manner. "Dad is it ok if we go to that party at Knotty Beach with Lexi and Ted tomorrow night?"

"If it's alright with G.R., it's alright with me," Mr. Winter said. "We've got a horseshoe tournament at the VFW tomorrow afternoon."

Dad looked at me in the rearview mirror. He took a second or two longer than I'd hoped. He looked out the windshield and then looked at me in the rearview again.

"That place ain't home," Dad said. "You two be careful."

Well, that could have meant a gazillion things. But we were going. Darlene also managed to tie Lexi and Ted into it, so I think they may have already planned that part. You know how girls are about that kinda stuff.

By the time we got to our house, the usual Friday night board game madness was in full swing. It was the game of Life this time. My great aunts were slugging it out with my mom, my sister, and one of my sister's new school friends. Darlene and I mingled for a few around the celebration of family and fun and then headed out to the beachside deck. Dad grabbed a couple of beers. He and Mr. Winter sat on the street-side deck.

"I think we'll have a lot of fun at the party," Darlene said. "A bunch of kids from my school are going."

"Yea should be alright," I said, as we leaned on the front railing looking out at the ocean.

"Something on your mind or are you just tired?" she asked.

"No, no, I'm good," I said. "Lot on my mind."

"Tell me," she said.

"Nah, it's cool," I said. "Just some of the fellas are wanting me to bring goodies and I don't think that's the right call."

"Yea, I think you're right," she said. "Maybe just enough weed for us four, a few joints."

"Yea, I agree," I said. "Let's walk downstairs."

We walked hand-in-hand down the steps and went under the deck. We made out for a few and I picked her up and sat her on the bottom portion of the china cabinet. I was kissing her and reached into the drawer where I had hidden her undergarments after our night swimming session.

"Here, these belong to you," I said. "Oh no, sorry, those are someone else's."

She smiled and joke slapped me lightly on the shoulder and wagged her right index finger at me.

"You planned that all along didn't you?" she said tilting her head.

"Of course," I said. "Since the night you left them. You got a few shirts and other crap here too. I'm going to start charging you a storage fee."

"Darlene, Darlene," my little sis yelled from the deck. "Your daddy says time to go home, meet him out front."

"Ok, ok," Darlene yelled back. "I'll come by the shop and see you tomorrow. Your car's going to be here then, right? I can't wait to see it!"

She gave me a peck on the lips and ran to the front. I shoved her underthings back in the drawer. I headed back upstairs and helped clean up after the game night crowd.

"Thank you son," my mom said. "You played really great tonight."

"Thanks Mom, no problem," I said giving her a kiss on the cheek as we finished up around the sink.

I hit the hay, looking out at the ocean for a bit. The gentle swish-swash sound of the waves led me to a dreamland filled with good things. I'd some pretty intense scenes involving Lexi leading me to blast awake real early with a raging boner. I felt a little guilty. Of course, I'd thought of Lexi like that. Don't judge! I was a kid. But I never seriously gave ANY thought to making a move on her and she never made one on me.

I wanted to catch a few waves before I went to the shop, so I hustled outside real quick without so much as a bathroom stop. I grabbed my board and sprinted across the empty sands and flung myself into the water. The shrimp boats were passing by and the seagulls were screaming a siren song chasing their breakfast as the sun rose. The brine of the saltwater was my morning meal as I tumbled off the board a few times. I managed a couple of decent rides then showered quickly using the one near the end of our walkway.

A quick change, teeth brushed, deodorant applied, and off I went to make the doughnuts. It being Labor Day Weekend, Saturday flew by as we were busy all day. Darlene and Lexi came by for a bit after hitting the beach, but I was so swamped we didn't have much time to talk.

"Ok, if we come around bout seven and we'll all get supper?" Darlene asked.

"Sounds good," I said. "Ted coming down here?"

"Yea, he's picking us up at Lexi's then," she said. "So we'll be by right after."

"Cool," I said.

Waves exchanged.

I did some business right after work, hitting the arcade, the Rec Hall, and the pier. Some of my usual customers had started getting a bit more and it about wiped out my various stashes. I made sure to keep enough for us four, but that was about it. I let Dutch know I needed to re-up big time on Sunday. I pulled the last of my personal stash from the spot where I'd taped it under the china cabinet. I showered (inside this time) to get the baking/grease funk off and was in my room when I heard my friends come in through the front.

"Go on back," my mom told them. "You want something to eat?"

"No thank you," Darlene said. "We're going to get some Italian."

"Oh, that sounds great," Mom said. "That's Lenny's favorite. Well, Lexi it's so nice to see you, it's been ages."

"I know," Lexi said. "This is Ted."

"Hi Ted," my mother continued. "You sure you don't want a drink or something?'

"No mam," Ted replied. "Thank you though."

Darlene knocked on my half-open door.

"C'mon in," I said. "I'm decent."

"You're never decent Lenny," Lexi laughed.

"Funny," I said.

"Cool room man," Ted said. "I dig that Zeppelin poster."

"Oh, thanks," I said. "I got to go see them in concert soon! Once I get my license, I'm rolling to wherever they are."

"That's Lenny's big dream," Darlene said. "Not to be rich or famous, or go to college, but to see Led Zeppelin."

"Sounds about right," Lexi laughed. "That's Zep IV playing now isn't it?"

I nodded as "The Battle of Evermore" was coming to a close on my turntable that was suspended from the ceiling (to reduce vibrations silly).

"You guys ready to rock?" I asked, showing them a handful of J's.

"Hell yea," Ted said. "Let's move."

We piled into Ted's big ol' black 64 Mercury convertible and burned a doobie on the way to the Italian joint on the mainland. The girls had their party attire on, sundresses and ribbons in their hair. Lexi's was a yellow print with matching ribbon in her short ponytail and Darlene's was light blue with a white ribbon holding her much longer ponytail. They both had on flops and matching white paint on their nails that looked fresh. It was a great end of the summer evening with the temp in the low 80s and early music from "The Boss" on the radio. Darlene was snuggled up close with my arm around her shoulders and her head nestled on my right pec.

"Damn, this is good shit Lenny boy," Ted said passing the joint to Lexi. "I need a damn beer now. Think you can get me an o-z (ounce) of it?"

"Yea, yea," I said. "But will prob be Monday before I can get it to ya."

"Hell yea," (apparently his go-to phrase) he said. "How much?"

"$45 an ounce," I said.

That year, I usually got a half-pound at a time for $150-175 and broke it up into ounces (4) half's (2) and quarters (12). The prices ranged from O-Zs for $45, half's for $30 and quarters for $20. I could clear between $250-$350 bucks on each "turn" and that included keeping a half for myself and friends. On a good weekend, I'd sell out. It was a lot of money for a kid, and that's not counting the every now and then sell of "ludes" or once or so a summer, a ½ sheet of acid broken into "tabs" or "hits", but ninety-five percent of my business was weed.

Ted nodded in the rearview as Lexi blew him a sideways shotgun. Darlene and I kissed a few times. I slid my hand up her sundress a couple of times. She kept giving me this evil grin that I always loved to see, but either meant "stop that", "not here", or "not now". I think that one meant "not here". The herb was kicking in and I was feeling really free as the wind whipped around the open air car. I had a nice buzz, great friends, the smartest most beautiful girl around, a pocketful of cash, and was going to a my first big high school party. Life was tasty and sweet!

We destroyed our food at the Italian place. Marijuana will do that for ya. Nothing like satisfying a good dose of the munchies. I thought Doritos missed the mark when they didn't open outlet stores next to all the newly legal marijuana dispensaries. I cleaned out a plate of spaghetti and Darlene did the same to some lasagna. No takeout boxes were needed as we loaded up and headed to the party.

We drove to the south end of Knotty Beach and the shindig was at one of the big beachfront houses near the far end of their barrier island. It was quite the gathering. There were tons of people milling around outside. Plenty more on the wrap around porch above and inside. There were cars jammed along both sides of the road. The music was loud. I don't remember exactly what was playing, but it was upbeat party music. We all still had a good buzz as we rolled toward the house.

"Let's see if we can find Ike and see where the booze is," Ted said.

"Uh, back there," I said, pointing to the beachside of the house.

Two guys were holding up another dude upside down over a beer keg. He was doing a "keg stand". That was the first one I'd ever seen and it looked awesome!

"Back there it is," Ted said, and away we went.

Several of our teammates and a bunch of guys from our cross-county rival were trying to outdrink one another. A dozen or so kids were waiting to participate or egg each other on. It appeared the crowd was about split between our school and our county rival with a few of Darlene's classmates hanging out as well.

"Woo-hooo Ted!" a few of our teammates yelled out. "Take a turn, Go Ted Go Ted!"

Well, Ted certainly didn't need any prodding and downed copious amounts of cold brew upside down. We all managed to get a cup of beer and after Ted got his fill, we walked up the back deck stairs to the second level of the three-tier house to try and find Ike, the host. Ted was a bit wobbly.

"This is really fun stuff!" Lexi said as we made the top of the stairs.

"Seems like a cool party," Darlene said, then wagged her right index finger at me. "Best behavior young man."

"I don't know what that is," I laughed and kissed her on the cheek.

Ted spotted some other guys he knew and walked over to them, leaving Lexi with us. Lexi and Darlene looked at one another, one of those girl looks where they're communicating and you have no idea what's going on. When that would happen, I often felt like

Heinlein's alien in "Stranger in a Strange Land" or a foreigner who couldn't speak the language.

"We'll be right back, we're going to find a bathroom," Darlene said.

I just nodded. Man has been perplexed for centuries by this mystery. Why is it girls can never go to the bathroom alone? I think it's one of the last greatest unsolved mysteries, right up there with who killed Kennedy or what happened to the Lost Colony. So, I was just standing there looking around when three or four of my classmates approached. They all had red solo cups with varying amounts of beer.

"Hey Lenny, how's it going?" asked Brigitte, a tall, willowy blonde with legs for days.

"Good, rock'n party," I said.

"Yea, fun," Brigitte, who was on the cheer squad with Lexi, continued. "Ike, here, this is Lenny, the one I was telling you about."

Brigitte, a fellow sophomore, and I had a couple classes together. We'd talked some that week. Ike, a junior who attended the academy, was her on-again-off-again boyfriend of a couple years. Brigitte had been bugging me about coming during our English Lit class Friday.

"Oh, hey man," Ike said. "I know you from, uh, uh, soccer?"

"Yea, we played against each other several times over the years in youth league," I said.

"Yea, I remember," he said. "You're with that Crazy Beach crowd, man you guys play rough."

"Been known to," I smiled. "But you guys beat us a time or two as well."

"You playing for HHH?" he asked.

"Yea, football too," I replied.

"Damn bro, that's a bunch of work," he said. "Hey, Brigitte said you're the new hook-up at school."

"I don't know about that," I said. "But...."

I shrugged my shoulders.

"Oh, I gotcha," he said. "You don't know me and all. Well till ya do, how bout working with Brigitte to help us out?"

I smiled.

"Want to burn one?" I asked.

"Oh yeah!" he said. "Let's go up to my room, c'mon Brigitte, we gotta go talk to Lenny."

Brigitte brought along a girl she was talking to I'd seen at school but hadn't met. We went up a side flight of stairs from the second level leading directly into Ike's room on the third story. It had a cool vibe with lots of rock and surfing posters on the ceiling and a long beach mural with several palm trees painted on the wall behind his bed. His room, along with a bathroom, occupied the entire tiny third floor of the triangle shaped housed. He had his own small beachside deck with a panoramic view of the southern tip of their island. Hendrix was playing on his stereo.

"Lenny this is Emily," Brigitte said.

"Hey," I said.

"Hi," she said. "I've heard a lot about you."

"Don't believe any of it," I said. "Well, maybe right much of it."

Everyone laughed.

Emily had shoulder-length dark hair, green eyes behind John Lennon wire-rim glasses, olive-skin, and was bout the same size as Lexi. She had on cut-off Levi shorts and a black off-the-shoulder silk top. She exuded smarts and confidence, the real kind.

"Well, my brother Vince saw some of it," she said. "He's on your football team. He told me about you almost slamming his Mustang into the field house."

"Wasn't even close," I said laughing. "Well, maybe a little close."

Everyone laughed even harder as I fired up a joint.

"Let's walk out on the deck with that," Ike said.

A decent breeze was coming in off the Atlantic and the party was really rocking all around us below. I looked for Lexi and Darlene but didn't spot them. I found Ted pretty easy, he was doing another keg stand.

"So Brigitte says your all that," Emily said smiling just before blowing me a shotgun.

"All what?" I laughed after accepting her smoke.

She gave me a flirty little look that suggested she knew more about me than she was letting on.

"Well let's see," she continued. "I've heard from about a dozen people how smart you are, Brigitte included. Hmm, a good ballplayer from everyone, a crazy driver from several, main connection from many and….."

She looked me up and down like I was a decent piece of luggage on sale at Sears.

"All that."

I laughed.

"You're too funny," I said. "I love a great sense of humor. What class are you?"

"I'm a junior," she replied. "How old are you?"

"16 next month, sophomore," I said.

"You don't look like no damn sophomore," she said. "I thought you were a junior or senior transfer."

"Well, I guess you haven't heard ALL about me then," I laughed.

"Well, tell me some more," she said.

Ike and Brigitte had started making out in his room. Emily blew me another shotgun and let her fingers linger on my face a bit too long as she finished. She smiled a dirty girl smile. I knew I was in trouble.

"Nah, I want to hear some about you," I said, trying to bring it down a notch. "But let me guess first. You live in Lansdowne, Dad's a lawyer, Mom was prom queen, Italian descent, one sibling Vince, and one yappy dog named after a philosopher. How'd I do?"

"Well," she started, eyeballing me up and down again. "You might be all those other things, but you damn sure aren't a psychic! I live three houses from here, my parents own the Yankee Clipper (fanciest hotel on Knotty Beach), Greek, two siblings, no pets! You suck!"

We both laughed a serious, crazy laugh. Ike and Brigitte were under the covers now and there were several pieces of clothing on the floor. They were attacking one another like mad dogs fighting over a chicken bone.

"Damn!" Emily exclaimed. "I think they're doing it right in front of us."

"Great, a free show!" I said. "Where's the popcorn?"

The sliding glass door was open and Brigitte had mounted Ike and was riding him like her life depended on it. She had one of her silky, deeply-tanned legs on the floor for leverage and was definitely using it to her advantage. She still had her top on, but it was quite a sight nonetheless.

"Wow, now that's going for it!" Emily noted.

I nodded. Emily's breathing was getting a little heavy and I could tell something was about to go down. I didn't want to cheat on Darlene, but there were no deck stairs and I didn't want to just walk right on into Ike's room with them going at it like that. I turned to say something to her and yep, you guessed it, she kissed me right on the lips. I quickly pulled back.

"Hold on," I said. "I want to, but I have a girlfriend, right downstairs, somewhere."

Damn, I thought I would never stop a hot girl from hooking up with me. But I did, first time for everything! I didn't want to, but I did. That was the first time I called Darlene my girlfriend to someone else. Right after being kissed by another girl. Emily laughed.

"Oh, okay lover boy," she said. "Ah, and you're true too, guess you're the real deal. Look me up if you ever get rid of her."

She gazed at me for a moment to see if I might change my mind. Satisfied I was going to just stand there, she turned her very pretty little ass around and walked away. She strolled right past the still copulating Brigitte and Ike who paid her no mind, leaving me to be the lone voyeur.

Track 27-Born Under a Bad Sign-Albert King (3:33)

We found a decent spot near where we'd been Friday afternoon just as Joe Cocker joined the Grease band on stage around two. Mandy acted like she'd lost her mind, her love for Cocker was so intense she went into convulsions like Cocker himself. At one point she whacked Hitch right in the chest with one of her arms. We were in a sea of hippies and melted right in as Cocker blew through a raging set that included the Beatles' "A Little Help From My Friends" and one of my favorites of the weekend, "I Don't Need No Doctor".

As Cocker's set was drawing to a close, a massive series of dark clouds burst open and pelted the dairy farm with torrential rain. We hauled ass back up the bowl to our campsite. The rain was coming down so hard it was knocking down some tents, the girls' included. We all hustled into the VW. We were all grabbing towels, rags, and dry clothes, anything to get rid of the wetness. We all peeled off our shirts and sat there laughing. It was like a funky, hippy sauna. It was one of the best moments of the weekend. The storm lasted a couple hours and we passed the time mostly talking music.

"Man, it's going to be rough out there tonight," Hitch said. "Mud, mud, and more mud."

"Yea, everyone wear your crappiest clothes and no shoes," Leslie suggested. "Whatever you have on tonight, isn't coming back in this van. And we're going to start heading back first thing in the morn if not before, so stay close."

"Hey, Lenny, you and Davey go help the girls get their tent back up," Hitch said.

The storm clouds were still around and it was much darker than any summertime suppertime I ever remember.

"This is kinda creepy," Mandy said. "Don't you guys feel a little weird?"

"It's just weather," I said. "It'll pass."

We noticed about half the crowd left during the storm or shortly thereafter. Putting the tent back up was a chore, it was somewhat water-logged. We struggled to get it set-up right. We finally managed with the help of some other festival-goers. Hitch and Leslie had closed up Henrietta when we got out. Guess they needed some alone time.

They re-emerged and Leslie made sandwiches for us with the last of the bread. The peanut butter also got finished off, as did the Vienna wieners and chips. The last sodas disappeared as well.

"Ok, look," Leslie said as we all finished up. "That's it for the food, till we leave. We might have a couple packs of crackers, but that's about it."

"Yea, our last bit of stuff got soaked," Dani said.

"We'll be fine," Hitch said. "We can roll out after the last act tonight."

We elected to stay kinda near the campsite for a good part of the evening. Mainly because it was drier than anywhere else around. We heard Country Joe, with the Fish this time, crank things back up just as we were finishing our food around six or seven. Ten Years After was next, then The Band rocked it pretty good for about an hour. The Winter Brothers came on next, Johnny was the named act, but Edgar came on and played several tunes with him. By the time they finished it was midnight and Leslie suggested we hit the road. It was her only bad call of the weekend. A ton more folks had departed as well.

"Nah, I want to hear Hendrix," Hitch said. "Let's wait a bit and see if he is up soon."

A prolonged, rather heated discussion ensued with Hitch prevailing for one of the few times I can remember. While those acts played, most of our crowd sat in Henrietta's side doorway or on logs by the fire. Hitch had a hard time getting it lit but finally managed about halfway through an Alvin Lee solo. I walked around the campsite mostly, a little restless. Davey slept a couple hours in the back of the VW. Mandy and Dani talked to some boys who'd been regular visitors to our campsite.

"Who wants to go down closer?" Hitch asked as Sunday turned to Monday.

Everyone was up for it except a still-seething Leslie who remained behind. We only went down a hundred yards or so as the mud made movement a risky endeavor. The bowl was only about 1/3 as full as it was at peak attendance. Mandy slipped and fell. Davey and I tried to help her up, but only managed to bust our asses too. The three of us looked like mud monsters and Hitch and Dani got splashed and covered as well.

We heard great sets from Blood, Sweat, and Tears, who absolutely crushed "Spinning Wheel" and a new group who were making only their second public appearance, Crosby, Stills, Nash, and Young.

"We're scared shitless man!" Stephen Stills famously said from the stage.

One of the first super-groups played an acoustic set and an electric set with the highlight for me being "Find the Cost of Freedom".

"Want to get a little closer?" Hitch said as Monday's dawn began to make an appearance.

He didn't wait for our answer and we all got within about 50 yards of the stage. It was the closest we had been since Thursday at sunset.

The Paul Butterfield Blues Band greeted the sunrise with a blistering take on Albert King's "Born Under a Bad Sign." It was my favorite song performance of the weekend. Up to that point I'd little awareness of the blues. My minimal education was that almost all the major British Invasion bands made sure to make it known they were influenced by the blues. After Paul Butterfield, I was hooked on the blues. If you walk into my house today, you'll certainly hear some blues in my music rotation pretty quick. I made it one of my life's goals to become immersed in the blues. There's a giant checkmark by that objective.

A fun, goofy, 1950s throwback act, Sha Na Na, took the remaining crowd, which historians indicate had dropped under

100,000 (or about 20% of estimated peak attendance) through a medley of classic doo-wop and 50's hits including "The Duke of Earl". The group was one of the first "nostalgia acts" so prevalent today as "tribute bands". They also opened the door for the 1950s to become cool again, helping lead to movies like "American Graffiti" and TV shows like "Happy Days" and "Laverne and Shirley". They even had their own variety show on TV for awhile.

A sleepy-eyed Leslie re-appeared near the end of Sha Na Na's set. She had her camera with her. She'd taken a few photos the day before as well.

"Don't you think we should start heading back?" she asked Hitch.

Davey was asleep on a mud-soaked blanket that had been left behind.

"Waited this long for Hendrix," Hitch said. "Glad you brought the camera, let's get a shot of the infamous Woodstock Six."

He asked a guy near us to snap some photos. We tried to wake Davey up, but he was out cold. So the staged shot has us, arms around one another's shoulders and waists all smiles with Davey out cold on the mud blanket below. We got lots more pics of one another in smaller groups and later, of our camping spot and Henrietta.

Just as Davey was beginning to wake up, the crowd began a low rumble. We all turned to face the stage and there he was, the man, the myth, the legend-to-be, Jimi Hendrix. We instinctively moved closer to the stage along with the estimated 80,000 other folks still there. We got to within about 30 yards. In one of my favorite photos ever, Leslie told Davey and me to face the camera (backs to the stage) and she took a couple of shots with Hendrix playing in the background. We were covered in mud, dirty all over, but our teeth shone like the first snow of winter. Two Crazy Beach boys at Woodstock, in a photo with Jimi playing away behind us. The National Anthem never sounded so good!

Track 28-(It's So) Nice to Be With You-(The) Gallery (2:21)

Well, I watched Brigitte do the reverse cowgirl for a bit. She finally dismounted and headed to the bathroom. I took the opportunity to head back inside.

"Later Ike," I said.

"Yea, thanks for the buzz man," he said. "Don't make too much of that Emily man, she's probably already out on the beach with somebody else. She has an appetite for boners."

I was at once relieved and deflated. Plus, I'd no idea he (and Brigitte?) even noticed. I bounded down the stairs to the living room and began looking for my people. The party was at its zenith by this time with people all over the house, the decks, on the dunes, and around both sides of the house. I walked out to the edge of the dunes, looked all around both decks, and then did a complete circle around the house. It took me awhile as people were talking to me, asking me questions, and general party banter over and over. I just wanted to find Darlene.

"Hey Lenny, what's going on?" it was Donnie.

"Not much Donnie," I said. "You seen Darlene, Lexi, or Ted?"

"Yea, yea," he quickly responded. "They're having a three-way in the surf!"

Donnie was blitzed and his usual good-natured X-rated banter was a bit much.

"Man, I'm serious Donnie," I said. "I haven't seen them in a while."

"Nah, man, nah," he said. "I haven't, but if they are with Ted, you never know."

He slapped me on the back.

"Got any ganga?" he asked.

I just shook my head no and continued my safari in the wilds of Partyland. After two conversations about dope, one about sports, and two about surfing, I'd made my way back around to the keg. I poured myself a fresh red solo cup full and drank about half of it down in one gulp and refilled the cup. I was starting to get a little concerned. Then I thought to maybe check back at the car.

I strolled back around to the front of the house without too many stoppages and looked down the street to where we'd left the car. There was a pile of people around it. I quickly walked in that direction and spotted Darlene and Lexi sitting on the trunk surrounded by guys. Ted was nowhere to be found.

"Hey y'all," I said.

"Hey Lenny," Darlene said. "Where the heck did you get off to?"

"Burned one with Ike and them," I said. "Thought I lost you again."

"Oh," she laughed a little. "That's like the eighth time we've lost each other when we're supposed to be together."

She then introduced me to some of our cross-town rivals and her schoolmates. After grunted exchanges, I got a little closer to Darlene.

"Where's Ted?" I asked.

"Passed out in the backseat," a drunken Lexi offered.

"Shit," I said.

"Yep," Darlene continued. "He kept doing keg stand after keg stand."

"Yea, yea," Lexi slurred. "He won the drinking contest for our school!"

"All hail the victor," Darlene said.

Everybody laughed, except Lexi.

"That's cold," Lexi said.

At that moment Ted flung open the driver's side back door and puked on the roadway.

"And that's warm," Darlene said sliding down off the trunk.

Lexi jumped down, her dress flying everywhere and went to tend to the drinking champion. It was the first time I'd seen a girl holding back the hair of a dude. Not a pretty sight.

"I'd like a mixed drink," Darlene said, taking my hand and leading me toward the house. "You know he's not going to be able to drive us home right?"

I nodded in the affirmative.

"We can't leave Lexi here either," she continued. "I'm not driving this tank and I'm not going to let you cause you've been drinking. I can smell it. I don't want you to lose your license before you even have them."

I nodded again. I had a very smart girlfriend. And beautiful, oh praise Elvis! How beautiful!

"Call Hal and see if he can come get us," she basically ordered.

I nodded again. I take it you've figured out I always nodded a lot. Mostly when Darlene or anyone wanted me to agree with them. I hate conflict. I would just nod unless something went against my principles.

"Why don't we see if there is someone here headed back our way?" I asked.

"I already thought of that Einstein," she said. "There's nobody here from our island but us and Donnie and he's stumbling drunk, hell there's no one even here from the entire south side but us."

We went in the front door and I quickly found the phone. Darlene went to make a drink. Thankfully, Hal answered the phone. His mom would talk you to death.

"No worries man," he said. "But Lenny, I'm going to need some gas money, I'm busted."

"I gotcha man," I said.

"Ok, ok," he said. "On the way, see you in about 30 or 40."

"What did he say?" Darlene asked.

"He's on the way," I said. "Good ol' Hal."

"Let's go on the beach," Darlene said. "It'll probably take him an hour to get here in that old junk pile."

"That junk pile is our rescue ship," I laughed.

"I know, right?" Darlene laughed too.

We sat on the beach and watched the tide come in. We didn't say much, just watched. There was a slight breeze, just enough to move Darlene's ponytail a bit. I put my hand up to hold it and she turned to look at me.

"I think I'd rather hang out just you and me," she said.

"One hundred percent," I chuckled.

We made out for a few minutes and just as things were starting to heat up, yep you guessed it, Emily and one of my soccer teammates, Anson, stopped right in front of us.

"Hey Lenny, sorry to bust in on ya man," Anson said. "But you got any weed I can get from ya?"

"Nah," I said. "Out till tomorrow."

"Oh, ok," he said. "Me and Emily are rolling your way then, ok if I snag some?"

Well, Ike was right, she was a fast worker.

"Sure, sure," I said. "I'll be at the shop till four, prob on the boardwalk after that."

"That'll be cool," he said.

I introduced Darlene to them as we got up off the sand.

The ladies eyed one another like girls do when they first meet. I always thought it resembles two gunfighters stepping into the street at sunrise. I hear music from "The Good, The Bad, and The Ugly" play when it occurs … wowwowwow…

"We gotta get back," I said. "One of our buds is coming to pick us up."

"Cool" Anson said. "Next time you need a ride, let me know. We'll see you tomorrow."

We walked back straight over the dunes, avoiding the masses at the party. Just as we reached the car-lined street, Hal pulled up in the old Scout. For some reason, Hal had his sunglasses on.

"Your carriage awaits my king and queen," he shouted over the Scout's rumbling engine, dipping his shades for emphasis.

"Thanks for rolling this way man," I said.

"We really appreciate it," Darlene said. "Let me go grab Lexi."

"Her dude pass out or what?" Hal asked.

"Yea, puke city over there," I said pointing to Ted's ride.

"Here, I brought ya a beer," Hal said. "Figured you might need one."

"10-4 on that," I said laughing.

I jumped into the back seat as Lexi and Darlene approached on the passenger side.

"I hate to just leave him like that," slurring Lexi said. "You sure he's going to be ok."

"Yea, he's just shitfaced," I said. "And we got to get you girls back home before this thing turns into a pumpkin."

"Woof, woof," Bluto awoke from a slumber behind us.

"Do you go anywhere without that damn dog?" Lexi asked.

"School, that's about it," Hal laughed.

The ride back to our little island was fun. The Scout was great for evening cruises, though at stoplights the exhaust could get ya. The night air blasted us as we tore down the really empty back road that ran parallel to the Intracoastal Waterway, Hal taking us home through a mostly undeveloped part of the county. We heard tunes like "Radar Love," "I'm 18," and "Blackwater" as we barreled past forests, creeks, and the lone house or two.

We pulled into a convenience store at the convergence of the loop road and the main roadway to the island, just a mile or so from the bridge. We stopped to get some gas. The girls had to use the bathroom, Bluto did too.

"Think I should go for it with Lexi tonight?" Hal asked.

"Yea, sure," I said. "If what you're going for is a smack in the face. She's really into that Ted dude."

"Are they banging?" he asked.

"I don't know," I lied.

"Yea, I bet she's giving him that good stuff, him being a senior and all," he continued as we waited with Bluto as he finished up behind the store. "Hey, they took down the Plantation Acres sign over there. Heard it got sold, going to build a development or some shit. Man, we've had some fun there, hate it's the end of the old girl."

"Yea, my aunt Pat told me," I said. "They gotta move. All that sucks."

Plantation Acres was a thickly-wooded campground along the waterway about halfway between the store and the bridge. My aunt Pat and Uncle Ed had managed the property since 1968 and lived on-site in a trailer. I'd a lot of fun there over the years. Darlene and I'd one of our best adventures there the summer before, right after eighth grade.

We'd been hanging out with two of my half-uncles (wait till you hear more about mom's side of the family in CBII) from out-of-town, who were down for the summer working. One was just a year older than me and one the same age. They wanted to go swimming in the pool at the campground. They talked Darlene and me into hitching a ride to the campground with them. They figured the sight of Darlene in a bathing suit would guarantee them a quick ride. We were toward the north end of the island already. We'd walked with them to get the older one, Trick's, paycheck from the Mermaid restaurant. My maternal grandfather was the chef that year.

"What if somebody we know sees us?" then 14.75-year old Darlene said. "My dad will kill all of you and then me!"

"Don't worry about it," Rich, the younger, said. "The first dudes come by will give us a ride, we won't be out here two minutes."

And sure enough, he was right. With Darlene standing in the front by Bud & Joe's Bar, in a one-piece black bathing suit, and the three of us behind her, the first vehicle spotted her stopped. It was a like-new, light blue, street-legal dune buggy. Trouble was, it only had four seats, so Darlene sat in my lap up front. I know, I know, some of you are cringing at the thought of a 14-year old girl hitchhiking with three boys and getting in a seatbelt-less dune buggy, but lots of young people hitched back then and no one wore seatbelts, not even the guy that invented them.

The wind blew Darlene's hair all over me, so I didn't see much of the very quick two or three-mile ride to the campground. Our driver was a curly-haired shirtless guy, with cut-off jeans who looked to be in his late 20s. Pink Floyd's "Dark Side of the Moon" cast the perfect spell from the radio.

Trick and Rich carried on most of the conversation with the driver. I just enjoyed Darlene sitting in my lap. She leaned hard against me with her left arm draped around my right shoulder and neck. Her left breast continually brushed against my right cheek and her face looked so beautiful. I held her tight with my right arm around her waist and my left on her left thigh. It was six or seven of the best minutes of my life.

"You guys ready?" Darlene yelled from the side of the convenience store.

"Yea, yea," I yelled back. "On the way."

Track 29-Homeward Bound-Simon and Garfunkel (2:42)

Leslie made us all hit the pond after Hendrix. There were still thousands of people milling about and some areas were pretty messy with litter, old blankets, and collapsed tents. The pond was pretty refreshing, but most kept their bottoms on this time around, though there were a few naked folks bathing. Dani and Mandy went topless and that was a great farewell to Woodstock treat!

"Let's get rolling," Leslie said as we all emerged from the water at about the same time.

I was down to my last pair of shorts. I had no clean shirts left and of course, was still barefooted. I looked like a little hillbilly hippy. The final walk back up the bowl was pretty much done in silence as everyone was dog tired or just taking it all in. We reached Henrietta and began clearing our campsite and packing up for the trip home. We tried to clean our area up as much as possible.

"We'll drop the girls off at the farmhouse," Hitch said.

"Thanks, that'd be great," Dani said. "Lenny, will you help me with our tent?"

"Sure, sure," I said.

Davey was already asleep in the back of the VW and Mandy was loading the girls' bags.

"Hey man, you got any food left?"

No shit, it was bathrobe guy, his pregnant ol'lady and rotund guy.

"For the little lady, we got quite a walk to try and find our car, we left it out beside the Thruway."

"Anybody want this crap?" Leslie asked, holding up our last can of spam.

No one answered save a few negative nods. Leslie gave it to the pregnant girl. She looked at it like it was lobster.

"Thank you," she said. "I hope you have a safe ride back home."

"Come on," Hitch said. "We'll take you guys up to the road."

Those three acted like Hitch told them they won the lottery. It was going to be a tight squeeze for sure. Guess she didn't give birth during the festival after all. Dani and I got the tent strapped to the top of Henrietta and were the last ones inside. Davey was splayed out where we had first snoozed what seemed like a lifetime ago. Mandy was in the middle section with the pregnant girl, her hubby and rotund dude taking up the floor space.

I headed to the back. Instead of plopping down in the small space Mandy had saved for her best friend, Dani followed me to the back and sat right in my lap. I was pleasantly surprised. Parts of me were really pleasantly surprised. She just smiled real big, raised her eyebrows, draped her right arm over my shoulders, and wiggled her cute little butt a few times. The ride up to Mr. Max's farmhouse only took a few minutes but we made the most of it. Dani got a pen from Leslie (who always had everything) and we exchanged numbers and addresses. It was a dream lap ride (my first almost lap dance?) for an 11-year old boy. Hitch's booming voice saved me (killed me) from messing up my last pair of shorts.

"Next stop, Yasgur Farms" Hitch said. "With connections to Monticello, Cleveland, and wherever that sweet robe hails from!"

Henrietta came to a stop in the main driveway of Yasgur Dairy Farm. A U.S. Mail truck sat idling by the mailbox. A tall man who looked like a young Tom Selleck in a postal service uniform was smoking a cigarette nearby.

"Oh wow, Dad's already here," Dani said.

"Boy, I'm glad to see him," Mandy said.

Hitch and I retrieved the girls' tent and Leslie and the girls started on their good-byes. Our new hitchhikers thanked us again and began walking east in search of their car. Maybe she gave birth between there and the car or in the car? It would be cool to have a connection to the legendary Woodstock baby (if there really was one born at or near Yasgur's farm).

"How all of you doing?" Dani's dad asked. "You ok honey?"

The girls reassured him all was well and they'd a blast. They introduced him to each of us and Dani quickly explained Mandy's situation.

"That's fine honey, we'll make arrangements for her to get home," he said smiling. "You girls are going to have to ride along for a bit before I can drop you off at the house. Well, I need to get to the rest of my route. Thanks for watching out for them."

He got into the postal truck with the tent. Mandy tossed her bag inside and jumped in. She paused in the doorway.

"Bye," she loudly proclaimed with a big smile. "Thank you so much and I'll never forget any of you, this weekend, and all the fun we had!"

"It went so quick," Dani said. "Thanks Hitch and Leslie, you really saved us."

"Glad to have met you kid," Hitch said. "Have a great life!"

"Bye Dani," Leslie said, misting up a little. "Thank you for helping me with that little fool."

"My pleasure," she said grabbing my cheeks with both hands. "Bye Lenny, you better write me."

"I will," I declared. "Bye Dani."

"Bye Lenny, take care," she said as she kissed me on the forehead. "Call me when you can. This better not be goodbye!"

She tossed her bag in and started to get in the truck. I ran over to her and gave her a quick bear hug. I probably squeezed way too hard.

"It won't be I promise," I said.

I watched as the mail truck rolled away in the opposite direction we were headed.

"Ok, Lenny, move it," Leslie said. "Long ride home."

Track 30-The Rain Song-Led Zeppelin (7:39)

I made my "connection" with Dutch on Labor Day Sunday and had a steady stream of customers, old ones, new ones, and a couple of surprising ones. I was standing on the pier after work. I thought I'd most of the deals done for the day. I was about to head home thinking I'd been stood up by my last scheduled customer. As I turned to head home, Darlene and Lexi exited the pier house.

"Hey girls," I started. "What's up?"

"Came to see you, big boy," Lexi laughed.

"That so," I said. "And why might that be?"

Darlene came over and gave me a kiss on the cheek.

"I need to get some herb," Darlene said.

"Sure no worries," I said. "Hey Lexi, how's Ted feeling today? "

"He's ok, embarrassed, but ok," she said. "He said to tell you he's sorry for not being able to get us home."

"No problem," I said, turning my gaze from Lexi to Darlene.

"You know where my personal stash is at the house, just grab some for y'all. I'm waiting for one more friend."

"No, no, not for us," Darlene said. "I need to buy some for my mom, she's not getting better and is hurting so bad, she won't tell anyone, especially my dad."

"Ok, ok, if it will help, sure," I said. "Just take it out of my stash, no charge."

"No," Darlene said firmly. "She doesn't know where I'm getting it from, she wants to pay."

She tried to hand me a $20 bill.

"Nope, not taking it," I said. "Take a quarter bag from my stash and you better not leave any money or I'll be pissed!"

"You're a stubborn ass," Darlene said smiling.

"Yep," I said.

"But I do love you so," she said.

"Good thing," I said. "Because I'm kinda fond of you."

She gave me a hug and a kiss on the lips.

"See you later tonight, after supper?" she asked.

I nodded yes.

Lexi came over and hugged me too. The only time she ever did when we were kids. She quickly whispered in my ear.

"You better love her right."

Darlene gave me our little half-wave and I returned the gesture.

"Bye girls," I said.

No sooner had they walked out of sight into the pier house, but who wandered out? Ahh, don't know if you guessed this one…..I'll give you a sec…..no cheating now… did you say Eggs? I didn't think so. I wouldn't have either. He wasn't the friend I was waiting on. That friend never showed. There Eggs was, even more ragged and confused than usual.

"Mumble, mumble, raff, snaff," he said.

"Hey Eggs," I said. "You ok?"

"Rumble, grumble, raff," he said.

"Oh," I said. "Something I can do?"

I thought he might need a dollar or something. He pulled a five dollar bill out of his filthy overalls and shoved it in my hand. It was pretty greasy.

"Thank you Eggs," I said. "But, I'm ok I have some money."

I tried to hand the slick Lincoln back to him. He wouldn't take it, so I shoved it in his breast pocket. He raised his right hand to his mouth and made a smoking motion.

"You want me to buy you some cigarettes?" I asked.

He violently shook his head no. I was afraid he was going to hurt himself. He made the smoking motion again, but with a long inhale motion.

"You want a joint?" I asked.

He held up two fingers.

"You want two joints?" I asked.

He shook his head yes. I was becoming the best speaker of the Eggs' language on the planet.

"Ok, ok," I said. "I only have one rolled up right now. I'll have to go to the bathroom and roll another one for ya, you wait here."

He started to follow me.

"No Eggs, wait right here," I said. "I'll be back in five minutes, I promise."

He shook his head yes and I hustled into the bathroom, rolled a couple real quick and headed back out. You're probably wondering about me standing around on the pier with herb like that. First of all, I never carried much out there at a time (I hid the bulk in the bathroom vent and would return as needed) and if the coppers had tried to bust me, I would've just let the grass fly out onto the seven seas. The kids that worked behind the counter were all my pals and got free goodies for keeping an eye out. Getting nabbed by the coppers for drugs never happened, but that was my plan, I always tried to have a plan. Many times they weren't worth a crap, failed, or got me in trouble, but I thought that was a good one.

"Here ya go Eggs," I said. "Be careful where you smoke them, don't want Dad to come have to bail you out again."

He shoved the five back into my hand and nodded his head yes. His eyes looked softer than usual. He put the joints in his overall's breast pocket. I shook my head no and motioned for him to take the joints (they were sticking up in plain sight) and put them in his waist pocket. He complied and walked away.

As you know by now, marijuana is great for helping people address a wide variety of ailments, especially pain, some eating disorders, and glaucoma. I think my last two transactions that day helped ease the pain of a couple of people, at least, maybe more. They remain my favorite drug-related deals.

"Darlene's on the phone for you son," my mom said from the kitchen.

I was out on the street side deck cleaning up one of mom's plants the wind or a drunken relative had knocked over. I was a little surprised it was Darlene calling, it had only been an hour since I saw her on the pier.

"Hey," I said. "You already had supper? We haven't."

"Good," she said her voice a little excited. "Mom wants you to come eat with us. It'll just be us three, Lexi's going out with her folks and our dads are in a poker tournament at the VFW."

Once again she knew where my dad was as much as me and more so the last couple of years. I had no idea. I thought he was at work, the car was gone.

"Hang on," I said. "Let me check with mom and make sure she doesn't have something special planned. Mom, ok if I eat at Darlene's?"

Mom nodded yes.

"All clear," I said. "What's the occasion?"

"Mom just wanted you to come over," she said. "She's making your favorite, spaghetti."

"Oh wow," I said. "That's awesome. What time?"

"Dinner served in 30 minutes you beach bum," she said. "Don't be late."

"I won't," I said.

I took a quick shower, threw on my favorite Duke t-shirt, kissed Mom, and jumped on my bike for the ride over. I had my learner's permit but didn't dare take my car, even if it was just a half-mile to her house. For one, my dad would've killed me, for two, my mom would've had a heart attack, and for three, no not the coppers, see number one.

"Hey gorgeous," I said giving Darlene a peek on the cheek as I entered.

"You smell good, go on over to the table," Darlene started, giving me a little shove. "Mom's bringing the food out now."

"No, it smells good in here!" I exclaimed. "You guys move an Italian restaurant in here or something?"

The Winter's home was always very neat as befits a military family. A WWII-era frame house, tastefully decorated with patriotic themes showcasing Mr. Winter's military career, Ms. Winter's athletic and academic achievements, and Darlene's school awards. There were lots of family photos and no pets since Connor's death.

"Well, here we go," said Ms. Winter as she placed a big bowl of noodles on the table.

The steaming sauce was already on the table with a giant ladle sticking out of a crescent-shaped bowl. Darlene had yet to make eye contact with me, which I thought was pretty weird.

"I hope you like it Lenny," Ms. Winter said. "I haven't made any in a really long time."

"I'm sure I will Ms. Winter," I said. "And thank you for having Darlene invite me over."

"Yes, oh my yes," she said taking a seat at the head of the somewhat large for the room, eight-seat solid oak table.

"I wish you'd come over more often," she said. "Like you did when you and Darlene were just little sixth and seventh graders."

"Mom!" Darlene said. "You're embarrassing us!"

"Oh hush Darlene," Ms. Winter said. "It's hard to believe that this is the fourth summer since you met one another."

I filled my plate with a heaping pile of noodles and drenched them in sauce. This was the first time I'd got to eat Ms. Winter's great cooking in over a year.

"So how's high school?" Ms. Winter asked. "I wish Charley would have just let Darlene go to school where you are. I know you would've looked after her."

"Mom, I don't need looking after," Darlene said, yet to put any food on her plate and yet to look me in the eye.

"You know what I mean sweetie," Ms. Winter said. "It's just, it's just….her voice trailed off.

"Darlene, you get yourself some food right now," Ms. Winter ordered her only child, pointing to the noodle bowl.

Darlene obeyed and we all ate a few bites before Ms. Winter asked a round of questions about my family. She talked about how she missed seeing all of us. She said her health had just not allowed her to do much.

"Mom, can we finish dinner first?" Darlene said. "Please?"

"Of course," Ms. Winter said.

A few minutes later I was up for another plate, but sensing that the meal wasn't the only reason I was there, I placed my linen napkin over my plate and asked to be excused. I could hear their voices in conversation as I made my way down the hall. I couldn't quite make out the subject matter.

When I returned, the table was cleared and Ms. Winter was sitting in her favorite burnt orange recliner. Darlene was sitting in the middle of the black leather couch, leaving an obvious spot for me between her and her mother. Ms. Winter was smiling the smile you see from authority figures when you know you're in trouble, or they're about to burst your bubble about something. Darlene's head was down.

"Sit Lenny, sit, please," Ms. Winter said.

I did as directed like a dutiful pet. Were Darlene and I about to get THE sex talk? Darlene looked up and at me for the first time. She gave me the exact same smile and placed her right hand on my left knee. I raised my eyebrows at her, questioning what was about to go down. She just squeezed my knee a little harder and looked back down. I turned to face Ms. Winter.

"First of all, Lenny," she began. "I want you to know how happy I am that our families have been close for all these years. It brings me a lot of joy to see Darlene so happy most of the time. I know you play a large part in that."

Another even harder squeeze from Darlene. Much more and I was going to have a sore knee. My heart began to race a bit, my mind was already speeding.

"But you see Lenny, you know I've been very sick," she said. "The doctors just haven't been able to do much to help me. Well, the fact is, the fact is, I'm dying."

Dagger!

Darlene put her head on my shoulder. I put my arm around her and pulled her even closer. She buried her face in my shirt.

"The doctors say six months or less, but if I get some special treatments several times a week, a bit longer" she continued. "But to get the treatments, I have to be in Durham at Duke and will be too weak to travel."

Darlene started to cry. Dagger number two. I was crestfallen.

I was a bit misty already myself. Ms. Winter was handling it all in line with her very Nordic heritage, stoic, and matter-of-fact. I was trying to keep it together for Darlene, who I later learned had just found out herself in the moments just after she called me. Darlene also said her mother wanted me there for her right after she was told. I was still holding Darlene around her shoulder, her face now in my chest, sobbing. You ever live a moment you can't get out of (kinda like the U2 song and video)? That was and is, the moment I can't get out of...

"Charley's telling your father tonight as well," she continued. "And it's fine if you let your mother know. I'm going to miss all of you."

She was talking like she was already dead.

"The treatments may extend my life another year or so," she said. "But as I said, we're going to have to be in Durham."

Then it hit me, you know how sometimes when you kinda guess what's coming next, you don't really let yourself believe it, but you know it's coming anyway. That's where I was right then. I guess I blanked out for a sec.

"Lenny, do you understand?" Ms. Winter asked.

"Yes Mam," I said. "You're very sick and have to get some special treatments at Duke."

"Partly," she said matter-of-factly. "Lenny, I'm dying before you two graduate. Darlene, her father, and I have to move to Durham right away."

Dagger number three, masterstroke.

I just nodded, Darlene was still sobbing. Darlene's very proud mother did her best to stand erect, passed Darlene a box of tissues, and laboriously walked to her bedroom. It was a slow, agonizing walk. It was the last time I'd ever see her stand.

"Good night Lenny," she said. "I'll see you again before we go, please stay as long as you like."

She was leaning against her doorframe. She gave a small downturned smile in her daughter's direction. I was too stunned to say or do anything, except hold Darlene.

Track 31-The Letter-Joe Cocker (2:35)

"Jane, will you please get the table set?" Mom asked little Sis.

My sister hustled to the kitchen and began gathering the necessary stuff. Skinny, bowl-cut brown bangs, glasses with a goofy smile, and a personality capable of melting the Grinch's heart, lil'sis was the apple of my mother's eye. Jane always loved helping Mom around the house and fishing with Dad, and good thing, cause as you know, I damn sure wasn't going fishing.

"Anika you want wine?" my mom asked Darlene's mom.

It was the start of the Winter family's second summer at the beach. Darlene and I'd just completed seventh grade. We'd been hanging out more and more.

"That would be great Ginny," Ms. Winter replied. "Here Jane let me help you with that."

"Lenny, tell your father and Charley supper's ready," Mom said to me, as Darlene and I played checkers at the bar.

I hopped off the stool and went out to the beachside deck and called the men for supper. The sky out over the ocean was pretty ominous looking. You could see heavy rains on the far horizon.

"Grab Charley and me another beer," Dad said as they began to make their way inside.

"Looks like that monster storm is heading our way," Mr. Winter said eyes fixated eastward.

"Three days in a row," my dad responded. "Haven't seen it like that before."

The rains, thunder, and lightning would come during supper, a heaving drenching eastern systems sometimes produce. It was strong enough to knock the power out as we were finishing up, the second time in three days the electricity had been k'od by Mother Nature. It wasn't quite dark so there was no need for candles yet.

"How about some Monopoly?" my mom asked as she whisked away empty plates and leftovers.

"That would be fun," Ms. Winter said. "Don't you think Charley?"

"Yea, ok," Mr. Winter responded. "I'll whip you guys like I did when we came over for the first time last summer."

"That'll be the day," my dad said using the old John Wayne line from the John Ford film "The Searchers" (that Buddy Holly used for his massive hit song).

Everyone laughed. My sister already had the game out from under the couch and on the table before anything else was said. She was just about to start setting it up.

"You kids wash up a bit," my mom said. "Anika you be the banker, I think Lenny may have helped the fellas a bit last year when he was the banker."

"No way," I protested while waiting my turn at the bathroom door.

"Charley, next month why don't we cookout for our turn," Ms. Winter said.

"Burgers and dogs or steaks?" he asked.

"Let's do burgers and dogs on the fourth and we can watch the fireworks after," Ms. Winter replied.

I didn't hear the rest of the answer as the girls clamored out of the bathroom talking loudly. By the time I returned, the game was on. Dad and Charley on the beachside of the table and the ladies on the other, lil'sis was at the end by Mom and her room. Darlene and I squeezed together in one chair on the other end nearest my room.

Darlene always had the prettiest smile, much like her mom's which was still bright and radiant that summer. It would be at their house during the cookout when she took her first turn for the worse. At this point, you couldn't tell a madly progressive debilitating disease was tearing her down piece by piece.

"I'll buy it," lil'sis yelled when she landed on Boardwalk.

She loved to get Boardwalk and Park Place. I favored the railroads, the red properties, (Illinois, Kentucky, and Indiana) and one of the cheapo packages after the GO! space. The game was fun and I always enjoyed being so close to Darlene. She had on little terrycloth red shorts and a spaghetti strap black tank top. She was already nice and tanned and it was hard not to stare.

"Ok, no whispering you two," Ms. Winter said to us as Darlene pulled back from my ear. "You two are ganging up on us."

Everyone laughed. Actually, Darlene was trying to get me to throw the game so we could go to my room and listen to music. As much as I wanted to, I was such a competitive little shit, I found it hard to take a dive. But I did, as much as you can with the luck of the dice and without being too obvious.

Darlene went out first simply by not buying any property. Her mom gave her a quizzed look when she turned down, for the second time, an opportunity to buy one of the green ones.

"Phooey," Darlene said, doing her best acting job as she hit her dad's hotel on Atlantic. "That wipes me out."

"You should have stayed in jail instead of paying your way out young lady," her dad told her.

It took me a few turns of really poor decisions and a roll of snake eyes to bust out, but I managed.

"Ha-ha, I beat you," lil'sis said. "First time ever!"

Darlene was smiling a little too big as I mortgaged off my properties to pay lil'sis after hitting her Park Place and Boardwalk hotels back-to-back. I was trying to act upset. I don't think my dad was buying it.

"Sixth place?" my dad began. "You know…."

He stopped mid-sentence and just half-smiled at me.

"May we be excused?" Darlene looked at her mother.

I thought it was a little quick, but it worked. Also, our quick loss wasn't without consequences.

"The dishes," my dad intoned. "Losers do the dishes."

A full smile this time from G.R. That was a game night rule, first two out do the cleaning up. Darlene and I didn't mind. We playfully did the chore all the while bumping each other with our hips and legs. The bar kept us mostly hidden from the waist down from the view of our dads. Then the power came back on!

"All finished," I said. "May we listen to some music in my room?"

"If it's ok with Darlene's folks," my mom said looking at Darlene's parents.

Ms. Winter nodded yes after glancing at Mr. Winter. We walked (I wanted to run) very briskly to my room. I started to close the door.

"Leave the door open son," my dad yelled.

I figured as much, but you can't fault a boy for trying. I'd thought many times about Darlene and I being in this situation. Now it was here. She'd seen my room before, but this was the first time we got to be alone for more than a few seconds in my sanctuary. The rain danced on the windows.

"Let me pick?" Darlene asked.

I nodded.

"Let me see," Darlene said, pouring over my albums and eight-tracks.

"Where are your 45's?" she asked.

"Behind the albums," I said. "Right below that picture of us on the beach."

I kept my albums in a wooden crate used for shipping fruits and vegetables. The crates are still around, people use them for planters now. The eight-tracks were stacked in alphabetical order by band name atop my most prized possession, a Teledyne Packard-Bell receiver and eight-track player I'd received for my 11th birthday a few weeks after coming home from Woodstock. Darlene was on both knees with her back and the soles of her feet facing me. Her hair was cascading down her back in golden waves to the bottom of her shoulder blades. I decided right then she was perfect.

"Oh crap," she said over her shoulder. "You have the new Stones' album!"

She didn't ask, she just pulled the Rolling Stones' "Exile on Main Street" from the crate and placed one disc on the turntable beside the eight-track player. I wouldn't suspend it from the ceiling until the next fall when I read an article in Creem magazine. Darlene helped me with the project. She was great at that kinda stuff.

"It's already number one!" she said triumphantly of her favorite band's opus.

"Yea, it really kills," I said.

Keith Richard's soon to be classic "Happy" (first track, side three) began just as Darlene turned around. She sprang to her feet grabbing one of my trophies and using it as a mike, began singing. She rhythmically swayed her hips.

"I need a love to make me happy…baby (pointing at me)…baby want you make me happy…"

"Turn it down son!" my dad yelled from the table.

Darlene laughed and turned it down.

"Sorry," I said.

We both laughed some more. She always had a way to take the tension out of any situation. She saved me many times from what I'm sure would've been a few ass whippings, with maybe a win or two thrown in as well.

She came over and sat down on the bed beside me, our bare legs touching. We studied the album carefully, discussing the cover, the liner notes, even the vinyl itself. Hey, if you've never owned an album, if you've never bought an album, go buy one, order one, or steal one! You don't need a turntable, do it for the art. Or just because albums are super cool, always have been, always will be.

The act of listening to music is much more encompassing when you have something to hold and read. The album itself was art, with tons of info and other goodies. You can try and dissect every word looking for hidden meaning, and the intent of the band/artist/designer. For us, it was a whole book, hell it was a whole encyclopedia. It was a huge part of our world.

After careful study, we decided this was the greatest album ever. Darlene said she was going to marry either Keith or Mick unless I proposed right away. I said I'd be glad to be her clipboard holder in case Keith or Mick didn't come through.

You know who the clipboard holder is, right? The poor third-string quarterback (QB) for an NFL team who never gets to play unless simultaneous lightning strikes, toasting both the starting QB AND his back-up, the second string dude. The poor sap just stands on the sidelines clutching a clipboard (a Microsoft Surface Pro nowadays, I guess?), charting some statistical crap. I've held a few clipboards and had many clipboard holders in my time, but those are tales for other days.

"This summer has started so great!" Darlene said. "You got a job right?"

"Yea, I am working for Carlos, washing dishes at a couple of places, the Corner, beside The Landmark, and the Blue Marlin, across from the raft rental place. I got a few regular yards to mow too."

"I wish I could babysit some," she said. "But we don't really know anyone with little kids around here."

Come to think of it, there weren't many little (ages 2-6) kids around. Maybe we just weren't paying close enough attention. Darlene did notice some letters laying on my desk.

"You have a new pen pal?" she asked.

"Nah," I said. "Same one, it's from Dani, that girl I met at Woodstock."

"Oh," Darlene said. "Does she write very often?"

"Sometimes," I said. "That's the second one this month, but she also goes a long time and doesn't write at all."

"I just love it when you talk about the festival," she said. "I hope we can have a big adventure like that one day."

Just as the last track ("Let it Loose") of that side of disc number two came to a close, my mom asked me to come help her out. Crap, I was hoping for more time with Darlene in my room. We hadn't done a damn thing, but at least she'd been in my room and by her words and actions, I think she felt comfortable. I know she loved the music. Music was one of our special connections. I felt our bond grow much closer that day.

"Will you please take that box down to my grandmother's china cabinet," Mom said, pointing to a cardboard box filled with kitchen junk on the floor by the open sliding glass doors. "I need some more space. Aunt Pat and Aunt Nina are coming over tomorrow. We're going to can some vegetables."

The rain had stopped, but the sky was still covered by dark, foreboding clouds, and dusk was coming quickly. I don't think it was urgent for the stuff to get stored, I think Mom may have felt our budding romance was overheating a bit, like Chuck Berry's hot rod in "Maybelline".

The game was still going, down to just the Winter parental units and my dad. Ms. Winter looked to be in control and about to K.O. her hubby who landed on her Pennsylvania Avenue hotel.

"Sure Mom," I said, picking up the box.

"Ok if we stay downstairs on the carport and shoot some pool?" Darlene, always a step ahead of me asked.

"Sure, but come back up if the weather turns bad again," her dad said, popping another top while leaning on the bar and surveying his game options.

Thank goodness Jane was in her room. I'm sure she would've tried to bust in on me and Darlene. We hurried down the back deck stairs, around and underneath the deck to the cabinet which was up against the back wall of the carport closet. The box was too big for inside, so I placed it on top and we went around to the carport side.

"I don't know if Dad would want me to uncover the table," I said. "It's pretty messy down here."

"That's ok," Darlene said, a mischievous smile slowly crossing her face. "They can't see us down here."

And so began our first serious make-out session. We'd stolen a kiss here or there in the year since our lips first met, but this was the first time we did some serious kissing and caressing. It was hot! Well for a junior high make-out session of that time period anyway, I think. It just didn't last long enough (10 minutes?). Does anything truly great?

"Darlene, time to go honey," Ms. Winter called from the front deck above us.

We broke our embrace just as her parents descended the steps. Looking at the still covered pool table, her dad cocked his head, the way I've seen Darlene do dozens of times when she is suspicious of me or about my answer to something. It usually doesn't end well for me.

"Who won?" he asked.

"Too messy to play," Darlene said, holding her arms out to her sides with both palms facing inward and fingers pointing down like a flight attendant pointing out the oh-so-obvious lights that will illuminate in case of emergency.

"Oh," Mr. Winter said smirking.

"I'll see you tomorrow for canning," Ms. Winter said to my mom, still atop the deck.

Darlene looked back just as she cleared the carport. She smiled a naughty-girl guilty smile. She bit her bottom lip and flashed our little wave. I smiled and returned the gesture.

Track 32-The End-The Beatles (2:20)

My mother was so stunned by the news about Darlene's mom, she was speechless. My dad, who never said much anyways, barely spoke for several days. I was numb. I didn't know what to do or say, to anyone. School was a daze, and for the first time in my life, I felt sports weren't very important. I went through the motions. It appeared most of the people in my circle of family and friends were doing the same.

The week after Labor Day weekend the boardwalk devolved into its semi-hibernation for the fall and winter. Today it still rocks right on well into fall, but back then, almost all the boardwalk businesses closed after Labor Day. The carnival rides packed up and headed for the warmer climate of Florida, the arcades shut down, and all but a couple of bars and The Landmark closed. The Rec Hall stayed open and was our lone off-season refuge. I wandered in after a soccer match a couple of weeks later.

"Hey Lenny," Candace said.

She was sitting with Jade and a guy I didn't know at the first table.

"Hey y'all," I said and walked on by.

I was looking for Dutch. I needed to tell him why I hadn't been by in a while. He was behind the bar. Of course, he already knew. I guess most everyone on the island did.

"Hey Lenny," he said.

"Hey Dutch," I said.

No one else was nearby.

"I think I'm going to take a break from stuff," I said.

He just nodded.

"I'll be here Son," he said.

I got up and left. I walked the deserted boardwalk. Where just a few weeks earlier were hundreds of happy, smiling faces, now there was almost no sign of human life. The bumper cars were boarded up, the donut shop was closed. The theatre had a sign that said open Friday/Saturday only and the movie advertised was X-rated. They'd dropped all pretense of being a regular theatre and were now showing X-rated fare exclusively, albeit only on the weekends.

I walked around the corner, past the shuttered "ring the bell" game. I headed up to the dunes. I walked out on the beach. Back then, and to a large extent still today, September is the best time to be at or on the beach; few tourists, water still warm, and the days still long enough to do things after school, even if you have practice.

I walked out on the sand, kicked off my flip-flops and made my way to the ocean. I didn't have my baggies on and didn't even bother taking off my shirt. I just walked out into the water and let the briny-scented mist overwhelm me. I fell straight in face first after a few yards, rolling over to float. I just floated and floated looking up at the sky thinking about what had transpired the last few weeks. It was a blur, it gave me knots in my stomach. Days creeped by. School sucked. I was struggling to stay focused not only at school, but at practice, and life period.

"Are you going over to see the Winters off Son?" my mom asked.

"Yes Mam," I said from my spot eating lunch at our bar. "They're heading out about two, so as soon as I finish up I'm heading that way."

My dad was at work and my sister was at a friend's house after church. My mom still didn't know what to say. I didn't expect her to. She just did what she always did in times of trouble or crisis, she just cleaned.

"I need that old, big wooden bowl Son," she said looking over her shoulder from the sink. "You put it in the china cabinet a long time ago."

"Ok," I said. "I know the one. I'll grab it."

I headed down the ocean-side deck and underneath to the old cabinet. I quickly reached up to pull the bowl down from its perch atop the cabinet where I put it the night we played "Exile" and yanked it down. I was hit in the face by one of Darlene's shirts. I breathed in her scent. I couldn't help but smile. She probably left 10 or 12 pieces of clothing in or around the cabinet over the years.

I took my mom the bowl and went into my room and thought about what to wear. Cat Steven's "Moonshadow" was playing on the radio. I didn't think long. I just went with what I had on, a black t-shirt with a picture of the new band Kiss' first album cover, showing the four members' painted faces. I had on my blue baggies. I'd written Darlene a note and had her a present. It was in a small gold box with a silver ribbon my mom tied for me.

"Please give Anika a hug from me," my mom said as I headed out.

I decided to walk. I didn't even feel like riding my bike and I was still a few weeks from my license. I have tried to recall what I was thinking as I made the six-block walk one last time. For the life of me, I can't remember. I mean, I wasn't in shock at that point or anything. It's just a blank. I'm sorry.

"Hey Lenny, come on in," Mr. Winter said.

The movers were packing up the last of the Winter's belongings. One of the guys was the younger, skinnier dude that helped move Melissa. We glanced at one another.

"Hey," he said, obviously recognizing me.

"Hey," I replied.

The other mover got Mr. Winter to sign something. He and I entered the empty house. No big old oak table, no recliner, no nothing, except the three of them with Ms. Winter now in a wheelchair. They'd been going back and forth to Duke three times a week for a few weeks until they could get all of their affairs in order.

"Lenny, I'm sorry, but we've got to be going," Mr. Winter said.

I nodded and leaned over to give Ms. Winter the promised hug.

"From Mom," I said.

She smiled. Mr. Winter began to push her toward the door. He stopped and looked around the room.

"Darlene, come on out in a few," he said. "Lenny, lock up for us."

I nodded. She nodded. She was wearing a little black sundress, small golden hoop earrings I'd given her for her birthday and flops. We just stood there for a second looking at one another. Due to their travel, school, and the situation overall, we'd spent zero alone time together since her mom told me. When we'd been together with our families for her birthday and a couple other times, it was just too sad and I mostly just held her. She managed a half-smile.

"It's only Durham," she said. "Like three hours or something."

I nodded, words weren't going to come easy. We held hands at her waist.

"I'll have my license in a few," I said. "And I didn't get into too much trouble for that last boardwalk brawl."

"I know," she said. "I know you're mad at life, but you've got to try and behave. I know you hate it, but we can talk on the phone till you get your license and I'll write you letters too."

I nodded.

"Here," I said, pulling the gold box and note from my baggies' left pocket.

She cocked her head and gave me the precious, mischievous smile I knew I would miss so much. She loosened the ribbon and let it fall. She gently tugged at the top and looked inside. She looked up with tears in her eyes.

"This better not be because…" she started.

I placed my right index finger on her lips and smiled a little.

"You know better than that, I bought it the next day," I said. "After our fight."

She pulled the little silver promise ring out and placed it on her left ring finger. It fit fine. I knew those fingers well. She was beaming.

"My birthstone," she said of the small sapphire stone.

"Mom helped me," I said.

"Oh, I knew that," she laughed-cried. "You were supposed to wait for your birthday."

"Darlene," her dad said peeking in the doorway. "Bye Lenny."

"Good-bye Mr. Winter," I said.

He left us alone again. We smiled at one another and began kissing. It was the best, most bittersweet kiss I've ever had. I could taste her tears and mine intermingled, I'm sure she could too. We broke our embrace and she wiped the moisture from my face. I did the same for her.

"I'll call you tomorrow after supper," she said.

I nodded. She didn't turn around. No final little wave. She was just gone.

Track 33-The Last Picture Show Soundtrack-various artists

The next few weeks were pretty much like the ones before. I kinda felt like I was sleepwalking sometimes. School and sports were blah. Friends were blah, blah, and life at the house and around the beach were blah, blah, blah. Darlene and I talked on the phone about every 3-4 days. We would take turns calling one another as both our dads were sticklers about not giving the phone company one penny more than required. Her first letter arrived just before my birthday. It was four pages long.

"….I hope you have a good birthday and Halloween this weekend! I miss you more than I can say. Mom's not doing very well at all. Dad is just quiet, even more so than usual. …."

She talked about her new school, talked about Lexi and asked about my friends, sports, and the beach. She sounded lonely and way down but was trying to cover it with cheery drawings of flowers, birds, and the bees (with our names on the bees). She said she was counting down the days until I got my license and could come see her.

She apologized for not being able to be with me on my birthday as she'd been for numbers 13, 14, and 15. She said a couple of girls she'd talked to at her new school loved her ring and thought we were a cute couple. She'd showed them some pictures. She included two in the letter. It was half of the black and white four-pack you used to get at photo booths for a quarter back then. I remembered the day we took them the summer before.

They showed us being goofy, one with us sitting side by side making faces and the other with Darlene on my lap sticking her tongue in my ear. It was a good day. It seemed so long ago. My stomach ached, my heart, I don't know what the hell it was doing, but it damn sure didn't feel good.

My coaches could tell I was bummed and I got called into the football coaches' offices on game day, the day before my birthday. My soccer coach was there as well.

"Hey Lenny," we just want to have a word with you son," my football coach said. "We know you're going through a tough time. If you need to talk about anything we're here."

I just nodded.

"It's not like you Lenny to be moping around," Coach Nwsou, my Nigerian soccer coach said in his very heavy accent. "Better days are here."

He didn't have quite a full command of English yet. I think he meant ahead. I listened to their very well-meaning spiel, said little, and was glad to leave. The game went ok and I was glad to just go home. I wasn't even excited about my birthday, my license, or anything.

Mom made me a cake, relatives came over, and we had a subdued party. I went and got my driver's license the next week. I pointed out an error in the test. The old examiner smiled.

"I been giving this same test for God knows how many years young man," he looked at me shaking his head from side-to-side.

"You know how many thousands of people have looked at this thing? But damn if you're not right."

I didn't even bother telling my dad. Of course, he let me drive home and he even let me pick the radio station. That was always his rule, the driver gets to pick the station.

"Son, your mother and I know how hard the last two months have been," he said.

And I'm sure what my dad said next was probably a tough thing for him to do. He turned the radio down. Clapton's "I Shot the Sheriff" was playing.

"We're thinking about going up to Durham and the Piedmont next week to visit relatives during my long weekend (four days off). Your mother wants to see Ms. Winter, so we'll likely go by there next Saturday. If Darlene's folks let her go off on a car date with you somewhere, you better be smart, you know what I mean?"

Uh, kinda?

"Yes sir," I said. "I know what you mean."

"Ok, good," he said. "Do we need to talk about any of that kind of stuff?"

"No, no Dad," I said. "I'm good, we had classes on it. I've read books."

"Look, I'm not okaying it," he said. "It's just, you guys are at the age and have known each other a long time."

"I know Dad," I said, uncomfortable as I'd ever be in my life. "I got it."

"Hey you guys here what happened last night?" Lil'sis said before we could even get through the front door.

"No what?" my dad asked

"Some guys broke into the bank and tried to blast open the vault," she said. "They came in through the roof, but they got caught though because their escape rope broke and they blew themselves up! Isn't that funny?"

We still only had the one bank on the island, right on the main drag. Mom had walked with little Sis and me to start a savings account on its opening day five years earlier. We each got a silver dollar and Mom got a toaster. I still have the silver dollar.

"You're kidding," Dad said as I tossed my license on the bar for Mom to see.

"No, no, it's true," my mother said. "And to top it all off the Wave caught fire and burned to the ground too!"

"That's too far-fetched," my dad said opening a beer. "I'm going to go see the Chief and find out what this is all about."

"I'm going over," I said.

"Oh, that's such a good picture," my mom said. "Be careful."

I started to jog toward the boardwalk, not even thinking I could've driven. I could see a bit of smoke rising from that section of the boardwalk by the time I reached the pier. As I approached the scene, there were a dozen or so locals near the shop, which was unscathed, and another five or six on the other side of the caution tape by the gift shop and arcade. Sure enough, the theatre was gone, almost totally burned to the ground, save the ticket window on the far left. I couldn't believe it at first, but there it was (or wasn't) right before my eyes.

"Too weird," Hal said coming up the alleyway by the shop with Bluto on a leash. "You know the deal right?"

"Nah," I said, bending over to pet the dog. "Just what's here and somebody tried to rob the bank too."

"They got that whole crowd in jail," Hal said. "Two of'em already confessed."

"How could you know all that?" I asked.

"My uncle's a firefighter and Chief Hall's cousin," Hal beamed. "He was one of the first here and went with the Chief to the bank."

"Well they didn't do shit for the theatre," I said.

"It was toast time they got here," Hal said. "Guys dropped their rope after they got in the bank and couldn't get out. They tried to blast the vault open, but all they did was blow themselves and all the furniture inside up. They're lucky to be alive. Knocked one guy through a wall into the bathroom. Huge fireball, they got no hair! Look like aliens my uncle said."

It would take a few days for everything to sort out, but Hal was basically right on the bank part of the story. What he or anyone else didn't know at the time was that the two events were linked. One of the robbers was the redhead from the theatre. Sans hair, the police didn't connect him to the theatre right away. After a few days in medical isolation, he confessed to an elaborate plan devised by Gerald to make quite a few "sweet bags of cash".

Months later at the sentencing, it came to light Gerald increased the insurance on the theatre to $500,000 from the $150,000 Mr. Brockington always kept. His plan was to burn the theatre down as a diversion in order to rob the bank in the middle of the night. His logic being the small police force and tiny firefighter brigade would be too overwhelmed by the boardwalk fire to even hear the commotion at the bank. He'd collect the insurance money and have the vault proceeds to boot!

The plan worked for about half an hour. The fire did tax all emergency personnel on the island to the limit. But the bungling robbers, led by the redhead, couldn't have made any poorer decisions had they tried.

They clipped the alarm ok and got in through the roof ok, using a rappelling rope to drop to the floor. Problem was, the rope came down with them and despite all kinds of hilarious attempts to get it back into place like getting on one another's shoulders, using furniture, etc., they failed. So, they decided to use twice the amount of dynamite Gerald had instructed to blow the vault, trying to bust out some of the shatter-proof glass.

They were hoping their amended plan would provide for their escape. Instead, the vault only suffered some serious dents. Some glass did get blown out, but the explosion ignited the gas lines. The bumbling robbers got knocked out and almost roasted. The sound of the blast alerted the first responders, who quickly sent a group over to the bank to find the interior on fire and the three-stooges like bandits almost naked but for their shoes, mostly hairless, bodies smoking, and knocked out stone cold.

It took them a few weeks to clear the rubble of the old theatre. I strolled by one day and tentatively took a few steps inside the caution tape when no one was around. Everything was mostly just burnt wood and ash, with a door handle here or there, and some other odd things, like the lid of the popcorn popper, still resembling their original selves. I wasn't really souvenir hunting and was about to leave when I glanced over at the still standing ticket window. There on the ticket window shelf, as if left on purpose, was one perfectly pristine ticket.

Made in the USA
Columbia, SC
24 January 2020